On a dark, wet December evening only five days away from another Christmas his mama couldn't afford, Rickey Jefferson looked away from the hard stare of the man in the $2,000 coat, trying to be brave. The man grabbed Rickey Jefferson by the chin and pulled his face up until he and the boy were nose to nose. The man's lips curled into a mocking grin. Then Rickey Jefferson pulled away, and started crying, standing there, shivering in the thickening sleet, bawling in the darkness, until a bullet blasted a neat, nickel-sized hole in the back of his skull.

"ENGROSSING . . .
A MODERN NIGHTMARE . . .
AN URBAN FABLE OF VIGILANTISM
GONE WILD"
Quincy Patriot Ledger

"A THRILLER . . .
GRITTY AND VIOLENT"
Shaker Magazine

"RESTRAINED ACTION AND
INTELLIGENT PLOTTING . . .
KINKOPF VEERS SHARPLY FROM THE
PREDICTABLE . . .
A WISE AND WELCOME NEW VOICE
IN CRIME FICTION"
Mostly Murder

SHOOTER

ERIC KINKOPF

AVON BOOKS NEW YORK

To Stan.
I know you're out there, somewhere.

Thanks to John Camp; Esther;
my editor, Neil; and my good friend, Dan Kelly.
Special thanks to my best friend, Robyn.

This is a work of fiction. The events and characters portrayed are imaginary. Their resemblance, if any, to real-life counterparts is entirely coincidental.

AVON BOOKS
A division of
The Hearst Corporation
1350 Avenue of the Americas
New York, New York 10019

First Avon Books Printing: June 1994

AVON TRADEMARK REG. U.S. PAT OFF. AND IN OTHER COUNTRIES, MARCA REGISTRADA, HECHO EN U.S.A.

Printed in the U.S.A.

RA   10   9   8   7   6   5   4   3   2   1

Rickey Jefferson stood silent. He stared down hard at his black, high-top sneakers. His feet were cold.

"Man, you ain't gonna be breakin' no big law. Never gonna be caught, neither." The lanky man in the black, full-length cashmere coat was getting impatient. "And if you do get roosted, you're gonna be out in a goddamned New York minute." The man took a quick glance toward the street. Nothing. He wiped some sleet from his shoulder, then stuffed his hands deep into his pockets. "C'mon, baby brother, it's put-up time. In or out?"

One of Rickey Jefferson's friends had put out the word that Rickey might be interested in some work. The man usually had "Swee Pea' " handle his street-corner shit, but "Swee Pea' " was sick tonight, or getting laid or something, and someone had told him this Jefferson kid would be a quick hit. But Rickey was just standing there, staring dumbly at his shoes. The man took another look over his shoulder, into the darkness, then reached into his coat and pulled out a lighter. He pushed the boy deeper into the shadows, then cupped his hand and flicked the lighter; a tiny blue flame appeared. The diamonds on the casing flickered. Rickey Jefferson looked up.

"Five bills, baby brother." The man's voice was soft now. "Five easy bills for this custom-made flamethrower." Rickey stared at the fire. The man pointed at the ground. "You work for me and you won't be needin' those raggedyass moccasins. You'll have a different pair of footwear for every day of the week—Mikey's Nikes, Cons, BKs, you name 'em." Rickey looked down at his feet, then up again. His toes were numb. The man opened his coat and Rickey saw a gun

1

tucked into the man's belt and another in a shoulder holster. The man reached into an inside coat pocket and pulled out a bill.

"You never seen Mr. Cleveland up close?" He held a bill under Rickey's nose, then lit a corner. Rickey took a step back. The man dropped the burning bill to the ground and waved his finger at Rickey. "Don't be foolin' with me, now, sonny. I ain't got time to be wastin'. I'm runnin' a business here. Understand?"

Rickey Jefferson remained silent. He was tall for his age—as tall as the man who stood before him—and dark-skinned. He didn't smile much because of a chipped front tooth. It embarrassed him. Looked like he had this big gap between his teeth. The result was a stern, morose, often angry stare that could scare the crap out of the neighborhood folks, black and white both—what was left of them. He looked a street-tough eighteen, but was really just a gawky mama's boy, an eleven-year-old with a shy, jack-o'-lantern grin and a hard stutter.

Every morning on his way to school, Rickey Jefferson passed a faded, peeling billboard across from a gutted gas station that showed a cool dude up front, a brother, slick, successful, dressed right. Behind him was a lady, a sister, barely covered, her finest parts pushed up and out—the kind of woman you see in your best dreams. The ad was for wine or beer or malt liquor, some sort of alcohol, Rickey never could remember. The couple looked happy. The picture made Rickey Jefferson sad.

A few years earlier, when the billboard was clean and new, Rickey had come home from school one day and told his uncle Tad that he wanted to grow up to be like the man in the ad. Tad Harrison was no real kin to Rickey. He was a big, vulgar man, about thirty-five, a neighborhood blow-hard with a thick tire of fat that drooped six inches below his T-shirts. Uncle Tad sometimes sat around the house when Rickey's mama was off cleaning rooms at a small downtown motel.

The way Rickey remembered it, Tad had begun laughing, then called out to everyone in the house. "Listen to little Rickeyboy here." Three of Rickey's cousins were horsing *around in the kitchen and came into the room. A few other neighbors were there, too. They all stopped what they were doing. Tad repeated Rickey's wish, still laughing. "Boy, you some crazy nigger already." Everyone else laughed, too. "You might as well try to be one of those damn shuttle astro-nuts, Mister Rickey, 'cause you got a better chance gettin' your ass blown into outer space than gettin' onto that billboard."*

Rickey smiled along, but he was embarrassed. Later, after dark, he went back to the dimly lit street corner and looked up at the man in the picture. The man looked back at him. Rickey picked up a can and tried to hit him with it. He missed badly. He threw a bottle, and missed again. Then, as Rickey stared through tear-filled eyes, the man's smile grew into a taunting smirk. Rickey tried to hit the face again and again. He couldn't. It was just plain out of reach.

Now, on a dark, wet December evening only five days away from another Christmas his mama couldn't afford, Rickey Jefferson stood across from that same billboard, looking away from the hard stare of the man in the $2,000 coat, trying to be brave, trying to sound tough.

"I d-d-d-don't th-th-th-think I c-c-c-c-can."

The man sniffed and shook his head. "N-n-n-no f-f-f-fuckin' foolin'." He grabbed Rickey Jefferson by the chin and pulled his face up until he and the boy were nose to nose. The man's lips curled into a mocking grin, and Rickey Jefferson suddenly realized that the man looked an awful lot like the dude on the billboard. Then Rickey Jefferson pulled away, and started crying, standing there, shivering in the thickening sleet, bawling in the darkness, until a bullet blasted a neat, nickel-sized hole in the back of his skull.

◇ 1 ◇

The ball came rocketing out of the late-afternoon shadows. It was halfway to the plate before he finally picked it up, and by then it was far too late. He told himself to back up, to bail out, but the ball kept boring in, following him, and rising. Again. And he was frozen. Again. He couldn't drop his bat and fall away, couldn't turn his shoulder into the pitch, couldn't throw up his forearm. He could only wait—all alone in the empty stadium, teeth clenched tight and eyes shut hard—for the ball to smash into his cheekbone.

And it did, just as it always did, striking with a dull, painless thud. That always seemed odd; he always prepared himself for a sharp crack and a piercing stab. Then everything would go black, but he would remain perfectly conscious. It wasn't until after the thud, long after, when he was already lying on the ground, that he heard his cheekbone shatter, like a picture window splintered by a brick.

Strangest of all, he knew it all was a dream, but he never could wake up. Not until he felt something thick and warm on his cheek, until he felt his left eye droop, then drop and slide forward, leaning heavy against his eyelid. Not until he heard again the screams ringing sharp and brittle.

This time, it was the telephone.

Stan Kochinski stared wide-eyed at the ceiling, breathing hard. He exhaled in a short burst and raised his fingertips to his face, feeling gingerly for shattered bone. He swiped at his cheek and jaw. They were wet, but with sweat. He touched his left eye. It was there, where it was supposed to be. He caught his breath, then exhaled again, long and heavy this time, shook his head slowly, swung his legs onto

4

the floor, sat up, put his head in his hands, and tried to get his bearings.

It didn't take long. The chill in the room helped. He had turned up the thermostat before he got into bed, but maybe the furnace was busted again. He turned and glanced out the window on the near wall—the sleet had turned to snow—then raised his right hand and squinted through the darkness at his watch—2:13. He had been in bed for only two hours, asleep for maybe one. He glanced toward Marlyss. The phone had woken her, too. It had rung at least six times. She hugged the covers tight to her chest as the answering machine kicked in. Johnnie Pisarcawitcz didn't wait for the end of Stan's taped message.

"Eight fuckin' times. Eight *mother*fuckin' times." The desk sergeant's voice was always painfully shrill, but this time of the morning it seemed at least another torturous half-octave higher. "Ya aint' gonna answer, ya got yer noodle stuck in somethin', set the fuckin' thing on two. Two, asshole! Or one. I ain't got time for this eight times shit."

Pisarcawitcz stopped to catch his breath. Stan rubbed his face again and lay back down while Marlyss cuddled close, tossing the covers over Stan, then molding her body to his.

Pisarcawitcz was back. "I know you're there, Stooshie boy, so listen up and listen good. Negro kid"—Pisarcawitcz pronounced the word with a short *i*—"took one in the brainlocker over at Drexel and Kercheval 'bout 20 minutes ago. Same old, same old." Pisarcawitcz sniffled loudly, sucked in hard, then swallowed. "No fuckin' shooter, no fuckin' witnesses, no motherfuckin' nothin'."

Pisarcawitcz paused again. Stan heard him take a slug of something—cold coffee, probably, one half of Pisser's diet. Cold coffee and stale donuts, the stuff of life for the foulest mouth in the entire department, which was saying a lot. Stan shook his head and shifted a bit. Marlyss moved with him.

The desk sergeant sniffled noisily again. "And it's all yours, hotshot." He stopped and blew his nose, and reloaded. "And like the chief's been sayin', Stoosh-head, let's not be finger-fucking this sort thing to death."

Stan bit his lip and shook his head. Pisarcawitcz just grunted, then hung up.

Marlyss waited for a moment, then reached across and pulled Stan toward her. They lay silently in the pitch dark for three or four minutes, holding on, and holding back.

Then Stan took a deep breath, and pulled away. Marlyss touched his forehead. "You're so tired." Her voice was a whisper.

He shook his head, his voice low, too. "I know."

"I'm sorry."

Marlyss got out of bed first, took a few steps into the darkness, then turned back to Stan. She couldn't see his eyes now, but she could feel them. She looked at him for a few seconds, then began to cover herself with her arms, as though she were suddenly embarrassed by her nakedness. But it wasn't that.

She shrugged, hugging herself. "I love you, you know."

He nodded.

She shook her head. "I can't wait here for you."

It was more a question than a statement, and he knew that. But he didn't know what he should say.

Worse, he didn't even know what he wanted to say.

Stan Kochinski had never planned to be a cop. From the very beginning, he was going to be a ballplayer, a pitcher. And a star. That was just the way it was going to be. It was almost as if he'd been conceived under some sort of sign. The day Stan was born, his father, Wladyislaw, a Detroit cop, found an almanac, looked up March 29, and saw that his son shared his birthday with the legendary pitcher Denton True "Cy" Young. Wladyslaw Kochinski beamed as he took the book to his wife, Margaret. She was sleeping. He didn't wake her. She wouldn't know Cy Young from the corner grocer, anyway. So, Laddy Kochinski, a devout Catholic and World War II dogface who'd lost a promising baseball career to the war, went to the nursery and looked through the glass at his first—and only—child, then closed his eyes and prayed—not that his little Stanislaw Cyrus Kochinski would become another Cy Young, but that his boy's dreams would have the chance to come true.

And for a while they did. Anyone who saw Laddy's kid throw a baseball knew Stan had something special. Some marveled at the grace of his delivery, stylish even in Little League. Some whistled at the crack that split the air when Stan's fastball slapped deep and hard into a catcher's mitt. Others just admired his love for the game. When Stan was eleven, the mother of one of his teammates on the Value Vacuum Cardinals turned to Maggie Kochinski at a game and said, "I've never seen such joy in a boy as your Stanley has out there." Maggie Kochinski, a frail, wonderful woman, just smiled and nodded and said, "Yes." For it was true. Stan was born to baseball.

Professional scouts—cynical, sweaty, cigar-chomping birddogs—were coming to watch Stan pitch when he was a freshman at Catholic Central on Detroit's west side. He rarely disappointed them. Stan pitched sixteen no-hitters for the Shamrocks, losing only one game in four years, and the word spread. Pretty soon, baseball writers who came to town to cover major league games at Tiger Stadium were stopping by, too. And the breezy, sunny summer afternoons on the city sandlots could entice even the most hard-bitten scribes into waxing poetic, comparing Stan to the greats, predicting his place in baseball history.

After sitting through a game with Laddy, a particularly cynical columnist for the *New York Post* broke down, too, and wrote:

"Twenty years from now, on some March 29, some giddy new father, a dreamer himself, will grab an almanac on the event of a son's birth and go down the list of notables born that day—looking for a sign, a clue that only he will know, that only he can embrace. He'll never get to the Ys, where Cy Young's name will rest. He'll have stopped long before, at the Ks—and the name Stan Kochinski."

In 1965, Stan was the seventh player chosen in the inaugural major league baseball draft. Minnesota grabbed him. Stan had just graduated from high school and didn't have to worry about the Army and Vietnam; a bundle of allergies had earned him a 4F. The Twins offered a $30,000 signing bonus, a nice sum at that time. And although Maggie desperately wanted her son to get a college education, the money was more than enough to help Stan win Laddy's support in turning down a baseball scholarship from the University of Michigan and signing with the Twins—and chasing after *their* dream.

Before Stan left that summer to join the Twins Single A team in St. Cloud, Minnesota, he married Jenny, his hometown honey and literally the girl next door. Stan figured life couldn't get much better. But it did. A month after his twentieth birthday, after less than two years in the minors, he hit the big time, "The Show."

His first major league appearance came in relief in late April at Cleveland's Municipal Stadium. He entered the game in the seventh inning with the bases loaded and no outs, and struck out the side on the minimum nine pitches. He threw only twenty-eight pitches that day. Twenty-four were strikes. He struck out seven of the nine Indians he faced and received a standing ovation from the normally surly Cleveland fans.

Laddy and Maggie's kid truly was going to make it. Everything was unfolding according to some wonderful script. By mid-August, Stan had compiled an 11-4 record and was second in the league in strikeouts. He was a shoo-in for Rookie of the Year. The Twins weren't doing badly, either. In fact, they were on their way to winning their first American League pennant. No one imagined that they would pop the champagne without Stan.

It was late August when the Twins returned to Cleveland's lakefront stadium for a crucial four-game series. Stan started the first game of a twi-night doubleheader and had a 3-2 lead entering the bottom of the seventh inning. He retired the first two Indians on routine plays, but the next three hitters got on base on a ringing double down the line to left, a Baltimore chop just over Stan's head that dribbled into center field, and a walk. That brought Billy Rogine to the plate. Rogine, twenty-seven, was a husky, handsome, budding star. He was hitting .283 with seventeen homeruns and seventy-three runs batted in. He was an aggressive player, the type who liked to crowd the plate, and he was tough and proud—the kind of batter Stan liked to face.

Stan had been feeling particularly strong that afternoon. It was a cool summer day, seventy-two, maybe even a few degrees cooler with the breeze coming in off Lake Erie—Stan's kind of weather. On days like that, Stan felt like he could throw the ball through a brick wall—and through any particular brick he picked. And despite the bases being suddenly full of Indians, Matty Simmons knew that, too.

Simmons was the Twins' veteran catcher. He had spent sixteen yeas in the big leagues with six different teams and had seen rocket arms like Stan's fire for a week, a month, maybe a year, and then fizzle forever. But Stan would be different, Simmons knew. He even gave Stan a nickname: Gillette. Simmons was a bona fide character and would hold court in the dugout before every game Stan was to start, feeding reporters the same spiel over and over again until they could almost mouth it from memory. "Speed don't mean a pile of ratshit, gentlemen, if you roll the fuckin' apple right over the plate. Ya gotta shave these guys close, move the pill inside, get 'em off the dish—scare the bejeezus out of 'em. My boy Gillette's tough as they come. Kid's got guts. He ain't afraid to nick no one." Then, as if one cue, Simmons would pause, unload a thick glop of tobacco-laced spit on the shoes of an unsuspecting out-of-town reporter, and point to Stan warming up in the bullpen. "There was only one Sal 'The Barber' Maglie, gents, but this kid could carry his fuckin' strop. I'm tellin' ya. I'm tellin' ya."

Simmons walked to the mound now as Rogine moved toward the batter's box.

"You okay, kid?"

Stan nodded.

"Good." Simmons still had a huge chaw of tobacco stuck in his right cheek. "Skip wants us to loosen this shithead up." His face was streaked with sweat and dirt. He was grimacing slightly and the wrinkles that creased his eyes seemed hard and deep. He suddenly looked older than thirty-eight.

Stan glanced toward the dugout. Sam Francis, the Twins' manager, had one foot on the top dugout step and was nodding his head slightly, almost imperceptibly.

Stan looked at Simmons. "Back him up?"

Matty let loose with a stream of tobacco juice. "Nope." He handed the ball to Stan and smiled wickedly. "Put him on his bigfatass." The last three words came out as one. "Hard."

Stan nodded.

Simmons did too, then took a quick look around. It was early evening now. The pitcher's mound was in the shadows, but home plate was bathed in the remaining sunlight, making it tougher for batters to pick up the ball. Simmons smiled again. "This'll scare the goddamn crap outa him." Then he chuckled. "You and me, Gillette."

Stan began to smile, then fought it back. Unnerve Rogine with the first pitch, then go after him. He nodded to himself. Just like it's supposed to be done.

Simmons set himself behind the plate and gave Stan a target on the outside corner, just in case Rogine tried to sneak a peek. Then he eased his glove to the left until it was almost under Rogine's right armpit. Stan nodded, wound up, kicked, and delivered. Good brushback pitch. He could feel it as soon as it left his hand. The ball came thundering out of the shadows toward the inside corner of the plate, then began cutting in toward Rogine and rising. Stan began to smile, then stopped. Something had gone haywire. It was Rogine—he wasn't moving. He was just standing there like a statue, waiting, waiting, waiting.

By the time Stan screamed, it was too late. Rogine never reacted at all, never flinched, never moved, until the ball hit him just below the left eye, slicing open a three-inch gash and sending him to the dirt as though he'd been shot.

For a few terrible seconds, Billy Rogine lay in the batter's box alone, quivering and whimpering. Then Stan rushed from the mound, ripped off his jersey, dropped to his knees in front of some 22,000 fans, and tried to staunch the blood oozing from Rogine's shattered eye socket. Within seconds, three men announcing themselves as doctors jumped from the stands and pushed Stan to the side. Stan stayed on his knees on home plate until Rogine was carted from the field on a stretcher. Then Stan left, too. He got as far as the runway between the dugout and the players' clubhouse before turning to the wall and vomiting his guts out.

Doctors said Rogine's eye was irreparably damaged and that he would never play again. He did, but not for long. Two months into his comeback the following spring, he was finished. Stan lasted a bit longer. But not much. He'd lost his confidence. And worse, he'd lost his nerve. He pitched in only three more big league games, lasting a total of six innings before he was sent back to the minors. He fared no better there, getting rocked repeatedly by banjo hitters who wouldn't even make it to the bigs for a cup of coffee. Stan Kochinski was out of baseball, and back home by the middle of the following season.

Jenny took it all in stride. She handled the adjustment just fine. She found a job at a bank and went to college at night; she wanted to be a teacher. But Stan was lost. He didn't want much of anything. He started hanging out with some old high-school pals, but they had jobs and didn't have sixteen hours a day to fritter away keeping Stan company. Stan did little or nothing for about nine months, living off Jenny's small salary and what was left of his baseball money. He hung around the house, around gyms and parks, he became a regular at three local bars. Then, one day, right out of the blue, he went downtown and took the test for the police academy.

Stan never really understood why he decided to become a cop, not that he cared to think about it all that much. Being a cop was more than just something to do. But there was no romance in it. He had no illusions about a cop's life. Maybe, Stan would tell himself, it was just fate. Years earlier, when Stan had regaled his father with wonderful visions of his baseball future, Laddy Kochinski, in a tough moment of truth, had rubbed his boy on the head and hugged him, then blinked away the sadness in his eyes and said, "Just remember, Stan, you're the son of a cop, and that's something even your best fastball can't outrun."

But Jenny knew that Stan's decision to become a cop wasn't fate at all. It was some sort of grim, horrible test.

"This is the way you're going to find out how tough you are?" The question was full of anger; it came with tears. For weeks, Jenny prayed herself to sleep, asking God to change Stan's mind. Jenny worshiped Laddy Kochinski, and he her, but she had watched him die like most big-city cops die—slowly, painfully, from the inside out. She didn't want to have to watch Stan die, too.

But Stan was undeterred. He graduated from the academy and became a policeman. Now, twenty years later, he was on the other side of forty, a long-forgotten baseball phenom, a divorced homicide dick, with a six-year-old son who rarely saw his father. Twenty years later, he was a tired cop trying to get some sleep between nightmares and phone calls, while struggling, like Sergeant Wladyslaw Thaddeus Kochinski before him, to keep the scum of the earth from turning his heart hard.

It was 3 A.M. now and Marlyss stood with her back to her car. The snow was coming down in big, thick flakes. It was beginning to look a lot like Christmas. She stared into the black, starless sky, then smiled and shivered. "Just a few shopping days left, detective—and I'll settle for nothing but mink."

Stan tried to smile back, and did, a little. He reached around Marlyss and opened her door.

She intercepted his hand and wound her fingers through his. "Okay, lieutenant, okay. It doesn't have to be mink. It's the thought that counts." She looked up at him with dark eyes that sparkled with a hint of mischief, and winked. "Something satin will do just fine."

She kissed him on the neck, got into her car and headed home.

Stan stood in the driveway and watched Marlyss drive off. Then he got into his car and headed back into the brittle, windy, pitch-dark Detroit night.

◇ 2 ◇

Most of the side streets on the city's lower east side were deserted at 3 A.M. Many were deserted at 3 P.M. too. The area had once been a proud, picturesque working-class neighborhood anchored by a sprawling, smoke-belching Chrysler assembly plant that fired on all cylinders twenty-four hours a day. The old plant was gone now, and a new, shiny one was up and running, but chronic auto-industry woes had taken their toll. The round-the-clock boom days had gone bust long ago—and all that was left of many of the neighborhoods were bittersweet memories. The area was literally an urban ghost town with only pockets of civilization—a block, or maybe just a row here and there, of three or four, or one or two, well-kept houses. Large, sweeping splotches were home only to rotting, abandoned buildings; empty lots, where the rotted, abandoned buildings had been bulldozed; ruthless drug dealers, and the few plain folks who had no place else to go. Even the two-bit pimps and their fearless hookers had long evacuated to the west side.

A reporter from *Time* had recently flown in to research a feature story about the decay. She'd written: "A planeload of explosives surely could wreak no greater destruction than poverty and drugs have wrought here. This is Dresden, American-style."

In fact, some city fathers had even given up trying to defend the place to smug, self-righteous outsiders. The reporter's characterization was a direct quote from the Reverend Thomas Gibbons, a staunchly loyal Detroit councilman.

Stan cruised slowly through the icy, eerie stillness. Sometimes he would drive the streets at a crawl, trying to picture

13

them as they once were, the way he remembered them when he was growing up, not far from here, with flowers blooming on neatly trimmed lawns and gaily shrieking children spilling onto the streets. Not tonight. He drove slowly now only because there was no need to hurry. It didn't take Sherlock Holmes to figure out that the gunman probably wasn't hanging around, waiting for someone to read him his rights. Especially in this neighborhood, where enforcers from rival drug gangs—the Satin Knights, the Pony Boys, the DeeJays—stole in and out of the darkness nightly to intimidate and assassinate.

Stan had rushed everywhere when he was a young cop. He'd figured he might be able to keep someone from getting killed, save a life, maybe even collar a scumbag or two. Be a hero. But "young cop" was a long, long time ago, and he wasn't thinking about any of that now. He was simply compiling a mental list of the people he'd need to question: any witnesses, nearby residents, the kid's mother, his father, friends, teachers. And he wondered what the kid's number was—646? 647? For all the good it ever did, which was none, the *Free Press,* one of the city's two daily newspapers, had started running the annual homicide tally again. Numbers were big news lately.

Stan turned right on Kercheval and glanced down a side street. Three kids dressed in summer jackets and sneakers were playing in the snow outside a ramshackle blue bungalow, its shattered front windows repaired with cardboard. He checked his watch. It was 3:17. He shook his head, then wondered if the kid he was about to meet had been scared, if he'd seen death coming. Then he stopped wondering, and promised himself that the kid would remain a number, just a number.

It was 3:21 when Stan turned right onto Drexel and eased his maroon Ford Galaxie to the curb. He radioed his position to the homicide desk and got out of the car. The wind whipped across Stan's face like a cold slap, blowing open his unbuttoned overcoat. He pulled his coat together and yanked the collar to his ears as he crossed Kercheval and headed toward a uniformed cop standing near the "meat wagon," the battleship-gray, hearselike vehicle used to carry bodies to the morgue. The meat wagon coughed its thick exhaust into the sharp winter air; the cop shivered, Stan flashed him his badge.

"Victim's name was Rickey Jefferson, sir." Officer Jeremiah Williams was a rookie patrol cop from a nearby precinct. Laddy'd worked with his dad, Oliver. The rookie didn't look good.

"Pisser said on the phone that he was a kid."

"No kid, lieutenant—another baby. A fifth grader." The wind blew hard again, choking off Williams's words.

Stan nodded and moved on, toward a TV crew taping footage for the morning news from behind the yellow-tape, crime-scene barrier. The cameraman was shooting a gas utility billboard ad that read WE WANT TO KEEP THE WARMTH IN YOUR LIFE. The sound man just watched. He looked cold, his hands stuffed deep into his pockets. Stan nudged his way past the men and headed for the small, bombed-out building on the corner and an opaque plastic sheet that lay across a large bump on the ground near the back wall. Stank took off a glove and pulled the covering back. Rickey Jefferson's mouth was wide open, and so were his eyes. The death stare. Stan had seen it hundreds of times. A crime-lab photographer excused himself and moved in for more pictures. Stan stood and put his glove back on as Williams approached him.

"His mama's in my car, sir. Been here about a hour. We asked her to wait here for you."

"Anyone else?"

"No, sir."

"Witnesses?"

"No one that'll do any good. We got a lot of folks who say they heard a shot."

"When?"

"In this neighborhood?" Williams shrugged and looked down nervously at his notebook. "At 8:05, 9:40, 10:30, 11:25 . . ."

Stan put up his hand, nodded, and headed for the patrol car. Williams followed. Myrtle Jefferson didn't see the men approach. She was sitting in the back seat, staring the other way, out the far window. She was still wearing her housekeeping uniform from the motel. It was pink. Her eyes were swollen from crying. Stan suddenly wished he had been here sooner so she could have gone home.

Williams caught up to Stan, opened the door to the cruiser, and called quietly to the woman. "Mrs. Jefferson, this is Detective Kochinski."

Myrtle Jefferson looked toward the front of the car. She sat erect and held her head high. "My son was not a bad boy, he . . ." She stopped suddenly and took a deep breath, then wiped the tears from her eyes with the back of her hand. Stan said nothing. The silence was painful. Stan had been here hundreds of times, too. He had heard all races, colors, and creeds of parents defend their kids. It didn't matter if the boy was a drug-gang hitman, a serial rapist, or a child molester. There were no evil boys; no good boys, either—only boys who weren't "bad." Somehow parents saw some sort of difference. Stan had nothing to say, so it was best to say nothing. He counted to ten, slowly.

"I'd like to talk to you sometime later this morning, ma'am." Myrtle Jefferson nodded. Stan lowered his voice. "I'll call first."

Myrtle Jefferson nodded again. "Yes, you will."

Stan closed the door and turned toward Williams. "What number'd Pisser give you?"

Williams flipped through his notebook. His hands were shaking. Maybe it was the cold—probably not. "Six. Four. Seven." Three sentences.

Williams watched as Stan took his dick book out of his coat pocket, blew on his hands, and wrote, "R. Jefferson, 6-4-7."

Williams pointed to the scribbling. "R. *Freeman* Jefferson, sir." His voice was shaky, too. He shrugged. "Mrs. Jefferson asked that we use his middle name, too."

Stan closed the book, nodded, and turned to Williams. "I'll meet you at homicide in forty-five minutes. We'll do the paperwork there."

"As soon as I get Mrs. Jefferson home."

"Right."

Stan looked Williams in the eye, then back toward the dead boy. Williams headed around to the driver's side of the squad car. "Williams?" The officer stopped. "If you get the chance, tell her I got a boy, too, and . . . that I'm sorry."

Williams nodded, then looked at Stan. "Why don't you just tell her, sir?"

Stan didn't hear the question. He was already turned back into the wind, with his collar drawn tight again, heading toward the building and Myrtle Jefferson's lifeless baby, lying in the new-fallen snow under the plastic comforter. He wanted to make sure someone had closed the boy's mouth. And his eyes.

◇ **3** ◇

Detroit cops referred to headquarters by its address—1300 Beaubien, or just "thirteen hundred." The building, a few blocks east of downtown, was a nine-floor 1920s monument that had been designed by industrial architect Albert Kahn. Decades later, the exterior was as statuesque as ever; inside was another story.

Homicide took up half of the fifth floor. Its central office, where a desk-bound sergeant held court, was a pale, institutional green, and dimly lit, with two grimy windows that looked out on the tired, old Wayne County Jail.

The filing cabinets—there were seven—were a mishmash of sizes, styles, and faded colors, and the place smelled, at various times, like industrial-strength disinfectant, burned coffee, cigarettes and stale cigars, or gas—the human variety. The detectives' squad rooms, five of them, were painted a dull gold that had aged to a dingy mustard. Each squad room had seven plain wooden desks, one for each of the thirty-three men and two women investigators. Some of the desks had brass or plastic nameplates. Some had pictures of smiling wives or kids. Others had bumpersticker-type slo-

gans that read "GO AHEAD, MAKE MY DAY" or "IN SMITH &
WESSON WE TRUST." All were sloppy with brown case files.
The walls were generally bare, save for a few yellowing
FBI most-wanted posters tacked here and there, as if hung
by a Hollywood set designer for maximum spartan effect.

The desk sergeant's office was the nerve center, or as
Pisarcawitcz called it, "sphincter control." The names of the
detectives were listed on a chalkboard across from the desk
sergeant's desk. The board had three columns: "IN," "OUT,"
and "NOTES." Pisarcawitcz has written "F—YOU ALL TO H—"
across all three columns alongside his name. The salutation
had been toned down a bit and the dashes added after a
newly elected city councilwoman had complained about the
previous message during a tour of the offices three weeks
ago.

Pisarcawitcz—a short, skinny, balding man—was the
third-shift desk dick. He had what the younger, hipper detectives called "a 'tude." The older detectives knew better.
Pisarcawitcz didn't have an attitude problem; he was just
burned out—to a crisp. In fifteen years as a homicide inspector, he had investigated more than one thousand mur-
ders. His commitment to truth and justice had long been
supplanted by a total disgust for the people he was sworn to
serve. Plus, he was clearly embarrassed by being put to pasture on the desk.

Any rookie who looked at him cross-eyed, challenged his
authority straight up, or worse, snickered under his breath at
him, got a standard response. "You crime-dog hotshots'll be
pissin' all over each other someday to get your gonads in
this seat, you watch." Then Pisarcawitcz would grumble
about "when cops was cops" and launch into stories about
the shootouts his grandfather'd had with members of the old
Purple Gang. No one knew exactly what was true. No one
really cared, either.

Pisarcawitcz was picking his ear with the eraser end of a
pencil when Stan walked in. The desk sergeant's face lit up;
his lips curled into a smirk.

"What'd I tell ya, Stosh boy? Easy pickins, huh?" Stan
didn't say anything. "Told you you'd be in and out. You
owe me one, pal. Gimme a line for the ol' log book."

Pisarcawitcz grabbed the hardbound green record from the corner of the desk, opened it to December 21, flipped the pencil to the lead end, and poised himself to write.

"Estimated, T.O.D., 12:42 A.M. Corner of Drexel and Kercheval . . ."

"Gr-r-r-eat fuckin' 'hood." Pisarcawitcz snickered. "Talk to mama?"

"Briefly."

Pisarcawitcz leaned across the desk, smiled, and lowered his voice to a whisper. "Let me guess. Mama says the victim was—let's see now—a future NBA star? Or maybe—a budding Supreme Court Justice?"

"Victim was black. Age eleven."

Pisarcawitcz's face took on a look of exaggerated—and transparently phony—concern. His voice grew quiet. "Oh, my."

Stan grabbed the last jelly donut from a box on the sergeant's desk. The donut was stale. "I'll have the paperwork done in a couple hours."

Pisarcawitcz sat back in his chair, then leaned forward and whispered again. "Sooner, pal. This one ain't goin' nowhere. I can smell it—and it smells like one less nigger kid to peddle dope and shoot cops . . . *white cops.*" Pisarcawitcz slapped the log book shut with a crack. "Case closed." Then he laughed, louder than you'd think such a little man could.

Stan headed down the hall to Squad Room Seven, opened the door, and switched on the light. Pete Dawlson, Stan's partner on a half a dozen cases a few years back, was asleep on a couch in the corner of the room. Dawlson, dead to the world and snoring like a sputtering chain saw, had returned to homicide six months earlier after a year's leave. The word after his rather abrupt departure was that he had escaped south with some bigshot lawyer's stuningly gorgeous wife, Kitty something.

When Dawlson's name would come up, Pisser would giggle and grab his crotch. "Our boy Pete has apparently rethought the, um, true meaning of life."

But when Dawlson had returned to the department, almost as suddenly as he'd left, he'd explained, quietly and almost sheepishly, that his mother, a widow living in a trailer park somewhere in Tennessee, had been stricken with Alzheimer's and that he'd headed there to care for her, to get her meager estate in order and, finally, to put her in a nursing home.

When Pisser had gotten the lowdown, he'd just shaken his head. "End of legend."

Stan flicked off the light, walked to his desk, put down the donut, sat down, and laid his head on the blotter. It felt cool, and good on his burning eyes. He reached for the donut and took a bite: Custard. Christ, he hated custard. He tossed it into the wastebasket, where it landed with a thick thud, then looked at his watch. 4:05. Dawlson was still snoring. Stan wanted to join him, but as soon as he closed his eyes, the phone rang. He felt across the desk for the receiver, lifted it from the cradle, and pit it next to his ear.

"Kochinski."

"Your pal, Johnny P."

Stan didn't answer.

"I wanna get outa here on time. I wasn't foolin' about gettin' that report ASAP pronto lickety-split. Garbage in, garbage out, Stosh. Put it on cruise control."

Stan opened his eyes, lifted his head, and while Pisser waited for an answer, placed the receiver gently back into the cradle. Dawlson was beginning to stir. Stan got up and switched on the lights, then went back to his desk. He stared down at the forms in front of him. The top line on the top sheet read: INCIDENT REPORT. He printed RICKEY FREEMAN JEFFERSON in large capital letters in the blank labeled VICTIM # 1. He rubbed his eyes and put down the pencil. He was exhausted.

"What's up, Stan?" Dawlson had sneaked up behind him. He clapped Stan softly on the back, then stretched and yawned.

Stan groaned, then turned and gave Pete the once-over. Dawlson was wearing black jeans, a black turtleneck, and a black sweater. Everything was rumpled. He was a well-dressed mess. Pete stared down at his jeans, then tried smoothing himself out. It didn't work, but he didn't seem terribly concerned.

"Coffee?"

Stan nodded. "Black—and strong."

Dawlson walked to the coffeemaker. "Strong, coming up."

Stan surveyed Pete's getup again. "You gone undercover, pard?"

"Yeah." Dawlson laughed, then winked. "As Johnny Cash—and I'm hot on the trail of the ironing-board bandit."

It was a silly joke, but it was good hearing Pete laugh. Maybe he was starting to thaw a bit. When the two had met some twenty years earlier in Police Academy Class 0170, Pete would talk for hours on end with Stan, about almost anything. When Pete broke up with his wife, Cindy, he spent a week crying on Stan's shoulder. Before he'd left on leave, he and Stan would play basketball with a group of guys at Romulus High School once or twice a week, meet after work at a coppers' bar for a few beers, maybe go to a basketball or hockey game every now and then. But Pete had been different since returning. He was friendly, all right, but in a cool, distant way—a polite friendliness. Stan hadn't seen him away from work since Pete had been back.

"Black and strong, Stosh." Dawlson handed Stan a cup of coffee. "What're you working on?"

"Dead kid. Bum found him a few blocks east of the Chrysler plant. Took a round in the head."

"Drug shit." It was a statement.

"Yep."

"Kid clean?"

"Was tonight." Stan took a sip of the coffee. "Good coffee, Pete. I needed this."

Dawlson smiled. "Figure he was rollin'?" He walked to his desk, sat down, and put his feet up.

"I guess. What else?"

Dawlson shrugged, then rubbed his eyes. "What's next?"

"The usual. Talk to the kid's mother. Rustle up a few friends. Just do what we do."

"Ad infinitum." Dawlson's eyes were closed again.

"Pete?"

"Uh-huh."

"This ever get to you?"

Dawlson's eyes were still closed. "Nope."

"Not at all?"

"You're frayin' around the edges, Stosh." Dawlson opened one eye. His voice was calm. It always seems to be calm. "Ease up. Get those reports to Pisarcawitcz, and move the hell on." He took a sip of coffee and put his feet on the floor. "If there's something out there, you'll find it. Something needs to be figured out, you'll figure it out."

"The kid was eleven."

Dawlson shifted in his chair and put his feet back on his desk. "Won't be twelve—and that's all you need to know right now."

Stan nodded. He took a deep breath, then exhaled long and slow. "How about you?"

Pete's eyes were closed again. He smiled. "I'm onto some heavy shit, Stosh—trying to score us some primo tickets for a Pistons game."

Stan smiled. "Get serious."

Dawlson opened one eye again. "Okay—I just went on loan to Internal Affairs. Some renegade cop shit over in the Fifth."

"Doesn't sound like homicide work."

"Never know."

"Sound interesting?"

Dawlson shook his head. "Not yet."

Stan's phone rang again. It was 4:18. He lifted the receiver to his ear. "Kochinski."

"I couldn't sleep." Marlyss's voice was a soft whisper.

Stan nodded and smiled again. He rubbed his forehead and looked over at his partner. Pete wasn't stirring.

"Just wanted to make sure you were okay."

Stan lowered his voice, too. "I'm better now."

"Good." Stan could hear the smile in her voice. "Meet me tonight?"

"Where?"

"New place. I've got to go now. I'll call you later with directions."

"When?"

"Eight."

"Whoa." Stan walked to talk. "Let me check my date book."

Marlyss giggled. "No—and bring a pillow. Bye."

"A pillow?"

"Yes." She laughed, quietly. "If you don't, you'll be very sorry, detective."

◇ **4** ◇

Frank Sims was sitting at the kitchen table in his robe and boxer shorts, reading the morning paper and waiting for the coffee to percolate, when his beeper went off. He looked at the clock in the microwave. It was 6:42. Must be headquarters. The Detroit police chief put down the paper, ran a hand through his thick blond hair, got up, and walked across the room to the snack bar. He picked up his beeper and pressed the red button on the side. A phone number appeared in the little window. It looked familiar, but Frank didn't recognize it immediately. He rubbed some sleep from his eyes. It wasn't headquarters. It wasn't the mayor. Colbane—that was it. Must be his home number. Bill Colbane was a judge at 36th District Court. But why would he call so early? Frank put down the beeper and dialed the number. Colbane answered on the first ring.

"Frank?"

"What's up?"

"Trouble."

"What? Someone grab our racquetball court?" Frank chuckled.

"This isn't a joke, Frank." The judge's voice was wavering.

Frank rubbed his eyes again. Colbane had a flair for the dramatic, some would say the melodramatic. "What is it, Bill?"

"What do you think?"

Frank sniffed. "I think I'm not interested in guessing games this early." He tried to remain calm. It was tough. Colbane could get on your nerves.

The judge swallowed hard. "Read the paper yet?"

"Just started."

"Take a look at 3B."

Frank went to the table, picked up the *Free Press*, and rifled through the pages until he got to 3B. The bottom half of the page was filled with a lingerie ad. Two-thirds of the top half was filled with a story about an oil spill in the Gulf of Mexico.

"Let's see—a rather uninspiring bra-and-panty sale at Hudson's, and dead fish in the Gulf."

"Quit screwing around, Frank."

Then Frank looked in the upper right corner, at a tiny, two-paragraph short. Colbane read Frank's silence. "Frank"—Halfway through the first paragraph Frank knew what the judge was about to say. A chill spilled down his spine—"that was our corner."

Colbane's voice had turned into a panicked whisper. Frank remained silent. His mind was already racing, trying to sort things out.

"Ours, Frank."

Frank had overfilled the coffeemaker again, and the liquid in the carafe was bubbling over onto the hot plate. He didn't notice the acrid smell.

"What do we do now?" Colbane again—and, Jesus, the judge was crying.

Frank Sims, eyes to the floor, paced slowly across the kitchen. He wasn't the fastest-rising politician in Detroit or Michigan politics, but he was easily the most ambitious—and daring. Smart, smooth, slick, quick, Harvard and Columbia Law School-educated, a former collegiate boxing champion and Special Forces officer, the former county prosecutor—Frank Sims hadn't been born to political status, but he had slaved, schemed, paid, and maneuvered to cultivate it. And now everything could be in jeopardy. He wished Colbane were there with him. He wanted to slap the panic out of him. He told himself, instead, to calm down. He cupped his hand over the phone and took a deep breath, then exhaled slowly, and began speaking in a cool, controlled tone. "Listen to me, Bill." His voice dropped to a whisper. "Settle down. It'll be okay." Colbane didn't answer. "Bill?"

"I'm here." Colbane was slowing down.

"Good. You sound better." Frank slipped a reassuring smile into his voice. "Now, first things first." Nice and slow. "Let's get off the phone. Call Hatch and Stone. Get them over here." Frank stopped. "No, I'll call them. You come, too . . . eight-thirty. We'll talk." There was no response again. "Bill?"

Colbane's voice was low. "This isn't what I agreed to, Frank."

"None of us did, Bill." Frank tried to sound a bit apologetic. Colbane needed that. "A little setback, that's all this is, if that. Stay calm. Okay?"

Nothing.

"Okay?" Frank's voice was more insistent.

"Okay."

"Right." Frank paused for a split second. "I'll get hold of the others. Eight-thirty."

Colbane didn't want to hang up. "Call Shooter yet?"

Frank shook his head. "No, don't worry about that. You just worry about staying calm." Pause. "And remember *why* you signed on, Bill. Remember?"

Nothing, then— "Yes."

"Eight-thirty. We can control the damage, Bill—if there even is any. Okay? Bill?"

"Okay."

Frank hung up the phone, put his arms on the end of the snack bar, and leaned forward. His robe fell open. He rubbed his chest, then sucked in a deep breath. Our corner—a goddamn, motherfucking mistake. The first one. But who knows if they could even afford a first one. He rubbed his forehead. The next few hours would be the most important of his life. Damage control. Those were the right words. He repeated them out loud, slowly and softly. "Damage control. Damage control." It was a soothing mantra.

He walked across the kitchen to the coffeemaker and studied his reflection in the door of the microwave. His forehead was creased, and he rubbed it again, trying to massage away the tension. He stared at himself for a few seconds more, then reached to pour himself a cup of coffee. He grabbed the carafe handle, but the pot wouldn't budge. The burned coffee had cemented it to the hot plate. He tugged again, then again without luck; the pot finally came free on the fourth pull. Frank looked at the carafe for a second, as though he were studying it, then lifted it over his head, gritted his teeth, exhaled loud and hard, and slammed it to the counter, sending splintered glass and hot coffee flying, showering himself with both—and hardly flinching.

He dropped the carafe handle to the floor and struggled to catch his breath. His lungs burned; his chest stung. He looked into the microwave door again and took a deep breath. Better. Another deep breath. Calmer. Cooler. He stared at his forehead—no lines—then looked down at his palm. Blood was dripping from a two-inch gash into a pear-shaped pool on the floor. He would need help bandaging the wound. He took one more look in the microwave door. The reflection began to smile back at him, thinly at first, then broadly. He nodded. It would be okay.

He looked down at his bloody fist and flexed his hand. His wife was good at first aid; he would get her to help. It was early, but that was okay, too. He'd missed her last night. Marlyss must have been working late, again. Frank Sims smiled and headed upstairs, trailing blood behind him.

◇ **5** ◇

Myrtle Jefferson was a short, stout, proud woman. Her hair was speckled with gray, and her round, kind face carried a roadmap of lines that belied her age. She was only thirty-six, but she looked fifty. She turned toward Stan but didn't look at him. "Officer Williams told me you have a son."

Her voice was softer now than it had been at the murder scene. The edge, the hint of defiance, the anger was gone. She simply sounded tired, and she looked tired. She wore a faded blue housecoat over her housekeeper's uniform, and floppy, ragged yellow slippers. She was sitting at her dining-room table, staring into the kitchen, where a radio played in a crackling whisper on a counter in the shadows. Rickey Jefferson's mother wrapped her arms across her chest, as if she were hugging herself against the cold. The house was warm, almost uncomfortably so. It smelled of strong coffee and burned toast.

Stan stood in the living room, in front of a threadbare, lime-green couch covered with a stiff, multi-colored Indian blanket. It was still night outside. Inside, too. The only light was a dim lamp on an end table next to the TV. The shade was covered with plastic and looked new.

Stan looked around the room. There was a crucifix above the television and six framed pictures on the bureau. They were all the same child. One photo looked as though it had been taken about three years ago. The boy in the picture had a shy smile on his face and was missing his two front teeth. The wall nearest the door was decorated with a trio of eight-by-ten glossy photos: Martin Luther King, John Kennedy, and Jimmy Carter. A "Home Sweet Home" sampler was tacked, unframed, near the front door.

A Christmas tree stood undecorated in the corner near the stairs. Boxes of shiny bulbs were stacked nearby; strings of lights were balled on the seat of a brown recliner. The butt end of a shotgun was visible behind the curtain by the picture window. Stan sat on the edge of the couch, holding his dick book in his hand. He unbuttoned his coat but didn't remove it.

"What do you want for your boy, Detective Kochinski?" Myrtle Jefferson looked Stan in the eye. "Officer Williams told me you used to be some sort of ballplayer. You hope your boy does that?"

Stan met her gaze, tilted his head nervously, and shrugged almost imperceptibly. Myrtle Jefferson turned back toward the kitchen. "Rickey didn't like sports." She chuckled. "He was a tall boy, always worried that he was going to grow to be seven foot tall and some coach would make him play basketball. His daddy played basketball. He laid awake some nights worrying about that." She shook her head. "Imagine that."

Myrtle Jefferson picked up a stack of day-old mail from the table in front of her and shuffled the envelopes without looking at them. "Maybe you hope your boy grows up to be a police officer, or a doctor, or a businessman."

She got up from her chair and walked slowly across the room. She stopped in front of the Christmas tree and reached for a box of bulbs, took a bulb, adjusted the tiny hook attached to it, and placed the ornament on the tree. "I had those hopes. All of them. Just like you." Myrtle Jefferson turned toward Stan, brushing the tree. The bulb came loose from its branch and fell to the floor; it shattered quietly. Myrtle Jefferson didn't even seem to notice. "But I had one hope first. I hoped my boy would live." She closed her eyes and wrapped her arms around herself again, then walked back to the table, sat down, and reached into her pocket for a pack of cigarettes—Kools. She lit one and inhaled deeply.

"I remember this very clearly, like it was yesterday. I went to bed one night when Rickey was four, right after his daddy died. Gus was a school-teacher. He was a good man." She smiled. "Got killed in a car accident." Myrtle Jefferson paused. She looked toward the picture window in the living room. "The neighborhood here was different then. Things were prettier."

Stan looked through the window. It was growing lighter outside. He saw two abandoned homes across the street, their yards dotted with garbage, their porch steps rotted and crumbling, their doors open to the wind.

Myrtle Jefferson looked at Stan, then turned away. "I remember lying in bed, staring at the ceiling, staring at this crack in the ceiling and telling myself that nothing else in my life was important except my boy. Just him." She took another drag on her cigarette, extinguished it, then quickly lit another. "Then I started crying, because I began following this crack with my eyes and I realized that the crack was so short. There was a maze of them up there, and I was staring at the shortest one. Gus would have told me I was being foolish, thinking that was some sort of bad sign." She smiled again, this time in embarrassment. "But he wasn't there."

Myrtle Jefferson paused again. She started to wipe her eyes on her sleeve, then reached into a pocket and pulled out a ball of crumpled tissue. "I cried myself to sleep that night, I was so scared. But that's what I decided, that I was going to make sure Rickey survived. I was going to make sure he escaped . . . from here." Myrtle Jefferson looked toward Stan, then right through him. "And I couldn't." She shook her head, and focused on Stan again. Her forehead was scrunched into a field of wrinkles. "He died a block from here. Do you understand that?"

Stan cleared his throat and shook his head. "There was nothing you could have done." He wasn't sure he was telling the truth.

Myrtle Jefferson nodded. "I know." She wiped her eyes with the tissue and sat up straight again. "I think."

Stan wanted to get up, walk to the table and put his arm around Rickey Jefferson's mother. She looked so tiny all of a sudden, as though she'd shrunk before his eyes. Stan pushed himself deeper into the couch.

Her voice was strong again. Or stronger. "How many of these cases have you had, detective?"

Stan shook his head. "Too many."

She looked deep into his eyes. "What do other parents say?"

He looked away and stared at the floor. "They say they don't understand, either."

"Even the parents of bad boys?"

He looked at Rickey Jefferson's mom. "It's no different with them."

Myrtle Jefferson nodded and wiped her eyes again. "I guess it shouldn't be."

Suddenly the room was quiet. The house was deathly still. The only movement was the thin trail of smoke from Myrtle Jefferson's cigarette in the ashtray, curling toward the yellowed plastic light fixture above the dining room table. Rickey Jefferson's mother seemed frozen in her chair. Stan felt the chill that she had been trying to ward off, and pulled his coat tight. He didn't want to be the one to shatter the silence—it seemed heavy, but so peaceful—but he did.

"Maybe I should leave. I could come back later."

Myrtle Jefferson shook her head. "It'll be no better later."

Stan nodded, and pulled a pen from his pocket. "I have a few more questions. . . ."

She nodded. "I know." She exhaled deeply, but silently. "I don't think he was in any sort of drug gang. Lots of them around here. Most of them ignored Rickey because of his stutter. Kids teased him about it. They thought he was a sissy." Myrtle Jefferson ran her hands through her hair. "A speech teacher at school—right there, down the road, at Carsten's—was working with him on that. We'd practice at night instead of watching TV. He was getting better. Deep down, I was hoping he wouldn't. I figured the stutter might keep him out of trouble." She looked at Stan, then smiled to herself. "Funny how a mind can work."

"On that corner last night . . ." Stan's voice was low.

Myrtle Jefferson shrugged, then shook her head.

Stan nodded. "I need the names of some friends."

"I can get you some."

"Phone numbers, too."

"Yes."

Stan puffed his cheeks and exhaled slowly, then slid his notebook back into his coat pocket. Myrtle Jefferson watched him, then stood and walked slowly to the window. The sky was pink with the sunrise. Steam seeped silently from a manhole cover.

"You solve many murder cases, Detective Kochinski?"

Stan waned to lie, but he didn't. "Some."

"Think you'll solve this one?"

Then, he did. "I don't know."

"Can't you promise?"

Stan shook his head.

Myrtle Jefferson smiled a terribly sad smile. "I knew that. I just wanted to ask. I don't have anything left."

The house went quiet again, until an alarm clock went off

upstairs. It was the clock that would wake Myrtle Jefferson so she could get Rickey up for school. Myrtle Jefferson brushed the tears from her cheeks and slowly padded toward the stairs. She turned back toward Stan.

"I think you should go now."

He did.

◇ 6 ◇

Bill Colbane pulled into Frank's driveway at about 8:25. He sat in his car for a minute or two, staring through the windshield and studying the Sims house, a sprawling Tudor on Balmoral in the heart of the affluent Palmer Woods area on Detroit's northwest side. He admired Frank's home. It was beautiful inside, impeccably decorated, but it was the outside, the almost pastoral setting on the edge of a boot-tough city, that Colbane envied. In the spring, Frank's place was resplendently garnished with the large, white flowers of a pair of catalpa trees, and tiny pink blossoms from three small clusters of cherry trees. In the summer, lush ivy wound its way across the front of the house; stately hedges, painstakingly trimmed, formed the perimeter of the front yard. In the fall, two huge statuesque oaks exploded into a rainbow of hard colors. The wind never seemed to whip through the yard, even on blustery days. The breeze was always soft and soothing. It felt like such a gentle place.

But today, even with the blanket of new-fallen snow, everything looked dreary and solemn. The brick was bare and imposing, and the yard seemed too big, cold, and sterile. Bill Colbane took off his glasses and rubbed his eyes. He was frightened. Getting out of his car, he was stung by a slap of wind, and tugged his coat closed. He was impeccably dressed in a black, full-length cashmere coat and a stylish navy suit, but he felt rumpled.

Frank met him at the door. He didn't even have to ring. Frank was wearing a dark gray, pinstriped suit, a white shirt, and a blood-red tie. Ready for business. Bill Colbane handed over his coat in silence and headed down the hallway to the study. The smell of fresh pastry wafted in from the kitchen. Mindless banter from a local morning TV show buzzed in the background. As Bill Colbane entered the study, he heard Frank greet Marty Hatch and Sandy Stone at the front door, and the three men arrived in the study about fifteen seconds later. No one was smiling, but no one looked as grim and despairing as Bill Colbane felt.

Hatch and Stone sat on the black leather couch across from Frank's desk. Frank offered Colbane a seat alongside the desk, but Colbane shook his head and stood against the wall behind the couch. Frank locked the study door, strode to the window, and pulled opened the curtain. Sunlight streamed in.

"Coffee, gentlemen?"

Hatch and Stone nodded. Colbane shook his head. Frank served his guests from the silver tea service on the mantel, then pressed a buzzer on his desk. Within seconds, there was a knock on the door. Frank unlocked the door and took a platter of pastries from a young, attractive housekeeper, closed the door, re-locked it, and carried the platter to his desk.

"Help yourselves." Frank sat behind his desk, leaned back in his chair, placed his fingertips together, and studied the three men. Stone, the chief assistant Wayne County prosecutor and Frank's protégé from his county prosecutor days, was also dressed in a suit and tie. He looked more concerned than worried. Hatch was dressed in a dark brown pinstriped suit with his trademark pink carnation on his lapel. Early in his political career, the flower had earned Hatch the nicknames "Pinky" and "Bud." Neither had really stuck, though one or the other would pop up time and again when one of the local newspaper columnists took a run at him. Hatch had a stern look on his face. Frank switched his gaze to Colbane. There was no doubt about him. He looked scared.

Frank sat forward in his chair and grabbed a cherry Danish, then deferred to the mayor. "Marty?"

Hatch was staring at a flickering TV in the bookcase across the room. The sound was off. A film clip showed the murder scene. Hatch waved his hand at Frank without looking at him.

Frank took a quick glance at the TV. He had already seen the footage. "I assume everyone has read the paper." He men nodded. "I touched base briefly with Shooter this morning on the off chance that we weren't involved." Frank paused, then shrugged. "But we were. I didn't have time to get the whole story. I'm meeting him later." He picked up the pastry and took a bite. "We better review everything from the beginning. Sandy?"

Colbane was anxious to get to the point. "The beginning?"

Frank smiled at the judge. "Relax, Bill. We'll get there. Sandy?"

Stone was six years younger than Frank, and almost as calculating. He sat forward on the couch. "Our mark was Julius Caesar Cooper, top street lieutenant and the second in command in Dickie Broedinger's Satin Knights. The Satin Knights operate primarily on the lower east side." Stone stopped and looked around the room. "This was supposed to. be a—maybe *the*—big one. Cooper was . . ."

Frank caught Stone's eye and raised a finger. He turned toward Colbane. "What do you have, Bill?" Stone could have continued, but Frank wanted to get Colbane involved before he lost it.

Bill Colbane reached into his shirt pocket and pulled out a sheet of paper from a yellow legal pad. His hands were trembling. He swallowed hard before beginning. "Cooper . . ." The word came out in a whisper. Colbane cleared his throat and began again. "Cooper. Black male, twenty-two. Record includes three convictions for possession, two for distribution, and two for aggravated assault. Always manages to find a sharp attorney. Always manages to find a decent alibi . . ."

Stone interrupted. "Always manages to convince any and all witnesses to disappear."

Frank nodded. "Bill?"

"Total time served on all those—eleven months, two days."

Hatch was shaking his head. "Motherfucker." The word came out in a cold, vicious whisper. He reached for a piece of coffee cake.

Frank smiled at Colbane. "Thanks, Bill." Colbane nodded. He was coming back, slowly but surely. Frank turned to Stone. "More?"

Stone nodded. "Julius Caesar Cooper is so good at what he does that he gets recruited by drug gangs in other cities."

Hatch looked at Stone. "I suppose he does a little consulting, too."

Stone looked back at the mayor. "As a matter of fact, he does. We heard he was in Chicago a few weeks ago to work with some west side gang."

Frank interrupted. "Go on."

"We've been hot on him for three homicides this year, all execution-style drug hits. All the victims were bound and gagged, all took one round in the back of the head. We couldn't make anything stick. We always got close. But that's all—close."

Colbane went into a coughing fit. Stone stopped. Frank got up, walked behind the judge, and patted him on the back. "Okay, Bill?" Colbane nodded. Frank looked at Stone. "Anything else?"

"Yep. He walked again three days ago, right out of Judge Sowinski's courtroom. Preliminary exam. Rape charge, first degree. Fourteen-year-old girl. Ripped her up bad. Put her in the hospital for a week. We figured we had him clean, until the victim clammed up and all the witnesses . . . poof"—Stone snapped his fingers—"just like that. He's back on the street. No trial, no nothing." Stone made eye contact with each man in the room. "He put the word out. There wasn't anything we could do. He was a good choice, Frank. He's a real . . ."

Hatch interrupted again. "Motherfucker."

Frank nodded to the mayor. Stone resumed. "Dickie B's

been trying to expand his business lately, and Cooper's boys've been doing some late-night recruiting." Frank got up and walked to the window. "Latest word was he— himself, J.C.—was going to be meeting with some kids last night around Lenox, Drexel, that area, and Kercheval." Frank was staring out the window. It was snowing again. "It should have been a piece of cake: Wait 'till Cooper's alone, and drill him."

Frank turned and faced the group. "And we fucked up." Stone nodded. "Apparently."

The mayor hadn't taken a bite of his coffee cake yet. He looked at it, then tossed it back on the tray. "Goddamnit, you told us Shooter was the best. What the hell happened?"

Frank shook his head. He bit his bottom lip, softly. "I told you, Marty, I don't know yet."

Colbane removed his reading glasses and blew his nose, then turned and walked to the fireplace, put his arm on the mantel, and stared down at the flames licking the logs, his back to the rest of the group. Frank watched Colbane for a second, then returned to his chair and sat down. "Cooper was supposed to be, what—number . . ."

Colbane didn't turn around or look up. "Seven." His voice was still shaky.

Frank leaned forward in his chair. He put his elbows on his desk. "Six before this mess? Well, we must be doing something right." His voice was strong and confident. "Maybe we got lazy. Maybe we got careless. Maybe we just got a little ahead of ourselves." He paused and looked Stone and Hatch in the eyes.

Stone looked at Frank and shrugged. "Maybe we just got unlucky."

"Maybe." Frank nodded. "But we can't afford any more bad luck."

Colbane looked up, turned, and tried to speak. Frank put up his hand. "Okay, here's what we do. For starters, we suspend the operation. Agreed?" The men nodded.

Hatch raised his hand. "Who's got the investigation?"

"I'll get there, Marty. First, we all need to understand one thing." He paused. "We need to remember, to remind ourselves as often as we have to, that to just about everyone in

the city—except us, of course—that this is just another garbage case."

Colbane looked up and stared hard at Frank. "An eleven-
year-old kid?" Colbane's voice was strong now. Hatch and
Stone turned toward him.

Frank stared back. "Garbage, Bill. Fucking garbage. It's
what the boys on the street call shooby-do—a goddamn
drug-gang shooting on a deserted street corner at midnight.
Could've been a drive-by. Could've been a drug buy.
Could've been the kid stiffed someone and they took it out
on him. It happens all the fucking time. And as for his
age—thirty-seven kids've been already killed this year—this
just makes thirty-eight." Frank sneaked a deep breath, then
exhaled slowly and silently, trying to take the edge out of
his voice. "Okay, Bill?"

Colbane nodded. Frank continued. "Kochinski's got the
case, Marty."

"Who's he?"

"Mr. Baseball."

"The one who ended Roman's career?"

Stone jumped in. "Rogine's."

Frank sat back in his chair. "He can be tough, when he's
interested—which isn't so much anymore. Did a bang-up
job last summer on the Mendoza shooting. That case was
cold as it gets, and he cracked it. When he gets a bug, he's
good. Other times, he's pretty ordinary."

Hatch leaned forward from the couch. "He got a soft
spot?"

"What?"

"Will he make some sort of crusade out of this?"

Frank shrugged. "Don't know."

Hatch frowned. "Don't know isn't what we need right
now."

"I realize that. But there's not much we can do. I can't
pull Kochinski off it, at least not right now. I don't think we
have much to worry about. After all, why *should* he care
about this case? We'll just have to make it tough on him."

"How?" said Hatch.

"Don't know. Something will come up."

"Great." It was Colbane. The sarcasm was sharp. He was

getting rattled again. "We got an eleven-year-old kid here, for chrissakes."

Frank nodded. "You keep saying that."

"That's the fact." Colbane took off his glasses. "What about the goddamn press?"

"I was getting to that." Frank stood and began pacing behind his desk. He didn't want to loose his cool. Calm was too important right now. "The media will latch onto this thing, so Marty, you beat them to this one. Call a press conference this morning. Tell the press that you've had enough of this senseless violence, that this shooting is getting priority treatment, that, goddamnit, we're going to find out who shot the kid. Then schedule some trips to the neighborhood, the scene, mama's house. Take her some flowers—no, better yet, put a wreath at the scene. Get out there this afternoon. TV'll love that. Great pictures. We'll make it the lead story on the evening news."

Hatch nodded.

Colbane spoke up again. "Not enough."

"Correct," Frank said. "On my side, I'll sing the praises of Kochinski and build up his success on the Mendoza case. Tell everyone he's one of our top guys."

Hatch jumped in. "Someone's going to ask why we don't put more detectives on the case."

Frank nodded. "Well, maybe we do. But at the same time, we make it clear that we can't grind to a halt over one case."

Colbane wasn't convinced. "What if that doesn't work?"

Frank spread his arms wide. "We don't even wait to find out. At the same time we play Kochinski up, Marty appoints one of those blue-ribbon panels to study the drug and violence problem on the east side. We say we not only need to solve this case but we need to make sure this never happens again." Frank looked at Colbane. "Then Marty puts one district court judge—one *black* district court judge—on the panel." He nodded to Stone. "And one tough young assistant prosecutor." He smiled. "And, of course, the police chief."

Hatch was nodding, so was Stone. Even Colbane looked a bit relieved. "This is not as difficult as it sounds, gentlemen—as long as we don't panic." Frank's smile widened. "Then we stick this thing on someone. Sandy?"

"Cooper?"

"Wouldn't that be sweet."

Hatch shook his head. "Are we dreaming, Frank?"

"About hanging Cooper? Probably. But we'll get someone." Frank walked to the window and leaned against the ledge. He felt a rush of adrenaline. "Just remember, we're okay. All we have to do is make a few adjustments. Nothing fancy." He looked at Colbane. "And just remember, too— only we know. No one else knows. And no one else will."

Frank looked around the room. Stone was smiling. Hatch was nodding. Colbane was rubbing his eyes. Everything would be okay, at least for now. "Any questions?"

For a second, everyone was quiet. Hatch raised his hand. "What if the press gets wind of this meeting?"

"It won't, but if it does—perfect. In fact, maybe we ought to leak it to someone: four concerned city officials getting together before breakfast to discuss the tragic loss of a child's life. What could be better?" Frank grinned again. "You handle that, Bill?"

Colbane nodded.

Hatch stood up. "Was this kid clean, Frank?"

"Dunno yet. But we can fix that, too, if we need to. A fifth-grade choirboy or an eleven-year-old asshole—it all depends on what we want. Okay?"

They all nodded.

"Then that's it." He walked to the study door and unlocked it. Stone hustled out, Hatch right behind him. Colbane loitered a bit, following Frank into the living room. He shook his head. "I'm scared, Frank."

Frank watched from a picture window as Stone and Hatch got into their cars and drove off. "I know, Bill." Then he put his arm around the judge and squeezed his shoulder. "But don't be."

◇ 7 ◇

The navy Mercedes pulled to the curb next to the red brick Ebony Market at Lenox and Charlevoix. The right turn signal flashed once, then the left, then the car pulled ahead two blocks, turned left on Gray and stopped. On cue, Julius Caesar Cooper, lanky and quick, in baggy army fatigues, an overcoat and reflector aviator sunglasses, stepped out from behind a vacant apartment building and jogged to the car. He took a quick look up and down the street, then rapped on the smoke-glass window. When the door latch popped, he slid in neatly next to the driver.

Richard Broedinger sat behind the wheel. Wendy, his wife, sat behind him in the backseat. Broedinger was a short, thin, pasty-skinned man in his early fifties. He wore a mother-of-pearl pinkie ring and dark, wrap-around sunglasses. Wendy was a bleached blonde in her early forties who fancied push-up bras, lots of rouge, and the attention of younger men. Years ago, Wendy Broedinger had been an elementary school teacher, and a terrible one. Now, she ran a strip joint on Eight Mile, the road separating Detroit from its northern suburbs. Years ago, her husband had been a flunky real-estate agent. Now, he was the brains behind a multi-million-dollar drug ring on the city's lower east side. Julius Cooper was Dickie Broedinger's right-hand man. The two men met every day, usually alone. Wendy was along today only because her husband was driving her to work. The time and place Broedinger and Cooper met changed daily. The meeting room didn't.

Cooper slammed the door shut and shivered. He reached for the Heat switch on the dashboard, punched it, then flipped on the fan. "Let's get some fuckin' warmth in here, man." He looked at his boss. "And what say we change the station?" Classical music was playing softly. Cooper began punching the radio buttons, but nothing happened.

"It's a CD, Julius." Broedinger smiled and took the disk out. "Schubert." He reached into a coat pocket, pulled out a tiny, red cardboard box, opened it, and offered Julius a cigarette.

Cooper shook his head. "That shit kills, man—and that brand stinks."

Broedinger laughed, pulled out a short, stubby, filterless cigarette, tamped it on the back of his hand, lit it, took a drag, and exhaled. "Du Maurier, Julius. Five sixty-five a pack—*Canadian.*"

Dickie Broedinger laughed again. He liked yanking on Cooper's chain, but Cooper was all right. They had worked together for almost four years now. Cooper, strikingly handsome, smart, and athletic, was responsible for the daily operation of Broedinger's twelve crack and cocaine houses. He seemed to grow more efficient each day. Broedinger's business had never been better. Much of Cooper's managerial success was traceable to his ruthlessness. Even Broedinger, who had once taken a meat cleaver to the thumb of a light-fingered employee, was somewhat wary of his right-hand man.

Cooper had been involved in the drug business since he was six, when he'd been a courier for a small-time dealer. By eight, he was packing a gun. By nine, he was using it to 'cap chronic debtors. By eleven, he was a full-fledged drug enforcer, which simply meant that he was a killer. No one knew how many people Julius Cooper had murdered. Cops in the gang squad said maybe as many as a dozen. Street legend had the total at twice that. When anyone asked him, Cooper would laugh and say he had lost count. "A long, long, *long* time ago."

Now, Cooper was swiping at the air, trying to fan away the smoke from Broedinger's cigarette. A trio of thin gold bracelets danced on his wrist. "That shit makes you smell like one of those fuckin' bars. Me, too. C'mon, man." Cooper turned toward the backseat. "C'mon, Miz B., tell him to stop."

Wendy Broedinger looked at Julius, shrugged, and smiled politely, but Cooper didn't return the grin. She reached up and massaged her husband's neck. "He's right, D.B."

Dickie Broedinger laughed again, extinguished his cigarette, then reached inside his coat and pulled a piece of paper from a pocket. It was the Jefferson clipping from the *Free Press*. He wasn't laughing when he tossed it in Julius's lap. Cooper picked up the paper, read a few lines, then tossed the clip back at his boss.

"You've become a speed reader, Julius?"

Cooper shook his head. "Nope. Just none of my business."

"Not you?"

"Nope, not me."

Broedinger pointed to the article. "This is our corner."

"I know."

"But it wasn't you." It was a statement, not a question.

"Why would I lie?"

Broedinger bit his lip, then nodded. "You know this kid?"

Cooper turned toward Broedinger. "Sure, I saw him last night. Word was he was lookin' for work. I met him to check him out."

"And?"

Cooper looked out the windshield and shook his head. "He was a fuckin' geek. Looked serious enough, but had trouble talkin'. T-t-t-talked like th-th-this. Said he was in, then out, then in, then out. There was somethin' stupid about him."

"And?"

"And he was still breathin' on his own when I left him."

"Sure?"

Cooper was getting close to losing it. He wasn't used to being interrogated by anyone but the cops—and he had little patience with them. "Yes. I'm. Sure." He bit off the words. "He was standing there, crying like a fuckin' mama's boy."

Broedinger was silent. He was staring at the newspaper clipping. "Some other gang, perhaps? The Pony Boys? The DeeJays?"

Cooper shrugged. "Maybe—go ask them." He looked out the window. "What's the worry, anyway?" Cooper was annoyed. The smoke, still hanging thick in the car, was getting to him. "Another nigger kid. Bitch would've died sooner or later—period."

Broedinger folded the paper and put it back in his pocket. "No worry, then?"

"None."

"To tell you the truth, Julius, I didn't think you'd be stupid enough to shoot anyone, much less an eleven-year-old, and leave the body out in the open." Broedinger ran a hand through his gray crewcut hair. "But that doesn't let us off the hook."

Cooper nodded. "You got that right."

"Things will be hot around her for a while. Someone's going to be raising some hell about this kid. The cops are gonna take some heat. Which means we're gonna take some heat."

Cooper unbuttoned his coat. He reached toward the dashboard and switched off the fan.

"So, let's play it cool for a couple of days. Keep your ears open. Maybe we find out who killed this kid. Maybe we make a trade . . ."

"Maybe we screw someone with it."

Broedinger nodded. "But let's not get too creative. For starters, let's just get the word out: Anyone tips us on the shooter, and we got a nice little paycheck for 'em."

"Gonna cost."

"Whole thing's going to cost us. The cops turn up the heat, and our patrons keep staying home. That means money. We either got to hope the cops figure this one out soon, or we have to help 'em."

Broedinger took out another cigarette and tamped it on the steering wheel. Cooper watched him and shook his head. "Time to go." Broedinger flicked his lighter and laughed.

Julius Cooper opened the door, slid out of the car, walked to the rear, and headed carefully down the street. Within seconds, he had slipped back into the shadows.

◇ 8 ◇

Frank arched his shoulders and his neck, then relaxed, took off the hat, and removed the mirrored sunglasses. The customs guard on the U.S. side of the Detroit-Windsor Tunnel hadn't recognized him, nor had the one on the Canadian side. He hadn't figured they would. He slouched down in the seat of the black Caravan and looked around. Nothing was moving. He and Shooter had met here at the Pilot House Marina in LaSalle once before. It was a good spot. It was about ten minutes south of downtown Windsor, out past the racetrack; and it was deserted this time of the morning, especially this time of the year. Frank had pulled into a vacant space along a row of some twenty dry-docked cabin cruisers. The minivan wouldn't be visible from the street—he'd checked that out last time—but he was getting jittery, now, and cold—and angry. He shivered. He could see his breath. He pulled a blanket from the backseat, covered his legs, and looked at his watch. It was 10:12. Shooter was seventeen minutes late. Frank gritted his teeth and wondered how much longer he'd have to wait.

The date flashed on the watch: December 21. He had sold his plan to Hatch, Colbane, and Stone almost a year ago. Fifty-one weeks, to be exact. And everything had gone according to plan—slowly, at first, though flawlessly, and almost effortlessly. Until last night. Frank's eyes burned. He took off his gloves and put his fingertips over his eyes. Despite himself, he chuckled. Frank Sims rarely looked back, but when he stopped to consider the incredible arrogance of his plan, he was amazed that he had been able to persuade Hatch and Colbane to throw in with him in the first place.

Well, Colbane, at least. Frank figured Hatch had had little

choice, maybe none at all. Marty Hatch, fifty-two, a bachelor, the son of a former U.S. senator, was a third-term mayor with an eye on the governor's mansion in Lansing—and beyond. In public, he was energetic and charismatic; he worked hard to maintain a well-honed image as a cultured man of many pursuits, and a gracious, democratic champion of all races and creeds. In private, he was calculating and single-minded—a cut-throat political beast who talked about "niggers" and "kikes" and "wops" as though they were pawns on a giant chessboard and who, when push turned to shove, would do just about anything for checkmate.

Still, Marty Hatch had accomplished a lot for his town. He had bullied his auto-executive cronies into reinvesting in the city. He'd persuaded a handful of skittish developers to build a skyscraping super-hotel downtown and tony condos and exclusive high-rises on the banks of the Detroit River. He'd hired more mops. He'd reorganized the city's recreation department and resurrected hundreds of acres of ill-kept parks. He'd lobbied successfully for state funds to fix streets and improve the city's landscaping. One beautification project had included planting five thousand maple trees on neighborhood tree lawns decimated by Dutch elm disease. A *News* editorial had lampooned the idea, calling it "sappy," but the voters had bought it.

They'd bought a lot of what Marty Hatch had offered—but less and less all the time. Marty Hatch wasn't the problem. People liked Marty. During his three terms in office his hair had turned from black to silver, his public manner had become more mature, more distinguished, more stately. His trademark pink lapel carnation had looked a tad pretentious on a forty-one-year-old. Now, it looked right. It sprouted from the breasts of Hatch supporters on election days and even popped up as an unofficial city insignia on the corners of promotional pamphlets and posters. But Hatch's city had a problem that carnations couldn't hide—and the frustrated people of the besieged city, needing to blame someone, anyone, were more and more moved to blaming Marty Hatch.

The problem was the Satin Knights, the drug gang that had taken its name from the shiny, one-hundred-dollar athletic jackets its members wore. The Knights had been only a sporadic nuisance ten years earlier, when Hatch had taken office. But over the decade, as other splinter drug gangs flared and then fizzled, the Knights had systematically infiltrated the lower east side until they had become a vicious occupation army running a multi-million-dollar drug operation that drove—and continued to drive—the blue-collar German, Polish, Italian, and black residents to the safety of the suburbs. White flight—and black, for that matter—was costing Hatch his power base. It was threatening to end his career.

Following his first term as mayor, Hatch had seemed a virtual shoo-in to be governor someday. Four years later, political analysts were calling him "one of the favorites." Two years later, they listed him in the middle of a pack of seven possible candidates—behind two men he had defeated in mayoral races. Each decline in the polls was directly traceable to Hatch's failure to attack crime—particularly the drug problem, the Satin Knights, and the desecration of the east side. When the newspapers ran stories on Hatch's rating, the headlines invariably said something like: "Hatch lays another egg." Marty Hatch was growing increasingly weary of being the butt of jokes. But the simple truth was that he was getting his ass handed to him by a bunch of punk thugs. And when it came to fighting back, Marty Hatch—who was known to whisper boasts of herculean sexual feats to men and women alike—was impotent.

He was losing face quickly, and he was growing increasingly desperate.

Frank Sims knew that, and he knew two other things. One: Marty Hatch wasn't dead, but he had to do something soon to salvage his political career. And two: If Hatch was going to gamble, he had to gamble big. Frank also knew that the mayor wasn't the most creative thinker and that he'd listen to just about any idea from his loyal protégé, Frank Sims, short of arming himself with an Uzi and taking to the streets.

So Hatch was a cinch. Frank was, too. He really had no choice, either. Frank had gambled by tying his political wagon to Hatch's, as the mayor's appointed police chief.

"Hatch goes down, I go down, too," he would remind himself more and more lately, shaking his head. And though Frank had briefly considered keeping Hatch in the dark about his plan—there really was no need to get him involved—it was better for Frank to get the mayor's approval. If the idea worked, as it must, Hatch would be even more indebted to him.

After all, this was Frank's route to the stars. It was simple: Hatch became governor, and Frank became mayor of the seventh largest city in the country. Then Hatch became senator and Frank became governor of the eighth largest state. It was possible—no, probable. Not that Frank figured on being Hatch's boy forever. Someday, it could be Hatch and Sims, the senators from Michigan. Why not? And someday, when the time was right, when it really counted, he'd finally loose himself from Hatch's coattails. Maybe when it came down to him against Marty in some backroom battle for a presidential nomination. Frank smiled to himself, but he really thought that big. And if it came to that, he would kick Hatch's keister from here to wherever. Now, he simply had to save the mayor's ass—and his own.

Sandy Stone? Simple, too. Stone was a Frank Sims protégé, and for this plan, Frank needed an inside man in the county prosecutor's office. Stone had few friends, and certainly no pals, among his colleagues. It wasn't hard to understand why. Nobody mattered to Sanders Albert Stone except Sanders Albert Stone—and Frank Sims.

Frank hadn't recruited Stone as his stooge; Stone had volunteered the day Frank became the country prosecutor. Stone had worked under Frank for two years while Frank was chief assistant, and had watched him carefully. Sandy Stone was an arrogant son of a bitch, but he'd known he needed a mentor, and he'd known Frank needed a lieutenant.

Frank could see right away that Stone would never challenge him politically. At five-foot-three, prematurely balding, and boyishly chubby, Stone was all wrong for the spotlight. He was law-school smart to the point of being brilliant, but he had no magnetism or charisma, not even in the heat of court. Frank knew from the start that Sandy Stone was a follower.

Frank also knew that Stone—married to the only child of a wealthy, local financier, and the father of two young boys—was a closet homo-sexual. About a year before Frank had become county prosecutor, Stone had been arrested for soliciting a male undercover cop in L.A. Frank had been using the department receptionist's typewriter the day the L.A. chief assistant DA had called the department about Stone's arrest. Frank had absentmindedly answered the phone, transferred the call to his office, and persuaded his L.A. counterpart to drop the charges.

Only Frank and Sandy knew about the incident. It was the sort of arrangement Frank Sims lived for.

In time, Frank and Sandy had become good friends. Frank kept Sandy involved in as many of the top criminal cases as possible. They formed quite a prosecutorial team, with Stone doing the research and legwork and Frank handling the courtroom. Over one long stretch, the county prosecutor and his prized assistant won six consecutive high-profile cases. Fred Smithson, a *Free Press* columnist, called one of their triumphs a "monster conviction"—and nicknamed them Frank 'n' Stone.

But Stone's main job was to keep secret dossiers on community leaders and politicians. He had begun his files as a hobby about a year before throwing in with Frank. In fact, it was the files that had won Stone over to Frank completely.

"I find things out, Frank." Frank was sitting behind his desk. Stone was standing in front of him. "Personal things." The doors to Frank's office were closed. The shades were down.

Frank sat back and folded his hands across his chest. "How good are you?"

Stone grinned. "Try me."

Frank nodded, sat up, and gave him the name of a defense attorney who'd been giving him trouble lately. Eleven days later, Stone walked into Frank's office, tossed onto Frank's desk a folder containing details of a certain drug-filled party after which a girl had been hospitalized, and walked out. Two days after that, Frank Sims and Sandy Stone were in business.

Bill Colbane was the only soft spot. Frank had figured he needed someone in the courts, someone who knew the judicial system inside and out. Colbane was a stretch in some ways—but in others, he was the most perfect.

Bill Colbane was a man of impeccable conscience and honor. Most who knew him figured that Bill Colbane would someday end up on the state Supreme Court. But few knew what Frank Sims knew about William Baxter Colbane—or rather what he knew about Melissa Anne Colbane.

Missy Colbane was the oldest of Bill and Molly Colbane's three children. She was the couple's only girl, and Bill Colbane's favorite child. She was never "Missy" to her father. She was "My Missy." It was never that way with his boys, Samuel and Abe. Only with his Missy. He was smitten with her, and she with him.

Missy Colbane had been a tall, perky kid with braces, who wore her hair in a bushy ponytail. She'd been an A-minus student at the prestigious Eastman Academy, played first-chair violin in the school orchestra, and been an enthusiastic, though rarely used, reserve point guard on the Pintos varsity basketball team. She'd been planning to attend either Princeton or Stanford—she'd been accepted at both schools—and hoped to follow in her father's footsteps and become a lawyer, then a judge. Sometimes her mannerisms—the way she would stroke her cheek when deep in thought; the way she rubbed her nose when she had the sniffles—had reminded Molly Colbane so much of her husband that she began calling her daughter Junior. A few years earlier, Bill and Missy had been working in the yard on a bright, sunny summer day when Missy had suddenly announced that she was not only going to be the first black woman to serve on the U.S. Supreme Court but the first child to serve on the court with her father. Then, Missy had giggled flirtatiously. Bill had chuckled, too, but not too much. His mind was awhirl. He was a dreamer, too.

Or once had been, anyway, before he'd lost his Missy. A little over a year earlier, Missy Colbane had been snatched off the street by two men as she walked alone to her car following a post-game party at a basketball teammate's house on Detroit's northeast side. The men had dragged Missy into their car and driven around the city for the next three hours, stopping to park in vacant lots and repeatedly rape her. They'd laughed at her when she'd pleaded for them to stop. They'd slapped and punched her when she'd cried for her "Daddy." When they were through with her, they'd dumped her on a lawn three blocks from there they'd found her. When a passing motorist spotted her two hours later, Melissa Colbane was curled up in a shivering ball and whimpering like a beaten animal.

Bill Colbane couldn't find his Missy when he walked into the emergency room. The only patient he saw was a horribly disfigured woman. Her nose looked broken; her lips were bleeding; she was missing two teeth. Her left eye was swollen shut in a bulbous purple knot; her right was wide open and grotesquely blank. She was rocking herself slightly, trying—desperately, it seemed to warm herself with a heavy woolen blanket that had been draped over her shoulders. Bill Colbane took a deep breath and was about to ask a nurse to help him find his Missy when the woman on the examining table turned away and the blanket fell off her back. When Bill Colbane saw the ponytail, he felt the breath being sucked out of his body.

He didn't hurry to his daughter's side. He couldn't. He stumbled to a pay phone, waving off help from a concerned security guard, and called Frank Sims. And in a moment of intense, incredible clarity, almost as if he'd somehow planned for such a tragedy, he told Frank he wanted the attack kept quiet. He didn't want the hospital or the police to file a report. He knew the legal system. Police involvement, publicity, maybe a trial, would only mean more pain for his daughter—and only a slim chance for convictions. He wanted only two things: He wanted Frank to come alone to the hospital in a few days with the police mug books. Frank did, and Missy Colbane paged through the books, and silently, stoically, pointed out her attackers. One was pictured in a shiny athletic jacket. The other was older and strikingly handsome.

After Bill Colbane kissed his daughter good night, he walked out with Frank and told him his other request: He wanted a shot at the rapists. Frank shook his head, smiled

kindly, and told his friend to go home and get some sleep.
Bill Colbane shrugged sheepishly, shook Frank's hand and
nodded—then drove to a shadowy street corner a few
blocks from the hospital, walked up to a teenager in one of
those gleaming jackets, pulled fifty dollars out of his
pocket, and bought a hot, snub-nosed Saturday night special.

Two months later, Frank Sims rolled the dice. He came
up with a seven.

Hatch, Stone, and Colbane were acquaintances, not
friends, which was fine with Frank. It was better that way.
Frank wanted to keep everything as antiseptic as possible.
This was to be a strict business arrangement, not a boys'
club.

Frank had called each of the men on Christmas night to
wish him a Merry Christmas and invite him over to watch
an NFL playoff game the next evening. All three had accepted, each thinking he was to be the only guest. They had
been surprised to see each other. They'd become even more
than curious when Frank switched off the TV just before the
kickoff.

"Very funny, Frank." Sandy Stone was an NFL junkie.
"Ha. Ha." He got out of his chair and walked to the TV.

Frank blocked his way. "Just give me a few minutes,
Sandy." Frank had an almost apologetic look on his face. "I
think I have something here a bit more interesting." Stone
looked disappointed but turned around and sat back down.

Marty Hatch was sitting behind Frank's desk. He took a
sip from his drink, pulled a pack of cigarettes from his shirt
pocket, and put his feet on the desk. "Anyone mind?" Bill
Colbane did. He hated cigarette smoke, but he said nothing.
He was too busy trying to figure out what Frank was up to.

"My guy from the *Free Press*—Slade, the old cop
reporter—called me last night a few minutes before I called
each of you." Frank was standing in front of a wall-length
bookcase. Colbane was on his left. On his right as an antique Nativity scene displayed on a ledge. The exquisite
crèche figurines had been hand-carved and hand-painted in
Czechoslovakia. The set cost three thousand dollars. Frank

picked the infant out of the tiny crib and gently closed his hand around it. "They finished tabulating the results of a new poll today. The results will run tomorrow morning." Hatch exhaled, coughed, then squinted through his smoke at Frank. Frank shrugged "Marty, it keeps getting worse."

Hatch shook his head and took a deep drag on his cigarette. "Fuck the polls. And that goddamn newspaper."

Frank kept his gaze on the mayor. Colbane kept his on Frank. The police chief had tightened his grip on the infant. "Wishful thinking, Marty." Hatch looked away, toward the Christmas tree in the corner of the room. Frank continued. "Crime's up all across the city. It's worse than ever on the lower east side—and it keeps spreading north."

Hatch took another long, deep drag on his cigarette. Colbane had never seen Hatch's face so furrowed. Stone was struck by how gray the mayor's complexion had suddenly grown. Both men were silent. Both felt uncomfortable, like outsiders caught in some private family discussion.

Hatch put his feet on the floor and his elbows on his knees and shook his head. He was still staring at the tree. "We've lost the goddamn east side to that nigger gang, Frank." His voice first was sprinkled with anger, then showered with despair. It wasn't the first time Frank had heard the mayor use that word in the company of blacks, but it was the first time Frank had heard Marty Hatch sound so beaten, and it was rather startling. But the confession was a perfect setup for Frank—so perfect that Bill Colbane would wonder later if Frank and Hatch had performed by script.

Frank shook his head. He still held the infant tight. "Not yet."

Hatch looked at him. "You got the answer?"

"Maybe."

"Well, then, let's hear it." Hatch's voice was riddled with sarcasm.

Frank pursed his lips and shrugged. "We take them out." He placed the infant carefully, safely on the ledge, next to the tiny manger.

Hatch squinted his eyes again, but not because of the smoke. "We what?"

"We take them, out."

"Kill them?"

"Slowly . . ."

Colbane and Stone shifted their eyes to Frank.

". . . and systematically."

Hatch laughed. "Assassination, Frank?"

Frank looked absentmindedly to his right and noticed that he hadn't placed the infant back in the crib. He gently picked up the tiny baby and set him in the his place. "No, not assassination, Marty . . . extermination." He paused. "There is a difference."

Frank looked to his left and locked eyes with Colbane. The look the judge got was what he would remember most about the meeting—the viciousness that flickered cold and gray in Frank's deep blue eyes.

Hatch laughed again, then suddenly stopped. "The department?" There was a childlike wisp of hope in his voice.

Frank shook his head. "I wish."

"Who, then?"

Frank tilted his head. "Us." He looked around the room.

"Us?" Hatch stubbed out his cigarette.

"Somebody working for us."

The study was silent. Frank looked at his guests. Hatch had a faraway look in his eyes. His mind was flying. Stone was smiling. He seemed genuinely amused. Colbane was staring at the floor now. Frank walked to the window. It was snowing again. He put his face close to the pane, and he felt a rush of relief. Everyone had reacted as he'd thought they would. He was okay. He was better than okay. This was going to work.

Hatch broke the silence. "We're supposed to be the good guys, Frank."

Frank turned back to his guests and smiled. "I know, Marty, and we are. And sometimes the good guys just have to gamble if they want to win."

"But . . . the risk."

Frank shrugged. "No risk, no reward."

Hatch exhaled in a low whistle. "Well . . . can't give us the chair for talking."

Frank shook his head. "No."

"So, let's hear it."

Frank walked to the bar and poured himself a drink, then to the fireplace and jabbed at the logs with a poker. He turned and faced his guests. "First of all, one thing is clear—we're losing in the polls because of the east side."

Stone got up and went to the bar. "Mainly because of Broedinger's boys."

Frank nodded. "Right. The Satin Knights." He took Stone's seat, sat forward, and put his elbows on his knees. "We need to go after them."

Stone was by the fireplace now. "The top guys?"

Frank shook his head. "Not right away."

Hatch stubbed out his cigarette and lit another. "Why not?"

"Too obvious." Frank paused. "But we'll get there." He looked at Colbane. The judge was still staring at the floor. "We take out some of the small-timers first. Just a few. Then we climb the ladder."

Hatch sat back in his chair. "I'd like to pull the trigger on a few of those motherfuckers."

Frank nodded. "You would be."

Colbane spoke up. His voice was low, now. He was still staring at his shoes. "How does this solve the problem?"

Frank smiled. "After the bodies start piling up, we get some stories in the papers blaming the shootings on gang warfare."

"How?" It was Hatch.

Frank waved his hand. "For starters, Slade at the *Free Press* will print just about anything I tell him. And I tell him the Pony Boys or the DeeJays, for instance, are trying to cut into the Knights' business."

"They're small potatoes."

"Right. But if we don't screw up, the Knights aren't going to be any wiser to this than anyone else. The Pony Boys and Deejays may deny it, but screw 'em. Not even the Knights will believe them. We get the gang-war stories rolling and we step up police patrols. I think we can make things so tough on the Knights they take their business elsewhere. They'll think they're getting it from two sides."

"Then they move to some other part of the city?"

"Maybe."

Hatch shrugged. "So, they move. We still got the problem."

"Not if they move out of the east side. That's a win for us. We reclaim those neighborhoods—what's left of them. We win." Frank paused. "Because we buy time." He could see Hatch nodding. "By the time the gangs get up and running somewhere else, your ratings will be up, and you just might be sitting under the rotunda in Lansing." Hatch was smiling now.

"We not only save the neighborhood, Marty,"—Frank looked Hatch square in the eyes—"we can save ourselves."

Stone pointed at Colbane. "Why us?"

Frank stood and faced his guest. "All of us here have some special interests. And I figure we need someone in the prosecutor's office and someone in the courts to make this thing work."

"Why?"

"Just in case."

Hatch pulled out his pack of cigarettes. It was empty, and he wadded it up and threw it at the wastebasket, missing. "In case. In case of what? How *does* this thing work?" He began fishing through his sports jacket for another pack.

Frank took a sip from his drink. It was almost empty. "It's simple. We pick a target. We make the hit." He walked to the bar and put down his glass. "I know a guy."

"Who?"

"Can't say."

"Can't say?" Hatch looked perturbed. "We're supposed to sign on to this and not know who in the hell the shooter is?"

Frank nodded. "Only way to do it, Marty. I know the guy, but no one else does. Too dangerous to have too many bosses. The guy is good. Trust me."

"You're asking for a lot."

Frank shrugged. "That's right." He looked at Hatch hard. "I'm promising a lot."

The study was heavy with silence again. Frank dropped some ice cubes in his glass. The tinkle echoed through the room. Frank looked around the study. Hatch was nodding to himself. Stone was still smiling and watching Frank.

Colbane was standing in a corner now, staring across the room at nothing. Frank poured himself another drink.

Hatch had found another pack of cigarettes. He was unwrapping them. "Guy do this for free?"

Frank laughed. "Nope."

"Who's paying?"

"The Satin Knights—that's the beauty." Frank stirred his drink. "It'll cost us about ten thousand dollars for a punk hit, twenty-five thousand for a mid-level one, and fifty thousand for one of the top guys."

Hatch nodded. "And?"

"And I—we—use the money in the police department's Secret Service fund, what we confiscate in dope raids."

Stone jumped in perfectly. "You keep track of that, Frank?"

"No, but I can get to it and I sign off on the books. Last year we had close to two million dollars. Ten thousand can get lost pretty easy."

Hatch lit another cigarette. "So, we got a soldier—and we got a fortune."

"Right."

"Let's run through this thing again."

Frank leaned forward from behind the bar. "Okay. We sit down and come up with a hit list. We start with a street dealer or two. Maybe move up to a few enforcers. Then maybe a crack-house boss. Maybe we take requests." Frank looked at Colbane. "Finally, we get to someone like Julius Cooper." The judge's eyes met his again.

Hatch smiled. "That's right at the top."

Frank nodded, then smiled. "We can get there."

"Go on."

"We investigate the shootings. We find nothing."

"Sure?"

"This guy is good—we find nothing. I make sure we find nothing. Then we sell the shootings to the media as gang warfare. And ain't it a shame that these punks are taking each other out? The press buys it. They eat up this gang-warfare stuff. Love it. Sells papers in the suburbs. Then we turn up the heat. The Knights feel the pinch from both sides and move out."

"What if they don't?" It was Colbane.

Frank shrugged. "If they don't, we lose." He paused. "But they will."

Hatch was jumping back in. "How often?"

"What?"

"How often do we . . . exterminate?"

"I don't know. Maybe once every six weeks or so, to start. Then we see how things go." Frank looked around the room again. He tried to make eye contact with each man. Colbane avoided his gaze.

Hatch sounded like he was already sold. "How long is all this going to take?"

"We can start tomorrow."

"To get the Knights on the move?"

"A year."

"That long?"

"Maybe longer. Maybe shorter. But it's going to work." Frank walked to his desk and sat on the corner. "One more thing." He put his drink down and folded his arms across his chest. "I picked you three for specific reasons. We need each other. We either all agree here, or we don't do it. We're all in, or we're not."

Hatch leaned back in his chair. "Fail-safe?"

"Not quite." Frank puffed out his cheeks as he exhaled. "But close as we're ever going to get."

"How close?" It was Colbane.

Frank smiled and went to his desk, reached into the drawer, and pulled out a thin sheath of papers. He passed a piece of paper to each of the men. It was a photocopy of a mug sheet. One of the photos was circled in red—Timothy "Capone" Stallings, a seventeen-year-old enforcer for the Knights.

"You remember this kid, Bill?'

Colbane nodded. Timmy Stallings was a killer. He had a rap sheet two feet long and had walked scot-free out of Colbane's courtroom in late July after being charged with two counts of aggravated assault on a drive-by shooting in broad daylight. ·A three-year-old playing next door to the target home had been wounded, and ended up losing a leg.

The story had flared in the papers, smoldered for a few days, then died. The charges were dropped.

Stone shrugged. "We went after him. Just couldn't prove he was the one firing from the car. Our case was just too flimsy."

Frank nodded. "I know—isn't it always?"

Then Frank distributed a set of photos. They showed Stallings, wide-eyed, in living color, lying in the basement of an abandoned home. He was wearing a shiny new jacket and a dark red hole in the center of his forehead.

"August 5th, gentlemen."

Hatch grimaced at the picture. "So?"

"Two of my best detectives investigated the shooting—when they weren't laughing, that is." Frank smiled. "They weren't big fans of little Timmy's. Seems somewhere along the way Tiny Tim had taken a potshot or two at the boys." Frank shrugged. "If I remember correctly, their initial notes said, and I quote, 'Good fucking riddance.' 'Fucking' was in all caps." Frank walked to the bar. "Timmy Stallings is dead, and we don't have time to worry about it, not with my boys thinking it was some two-bit drug hit and not that they even care—not with six hundred-plus other homicides to deal with."

Hatch was still staring at Frank. "So?"

Frank leaned back against his desk, cocked his thumb and forefinger, and pointed it at the mayor. He dropped his voice to a whisper. "My guy."

"What?" It was Colbane.

"My shooter."

The silence was almost suffocating. Hatch broke it with a low, raspy whistle. "Quite the gamble, Frank."

"No, Marty. No gamble at all." Frank freshened his drink. "Care to try and prove I was involved?" He took a sip and smiled smugly. "Good luck." Frank looked around the room. "The Stallings murder is wide open. But, funny thing, if you check the case file in homicide, it's stamped closed. Done. Finished." Frank winked at the mayor.

The silence was thick again. Colbane broke it. "So, why not just go it alone, Frank?"

Frank smiled. "Good question." Frank had figured

Colbane would ask that. He'd been waiting. "A couple of reasons. One: I said a few minutes ago that I picked all three of you for specific reasons. The more ambitious this project becomes, the more help I may need—some backstopping, just in case some lucky cop or judge puts two and two together and gets thirteen. We put up a few roadblocks—you, Bill, in the courts; or you, Sandy, at the prosecutor's office. We make things a little difficult. Reports get lost, evidence turns up missing. We just discourage them."

"That all?"

"That's all it will take." Frank paused and looked down at the floor, then around the room. "Remember, gentlemen, we're not talking about the tragic death of a kindly grandmother. We're providing a public service." He took another sip of his drink. "More importantly, we're not a bunch of virgins, here, either. Like I said before, we all have our own little agendas. Marty has his. I have mind. Sandy." Frank stared at Colbane. "And Bill." He stopped. "Not that we need to turn this room into a confessional. Bottom line—I'm just a salesman tonight, Judge, gentlemen. Just thought you all might be interested in what I'm trying to peddle—self-respect, salvation, payback."

The silence was heavier this time. Stone was the first to speak. "I'm in."

Hatch nodded. "I do nothing, I'm dead."

Frank nodded. "Bill?"

Colbane didn't look at him. "I need some time, Frank."

Frank shook his head. "Can't have it, Bill. You're in, or we're all out. It's that simple. You're out, and none of this ever took place. And if we're in, it means we're in. No one drops out. Can't do it. Can't change your mind."

Hatch took a quick drag on his cigarette. "I'm still in."

Stone nodded.

Frank looked around the room. "Shall we drink to this, then?" He raised his glass. Stone raised his. So did Hatch. They all looked at Colbane. Finally, he raised his glass, too.

Frank smiled. "Three wise men—a Happy New Year to all." Then, he walked to the TV and flipped it on. "Football, anyone?"

* * *

Beginning in February and over the next ten months, surely, but too slowly for Hatch's taste, six members of the Satin Knights became line entries in Pisarcawitcz's green homicide log. There was nothing sensational about the well-spaced deaths, just six bodies—a lowly bag man, two mid-level enforcers, two crack-house operators, and one of Cooper's lieutenants—found on deserted street corners or in alleys. There was nothing linking the shootings to each other, or to anything else, until Frank floated the gang-warfare theory with Slade. Slade and the *Free Press* took the bait, and the *News* followed the lead. So did TV. Pretty soon, every drug-related homicide was being analyzed in print or on news shows as a possible gang hit.

Frank had been getting a bit worried until Slade came through. Frank was eager for reports from his narcotics squad about confusion and panic among the Knights. He got none—until the media jumped on the bandwagon. The gang's business began to suffer once stories of hit men and executions blossomed. The reports began to scare away the gang's wealthy suburban customers. And as business started to wane, even just a bit, frustration grew among the Knights, who made money only when Dickie Broedinger made lots of money. Members of smaller splinter gangs denied they were weaseling in on the Knights' operation, but, as Frank had predicted, who believed them? Skirmishes between the groups began to spring up, and within a few months a drug war had actually begun.

Still, Broedinger wasn't quite ready to relinquish the east side and move to more peaceful ground, buying Frank and Hatch the time they desperately needed. But business was suffering and Broedinger's boys were beginning to feel spooked. Dickie B was just about where Frank wanted him. Hitting Cooper might have finished the job.

Might have.

Could have.

Should have.

Would have.

Frank gritted his teeth and shook his head. He looked at his watch. It was 10:33. He started to sit up in his seat when he saw a flash of color out of the corner of his eye. The passenger door clicked open. Shooter slid in.

"You'd be easy pickin's, Frank." Frank Sims's hired gun was smiling.

Frank wasn't.

◇ **9** ◇

Frank started the car and headed out of the marina. Shooter reached back and pulled on his seat belt. "Nice touch—the Canadian plates. Must be an impound car." He smiled.

Frank didn't say anything.

Shooter pulled a pair of sunglasses out of his pocket. "Turn left. There's a decent little place about a mile down the road." The men drove in silence. "There it is—Millie's. Good food. Filthy silverware." Shooter laughed. Frank pulled in. He still hadn't said a word.

Millie's was busy. That was good; Frank was relieved. He and Shooter got a table in the back, near the kitchen. The room was loud with chatter, and smelled of bacon grease and maple syrup. The menus were dog-eared and spotted with coffee stains. Shooter picked one up and studied it, while Frank stared across the table. Shooter was still wearing his shades. "Where are you supposed to be now?"

"Work." Shooter rubbed his nose.

"You gonna be missed?"

Shooter kept scanning the menu. "Next question."

"Last night." A waitress arrived at the table. She looked about sixty, and tired. Frank waved her away.

Shooter didn't. "Three eggs over easy, hash browns, sausage, coffee—and a smile, if you've got one." The woman forced a friendly grin. Shooter smiled back.

"Last night."

Shooter took a drink of water and inspected his fork. The prongs were dirty. "Two stars, maybe less. You lose two stars, maybe two and a half out of four, right off the bat for dirty silverware." He shook his head. "Give me yours."

Frank handed his over. "Last night. And take off the fucking glasses."

Shooter inspected Frank's fork. It passed. "Settle down, Frank. We're okay. No one saw anything." The waitress brought Shooter's coffee. He removed his sunglasses.

"You hit the wrong target."

"You're not listening, Frank." Shooter leaned forward and whispered through his teeth. "No one *saw* anything."

"You made a mistake." Frank felt his voice rising, and fought it. Now he was hissing through clenched teeth. "How?"

"It was dark."

"No excuse."

"Okay. Drug corner. Two guys. Same size. Dark-skinned. Long coats. I turned around, and one was gone."

"Cooper?"

"Your guess is better than mine was."

"Not funny."

"Look, the way things've been going, I figured it didn't make a helluva lot of difference."

"Well, it did." Frank wanted to pound the table. His hands were clenched white. "The kid was eleven."

"A mistake, Frank. I didn't know they grew eleven-year-olds that big."

"We can't have mistakes."

Shooter shook his head. "Well, that's where you're wrong, Frank."

The waitress arrived with Shooter's breakfast. "I used a piece from my personal collection." Shooter smiled at the waitress. "Thank you." After she left, he made an *X* in the yolk of each of his eggs, then flipped back the white membrane covering the yellow. The yolk oozed across his plate. "Damn, I wanted some toast, too."

"I don't give a damn what you used."

Shooter nodded and smiled. "Oh, yes, you do. See, I have

this little arsenal at home, stuff I collected during some of my scouting missions."

"I thought we discussed those. You said you were going to cool it. We can't afford you getting caught in some off-duty commando crap."

"The point is, Frank, I did the kid with a special-order .31, a real Fancy Dan of a gun. Looks like Custer's six-shooter. Patton's. Remember that movie? Pearl handlegrips and etching all over it."

"So?"

"So . . ." Shooter's smile began with a hint of a curl, then spread across his entire face. ". . . the weapon of choice last night was a gun I took off Julius Caesar Cooper."

Frank's mouth dropped open. "What?" The question came out in a loud whisper. A couple at a nearby table looked over. Frank ignored them.

Shooter lowered his voice. "On one of those night rides you told me to quit." Shooter continued between mouthfuls of food. "I was out one night—sometime in October or November, I think; must have been about three or four in the morning. Just looking around. I pulled down Coplin, or what's left of it. You know the street?"

Frank nodded. "Sure."

"Pretty bad. Place is deserted. All the houses are falling down." Shooter took a sip of coffee. "Actually, I don't know why I'm on Coplin, but I'm cruising down the street, ready to call it a night, and out of the corner of my eye I spot this Beemer or Mercedes, not sure—a dark . . . maybe purple. I'm bad with colors, Frank. It's parked in back of this shack. I turn my lights off. It was blacker'n hell. Overcast. No moon. I get out and start walking toward this car, and I swear I see this hunk of bright yellow hair bouncing up and down in the backseat." Shooter finished his breakfast. He waved the waitress, caught her eye, and mouthed, "More coffee." He took the napkin off his lap and placed it across his plate. "Anyway, I'm think that this is gonna be fun. I go back to the car, pull a nylon over my face, put on dark glasses and a hat, and tie a big black bandanna across my face." The waitress poured Shooter some more coffee.

Frank motioned for some, too.

Shooter leaned back in his chair and waited for the waitress to leave.

"Anyway, I sneak up to the car and yank the back door open real fast." He smiled. "Guess who?"

"Cooper?"

"Bingo. Sittin' there with his dick twitchin' in the moonlight. The broad tries to cover up with her arms, but she isn't covering up *anything*. She looks pretty well-to-do. Nice clothes. She also looks like she's going to throw up. Cooper doesn't look too happy, either. I give him a few 'motherfucks' to establish my bona fides, and take his money. Then I see this piece sticking out of the waist of his pants. I grab it from him and tell him to get the hell out of there." Shooter took a big gulp of coffee. "Funny as hell, seeing him run off, with his dick flappin' in the breeze. Made my night."

Shooter put down his cup. "Anyway, I take this gun home, wipe it down good, and put it in a special place, for a special occasion. I figured Cooper's number'd come up sooner or later and . . ." He stopped and smiled.

"And?"

". . . and I'd drill him with his own gun." Shooter smiled. "Nice irony, no?"

Frank frowned. He was still trying to piece everything together.

"Now, Frank, all you do is find the gun at Cooper's place and wait for the ballistics report—.31 caliber."

Frank was silent. He was staring through Shooter. Shooter leaned forward again, his voice a whisper. "Do you hear me? This was Cooper's favorite piece. Everyone out there knows it's his. And what's he gonna say when it pops up during a search and it matches the bullet that killed this Rickey Whatshisname? That he lost it? That someone stole it from him?" Shooter reached for a toothpick and began unwrapping it. "Do you think this white broad, whoever she was, is gonna back up his story? 'Oh, yes, Your Honor, it's true, Your Honor. You see, I was playing the skin flute for this Negro gentleman when some guy dressed like Jesse James stole his gun.' Think about it, Frank. He's your guy.

Cooper takes the big fall—the big one. You're home free. You . . . are . . . home . . . free."

For the first time in hours, Frank felt a smile wrinkle across his lips.

"There isn't a jury on this planet that's gonna let Julius Cooper walk on this one, Frank. There ain't a lawyer in the universe who can squeeze Cooper's slimy ass out of this jam. We'll get him placed at that corner that night. We got a dead kid. We got Cooper's gun." Shooter laughed. "I missed Cooper, but you get him anyway." He paused and picked at his teeth. "And it's even better this way. Think how good this'll make you boys look. You solve this one quick—and you put Public Enemy Number One on ice and cripple Broedinger's operation all at the same time. This is a goddamn PR coup, Frank."

Shooter stopped and leaned across the table again. "Mistake, my ass, Frank. I just might ask for a goddamn raise."

◇ **10** ◇

It was snowing heavily as Stan pulled out of the garage at headquarters and turned north on St. Antoine. He drove carefully. The weather service was forecasting six inches of snow by nightfall, and there were already two inches on the ground. The trip to Big Time's place took about five minutes in good weather. It would probably take at least twice that today. Stan turned on the radio and hit the scan switch. A country song came up, then a rock oldie, another oldie, a classical recording, then, Martin Hatch. Stan punched a button to hold the station. The mayor's voice faded away for a second, then returned.

" . . . mendous tragedy. But we will find Rickey Jefferson's killer. I promise that. We will find whoever did this and bring him to justice."

Stan checked his watch, then the digital display on the radio. It was almost 3:30. The channel was 1430. He guessed he was tuned to "The People's Agenda," an afternoon talk show on WMKO. He was right. The host of "The People's Agenda" was Sonja Rowdoe, a stylish, fortyish redhead, mother of three, and self-made local media personality. Rowdoe was also a gushy Hatch admirer, and three years earlier, popular legend had it, had been caught bent over a floor polisher in a maintenance closet with the mayor during a City Hall Christmas party. The mayor was a frequent guest on Rowdoe's show, and the invariable recipient of a "Rowdoe tooter," as one of Stan's newspaper friends put it.

Hatch was getting one again today. "This must be terribly upsetting to you, Mayor." Rowdoe climbed all over the word "terribly." Her voice dripped with concern.

"Me?" Hatch sounded his incredulous best. "How about Myrtle Jefferson? This is a hard-working, honest woman. Her boy was her only child."

"I assume this case is getting top priority." Rowdoe spat out the word "top."

"We have one of our finest homicide detectives on the matter."

"I'm sure you do, Mayor." Rowdoe paused. "After these messages, Mayor Martin Hatch will tell us about the visit he made at noon to the home of Myrtle and Rickey Jeff . . ."

Stan switched off the radio. He shook his head and decided to make the rest of the trip in peace. It was only a few more minutes, anyway. He ran his hand through his hair. Hatch. And Rowdoe. He wondered if the broom closet story was true. And the floor polisher.

It was almost 3:45 when Stan pulled to the curb at Arndt and Elmwood. The driver had taken longer than expected. Still, Stan was in no hurry. He sat in his car for a few minutes and surveyed the desolation of what had once been a tidy, thriving, neighborhood intersection. One corner now housed an abandoned barber shop; another was home to a gutted grocery. A third was landlord to a once-stately brick chapel with boarded-up windows and a rotted sign that said APOSTLE REFUGE. The fourth was an overgrown lot with a rusting swing-set and a big sandbox full of glass, cans, old newspapers, used condoms, mufflers, used tampons, and hypodermic needles. A trio of scraggly hounds, one with only three legs, stopped their tug-of-war over an inner tube long enough to watch Stan get out of his car. A quartet of fat blackbirds in the middle of the street paid no attention to him; they were too busy picking away at a cat's carcass.

Stan stopped outside the barber shop, turned, and looked down the block. The streets were deserted as far as he could see. The only sound was a *flap-flap-flap* of a torn awning blowing in the wind. Stan looked over his shoulder again for signs of human life, and saw none. It was snowing harder now. That was good. A fresh coat of snow always made things look better here. For a day, anyway, maybe less, until the salt and dirt and soot turned the snow black and the devastation poked through again. He shook his head—black snow. He shivered, pulled his gloves on tight, then opened the door leading to the stairway to the second story.

Ralph "Big Time" Slaughter had lived in the Gratiot and Mack area his entire life, and above the barber shop for almost seven years now. Big Time was a six-foot-five, one-hundred-seventy-pound heroin addict. He was thirty-nine; he looked more like fifty-five. His hands were grotesquely bloated and pockmarked with deep scars from infected sores he had gotten from shooting up with dirty needles. Once a lightning-quick, all-city basketball player, Time now walked stooped over, with a limp. He told everyone who cared to listen that he had done time in the Army, and blamed his stiff-legged shuffle on shrapnel he'd taken during a firefight in Vietnam. The truth was that the closest he had ever gotten to the military was the surplus store downtown, where he bought the green Army jackets he would wear until they unraveled on his back. He'd taken some lead once, all right, but not from the Vietcong. He'd gotten his from a thirteen-year-old enforcer, who'd shattered his kneecap with a .22 three years earlier on the Fourth of July, when Time had tried to steal some dope.

Big Time had been "The Man" here fifteen, twenty years ago. He'd been the neighborhood tough, with a loyal following. If a gang had wanted to run some numbers in the "Four Corners" area, they'd come to Big Time and make peace with him first. Same with a gang that wanted to hawk dope. Even Jehovah's Witnesses would stop and visit to make sure it was all right to solicit souls. But that was long before fourth-graders began gunning down adults. And it was long before Big Time got hooked on heroin.

To the ruthless young outlaws who now owned the streets, Big Time was a faceless town drunk, someone to laugh at, another flea-bag mutt to kick around. Sometimes, when they had nothing better to do, the local punks would drag him out of his apartment and roll him. Mostly, though, everyone ignored him, and that was even worse.

Big Time stole or panhandled or, when he could get hold of some cocaine, sold a little dope to pay for his essentials—"The Two Hs," he called them: heat 'n' horse. He ate at soup kitchens; he lived atop the abandoned barber shop for free, a modern-day squatter.

Stan had met Big Time about six years earlier, during a small-potatoes drug bust when Stan was on temporary duty as a narc. Time had looked like shit. Stan had told him he could get him probation if he was interested in doing a little police work.

Big Time was sitting in a chair at the end of Stan's desk. "Like what kinds of work?"

Stan was completing some paperwork. He didn't look up. "Like keeping your ears open."

Big Time had some friends who worked as police informants. "That it?"

Stan was still writing. "Just about."

Big Time smiled a big, wide, mostly toothless smile. "And just what might this keepin' my ears open be payin' for a man such as me?"

Stan kept writing. "Today, it ain't paying shit, douchebag." He glared at Big Time. "Talking to me about the east side is gonna be payback for a while for me keeping you out of jail—unless you want to do some time where there ain't no horse, and the drunks are gonna be ponyin' up to take turns walloping your sorry ass."

Stan stole a glance across the room at another narc, Billy Castle, and winked. Castle was holding his nose and trying not to laugh out loud.

Big Time didn't see any of that. He just nodded. "Lemme think on this, Mr. Ko-chinski." He stood up and scanned the room as though he were going to claim a desk there, somewhere, then turned to Stan and held out his hand. "Well, I'm your man." Then, Ralph "Big Time" Slaughter grabbed his gut and vomited all over Stan's shoes.

The relationship continued when Stan went back to homicide. Big Time wasn't helping solve big cases, but he knew what was going on. He kept his ears open and his mouth shut, and Stan paid him well. Each time a payday rolled around, Stan would tell Big Time to buy food, not dope. And each time, Big Time used it on a fix. Stan was paying his street partner to kill himself faster. Stan thought about the incongruity of the arrangement often enough, but he didn't lose any sleep over it. He couldn't.

The door at the top of the stairs was ajar. Stan pushed his way into a hallway lined with musty mattresses, a refrigerator minus a door, a TV with a cracked screen, and other discarded furniture. The plaster walls were chipped and cracked. The floor was caked with a gummy filth. Someone had spray-painted CRACK CITY in black script on the ceiling, and CALL BT FOR A BJ in six-inch-high block letters, with an arrow pointing down the hall, on the wall. Stan had to step over four plastic bags of garbage to get to Big Time's door. He knocked three times. A tall, thin, cream-skinned woman answered. She kept the door chained, and Stan felt a rush of warm, sweet air. The woman's blouse was open to her navel and knotted at the waist. "Some white dude, BT." She smiled. "Kinda old, but kinda handsome." She looked about twenty-five, maybe younger. She had a magnificent figure. Stan tried not to stare. He wasn't doing very well.

A shrill voice came from deep inside the apartment. "Tell him we ain't open for business."

The woman pouted, shook her head, and began to close

the door. Stan put his hand against it and pushed. "Tell him I'm not leaving."

She turned her head, still smiling and keeping one eye on Stan. "White boy says he ain't goin' nowhere, baby."

Stan heard Big Time limping toward the door. "Shit. Who is it? Goddamn motherfucker." Time peeked over the woman's slender shoulder and saw Stan. "Goddamn motherfucker. What you doin' here? Goddamn. Goddamn. Goddamn."

Big Time pushed past the woman, shoved her away with a forearm shiver to the chest, unchained the door, and opened it. "I knew you'd be comin'. I knew it. Sonofabitch, I knew it."

Stan walked to the middle of the living room. The place was as bad inside as out. Newspapers, magazines, brown paper bags, cans, bottles, all sorts of garbage was strewn in various piles around the room. It smelled like stale beer. The TV was on. So was the radio. There were six wiggly lines of coke on the coffee table in the living room and a pile of cash on the bed in the next room. The woman backed toward the couch, sat down, and curled a leg up under her. She leaned forward toward the dope. The bottom curves of her breasts rubbed out two of the lines. She did two others, then sat back and smiled.

Stan stared at her for a second. She stared back. He took Big Time by the arm. "Let's talk."

Big Time looked like he wanted to get on his knees to ask forgiveness. He was nervous. "She's my fuckin' cousin, man. I tol' her not to be doin' this shit. I . . ."

Stan closed his eyes and shook his head. He lowered his voice. "Not her—and not here."

They went into the next room. Time circled behind Stan, took a peek into the living room, and shut the door. "She don't need to be hearin' this stuff, man. She gets around."

Stan looked around the room. Big Time's dresser was bare, except for a beer can filthy with cigarette butts and an open jar of Vicks. Two yellow-striped cats were asleep on faded newspapers in the corner. Another radio hummed quietly on the nightstand. The toilet in the adjoining bathroom was running. "You know why I'm here."

"The kid."

"What're you hearing?"

Time closed one eye and tilted his head. "This stuff is still fresh, man."

Stan walked across the room to the window. The pane was gone and had been replaced with cardboard and thick plastic. Stan fingered the masking tape around the edge of the plastic. "Don't bullshit me, T. Things get stale around here after twenty minutes."

Time nodded anxiously. "You're right, Stan. You're right."

Stan turned back to him. "So?"

Time shrugged, and stuffed his hands deep into his pockets. Stan could see Big Time's fingers poking out of holes in his pants. "Lotta talkin' goin' on."

"Like?"

"Normal stuff. Conjections, that sort of thing."

Stan looked over at the bed, and saw a sliver of green poking out from underneath a pillow. He walked over and picked up the pillow and uncovered a pile of cash. The bills were mostly fifties, with a few hundreds. He picked up the money and began counting it. "How about letting me in on a few of the ... conjections?"

Time was nervously eyeing the cash in Stan's hand. "Where you want me to start?"

Stan smiled, brushed off a spot on the edge of the bed and flopped down. "I'm going to start with the fifties. You start wherever you like."

Time stole a quick glance toward the bedroom door, walked over to it, and made sure it was still closed. He lowered his voice to a whisper. "Cooper." His eyes bugged out. Sweat began to bead on his forehead. "But this is the same stuff, man. Same name as always. You know people be sayin' that stuff just because that boy's bein' tough and it's his time. They used to talk that way about me. Every little big thing comes up, man, it was BT this and BT that." Time was spitting out the words faster and faster. "Man, back in those days, accordin' to the word, I was knockin' off more stiffs than Alan Capone and gettin' more play than Superfly. And Stan, honest to God, if I'd a been lovin' that much, my dick woulda fell off. That's the kinda stuff I been hearin'. I heard Cooper. Word is he was hanging around that corner last night. But who the hell knows?" Time stopped suddenly and took a big breath. He was shaking.

"Who says he was there?"

"Guys."

"Names."

"I-I-I-I can get some."

Stan had finished with the fifties. He picked up the hundreds. "What do you think?"

Time shuddered. "I think Cooper'll kill me if he hears me talkin' this way."

Stan shook his head. "No—the kid."

Time nodded. "Right. Things gotta shake down a bit, man. You know that. Someone out there knows somethin', and soon someone out there's gonna be sayin' it."

"You screwin' the broad?"

Time laughed nervously. "My cousin?"

Stan chuckled. "Yeah, your cousin."

Time shook his head rapidly.

"Why not?"

"Not my type."

Stan laughed. "Keep going. You're getting warm."

"She's a friend of Cooper's."

"Name?"

"Don't know. Calls herself Fine Thing. Strips at some joint—Niqui's, Eight Mile. Does a few tricks here and there, too. Word is she can make it so fine you'll think you never ever had it before."

"So, what's she doing here?"

"Cooper gets me some of his surplus stuff to hawk every now and then, and part of the deal is I gotta share. I get some spending money. She cops some dope. What's his is mine—and hers."

"He doin' her?"

"Her and anyone else he wants."

Stan finished counting the money. "Five thousand—about."

"Gimme a break, man." Big Time was pleading.

Stan threw half the cash on the bed. Time snatched the

bills and quickly stuffed them into his pants. Stan waved the rest of the money at him. "You get the rest back after I get some good stuff."

Big Time forced a smile. "Hey, no problem." Stan reached for the doorknob. Time grabbed his arm. He was really nervous now. "We got to make this look good." He rubbed his hand furiously across the stubble on his shaved head.

Stan shrugged. "Okay. What? I'll rob you."

Time shook his head. He gritted his teeth. "Now, man, that's weak." He was still nervous as hell. "She may be walkin' around half-naked, but she ain't dumb." He thought a second, then reached for the door. "I got it. Just follow me."

Time opened the door with a jerk and hopped into the living room. He turned and screamed at Stan. "No. No. No. Like I been tellin' you, man, I ain't got that kind of shit. I ain't got it. And it ain't gonna do you no good to be comin' back here, 'cause like I told you before, I had the stuff that one time. Just then. That one goddamn time. My man just ain't keepin' me stocked. Understand?"

Fine Thing wasn't watching. She had her eyes on the needle she was carefully inserting into a vein. Stan watched her out of the corner of his eye. He grabbed Time by the collar. "Then where are you gettin' all that cash, you skinny motherfucker? Your rich uncle just die?"

Time raised his voice an octave higher and got into Stan's face, spraying him with spittle through the gaps in his teeth. "I'm tellin' you, I ain't got stuff for you. You want some blow, go down three blocks, take a left, and take your pick. It's a damn department store down there. They be havin' white sales all the time."

Fine Thing pulled out the needle carefully, leaned back, put her hands behind her head, and focused on Stan and Big Time. She sat there a few seconds, then stood up, and walked slowly toward Stan. She pushed Time out of the way and turned and pressed herself into Stan. "Mr. Clean can have some of mine, T. Any way he wants it."

Time grabbed Fine Thing by the arm and pulled her away

from Stan. "He don't want your little bitty, babe. B'sides, he's leavin' now."

Stan grunted and turned toward the door. Fine Thing had circled behind him and was blocking his way. She stepped toward him. Stan looked her up and down. "Not now, honey. Maybe later." Then he sidestepped her, opened the door with a jerk, walked out, and slammed the door hard behind him. Time hobbled to the door and locked it.

Fine Thing had a dreamy smile on her face. Big Time tapped her on the shoulder and screamed at her. "What I been tellin' you about openin' that door like that, sister? You could get us killed."

Fine Thing's eyes rolled closed. "Where'd you meet that guy, T? He's nice lookin'. I wouldn't mind doin' him. But you know what I think?" She began moving slowly toward the couch. "I think he looks like a cop. He ain't a cop, is he?"

"Cop?" Big Time laughed. He took Fine Thing by the arm. "Baby, he ain't no cop. You're too fuckin' paranoid. That's what that stuff does to you. Makes you a nut case. He's a geography teacher from the suburbs. Them white folks're a crazy fuckin' breed. Creatures a habit." Big Time helped Fine Thing sit down. "Man gotta learn to shop around. He gotta be learnin' to do that."

Fine Thing had stopped listening. Her eyes were closed tight, and she was sitting on the couch, humming, her head rocking back and forth slowly in rhythm. Time took her by the shoulders and gently laid her down. He stared at her beauty for a moment, trailing his fingers tentatively across her flat stomach. He shook his head. "Maybe some other time, babe." He knelt alongside her and covered her with a blanket.

Then Ralph "Big Time" Slaughter put on his coat. He had to take a walk. It was time to go to work.

◇ 11 ◇

Pisarcawitcz was still running the desk when Stan got back to headquarters. The day sergeant had called in sick, and Pisser had been held over on double duty. He was sitting with his feet on the desk re-reading the paper. He handed Stan two messages without looking up. The first was from Mary Stimic, a reporter with the *Free Press*. She wanted Stan to meet her at 5:30 at the Copper's Kettle, a police hangout in Greektown, a few blocks from headquarters. Pisarcawitcz licked his lips, then grinned. "Better call the ol' Stimic babe back and tell her you'll be late. Sims wants you in his office at 5:00." He lowered his voice to a whisper. "The Jefferson kid. That's all anybody's been gassin' about."

The second message read simply, "Babe No. 2. Sounded blue. No name for U." Stan looked at it. Marlyss? No. Marlyss wouldn't leave a message. Someone might recognize her voice. If Stan's phone had rung through to the homicide desk, she would have hung up. She always did. But maybe something was wrong. Stan turned to leave.

Pisarcawitcz was watching Stan out of the corner of his eye. He cackled. "Yo, Stoshie. I was just kidding on the second note—it was Jenny."

Stan stopped and gritted his teeth. He turned back to Pisarcawitcz and ungritted them. "Petey okay?"

"Didn't say." Pisarcawitcz swung his legs off the desk and leaned forward in his chair. "Say, why'd she dump you, anyway?"

Stan turned to leave again. "She didn't like the people I associated with."

"Yeah, I don't blame her. Pimps, hookers, faggots." Pisarcawitcz lowered his voice again. "Negroes"—short *i*.

Stan shook his head. "Not them, Pisser. You."

It took a second for Stan's answer to sink in. "Me. Me? Good one, Stoosh." Pisarcawitcz leaned back in his chair, put his feet back on the desk, and howled. "Me." He put his feet back down. "Hey, don't forget. The boss. At 5:00." He looked out the window at the rush-hour tie-ups in the snowy street below. "Me. Good one. Fuckin-'ay me."

Dawlson was coming down the hall as Stan headed toward the squad room. He nodded toward Pisarcawitcz. "What's with him?"

Stan shrugged. "Simple mind."

Dawlson nodded. "I'll be back in a second. We need to talk."

Stan walked to the coat rack and hung up his coat. He went to the coffee maker. The stuff was thick as sludge. He put down the pot and shuffled slowly to his desk. It was 4:40. He should call Mary to cancel. He tried, but the line was busy. Dawlson walked into the room as he hung up.

"You get anything today?" Dawlson was carrying a cup of the watery coffee from the vending machine down the hall.

"Nothing yet. Still early." Stan walked back to the coffeemaker and poured himself half a cup of the black muck. "Give me a hit, Pete? I need to dilute this stuff."

"Got sugar in it."

"I can handle it." Dawlson poured some of his coffee in Stan's cup. Stan took a sip. "Not too bad." He sat down at his desk. "Got one of my guys on it."

"Big Time?"

Stand nodded.

"He still alive?"

Stan smiled. "Barely." He took another sip of his coffee, this time without wincing. "What's up?"

"Chief wants to see me."

"You?"

"Yeah." Dawlson sat on the couch against the far wall and put his feet up. He wriggled a bit, trying to get comfortable. "Someday the damn springs in this thing are going to shoot right through the fuckin' plastic and drill someone good."

Stan laughed. "Maybe we ought to take it into the interrogation room." Dawlson chuckled. He still looked uncomfortable. Stan noticed. "So?"

Pete shrugged. "I think I'm going to be pulled into this thing."

"The kid?"

"Yep."

"I thought you were working IA."

"Am. Was. Don't know." Pete shrugged again. "I told Frank I'd be busy with that at 5:00. Told me to cancel."

Stan scratched his head. "Internal Affairs usually gets top priority." He shrugged, then smiled. "It would be good working together again, though."

Pete nodded. "Like old times."

Stan nodded back. Dawlson winked and gave him a quick thumbs up. Stan reached to dial Mary again. His phone rang first.

"Stan?" It was Jenny.

"I was just about to call."

"I've heard that before." There was a smile in her voice. Stan was always glad to hear it.

Stan and Jenny had been divorced for three years. It had been a friendly breakup. They'd even dated a few times; Stan had spent the night once. But nothing rekindled. They were going in opposite directions—one deliberately, the other because he knew no other way. It sounded like a romance novel cliché when Stan explained it like that to himself, but it wasn't. It was true. Jenny wanted a life Stan could never provide. She wanted a husband and father who was a husband and father first, and cop, or anything else, second. She wanted a man who was alive and growing, not just trying to survive. Some days, she would walk past the photo of Stan and Laddy Kochinski on her piano and do a double-take. The men seemed to be hugging each other in such a sad, desperate, knowing embrace—one, she told herself, that no one but a cop, not even a cop's wife, could understand, much less share. Jenny would swear that the photo, taken shortly before Laddy had died, was a picture of twins, that Stan had already turned into Laddy, trapped by some hellish, foolish, irrational commitment. Then she would shake her head, because she had known, had realized long before she and Stan had split, that she had already become a widow. She still loved Stan, but she had told herself, convinced herself, that she had had no choice. She wanted life. She wanted love. And she wanted Stan. But she couldn't have all three. One had been lost, irretrievably. And no one really was to blame.

"What's up, Jenny?"

"Just about to head home." Jenny taught second grade at St. Clare's Catholic school in Grosse Pointe Park.

"Long day."

"Tell me about it. I just wanted to remind you about Friday."

Stan looked up at the calendar on the wall. Tomorrow was Petey's birthday.

Stan nodded. "Thanks." He paused. "Again."

"Need a shopping list?"

"Yep."

"Same as always—no toy guns."

"Right, no guns. Simple. Can I have him tomorrow?"

"Bad timing, Stan. Sorry." She did sound sorry. "Roger is taking me and Petey out." Jenny had been dating Roger Frayley for about seven months. He was an attorney. Okay guy. Good-looking. Tall. Lots of money. "How about Saturday—the Clown Café?"

The Clown Café had opened a few months earlier. Petey had called Stan and told him how all the kids in school were talking about the huge, plastic talking clown in the middle of the restaurant. Stan had promised Petey he would take him. He hadn't. He should have, but he hadn't. Some investigation had come up. Some investigation always came up.

Jenny waited a moment for an answer, then piped up again. "Saturday, Stoosh?"

Stan nodded. "I'll check. Good idea. I'll let you know tomorrow.'

Jenny's voice dropped a bit. "Just you and him?"

Stan shook his head. "You too, if you want."

"Me?" Jenny giggled, a bit nervously. "Not this fairy princess he tells me about?"

"She's a regular Mother Teresa."

"Petey says she's beautiful." There was a twinge of sadness and a sprinkling of jealousy in Jenny's voice now.

"Yes." He didn't say it to be mean. He simply couldn't think of anything else to say.

Dawlson poked Stan on the shoulder. "Two minutes to kickoff, Stosh."

"Gotta go, Jenny." Stan stopped, and the silence followed and hung heavy for a few seconds. There were still uncomfortable pauses in their conversations, but the lulls were growing shorter, less painful. They were getting better at them. "Thanks."

Jenny nodded. "See you—when?"

"Tomorrow. I'll stop by."

"Stan?"

"Yes."

"Brigitte Bardot?"

"Mother Teresa."

"Liar."

They both laughed.

Dawlson was heading out the door when Stan hung up. Stan hustled after him. Three TV mini-cam crews were waiting outside Frank's office on the third floor. Dawlson smiled as he pushed through the gaggle like a linebacker. Stan followed. Frank was sitting on the edge of his secretary's desk, waiting for them. He hurried the two detectives in his office and sat down. Stan and Dawlson stood.

"I've only got a few minutes. At 5:20, I'm going live on all three stations with a press conference about the Jefferson shooting. You boys don't need to be there, but I wanted to get with you before the day was over. Sit down."

They did. Dawlson raised his hand. "I'm temp duty with IA, Frank."

"Right. What's the deal?"

Pete looked at Stan, then at Frank. IA stuff was usually top secret, at least to other officers, sometimes even to the chief.

Frank nodded. "It's okay."

Pete shrugged. "McGinnity."

Frank smiled. He didn't mean it. "Tell me something I don't know."

"Can't say much more, Frank. You know that."

Frank rubbed his forehead. "This guy doing everything I'm hearing?"

"Like?"

"The renegade crap. Graveyard shit. Taking punks out."

"Like to say . . . can't."

Frank nodded. "Well, you're off McGinnity, for now."

Dawlson looked at Stan, then back at Frank. "You can do that?"

Frank stood. "Right now I can."

Dawlson wasn't convinced. "You check with Stinson?" George Stinson was the deputy chief in charge of Internal Affairs. He was a rung below Frank on the chain of command but reported directly to Hatch and the head of the police commission.

"Fuck him." Frank walked to the window, and stood there for a moment with his back to the detectives.

Dawlson shrugged and looked at Stan. Stan didn't look back. He was staring at a framed photo of Marlyss on Frank's desk. Stan had been in Frank's office before, but it was the first time he had seen the picture. Stan guessed the photo was about five years old. Marlyss looked younger, her smile brighter, her eyes darker, deeper, more alive. Or maybe the picture had been touched up. Stan felt Dawlson's hand on his arm. Stan looked at Pete, then at Frank. Frank was still staring out the window. The city was alight with Christmas decorations.

Frank turned around. "This thing is blowing up big. So far, we've got three community groups raising hell about police protection in the neighborhoods, and there'll be more. We've got black ministers coming at us like termites out of the woodwork. The NAACP is coming down on us like a sledgehammer. We've got the local media on our ass—been there since early this morning. And it's all only going to get worse when the networks tie all this together." Frank looked at Stan and Dawlson and sat back down. "We've got to solve this thing." He picked up a pencil and rolled it between his fingers, then snapped it. "Now."

Stan looked at Dawlson. Frank dropped the eraser half of the pencil in a wastebasket, then pointed the lead end at Stan. "Stan, you're in. You were there last night and you've got the head start." He nodded toward Dawlson. "Pete, you're in, too." Frank sat back in his chair. "You're partners again." He waited for Stan and Pete to acknowledge each other. They didn't.

Frank got out of his chair again, walked to the front of his desk, and sat down. "Here's the plan: Stan, hit the streets. Talk to as many people as you can. I want daily reports on what people are saying about the killing, about the cops, about crime in the city, about Hatch, about me, about anything. I want to know more about this kid, too. Good kid. Bad kid. Some of that. I want to know what we got to work with."

Stan rubbed his forehead. "Sounds like I'm taking a poll, Frank. Who gives a shit what Joe Blow's saying?"

Frank's lips tightened into a thin line. "We got more on our hands than just a dead kid, Stan."

"I know that, but . . ."

"No buts, detective. None. And, quite frankly, I don't think you do know." Frank switched his gaze to Dawlson. "Pete, I want a list of suspects. Do what you have to do, but get me a good list. I want five names by Saturday at 5:00. Five guys we can focus on. No, make that three guys. Three guys. Two days. Got it?" Dawlson nodded.

Stan tilted his head. And puffed out his cheeks. "Frank?"

"Yeah."

"No offense to Pete, but I got better contacts in that area than he does. I've got a guy's been working that part of town for five, six years now."

Frank stared hard at Stan. "And?"

"And I think I got a better chance than Pete of getting you a good list by Saturday."

Frank nodded, and took a deep breath to calm himself. "Number one, we're a team here, Kochinski. And two, that is precisely why I need you in the street doing the dirty work. You know that area. And, quite frankly, what you get for me is more important right now than what Pete comes up with." Frank paused and looked at both men. "Questions?" Stan was staring at the floor. Dawlson shook his head. "Good."

Frank stood and walked back behind his desk. Stan and Pete got up to leave. "Hold on just a second." Frank sat down and picked up a pen. "Kochinski, give me your years in the department, recent big cases, commendations, stuff like that."

Stan was still upset. He didn't try to camouflage the anger in his voice. "Twenty-one. The Mendoza thing last summer. No medals."

"Married?"

"Was. One kid. Almost seven."

"Seven. Seven. Seven." Frank wrote down the numeral, then underlined it. "Pete?"

Dawlson looked at Stan, then at Frank. Sims still had his head down, ready to take more notes. "Same time in service as Stan, Frank. Divorced. No kids. Silver Star in . . ."

"Doesn't count."

"Three citations for heroism. Two local, one national."

"Mayoral Badges of Courage?"

"Two."

"Refresh my memory. Didn't you get one for saving some black kid?"

"Pulled her out of a burning bedroom."

"Near east side?"

"Two months ago."

"Age eleven?"

"Nine."

Frank recorded the girl's age, then circled it. "That's it. We'll talk tomorrow."

Frank stood, adjusted his tie, ran his hand through his hair, and hustled the detectives out of his office as quickly as he had ushered them into it. The three were hit by blinding TV lights as they left Frank's office. Stan and Dawlson shaded their eyes as they struggled through the tangle of cameras, reporters, and cables. Neither the maze nor the glare fazed Frank a bit.

Dawlson put his hand on Stan's shoulder as they headed

back to the squad room. "Relax, Stan. It's okay. He's right. This is more than just another dead kid."

Stan didn't answer.

Pete stopped in the middle of the stairwell leading to fifth floor. "C'mon, Stosh. You know the drill: Everyone ignores the first six hundred forty-six stiffs. Then along comes number six forty-seven, and we start the tap dance."

Stan nodded, took a deep breath and continued climbing. "You surprised he took you off the McGinnity thing?"

"Nope." Pete shook his head. "No surprises. Frank's ass is in a sling. Nothing he does from here on out will surprise me. This is all politics, now."

They were back in the squad room, now, and Stan reached for his coat. Dawlson went to the TV in the corner and flipped it on. Frank was speaking. He looked perfect: concerned, energetic, apologetic, a little harried—he hadn't pulled up his tie all the way—but determined.

". . . of our best investigators on the case—Stan Kochinski and Pete Dawlson. Kochinski did superb police work last summer on the Mendoza case. I can refresh you on those details after we're through here. Dawlson was his partner on a few big cases a few years ago. They're our top team." Frank paused and took a piece of paper and a pair of reading glasses from his shirt pocket. He put on the glasses. "Dawlson won a Mayor's citation a few months ago for rescuing a young black girl from a burning apartment building. I've got more details for you on that. And Kochinski"— Frank pursed his lips and shook his head ever so slightly— "has a young son the same age—eleven, age eleven—as Rickey Jefferson."

Stan exhaled in a low whistle. Dawlson laughed. "Got to hand it to him, Stan. He's got it down."

"You think they buy it?"

Dawlson laughed again. "Those idiot reporters?"

Stan nodded.

"We find the guy . . . and Sims is golden."

"He'll owe us one."

Dawlson shook his head. "He won't think so."

Four blocks away, at the district courthouse, Bill Colbane was watching Frank's press conference and thinking the same thing: Frank had it down, all right. Colbane was sitting at his desk in his chambers, the doors to his office locked from the inside. His black robe hung on a coat rack next to a bookshelf filled top to bottom with law books. Colbane had his legs crossed and his pants leg hiked a bit, revealing the snub-nosed .38 in a leather ankle holster. He had a tall glass in his hand, filled with two fingers of straight whiskey.

Colbane grabbed the TV remote control and pressed the mute button. Frank's lips were moving now, but nothing was coming out. Colbane reached down and removed the revolver from the holster and held it in his palm, studying it. It was the gun he'd bought the night Missy had identified her attackers. For months, it had rested in the bottom drawer of his dresser, underneath a stack of cotton turtlenecks. Bill Colbane hadn't started carrying it, hadn't even brought it out of hiding, until two members of the Knights had shot up a courtroom where a third Knight was on trial for first-degree murder. One of the gunmen, a sixteen-year-old kid named Robby "Crazy Ed" Molinsky, had rushed the bench and shot the stunned judge right between the eyes. The other gunman had gone for the prosecutor, who'd wound up gutshot and in critical condition. Three other people, including two newspaper reporters, had been wounded in the crossfire between the gunmen and courtroom guards, who'd finally shot and killed the two gang members. That night, Molly Colbane had begged her husband to buy a gun. Bill Colbane had laughed. "They put the rush on me, honey, and I'm just going to duck under the bench and chew on a cigar until the smoke clears."

Molly Colbane had gotten no solace from her husband's weak joke. So she'd kept after him. Bill Colbane had held out for about a week, until he'd discovered that most of his fellow judges had begun wearing concealed pistols. He'd taken his revolver out of the drawer, gone to a gun shop, and bought an ankle holster. Slowly, but surely, the gun became a regular part of his courtroom wardrobe. Bill Colbane never really considered himself armed. He simply strapped the holster on before he took the bench, just as he put on his robe. This was the first time, in fact, that he'd removed the gun from its sheath. It felt good in his hand—solid, weighty. He emptied the six chambers, pulled the hammer back, and pointed the shiny, blue-black gun at Frank's noiseless image on the screen. He squeezed the trigger, heard a solid click, and felt a tiny rush of intoxicating, indiscriminate power.

Bill Colbane put the revolver on the desk, right in front of a picture of Molly and their three children. He sat there a moment or two studying the weapon. Then he spun it around. When it came to a stop, the barrel was pointing at him. He rubbed his eyes, then reached into his desk drawer for a piece of paper and picked up a pen. He grabbed the remote control again, aimed it at the TV, and made Frank Sims disappear. Then, Bill Colbane started writing.

Back at police headquarters, Stan had heard enough, too. He buttoned his coat, waved to Pete, and headed for the door.

Dawlson nodded. "Chin up, Stosh."

Stan headed to the elevator. He would be at least half an hour late for his meeting with Mary Stimic—if he even went. He didn't want to go. Hadn't said he would, either. Mary was probably involved with the Jefferson story and he didn't want to talk to anyone about it, especially her. He just wanted to be left alone. He stopped at a pay phone in the lobby and dialed Marlyss's number. The phone rang four times, then an answering machine kicked in. Stan couldn't leave a message, but he listened anyway. He just wanted to hear her voice. He listened, hung up, dialed again, and listened once more. Then he headed out into the cold.

◇ 12 ◇

Big Time hit the ground when he heard the first shot. He tried frantically to dig himself into the snow when he heard the second.

"Hey, hold the fire, man. Stop shootin'." He was facedown in an alley about three miles east of his apartment, lying directly under a streetlight. He looked to his right without moving his head. The snow near his thumb was turning red. "I'm hit. I'm shot." He'd been yelling before; he was screaming now. "Stop the shootin'. It's me, Big Time. C'mon, man, everyone roun' here knows BT." He spotted a rusted-out car about ten feet away, crawled on his stomach to it, and sat against it. He tried to catch his breath, but it wasn't easy. He looked at his thumb and saw that he hadn't been shot. He had ripped his thumbnail halfway back when he'd dived for cover. He reached into his pocket for something to use for a bandage, and pulled out a fifty-dollar bill. The money. He had stuffed it in his pants just before Stan left. He began to sweat. The money's a goner if these motherfuckers find it. Give them a reason to kill him, too. He stuffed the fifty in his shoe.

"Yo, old man, you still out there?" Time knew a lot of the boys in the Mack-Chalmers area, but he didn't recognize this voice. It sounded pretty young. "We was just having some fun. C'mon out, old man."

Time turned around and peeked over the hood of the car. He saw two shadows approaching. He got to his feet, but remained hunched over behind the car.

Two figures walked into the light from the street lamp. They were teenagers, probably no more than fifteen. One boy had a rifle. The other had what looked like a .22 semi-

automatic. Both were wearing shiny jackets, one lettered
"Georgetown," the other "Hornets."

The boy in the blue Hornets jacket was carrying the rifle
and holding a leash. At the end of the leash was a speckled
gray pit bull. The dog's rear end was attached to a harness
with wheels. His hind legs were missing. Hornets was doing
most of the talking. "You can't be trampin' around in this
alley like that, old man." Time could hear both boys howl-
ing in glee. "Come on out—or we'll send Gimpy in after
your raggedy faggot ass." The dog growled at the sound of
his name and lurched forward. The wheels squeaked.

Time wiped the blood from his thumb on his pants, took
a deep breath, closed his eyes, gritted his teeth, and bent the
nail back in place, then slowly emerged from behind the car.

The boy in the gray Georgetown jacket pointed his gun at
Time. "What you doin' here anyway, old man? This ain't
your neighborhood."

Time shrugged. "Used to be."

The boy in the Hornets jacket snickered. "When? 1950?"
The boys laughed and gave each other high fives. Time just
stood there. He wanted to slap them silly, but he decided
just to look as stupid as he could. He shrugged. His thumb
throbbed, but he tried to ignore the pain. "You right. You
right. You funny." He waited for them to stop laughing. It
took a few seconds. "I'm just looking for Coop." He stayed
as far as possible from the dog.

Hornets was still giggling. He jerked his thumb back over
his shoulder. "Coop's inside." He looked at Georgetown
then at Time. "You got an appointment?" They laughed
again.

Time was more angry now than scared, but he forced a
grin. "Don't be playin' with me so much. I ain't out for no
trouble. I just gotta see Coop."

"You wanna see Coop, we'll take you to see Coop, old
man." Georgetown was talking.

Time nodded. "I gotta go first."

Georgetown laughed. "There's a bathroom inside."

Time shook his head. "Can't wait."

Hornets nodded and waved his rifle. "Go ahead."

Time shook his head again. "Not here. Can't when some

one's watching." He began moving toward the car. "I'll go right over here. Okay?" He backed over to the front of the car, out of the glare of the streetlight, turned his back to the boys, unzipped his fly, then slipped his hand into his pocket and pulled out the wad of bills and stuffed it quickly into the grill of the car. He breathed a deep sigh of relief. He even tried to piss, but he couldn't. He was freezing cold and shriveled up tight as a knot. He zipped up and walked toward the boys. "I'm ready."

"No, you ain't." Georgetown was doing the talking. "We gotta frisk you." He did. "And you gotta put your hands on top of your head. You're our pris'ner." Hornets laughed. The dog growled again. Big Time did as he was told. The boys walked him fifty yards down the alley, then took a right turn onto a small walkway, then into a house.

When they got inside, the boys passed Time on to another boy. The kid was sitting inside a kitchen doorway. He had an Uzi slung over his shoulder and his arm around a woman sitting on his lap. He was wearing a Giants jacket; she was wearing a dirty white blouse and panties. She looked at least ten years older then he did. Georgetown told Giants that Time needed to see Cooper.

The kid didn't look at Time. "Coop's busy."

Time nodded. "I can wait, sir."

The boy jerked his head back toward the hallway. "There's a chair."

Big Time took off his hat, walked to the chair, and sat down. From his seat he could see the living room, dining room, and hallway. It was still early, but the place was already open for business. A pair of kids, maybe not even teenagers, were sitting behind a steel door in the hallway. The door had an opening like a mail slot but almost at eye level. Every few minutes, a wad of cash would appear through the slot. One of the boys would grab the money; the other would pass a baggie of dope—cocaine, crack, or heroin—out the slot. Four brown grocery bags were scattered behind the boys. One was already filled with cash.

"Whaddya think, old man?" It was Georgetown. He had been relived from sentry duty.

Big Time nodded. "I done this sort of business before. I ain't no rookie."

The kid laughed. "You ain't done it like this, old man." He pointed to the door. "Takes five of us to move that door in and out." He flexed his arm. "You ever do that?"

Time shook his head.

The boy pointed to the living room. There was no furniture, only a filthy yellow carpet. Half a dozen people were scattered along the walls, some sitting, some standing. All were shooting dope or smoking it. "You ever have a separate room for preferred customers?"

"For what?"

"That's what I'm sayin', old man. This is new-age stuff. You ain't seen nothing like this." The boy laughed and pointed to the kids manning the steel door. "We got drive-up"—he swept his hand toward the living room—"and we got full service." The kid nodded toward the living room again. "And we got preferred customers." He laughed. "We even got drive-*through* at some places."

Time waved at the kid. "You ain't showin' me nothin' I ain't seen before."

The boy laughed again. "Go on, ol' man. This ain't ancient history."

Time shook his head and sighed. "I just need to talk to Coop."

The kid nodded. "Third floor. Make it quick."

BT was out of breath by the time he reached the top of the stairs. He paused a second to rest, then pushed open the door. The room was dimly lit, and no one saw him enter. He stepped into the shadows and looked around. The unfinished attic was cramped and warm, too warm, heated almost hot by a trio of smelly kerosene heaters. A ragged couch was pushed against the wall to the left. The only other pieces of furniture were a card table and chair in the middle of the room. Cooper was behind the table, dressed only in black sweat pants and a black, silver-stitched shoulder holster. Four thick gold ropes hung around his neck. They looked almost incandescent against the sheen of his rich black skin. He looked as though he had just woken up. He leaned forward, his elbows on the table. His biceps bulged. Two figures stood in front of him. One was the kid in the Hornets jacket. The other looked older, maybe twenty.

Cooper rubbed his eyes and sat back. "Tonight."

Hornets nodded. He didn't look so cocky anymore. He was staring at the floor. "He's . . . my brother, Coop."

Cooper chuckled, then stopped. His smile suddenly disappeared, his face screwed itself into a grimace, and his voice grew into a low, frightening, thunderous rumble. "What you take me for, some fool-ass nigger? Huh?" Cooper stood, reached across the table, and grabbed the kid by the jacket. "Huh? Don't fuck with me, boy." He slapped the kid hard. "We ain't got no brothers here. This is business." He lowered his voice and pulled the kid closer, across the table. "You got two hours—no, you got one." He was whispering, now. "Then, I want him up here, squealing like a goddamn stuck rat." Cooper lowered his voice even more, then smiled. "He don't . . . he's dead." Another pause. "You, too." He leaned forward again. "You hear? That simple, boy. Him, your brother . . . or both of you."

Cooper threw the kid back and sat down. The boy was still staring at the floor. He'd seemed older before. Now, he looked about twelve. He nodded.

Cooper nodded back. "I got Sammy, here, to give you a hand. He goes with you. Now, get out."

The kid turned and left, brushing past Time. Cooper saw Time trying to squeeze into the corner. He wasn't happy to see him. "And what the hell you want, ol' man?"

Time cleared his throat and inched forward. "Fine Thing's gettin' pretty messed up over at my place, Coop. She been there for three days now."

Cooper leaned back and put his hands behind his head. His forearms looked as big as Time's thighs. "What the hell you want me to do about it? Huh?" He grunted and strained as he stood. "Do I look like her ol' man? Don't be wastin' my time with that crap. Throw her out." He shook his head.

Big Time shifted his feet nervously. He cleared his throat again. "It's not just her, Coop." Cooper was putting on his shirt. He didn't answer. "Cops are swarmin' around my neighborhood askin' questions about this kid"—Time swallowed hard—"and you."

Cooper was buttoning up. He didn't look at him. "This supposed to be some sorta news flash?"

Time shook his head furiously. "No, no, Coop. I just wanted you to know."

Cooper walked over to Big Time and put his arm around him. He squeezed his shoulder hard. Cooper smelled like sweat and sweet, expensive cologne. "You see that boy up here a minute ago? Kid's brother's playin' both sides. Works for me—and for the DeeJays on the west side. And people been tellin' me he trades a little information . . . to the cops." Time tried to swallow; he couldn't. Cooper tightened his grip on Time's shoulder. "You don't sing, do you, old man?"

Time shook his head rapidly.

"Of course you don't." Cooper slid his hand to Big Time's neck and squeezed tight. "What would a rag-ass like you have to croon about? Huh?" Cooper increased his grip and just about lifted Time off his feet. "So, why you come here interruptin' me with this lame shit about the cops and that dead-ass kid? What you expect, ol' man? A confession? Who'd you expect the cops to be lookin' for?"

The veins in Cooper's neck grew, almost grotesquely. He shoved Time against the wall, took the gun out of his holster, and put the barrel against Time's forehead. The steel was cold. Big Time wondered for a split second if Cooper was strong enough to jam the barrel through his forehead and out the back of his head. He began shivering. He stared at the barrel. But even in his blind fear, he noticed that something looked strange. He tried to slump to the floor, but Cooper held him up. "I'd blow your brains out if you had any."

Cooper let go of Time's neck and Time dropped to the floor like a sack of dirty laundry. Cooper turned and walked away. "Get outa here, ol' man. I ain't got time for your sorry shit."

Big Time did. He crawled to the door and backed slowly down the stairway. He didn't face downstairs until he reached the second-floor landing, where he stopped and tried to reassemble himself. He wiped the sweat from his face, then sat down for a second to catch his breath. Then he remembered Cooper. Then he remembered his money. Then he ran down the stairs.

The downstairs was busier now. More people. More customers. The boys at the front door were laughing and smiling and, between customers, beginning to count the take, sorting the bills into stacks. The kid in the Giants jacket was still guarding the back door; the woman was still on his lap. He put his leg across the doorway as Time tried to leave. "You see Cooper?"

Time nodded, tiredly. "Yeah, I saw him. He's not in a very good mood."

"He's been mad today, ol' man."

"Tell me about it."

The woman got up and walked to the living room. The kid didn't seem to notice. "I think he's worried the cops are gonna figure a way to stick him. I hear he's even talkin' about headin' out for a couple of weeks."

"Think so?"

Giants shrugged. "Not sure if the boss would let him."

"Why not?"

"Business been off lately. He goes, it's only gonna get worse."

Big Time nodded. "Probably."

"I'll tell you this, old man. I've never seen him like this before."

Time nodded again, this time more seriously. "Me neither, not that we's exactly friends like we used to be."

Giants laughed, hard. He waved Big Time away, and out.

Big Time passed Hornets and Georgetown going the other way as he headed down the alley. He was halfway to the car when he heard a shot and hit the pavement. Then he heard someone scream. He held his breath to make sure it wasn't him wailing, and lay there for a minute. Then he heard another shot, then another, and more screams. He counted to fifty, slowly, then climbed slowly to his hands and knees and crawled into the shadows of a burned-out garage. From there he made his way toward a car and reached inside the grill. Nothing. The bills were gone. He sat back in a heap, leaning against the rotting hulk and slapped his thigh. He wanted to cry. He reached up and rubbed his forehead. The spot where Cooper had shoved the gun was still sore.

"I'm too goddamn old for cops and robbers. Too goddamn old for these punks."

Then he looked down the alley—and saw another car. He turned and looked over his shoulder. Wrong car. Maybe. He crawled to the next car, knelt before it, and stuck his hand inside the grill. The money was there, but it was frozen to the car. Time cupped his hands around his mouth, put his lips to the freezing metal, and exhaled hard once, then twice, then again, and again. He pulled at the bills. Nothing doing. He sat there and thought for a second, then stood, cautiously, looked around, and unzipped his fly. The bills were loose in seconds.

Big Time was a mess by the time he got home, but he was as rich as when he had left. And he'd get more from Stan, maybe the rest of what was hidden under his pillow. He was sure of that. He'd done his job. Some sort of celebration certainly was in order. But there was no one to party with. The TV was on and the radio was playing, but Fine Thing was gone.

$$\diamond \ \mathbf{13} \ \diamond$$

Mary Stimic drummed her fingernails on the tabletop at the Copper's Kettle and checked her watch—6:03. She took a long sip from her gin and tonic. She wasn't looking forward to the meeting with Stan, either. *Free Press* assistant managing editor Ted Enders had dragged her kicking and screaming into the Rickey Jefferson story early Thursday morning—and she was still pissed.

Stimic was one of the best journalists in Detroit. She

wasn't the world's best writer, wasn't even the best word-smith at the *Free Press,* but she knew better than anyone in the newspaper's crowded third-floor City Room how to bulldog a story; when she found a live one, she didn't let go until she was done with it.

Her recent series on the battered wives of corporate executives—"Behind Closed Doors: Boardroom Brutality"—was a perfect example. The project had begun with an anonymous phone call from the friend of a frightened, desperate woman. Mary's immediate editor, one of Enders's assistants, had given her three days—and condescendingly, at that—for a throw-away quick-hitter on spouse abuse among the affluent. Mary had lobbied, then screamed and argued with whomever would listen—mainly Enders—for a nine-month project. She'd ended up with six months—and a startling, heart- and gut-wrenching series on white-collar wife-beating that had copped three national and two local newspaper awards.

Her hard work had paid off in other ways, too. Two weeks ago, on the heels of the last of the awards for the series, the *Detroit News,* the paper down the street, had offered Mary a column and a huge raise. The *Free Press* had countered with a column and a bigger raise. She'd stayed put. Her first column was scheduled to appear in less than two weeks—on New Year's Day. She figured on coasting painlessly until then, just playing with a few ideas. The series had taken a lot out of her. And besides, after eight years of chasing anything and everything that bounced across her desk, she figured she deserved a little down time, even if it was on the job.

Ted Enders had had an entirely different idea when he pulled Mary into his office.

"We're always talking about trying to really write—*really*—about what a goddamn mess life is in that part of the city. About what some kids got to go through . . ."

Mary had heard about the Jefferson kid, and she'd heard Enders's homily before—too many times to count. She wasn't in any mood to listen to it again. "You say the same thing every time some kid gets it."

Enders's face grew red. He had a short fuse. The color

was spreading to his bald head. "Well, maybe it's because we haven't got it right yet." He bit off the last two words.

Mary didn't back off. "I got it right last year—that piece I did on Rodney Stamm finished in the top three in the Pulitzers. Change the name and run the thing again."

Enders was nodding. "Didn't win—did it?"

Mary looked puzzled. "I must be missing something."

Enders fashioned a fake, toothy smile. "You are. This isn't another one of *those* stories. Listen to me for a second." Enders's voice turned conversational, almost plaintive. "I talked to the reporters working this thing—Hillers and Slade. They spent some time with the boy's mom and some of his friends. They think this kid was pretty straight."

"They think?" Mary said. "Terrific."

"Me, too. Listen to this. Kid finished second in a short-story contest. He hated basketball. His mom's an angel. His dad didn't run off and disappear; he died in a car crash."

"So?"

"So, this could be a killer story."

Mary nodded, tiredly. "Good, then let it kill someone else this time. I need a break from blood, sweat, and fears."

"I don't have anyone else"—Enders played his hole card—"except Smithson."

Fred Smithson was a long-time *Free Press* columnist. He was an asshole. He hated Mary. And he was damn good.

Mary gritted her teeth. "Don't do this to me, Ted."

"Look, I'm not asking you to spend six months on this."

"My column starts in a week and a half."

"Exactly. I want you to nose around, do some digging on your own, then write something for the thirty-first. You know: despair and hope and evil and good. Make 'em dry. Make 'em choke"—Enders sat forward for effect and lowered his voice—"on their fucking guilt." He stopped. "It's a great opportunity. We run that piece with a tag line that says your new column debuts tomorrow, and no one in this city is going to dare miss you on New Year's Day."

"No one will miss it anyway."

Enders took a deep breath. "I really don't have any choice, Mary."

Mary fought back anger. "Pulling rank is really chickenshit, Theodore."

Enders shrugged. "I know." He nodded. "End of discussion."

And it was. But Enders was right, Rickey Jefferson was a good story. But so were Rodney Stamm and Joshua Hart and Joey Sanders and little Keisha Stevens. And Mary had already done all those, and dozens of other stories about dead kids. Now, there was one more. In this town, there always was one more.

Mary checked her watch again—6:20. She spotted Stan at the door, waved to him, took a deep breath, and hustled up a reasonable facsimile of a smile.

"I ordered for you—Diet coke."

Stan sat down and nodded. "Close enough."

Mary took another sip of her gin and tonic. "I heard—no more hard stuff, huh?"

"Not tonight, anyway."

"Anymore?"

"Not much. Not often. Cut way back a few years ago. Made Jenny crazy."

Mary stared down into her drink and poked at the wedge of lime. "I haven't talked to her for a while."

Stan took a swig of his Diet Coke. "She's okay. You ought to call."

Mary Stimic and Jenny Matthews had been best friends from high school—inseparable—but they had been opposites in a lot of ways. Jenny had been quiet and industrious and attractive; Mary, outgoing and impulsive and striking. Jenny had been proper; Mary, elegant; Jenny, cute and girlish; Mary, precocious and sexy. Still, lots of people had thought they were twins. Both were blonde and green-eyed. Both had splashes of freckles. Both were a bit pigeon-toed, wrote left-handed, and had a single dimple, though Jenny's was on the left cheek and Mary's was on the right. And both had had schoolgirl crushes on the shy, crewcut neighborhood paperboy. Jenny had married him.

Mary was trying hard to be nice. It showed. "How's my little pal?"

"Petey? Good kid."

"You?"

"Been better."

"When?"

Stan shrugged. "Pick a day."

Mary studied Stan for a second, then shrugged back. "I know your problem, Stosh."

"I'm sure you do."

"Want to hear?"

Stan shook his head slowly. "Nope."

"Sure?"

Stan nodded. He stifled a laugh. "Yes. I'm sure."

Mary paused and sat back in the booth. "I'm surprised you showed up."

Stan nodded again. He knew he was going to be sorry for coming. He'd only come because he'd had an hour to kill before meeting Marlyss. Now, he suddenly wished he'd gone anywhere else—to the laundromat, even. "Me, too."

Stan and Mary were in the back booth at the Kettle. The place was half-shrine and half-tavern. One wall was lined with framed photographs of cops killed in the line of duty. The other three were covered with newspaper clippings, as far back as 1905, about police heroics. Mary had a few bylines on the wall. One was a *Free Press* Sunday magazine profile of Homicide Detective Stanislaw Cyrus Kochinski, published soon after he'd solved the Mendoza shooting. Maria Mendoza, a thirty-two-year-old mother of three, had been an anti-drug, anti-gang community activist in the southwest section of the city. She'd been sitting on her front porch one cool summer night when three DeeJays had driven by and riddled the house with machine-gun fire. Mendoza had been hit six times; she'd died two days later. It took three months, but Stan had tracked down the trio of teenagers in the car. The boys had been tried as adults, found guilty, and sentenced to forty years each in prison. Nailing the kids was the closest Stan had come to being emotionally involved in a case in at least ten years. He'd admitted as much to Mary during one of three long interviews.

"For once—for the first time in a long time—it all had a meaning," Stan had said. "It wasn't just a job. I could feel this one. For some reason, this one meant something."

The magazine's graphics editor had pulled out part of the quote and used it as the title for the piece. Mary had chosen the booth nearest the story. She was sitting directly beneath big, bold, black lettering that read: *"This One Meant Something."*

Stan had noticed. He pointed to the article. "This some kind of setup?

Mary took a sip from her drink, leaving a smudge of dark-red lipstick on the glass. She couldn't help but smile. "There you go again. You gotta lighten up."

Stan nodded. "Says the pot to the kettle."

Mary shrugged. "See what I mean, Chipper. Give it a rest."

Mary was the only one who called him Chip, and any and all of its variations. Stan had tried to give himself the nickname when he was a seventh-grader, when he was tall and beanpole skinny and thought Stanislaw Kochinski—Stosh—was a name for some thick, swarthy guy. A bulky, bow-legged third-baseman, not a graceful pitcher. But Chip never stuck, except when Mary used it as a needle.

The Kettle was busy tonight, and noisy, but suddenly not in their booth. Mary took another sip of her drink. Stan stretched out, his right foot resting accidentally against Mary's leg. She moved almost immediately—almost. She put down her drink. Enough goddamn foreplay; it was time to get down to business.

"Truth time, Stosh: I'm less excited about this Jefferson kid meeting his Maker than you are."

Stan looked across the room. "I doubt it."

"Don't."

Stan turned back to the table and looked at Mary. Her blonde hair was in a tight bun. Her eyes sparkled. She still looked a lot like Jenny, except that her blouse was unbuttoned about two buttons lower than Jenny's would have been. He didn't think Mary saw him looking. She did. He looked down at his Diet Coke. "You doing daily stuff?"

"No, another longer piece. But I need to get up to speed fast." She looked Stan square in the eyes. She had a tough stare. She'd worked hard to cultivate it. "It's your case, isn't it?"

"Mine and Dawlson's."

"Pete?"

"We were partners before." Stan sipped his pop.

"I remember." She nodded. "You don't look terribly pleased."

"This on the record?"

Mary shrugged. She wasn't staring anymore, but she was still watching Stan's eyes. "Doesn't have to be."

Stan began to relax a bit. "There's just something screwy . . ."

"Like?"

Stan shrugged. "Don't know yet."

Mary poked at the lime again. "Well, let's stop the presses."

Stan ignored her. "I do know that this thing could maybe make or break Hatch. Sims, too, probably."

"Stop 'em again."

Stan dropped his head. "Fuck you, Mary."

She pulled one of her legs under her and sat on it. "I'll bet you say that to all the girls."

"Only the assholes."

Mary nodded. "I'll take that as a compliment."

Stan and Mary sat silently for a minute, maybe two. They had been through this before, too many times. Mary finally broke the quiet. "Okay. Truce." They'd had those before, too.

Stan nodded. "Been a long day."

Mary nodded back. "Well, let's shorten it."

Stan sighed. "Okay. What do you need?"

Mary leaned across the table. He could have looked down her blouse if he'd wanted to, but he didn't. "A name."

"Jesus Christ, Mary." He laughed.

"Not his."

"You're doing a magazine piece, not some Page One nutcracker. Why do you always have to be right the fuck on top of everything?"

Mary shrugged.

Stan shook his head, then nodded. "Right." He paused. "Me lighten up." He paused again. "Well, it's too early. I don't have a name."

"I'll settle for a hunch."

"Don't have one of those, either."

"A guess, then."

Stan smiled, then whispered. "Yours is as good as mine."

Mary slid to the side and sat back against the wall of the booth. "Cooper."

Stan nodded. "That's what everyone is saying." He looked away from Mary, across the room. "But it doesn't make sense."

"No?"

He turned toward her. "Nope." He shook his head. "Why would he do something so stupid?"

"I don't know."

"I do—he wouldn't." Stan picked up his can of Diet Coke and drained it. "You know this guy?"

"Nope. Heard of him."

"He's ruthless." Stan swung a leg onto the seat of the booth and leaned back. "But he's smart, too. He's a businessman. This'd be *very* bad advertising." He tapped the empty can on the table. "Listen, we've run Cooper in for questioning dozens of times. But always for small hits. Some two-bit punk gets Cooper mad, and Cooper punches his ticket. Cooper catches someone with their hand in the jar, and Cooper drills him. It's part of his job. But it's always been scumbags, penny-ante motherfuckers. He's doing us a goddamn favor. Why shoot some eleven-year-old kid?"

"Maybe he made a mistake."

Stan shook his head. "Possible. Not probable. Cooper is sharper than hell."

"But possible. It gets pretty dark at night."

"It never gets that dark for guys like Cooper, Mary. For me and you, maybe. Not him."

Mary had finished her drink. She rubbed her forehead, then put her hand to her mouth, then back to her lap. "So, if you were me, what would you do?"

Stan looked at Mary and smiled, then stared across the room at the wall decorated with dead heroes. "If I were you? If I were you, I'd go get myself the richest sonofabitch I could find, get married, buy a house in West Bloomfield, and make a couple of pudgy little Stimic babies."

Mary smiled. "You're a dick."

Stan smiled back. "Mary, Mary, always so contrary."

"You're hopeless, Chipper."

"You asked."

Her smile faded. "I'll ask again."

Stan shrugged. "Okay. I'd find some good contact in the police department and persuade him to give you everything you ever wanted to know about Julius Caesar Cooper." Stan waved at someone across the room. "You'll probably be needing it, one way or another."

"You?"

"Nope, not me."

"Who then?"

"That's not my job, Mary. I think that comes under the job description of star investigative reporter."

"C'mon, Stan."

"Okay, try Dawlson."

Mary shook her head. "He doesn't talk to me. He doesn't talk to reporters. Period."

"Smart guy."

It was Mary's turn to shrug. "Looks like that leaves just you."

Stan laughed. "No, it doesn't. I don't know enough, Mary." Stan looked her in the eyes. "I'm just a dumb Polack."

"I doubt that."

"You'll see." Stan was looking off across the room again. He glanced down at his watch. "Two minutes to end of interview."

Mary swung her legs under the table and sat up straight. "Tomorrow night. My place. You bring the Cooper file." Stan grimaced, but she continued. "Dinner. Dessert. Diet Coke. And true crime stories."

"Nope."

"Why not? Don't know any true crime stories? Make some up."

Stan shook his head. "No imagination."

Mary nodded, smiled, and began inching slowly toward the aisle. "That's what I've heard."

Stan looked her hard in the eyes. "No letup, huh, Mary?" She smiled. Stan shook his head. "Sorry, can't."

"Got a good reason?"

"Don't need a good reason, Mary. Don't need a reason at all."

Mary nodded. Then she slowly gathered her things and got up to leave. She slid across the seat, stood at the end of the booth, put both hands on the table, and leaned toward Stan. This time Stan took a good, hard look at her. He could see clear down her blouse to her waist. She wasn't wearing a bra—only a cocksure smile on her face. "You're no dumb Polack, Chipper." She looked down her blouse, then coolly straightened and buttoned up. "You're not dumb at all."

◇ 14 ◇

Stan scratched his head. He'd left the Kettle and driven for about an hour and had expected to end up at a mall or a restaurant or at some sort of coffee shop hideaway. Maybe even a roadside motel. But Marlyss's directions had led him to an ice rink—an *ice rink.* Where, he wasn't even sure— Melvindale, Lincoln Park, Allen Park. Somewhere downriver. He was more than a little confused.

The place was pretty empty. A chunky, red-haired women was sitting at the front desk doing some bookwork. Stan said hello and tried to make a little small talk. The woman shrugged, then looked at Stan as though he were nuts. She looked tired; she sounded the same. "You want packed, pal? Try Friday, about nine—then, it's a zoo. Tonight's a school night." She shook her head and waved him in.

Stan nodded and smiled politely, took a quick look around, then headed toward a sign that said SNACK BAR. It really wasn't a snack bar, but a dingy little pea-green cinderblock room with six tables, a jukebox, and a row of five vending machines, two of which were out of order. The place was empty except for a couple sitting at the table near the music. The pair looked about sixteen, maybe seventeen—eighteen, tops. Kids. They were holding hands. They didn't see Stan; they were too busy staring at each other. Stan left and went to the rink. Hockey practice. The skaters looked ten, maybe twelve, and were doing two-on-one drills. The coach was screaming at them. Stan felt bad for the kids. He had had a baseball coach once who was a screamer, a big-time, bad, mean screamer. Laddy had gotten fed up one night after practice and popped the coach good. No one else was around, not even Stan. All Stan remembered was that Laddy had come back to the car with a fist-ful of raw knuckles and that the coach had showed up the next night with a shiner and a split lip and hadn't yelled so much after that.

Stan headed back to the entrance, interrupted the woman at the desk again, and told her he was looking for someone. He described Marlyss. The woman didn't look up this time.

"Jane's the only other one workin' tonight." She pointed to her left. " 'Round the corner."

Stan mumbled thanks, walked down a short hallway, and found a small group of adults standing along a Plexiglas window. They were watching a bunch of little kids on a smaller rink in a separate room. None of the children could have been more than four or five. Some looked even younger. Three had pillows tied to their backsides. All were watching the lone adult in the middle of their ring. The woman was demonstrating some sort of turn. Each of the kids tried it; each fell down. The instructor helped each one up, then dusted them off. Stan watched her. For some reason, he couldn't take his eyes off her. Neither could the kids. The woman looked over at the window, saw Stan, and smiled. It was Marlyss.

She moved across the ice with strength and grace. Stan laughed at himself. He hadn't even known she could skate. She looked a little different, too. He had never seen the coat she was wearing, and her hair—it was up and pulled back. She looked like some prim, proper librarian. Her makeup was different, too. Her lipstick seemed lighter, though her smile gave her away. Same smile. It made her dark eyes sparkle. No disguising that.

But there was something else that caught his eye: Marlyss looked really happy. Stan wanted to wave her over, put his arms around her, and hug her tight. He wanted to feel that joy in her; it looked awfully real. But he couldn't. Not here. So he faded to the back of the pack of parents and just watched. A stern mother told him the kids had ten minutes left.

He was sitting on a bench in the corner when Marlyss came off the ice. She sat next to him, but not too close, smiled again and wrinkled her nose.

Stan nodded. "Good evening . . . Jane."

"Jane Smithson." She giggled.

Stan closed one eye and surveyed her appearance in mock amazement. "Lady of a thousand faces?"

Marlyss shrugged like a little kid, still smiling. "Two or three . . . maybe." She giggled again, a bit nervously this time. "Hidden talent, I guess."

She noticed a little boy across the way. His parents were late and he looked as though he were going to cry. She stood to go and sit with him. "Raymie King." She shrugged. "He can be pretty weepy." She sat down, and quickly made Raymie smile, too. She looked across at Stan and winked. Stan suddenly felt incredibly jealous of the five-year-old. He wanted the kid to disappear.

Raymie did, finally. It seemed like twenty minutes; it was about five. Marlyss moved to the bench across from Stan. "Hey, Stosh, no pillow?"

Stan shook his head.

"Too bad." She smiled flirtatiously. "I was going to give you a private lesson." She looked down and began unlacing her skates.

"Since when?"

Marlyss laughed. "Since when, what? Skate? Since I was three."

Stan shook his head. "No—this. All this."

She laughed again. "A while, but not long enough." She looked up, still beaming. "No one knows me down here,

Stosh—no one. I can be me—once a week, for forty-five minutes. And the kids *like* me." Her smile had faded a little, but her eyes were still on fire. "I can feel that."

All of a sudden, Stan felt a little like an intruder; it made him a bit uncomfortable. "Pretty happy." It was a statement.

Marlyss nodded.

"It's nice to see you like this."

She bit her bottom lip. "I know." She giggled again, then smiled. "Sometimes I wish I had a mirror."

Stan smiled back. "Next time I'll bring a camera." He wanted to tell her that he had never seen her this beautiful, but he didn't know how to say that sort of thing.

Marlyss had her skates packed now. She moved to Stan's bench, looked around quickly to see if anyone was watching, then reached up and kissed him softly on the cheek. Her nose was still cold, her lips, cool. She slid her arm in his, but only for a moment. The tiny lights in her eyes twinkled. "No pillow—then buy me some hot chocolate, Stanislaw." She hardly ever called him that.

Stan nodded. "Deal. Where?"

"Here. In there." Marlyss pointed toward the snack bar.

Stan could see inside from his seat. He grimaced. The gooey-eyed couple was still there. Another youngish pair was there now, too, stuck in a lovesick pose. He shook his head. "Not here."

Marlyss looked over. "Why not?"

Stan shrugged. "I'm not sure I need to feel like some kid out on a date."

Marlyss grabbed his hand and squeezed. "That's exactly what you need to feel like, detective."

She smiled. Stanislaw did, too. Then he followed her to a table.

They'd met less than four months earlier at Tiger Stadium. Stan had promised to take Petey to a baseball game the summer before, and he was finally coming through. They were using a pair of box-seat tickets that Stan had gotten from Pisarcawitcz, who'd gotten them from Harry Morton, the homicide inspector, who'd gotten them from deputy

chief Dan Myers, who'd gotten them from Frank Sims.
Marlyss had been in the seat next to Petey.

Stan had known who Marlyss was; he was sure she didn't
know him. The last time he'd seen her was at the department Christmas party at the Polish Century Club on East
Outer Drive. It had been a shot-and-a-beer affair, but she
and Frank had been dressed for opening night on Broadway.
Frank had worn a tux, Marlyss a sequinned, navy cocktail
dress. She'd been stunning, the only woman the cops had
talked about, and probably dreamed of, for weeks.

She was much less intimidating at the ballpark, dressed in
faded jeans, yellow high-top sneakers, and an oversized purple T-shirt. At least to Petey. He spoke to her first, in the
bottom of the second inning, immediately after she'd made
a brave, but awkward, attempt to catch a foul ball that had
landed a few seats away and ricocheted in a high, lazy arc
toward their seats.

"Nice try." It came out, "Nfff trrr." Petey's mouth was
stuffed with half-chewed hot dog.

"Naw." She watched a pair of teenagers wrestle over the
ball, then turned to Petey and smiled at him. "Not even
close. But I caught one once before, you know . . ."

Petey was impressed. He'd known only one other person
who said he'd caught a foul ball: Benjy Studens, a pudgy,
wheezy kindergarten friend who was always picking his
nose. And Petey didn't believe him.

". . . on the fly." Petey's eyes grew wide; he looked at
Stan. So did Marlyss. Her smile was wonderful. Even Petey
noticed that. Stan grinned shyly and shrugged. He felt about
as old as his son.

Petey still wasn't sure. "What'd you do with it?"

Marlyss wrinkled up her nose. "I gave it to the little boy
sitting next to me."

Petey nodded, matter-of-factly, then reached under his
seat. "I brought my glove." He sat down and put the glove
in his lap. It was almost as big as him. "You can borrow it
next time."

Marlyss nodded back with a look that was as serious as
Petey's offer. "Thank you. I just might do that."

Stan didn't join the conversation until the fourth inning.

Then, they talked across Petey—mostly small talk, mostly about baseball. Marlyss said she was in love with baseball. He said that he had played once, then felt stupid for bringing himself up. She didn't ask much about his career, which was good. Sort of. When Petey announced in the eighth inning that he had to go to the bathroom, Marlyss offered to take him. She said it was okay; she had to go, too. As she left for the bathrooms, she asked Stan his name. "Just in case you decide to run off and leave me with the boy." He told her, and she smiled again, a schoolgirl smile this time. Petey looked at Stan and grinned, too.

It wasn't until the game was over and they were walking up the stairs to the ramp that Stan realized Marlyss was alone, and that he was suddenly out of time, and that he probably wouldn't see her again, at least not like this. He wanted to offer her a ride home, then he realized, too, how stupid that would be—the chief's wife. It was nuts. Besides, she probably had her own car. Instead, he offered her a handshake. That seemed pretty silly also, especially when he held out his hand long before they'd left the stadium and actually said goodbye. But she accepted it, early. She said she'd had a nice time, almost as if it had been a date. Her hand was warm and soft, but strong. It felt good. He would remember that—that, and feeling like a goofy teenager.

He never expected to hear from her—that would have been crazy—but he did, about three weeks later, on a Monday. She called him at headquarters from her office at the Long Lake Fitness and Health Center in Bloomfield Hills, and said she'd been at another Tigers game that past Saturday and had caught a foul ball . . . well, with a little help from a guy next to her. She laughed. She said she'd had the ball autographed by a few of the Tigers and that she wanted Petey to have it. Stan said that would be terrific. She said she could drop it off on Saturday evening and if they weren't home, she would just leave it in a box inside the door. He said that would be fine, too.

He and Petey were home when she came calling, just as she had hoped.

She was alone, just as Stan had prayed.

Petey met her at the door. "Can you stay for dinner? We're gonna have pizza." He hadn't even asked her in yet.

Marlyss smiled. "My favorite."

"No onions." Petey stuck out his tongue.

Marlyss did the same. "Yuck!" Petey laughed.

Stan had spent the afternoon cleaning up the place. He began apologizing for it as soon as Marlyss walked in the door.

She laughed, and ignored the thick dust on top of the TV. "Everything is fine."

She gave Petey the baseball and Stan ordered the pizza. It was 6:30. By eight, the pizza had come and gone and the dishes were done. Petey shook Marlyss's hand like a little gentleman when he said goodnight. "You're almost as pretty as my mom."

Marlyss smiled and shook her head. "I don't think so."

"Yes, you are." He nodded. "Almost." He turned to leave, then looked back. "You know my mom?"

Marlyss shook her head again. "No."

Petey stared at her for a few seconds. "I miss her when she's not around."

Marlyss nodded. "Your daddy's here."

Petey nodded back, then turned and walked down the hallway to the bedroom. Stan followed him and tucked him in. The house was still when he returned to the kitchen. Marlyss was sitting at the table, paging through the newspaper. Stan poured them coffee, then joined her. She was leaning forward, reading an article. He thought he noticed some dark splotches on her neck and chest where some makeup had rubbed away. He wanted to stare, but didn't.

She looked up at him. "Single parenting."

Stan shrugged. "I'm not very good at it."

She laughed. "No, this story. It's about single parenting."

He glanced across the page. "Maybe I should read it."

She shook her head. "You won't."

He nodded. "You're probably right."

"I don't think there's a probably to it."

Stan laughed, and so did Marlyss. "Your son's a nice little boy."

Stan nodded. "His mother's responsible for that."

They talked for an hour, often in short spurts. Some of the silence was uncomfortable. Some of the conversation felt silly or awkward or even, somehow, futile. But some of it was very good. Stan didn't bring up cop stuff, nor did she. When the coffee was gone, Stan checked his watch. It was 9:25, not very late, but Stan was nervous. He picked up his cup, walked to the sink, and deposited it. She gave him a mock glare until he rinsed it out, then shrugged. "I ought to be getting home."

He nodded and walked her to the door. It had gotten cool, almost cold, so he told her to wait second and tiptoed into the bedroom and got a sweatshirt. It was an extra-large, and it drooped to her thighs. She looked like a schoolgirl. She played with the cuffs a bit nervously, and he helped her roll the sleeves. "I'll walk you to your car."

She scrunched up her nose, rubbed it, and pointed to her car parked a few steps outside the door. "It's not a very long walk."

Stan felt dopey again. He rubbed his head. "Right."

Marlyss took his hand in hers. Her hands were soft and warm again. She had wonderfully long fingers. She leaned over and kissed Stan on the cheek. "I had a nice dinner. Take care of that baseball."

Stan turned to her and nodded. "Me, too—and we will." He wanted to kiss her back, but he didn't know what she wanted.

Then Marlyss left, got into her car, and drove off. Stan had half a mind to follow her, get out of his car and the first stop sign or stoplight, and ask when he could see her again. He might have, but Petey was asleep in the bedroom. He just watched her drive away.

He called her a week after at her office and told her he had gone to a Tigers game and caught a foul ball and . . . They both laughed, and then they both held their breath, for what seemed like minutes, waiting for someone to say what would, what should, come next. This time, it was Stan. And this time, Petey wasn't home.

And, so it began.

* * *

Now, here they were again, this time sitting in the corner of a skating rink snack bar, with two half-finished cups of lukewarm vending-machine cocoa, and two pairs of kids sitting at nearby tables making cow eyes at each other. And it was getting late. It was always getting late when they were together.

Marlyss studied Stan's face. "You look tired."

Stan nodded. "Still am."

Marlyss looked over at one of the pairs of kids. She smiled. "You ever been in love?"

"I think so. You?"

Marlyss shrugged. "Not sure." She stopped, then smiled nervously. "Does she know who I am?" Her voice was softer now.

Stan shook his head. "No."

"Anything about me?"

"No." he stopped. "Yes—Petey told her you were beautiful."

Marlyss smiled, a bit brighter now, and paused for a second. "What was she like?" She always politely avoided using Jenny's name.

"I have a tough time remembering." He played with his cup, without drinking. He wasn't telling the whole truth.

"It wasn't that long ago."

He shrugged. "Maybe I've tried to forget."

"Try to remember."

"Why?" He was looking down at the table.

"It's important . . . to me."

He looked at her this time. "It shouldn't be."

"I know." Marlyss nodded. "What happened?"

Stan took a deep breath, then exhaled slowly. "I'm not sure."

"Something . . . just happened?"

"I never saw anything coming."

"Did she?" Marlyss sounded concerned for Jenny.

Stan could feel that. "Says she did."

"Is that going to happen to us?"

"I don't know." Stan's voice was low now. It was almost as if he were talking to himself.

"I wish you did."

He heard the hurt in her voice. "I wish I did, too."

They were in the parking lot now, by her car. They spent half their time standing by her car, in the darkness. She looked up into the starry sky, closed her eyes, and took a deep breath. "What do you see when you close your eyes, Stosh?"

Stan shrugged. "I suppose I don't see anything. Not that I think about it all that much."

"Think about it now."

"Okay." It took him a few seconds. "I used to practice pitching with my eyes closed. I mean, I could see everything that I was going to do and everything that was going to happen, mostly. They've got some fancy name for that nowadays, but it worked, even back then. Everything made sense. Not like this." He was looking past her now. "Sometimes, I see my father—once, anyway. In his uniform. At least I think it was him." He paused and tried to change the subject. "Tell me about your father."

She shook her head. "He's dead. Long time ago."

"I'm sorry."

"Don't be." She smiled. "We're talking about you."

He shrugged again. "Now, there's mostly nothing. Now, I just close my eyes and go to sleep. Maybe my dreaming's done."

She was staring into his eyes. "Don't say that—ever."

"Okay, what do you see?"

"Sometimes I see a tiny little figure skater." She smiled. "And ..." She stopped.

"What?" He smiled. "Did you want to be a skater?"

She nodded, then smiled back. "America's sweetheart— Peggy Fleming. That was supposed to be me." She laughed. "But we were talking about you, detective."

The rink was closing now. The inside lights flicked off, then the outside lights. The two couples from the snack bar were walking toward their cars. Marlyss looked at them, then turned back and jabbed Stan in the gut. "So you got the old blank screen last night, detective. So what? Maybe you just had a bad night."

Stan nodded, and laughed at himself. "A lifetime of 'em."

One of the couples stopped alongside a rickety pickup, and embraced clumsily.

Marlyss watched them. "First boy ever kissed me was Wally House. He missed my lips and hit me here." She touched a spot just below her right eye. "Then he told me he loved me." She snapped her fingers. "Just like that."

Stan smiled. "You loved him?"

Marlyss nodded. "Of course. He was a lot like you, Stosh—same bashful, boyish charm." She laughed. "And besides, he liked me."

Stan laughed, too. "How old was he? Ten?"

Marlyss smiled. "Seven."

It was time to go—again. He was really bad at this, too. She wasn't. She kissed him softly on the neck, then got in her car. "Call? Tomorrow?"

Stan nodded. "I will."

She smiled. "I'm glad you came."

So was he.

It was almost one when Stan got home. The living room was dark, except for the tiny red light on the answering machine next to the pone on the end table. The light flickered twice, paused, then repeated its flashes. Two messages. Stan flipped on a light, hung his coat in the closet, and went to the kitchen. The messages had waited this long; they could wait a few minutes longer. He opened the refrigerator: milk, butter, orange juice, a few eggs, mustard, peanut butter, half an eggroll, three cans of cheap, low-alcohol beer left over from—he couldn't remember when. Stan grabbed a beer, popped the top, and took a long gulp. It tasted watery, and too bitter, but it went down cold. He went into the living room and turned on the TV. A cop show was on—"The Rockford Files." He grabbed the remote control off the end table and turned James Garner mute, then sat on the couch, reached over and hit the Play button on the answering machine.

The first message was from Big Time. "Made contact with Cooper. Got somethin'. Not much. If he's your boy, I wouldn't be wastin' my time before I grabbed ahold of him. Time is of the accents. Call me."

Stan smiled. "Essence, you wiseass." He nodded. Big Time wanted everyone to think he was an idiot. He was no idiot.

The second message was from Jenny. "Don't forget about the Clown Café. Call me. Bye." Stan nodded again, then closed his eyes.

The phone rang. Stan didn't answer it, and the answering machine kicked in. "Frank Sims, Stan. It's about 1:15—A.M. Let's move tomorrow's 5:00 P.M. meeting up to noon." Frank paused. It sounded as though he was talking to someone in the background. "Stan . . . ah, I talked to Pete a few hours ago and he doesn't think he'll need 'til Saturday on the list. Call me first thing in the morning."

Stan got up, walked to the hallway and switched off the light, then went back to the sofa and lay down. He looked around the room. It was an old place, with faded pastel walls, plastic light fixtures, and worn, chocolate carpeting in every room except the bathroom and kitchen.

Stan had rented the bungalow on Buckingham for two years, now. The house had finally begun to feel comfortable, or at least familiar. He'd even gotten used to the noise—he could look out the kitchen window and see the freeway, I-94. But tonight, everything felt different somehow. That happened every now and then. Nothing had been changed, but nothing looked the way he expected it to. Stan closed his eyes. Still nothing there.

He sometimes wondered if he was crazy to keep seeing Marlyss, considering who she was—his boss's wife, the *police chief*'s wife, for chrissakes—but he just as quickly dismissed it. He knew he couldn't let her go, so why wonder? Something else puzzled him, too, though: Why him? Why a tired, dog-eared, homicide cop? He had never asked her, and she had never said, but he had sensed something in their meetings. Beneath the laughing exterior, a deep unhappiness, darkness. He didn't know if it had to do with her marriage, but it was there, all right. And it somehow drew them together.

He sat up and reached for the phone, then dialed. She answered after one ring.

"Just wanted to make sure you got home okay."

"I did." Marlyss knew that wasn't why he had called. "He isn't home yet."

Stan nodded. "I figured. He just called here, sounded like he was still downtown."

"I'm glad you called."

"So am I." Stan lay back down and closed his eyes.

"Stan." Her voice dropped to a whisper. "Let's leave."

Stan chuckled and whispered back. "When?"

"Now."

"Okay." Stan laughed again.

Marlyss shook her head. "I'm serious—tonight, now."

"I can't."

"Why not?" She fought to keep the disappointment out of her voice.

"I just can't, that's all."

"You talk about it sometimes like you mean to. Could you give up being a cop?"

"Tonight . . . yes."

"Tomorrow?"

"I think so."

"What would you do?"

Stan exhaled slowly, then paused. He smiled, then chuckled, almost to himself. "I just got a Christmas card from a guy I used to play ball with. He's trying to set up a minor-league team in Montgomery. Says he needs some help."

"Where?"

"Alabama."

"Is he serious?"

Stan shook his head. "I don't know. I don't know a damn thing about running a baseball team."

"You could learn."

"Me—okay. You? You'd probably end up bagging popcorn in the concession stand."

"Alabama sounds . . . nice."

"Sounds nicer than it is. Hot. Humid. Bugs. Red clay—stains everything."

Marlyss got serious again. "What about Petey? Could you leave him?"

Stan shook his head. "I don't think so."

Marlyss knew that. What did she expect him to say? She stopped. Frank's car was coming. "I've got to go."

"Okay."

Marlyss held the phone tight. "Stan? When I close my eyes tonight, I'm going to see . . ."

"Wally House."

She laughed. ". . . Alabama."

Stan smiled and nodded. "Red clay."

Marlyss nodded, too. Her voice was a whisper, but her smile was back. "Everything."

Then Marlyss hung up. Stan waited for the click and did the same. He tried to see Alabama, too, but everything was still black. Maybe, he told himself, he was just too tired. Or maybe, he was just gazing up into a dark, starless Alabama sky.

◇ 15 ◇

Bill Colbane was an early riser. He would get up at 5:15, go downstairs and put on a pot of coffee, then shuffle to the front door and get the paper. Then he would sit at the kitchen table, in the chair nearest the bay window, and read the paper, from front to back, saving the editorial page for last. At about 6:15, he would go the bedroom in the rear of the house to wake Samuel, his loud, brassy, fifteen-year-old, for school. Then he would trudge upstairs to wake Abe, the eleven-year-old who slept in the bedroom at the top of the landing. As soon as the boys were up and moving at some reasonable speed, Bill Colbane would crawl back into bed, put his arms around Molly, hold her snug, and listen to the morning news on the clock radio. When the newscast was finished, Bill Colbane would rise again, do fifty sit-ups and fifty push-ups, shave, shower, dress, eat a bowl of corn flakes with just a touch of skim milk and exactly one-third of a banana, drink half a glass of apple juice, and head to the courthouse. Bill Colbane's weekday-morning routine was unchangeable.

Except today. Bill Colbane was awake early, but he wasn't sitting in his favorite spot in the kitchen. He was sitting on the couch in the living room, waiting nervously, listening intently for the muted slap of the morning paper on the front stoop. He hadn't slept. He'd lost count of how many times he'd been up. He'd vomited twice, he knew that. He'd told Molly he must have caught the bug that was going around the courthouse. She'd made him some weak tea the first time. The second time, she'd moved to the guest room on the third floor so he could rest easier. But Bill Colbane had never gone back to bed. First, he'd gone downstairs and looked in on Samuel. Then, upstairs to Abe's room. Then, down the hall, tiptoeing into Missy's room and standing just inside the door for five, ten, maybe as long as fifteen minutes, just listening to her breathe. She still slept fitfully. He'd wanted desperately to hold her; he hadn't even touched her. Then he'd gone downstairs and sat on the couch to wait for the paper, checking his watch every five minutes to see how much time had passed. He'd begun the vigil at 1:35.

It was now 4:30, and the antique mantel clock chimed once. The paper should have arrived by now. Bill Colbane, wearing a navy blue flannel nightshirt and black slippers, got up and looked out the living room window. There were tracks in the snow leading to the front door of his house. He hadn't heard the paperboy; the footsteps and thud of the paper must have been muffled by the new-fallen snow. He opened the door, his hands shaking, and lost his balance somehow and slipped, one foot landing on the stoop. A small dusting of snow kicked up into his slipper. He didn't even notice. He picked up the paper and carried it carefully and quickly into the kitchen. He didn't look at it. He forced himself to wait until he was sitting down, in his regular spot.

Bill Colbane held his breath as he took the paper out of its plastic bag and unfolded it. Suddenly, he was sure his picture was going to be on the front page, large and bold, with a caption that read: "Judge William Colbane; a conspiracy to kill." His picture, yes, and Frank's and Hatch's and Stone's—and Rickey Jefferson's. And while gripped by that crazy panic, he also held out a silly, childlike hope that nothing about the murder would be there, that the whole thing was simply a nightmare, that the big fat headline type would spell out: "Unemployment Up," or "U.S. Lifts Trade Embargo"; that Rickey Jefferson hadn't died after all.

But all he saw when he opened the paper was reality—or Frank Sims's version of it. The headline read: "Hatch, Sims Vow to Find Boy's Killer." Bill Colbane squeezed his eyes closed, then opened them and began reading, slowly, carefully. The main story recast what Frank and the mayor had said in front of TV cameras the day before—that they promised to solve the Jefferson shooting quickly. "This case will be the impetus for a renewed effort in the battle against drugs and violent crime on the lower east side," Hatch was quoted as saying. "We already have a lead in the case," Sims was quoted as saying. "We have two of our best detectives on it. They will have as much support as they need." The coverage included four shorter, related stories—sidebars—about the victim, the reactions of neighborhood activists and black leaders, the crime statistics for the city, and the detectives on the case, Stan Kochinski and Pete Dawlson.

Bill Colbane read about Senada Wilson, a teacher at Carsten Elementary, who said that Rickey Jefferson had been a good student, with a speech impediment, and had been polite and courteous and rarely was absent. He read about Esther Donovan, an elderly white neighbor of the Jeffersons, who told how Rickey had shoveled her sidewalk in the winter and cut her lawn in the summer—for free—and often run to the drugstore to pick up her medicine. He read about neighborhood activists calling for help from blacks like him, blacks who held positions of authority. Bill

Colbane read, and read, and read, then re-read everything again. He was still reading, when the refrigerator door popped open. It was Missy. She startled him.

Bill Colbane took off his glasses and rubbed his eyes. "What time is it, honey?" Missy was staring blankly into the refrigerator. She didn't answer. Bill Colbane really didn't expect her to. He only hoped. Missy didn't talk much anymore. She often went for days without saying a word, breaking her silence only to say yes or no. She closed the refrigerator door, then left the room as quietly as she had entered it, without even looking at her father. Bill Colbane checked his watch. It was 6:25.

He put down the paper and hurried to Samuel's room. Samuel was snoring loudly. Bill Colbane put his hand on Samuel's shoulder and shook him awake. Samuel groaned and pushed his father's hand away. He said he would get up in a few minutes. He always said that, and he always got up.

Abe was sound asleep, too. And even though he was late waking him, Bill Colbane stopped for a minute to watch his youngest child sleep. The light from the hallway bathed the room softly. Abe's chest moved in a gentle rhythm. Bill Colbane envied his son's peacefulness. He leaned over and kissed him on the forehead. It was the first time he had kissed one of his children in weeks, maybe months. He felt a sharp, painful flash of regret. He wished he had kissed Abe more often. He wished he had hugged Samuel more. He wished he had spent more time with Missy. He began to cry, quietly.

Bill Colbane had to wake Abe, but he was suddenly paralyzed with fear. What would Missy and Samuel and Abe think if they knew? Would they know? How would they find out? The tears burned his eyes. Abe turned toward him, awake. He was startled. "Dad?"

Bill Colbane swiped at his eyes and tilted his glasses forward so Abe couldn't see his tears. "Time to get up, son."

"Dad?" Abe squinted at him.

Bill Colbane backed up. He nodded. "I was just finishing this story in the paper. Lost track of the time."

Abe sat up. He looked over at the paper and read the

headline, moving his lips. Molly said Abe would outgrow the habit, but Bill was always on him about that. He didn't say anything this morning. "The story about that boy?"

Colbane nodded. "Yes."

Abe moved to the edge of the bed, rubbing his eyes. "We talked about him in school yesterday. One of the kids played on a baseball team with him last summer."

Colbane took a handkerchief from his pocket and blew his nose. "Your teacher talked about this with you?"

Abe nodded. "She talked about drugs, and all that stuff."

"Did she say this boy was involved with drugs?"

Abe swung his legs out of bed. "Said he maybe was."

Colbane slipped three fingers under his glasses. The tears were coming again, and he tried to squeeze them away. He turned and walked toward the door. He wanted to make sure Abe couldn't see his eyes.

"Pop?" Abe stood and began putting on his shirt. He stopped and turned on the light on the nightstand. "You've never been shot, have you?"

Colbane shook his head. "No."

"Must hurt."

Colbane turned back to his son and nodded. "Must."

The judge turned again to leave, and as he did, he saw Missy rocking herself on a chair in the corner of the room. She had been there the whole time. Colbane hadn't even noticed. He looked at Missy, then walked over to Abe and put his arm around his boy. He smelled fresh, like a child. He inhaled the fragrance, then hugged his son. "You're going to have to hustle to catch that bus."

Abe looked at his father. His voice became a whisper. "Does Missy talk to you, Dad?"

Colbane shook his head.

Abe nodded. "She talks to me sometimes, but I don't understand what she's saying."

Bill Colbane looked at his silent daughter, then at his son. "Listen hard enough, and maybe you will."

"You sure?"

Colbane shrugged, then nodded, hugged his boy again, then headed toward the guest bedroom. Molly was still asleep, snoring quietly and evenly. The judge went to the dresser and looked for a pair of scissors. He found a pair of cuticle scissors, unfolded the newspaper, and carefully cut out the picture of Rickey Jefferson. The caption under the photo said it was Rickey Jefferson's fifth-grade class photo. Bill put the clipping in his pocket, then threw the rest of the paper in the wastebasket.

Molly stirred and looked up. "Bill? That you?"

"Yes." He sat on the edge of the bed.

Molly sat up next to him. "How are you feeling?"

He smiled. "Better. Much better."

"The flu?"

"Maybe just something I ate."

"Your eyes look red."

"I didn't get much sleep."

"You sure you're okay?"

He nodded. "Yes." His eyes still stung from his tears. He wanted to rub them, but didn't.

"Want any breakfast?"

Colbane shook his head. "No." He put his arm around his wife. "Breakfast can wait. I think I'm going to take the day off."

Molly's eyes flared open wide. "You got a fever?"

Colbane laughed and shook his head.

"It's been at least seven years since you've missed a day of work."

He nodded. "Maybe it's time. I'm thinking I'll stay home and sit around, maybe see if Missy will go for a walk with me."

Molly put her arms around her husband and hugged him tenderly. "It'll be nice to have you home."

She smiled. Bill did, too. "It's a date, then?" Molly nodded.

Colbane hugged his wife, then walked to the dresser to call his court clerk. For some reason, he was feeling a bit hopeful. But the phone rang before he could pick up the receiver. It was Frank.

"We need to talk, Bill."

Frank Sims hung up the phone. He was propped up in bed, bare-chested, in a pair of blood-red silk pajama bottoms. He was feeling chipper. He was still in control. The worst wasn't over, but he could see the end from where he was sitting, and it looked okay. He had only one worry: Bill Colbane. The judge was the trip wire. If Colbane went, everything, and everyone, did. The key was keeping him busy. The more time the judge had to think about what had happened, the greater the chance he would blow.

Frank flexed his right arm and admired his biceps. It had shrunk a bit since his college boxing days, but it was still impressive. He closed his eyes and his mouth, then exhaled slowly through his nose. "Keep . . . a rein . . . on Colbane." It rhymed. "Rein on Colbane." He smiled again, then laughed. Marlyss stirred, rolled onto her back, hugging the covers to her chest, opened her eyes, looked at Frank, then turned away from her husband, pulling her knees up her stomach. Frank was still laughing as he watched her. Her back and shoulders were perfectly shaped, as if an artist had sculpted them. They were her most beautiful parts. Marlyss could feel her husband's eyes. She scrunched down and pulled the covers even tighter. Frank leaned over, pulled the blankets down, and ran his hand lightly down the back of her arm. Marlyss shivered, curled tighter into a ball, and pulled the covers back up.

Frank sat back. "My, we're full of spunk this morning. We must be feeling pretty good about ourselves." He reached over and played with Marlyss's hair. "Things must be going well . . . at work."

Marlyss didn't answer. There was no reason to.

Frank slid out of bed and went to his closet, trying to decide on a shirt. "Think Bill Colbane has any backbone, dear?"

She was still silent. She had no idea what Frank was talking about.

"Bill. Fucking. Colbane." Frank laughed to himself. He walked back to Marlyss's side of the bed and sat down, pulled down the covers again, leaned over, and kissed her on the cheek, then on the soft, round curve of her left breast. Marlyss tried not to flinch. She wasn't very successful. Frank smiled. "We've been missing each other a bit too much lately, don't you think?"

Marlyss closed her eyes as though she were trying to go back to sleep. "Late nights. Busy time of the year . . ."

Frank nodded. "Of course."

". . . membership drive, computer problems."

"Certainly. Computer problems at the health club." Frank rubbed her shoulder, softly at first, then harder. "Well, maybe we ought to make a date." Frank traced the outline of her lips with his finger. "Or maybe your date book is all filled up? I certainly hope not."

Marlyss lay perfectly still. Frank pulled the covers back up over her, patted her head, then got up. "Let's do something fun on this date." He went to the bedroom window and pulled back the curtains. It had snowed on and off throughout the night. "Not dinner." He surveyed the conditions outside, then turned back toward the bed. "Something really healthy. Tobogganing? Skiing? Skating—that's it." Frank nodded. "Ice skating. You skate, don't you, dear?"

Marlyss tried to maintain her blank expression, but her mind was reeling. What did he know? Everything? She closed her eyes.

Frank smiled. "But first, Bill Colbane. He'll be over in a few minutes. And I've got to get a rein on Colbane." He laughed. "After that, maybe I'll try to learn how to do a triple axel. With your help, of course."

Marlyss ignored her husband's gibberish. She was too busy trying to fight back the waves of panic—and losing. Frank could tell. He could always tell. He was headed to the bathroom to shower and stopped in the bedroom doorway. "By the way, how is dear old mom these days?" He didn't wait for an answer, he just laughed again. Then he shook his head and left.

◇ 16 ◇

Martin Wallace Hatch III sucked a few pieces of ice from the tall glass of grapefruit juice in his right hand, rolled them around in his mouth, then crunched them quietly between his teeth. He was sitting on the edge of his desk in his office on the eleventh floor of the City-County Building downtown; he was dressed in a blindingly white undershirt and brown, pin-striped suit pants. A TV remote control was in his left hand. "Nice-looking kid."

Chet Lyttle, Hatch's press secretary, was sitting at Hatch's desk. He had an unfiltered cigarette stuck in his right hand and a pen in his left, and was scribbling on a yellow legal pad. He didn't look up from his work. "I guess."

"She'll do okay." Hatch nodded. "In fact, she'll do great. I want her for that noon interview."

Lyttle still hadn't looked up. "Casey might raise a stink." Arne Casey was the news director at WKCY-TV. "He doesn't like to be bossed around."

"Fine. Then don't—just tell him my schedule's too tight at noon for an exclusive interview."

Hatch was staring at the wall to his right, which housed four big-screen, built-in TVs, one for each of the local network affiliates and one for CNN. Hatch had all four TVs going this morning. All but one were silent. Channel Six morning anchor Melanie Thompson had Hatch's attention. She was doing a report on a school board vote. Hatch walked to the screen and pointed the remote control at her lips. "The messenger." He smiled, then pressed the Volume button, and her voice faded away. "Yep—young and pretty. Impressionable. She'll do just fine."

Lyttle still hadn't looked up from his scribbling. He took a drag on his cigarette. "I'll see what I can do."

That meant Lyttle would get it done. He'd handled Casey before. It really wasn't all that difficult. Hatch nodded. The mayor was in his office a full three hours earlier than normal and he was in as good a mood as could be expected. Frank had told him late the previous night that they were going to stick the Jefferson shooting on Cooper, guaranteed, and Frank's word was good enough for him. He turned toward Lyttle. "We ever talk about Sims, you and me?

"Not much."

"What do you think?" Hatch got up and walked to the wall behind his desk, which really wasn't a wall, but a huge window that framed the bustling riverside district of his renovated, resurgent downtown. The city was creaking to life under a bleak, gray December sky.

Lyttle continued writing. "Smart. Slick. Sly."

Hatch nodded. "Yes. Yes. Yes."

"Maybe . . . too smooth." The last two words sounded like one—too smooth. "Maybe dangerous."

"Frank?"

Lyttle shrugged. "Just a guess."

"Why?"

"Not sure. History, maybe. Caesar and Brutus."

Hatch laughed. "Not Frank. He's too smart."

Lyttle nodded. "You asked." He looked up, but only for a second. "What say we just worry about Rickey Jefferson for a few minutes?"

Hatch nodded. He finished off his juice and turned back toward the TVs. "Looks like nothing new this morning." He picked up the remote control again and pressed the red Power button once. The wall went dark. Lyttle stood and walked around to the front of Hatch's desk, pulled up a chair from the corner, and sat down. Hatch hitched his pants absentmindedly and turned back to the window. The sun was beginning to break through the overcast. Traffic had picked up. "I've worked hard to rebuild this city, Chester."

Lyttle nodded and continued scribbling.

"I'm not going to let anyone take it away from me, especially not a gang of punk motherfuckers."

Lyttle shook his head.

Hatch laughed again. He reached to his desk and pressed the Intercom button. "Nancy, where's my carnation?" Nancy Grim was Hatch's secretary. The mayor released the button and walked to the closet just to the right of the huge window, selected a shirt, carefully took it off the hanger, and began to put it on. "You ready?"

Lyttle nodded.

Chet Lyttle was a husky, grumpy-looking sort. His general dishevelment—shoes unshined, tie down, shirttail out, even at this early hour—was a stark contrast to the mayor's trim, dashing, neat-as-a-pin countenance. Lyttle, about fifteen years Hatch's junior, constantly waved off suggestions, even from the mayor, often from the mayor, that he improve his appearance. His answer was always the same: He had no time to waste on the way he looked. Hatch's appearance was all that mattered. And he was right.

"You've got a meeting with the East Side Citizens for Community Preservation at 7:30 . . ." Lyttle extinguished his cigarette in an ashtray on Hatch's desk, then reached into his shirt pocket, pulled out another cigarette, tamped it on his knee, and lit it. "You've got the black ministers at nine . . ." He took a long drag on the cigarette and continued speaking, the butt dangling from his lips, the inhaled smoke drifting from his mouth and nose in short bursts. "You've got the trip to the boy's school after lunch to speak with his classmates. Look more aggrieved than debonair. Maybe even grandfatherly. Rumple your hair a little. WMET, WNOX and WKCY will all be there." Lyttle scribbled on the notepad. "You should also be able to get another audience with Mrs. Jefferson, this time at the funeral home. Wake's this evening. The TV crews should follow you there. We'll have a bouquet of red roses for her and a display of pink carnations for the casket. You'll present both. No sound bites, just video. I've already talked to the stations. Told 'em we don't want to make a circus out of this." Lyttle took the cigarette from his mouth and finally looked up at the mayor. "Do we know for sure that this kid was clean?"

Hatch shook his head. "Not one hundred percent."

Lyttle looked back down at the pad in his lap. "Right." He put his pen down and rubbed his eyes. "What do you hear from Sims?"

"That we have a suspect."

"We knew that yesterday." Lyttle looked up. "How good?"

Hatch smiled. "Good enough to canonize the kid."

"That's what I wanted to hear." Lyttle looked down into his lap again and made a few more notes. "Okay. From here on in, Rickey Jefferson's a victim—period. Anyone from the press suggests he wasn't an angel, get indignant, give 'em hell. Make sure Sims gets the word."

Hatch nodded. "You're preaching to the choir, Chester."

Lyttle grunted, then took another deep drag on his cigarette. "From 3:30 until, well, as long as you can hold out, you have newspaper, radio, and TV types lined up for interviews."

"Can't do them all at once?"

"No." A streak of smoke crossed into Lyttle's right eye. He shut it, then picked some tobacco off the tip of his tongue with his thumb and forefinger and flicked the pieces to the carpet. "Better to see you in person. We want this thing personalized—you care, you're concerned, you're going to solve this thing." Lyttle paused. "We'll run 'em in and out of here as quick as we can—twenty minutes per reporter, max. I should be here all the time, but in case I'm not, let's make sure you're standing against the west wall here for any newspaper or magazine photo ops or video." The west wall of Hatch's office housed a large built-in bookcase where the mayor stored his law books. The volumes were window dressing. Hatch hadn't practiced law in almost twenty years, but Lyttle considered the books to be a big part of his embattled boss's image—a man of the law fighting lawlessness. "I'll get Nancy to run a rag over the books."

Hatch finished tying his tie, then walked to the mural that decorated about half of the east wall of his office. The painting was supposed to depict the multi-national, multi-racial, and multi-religious backgrounds of the city's constituents. Hatch hated it. He thought it was clumsy, clownish, and it was. The people were horse-faced and their poses were unnatural. But for some obscure historical reason, the painting was almost sacred, and Hatch, like three of his predecessors, had to suffer it. He took a few steps to his left and stood in front of a pair of black workers in hard hats, then faced Lyttle again. "What about here, a photo right in front of the . . . brothers?"

Lyttle looked up and absentmindedly stubbed out his cigarette. "Next question?"

Hatch nodded. "Think I'll see any white folks today, Chester?"

Lyttle looked back down at his pad. "Nope. Do reporters count?"

"Yep."

"Then you'll see lots of 'em—and take advantage of it. They love this ghetto life-and-death crap. It's like war to them. Makes 'em feel tough, worthwhile. Besides, it's Christmas. They're looking for melodrama."

Hatch nodded. "How'd I do yesterday?"

"Sounded like Sonja was going to come right there on the air."

Hatch smiled. "She's a sweetheart."

Lyttle shook his head. "She's too soft on you. That isn't good, either. I'll talk to her beforehand next time . . ."

"Tomorrow, she said."

"Right. We'll get her some stiffer questions."

Nancy Grim knocked on the door and entered carrying the mayor's pink carnation. Hatch grabbed his suit jacket from the closet and put it on. Nancy pinned the carnation on Hatch's lapel. Lyttle watched. "Got a piece of black ribbon, Nancy?" She shook her head. He looked back down to his pad and made another note. "Find some."

Hatch looked at Lyttle. "For?"

Lyttle ignored the question. "Later."

Hatch studied himself in a full-length mirror. "Got anything from our Ms. Brooks?" Terry Brooks was Hatch's former campaign boss. She was on the city payroll as an attorney, but, in effect, was Hatch's political analyst.

"She works fast. Faxed me sixteen pages last night." Lyttle put his cigarette in the ashtray and pulled another from his pocket. He lit the new one with the old. "Still, not a lot new here. We've been through a lot of this before, so I'll keep it short." He shuffled through some papers. "She found similar scenarios in somewhat similar political climates in three other cities within the past five years. Facts are basically the same. Citizens are frustrated with crime, and their emotions boil over some kid or grandma who dies violently at the hands of some punk outlaw during drive-by shooting, stick-up, break-in, et cetera. Press makes a martyr out of the victim. Everyone screams and shouts."

Hatch nodded. "Cut to the chase, Chet."

Lyttle winced, then took the cigarette from his mouth. This time he just spit out the tobacco residue. "In one case, a vulnerable—and venerable—mayor and his administration take big-time heat and big-time hits. Not fun stuff. Time to polish up the old résumé. In the other two, the bosses, also extremely vulnerable, survive, even flourish." Lyttle brushed at his tie. Crumbs from a donut he'd eaten an hour earlier fell into his lap.

Hatch went to his desk and sat down. He leaned forward in his chair. "Because they solved the case."

"Close." Lyttle brushed at his tie again, this time to dust off some ashes, which also fell into his lap, and this time onto his pad. He didn't notice. "Because they solve it . . . fast. F-A-S-T. Within days."

"Days?"

"Any longer, and Brooks says the up side, for us, drops drastically." Lyttle tugged on his ear. "Because someone else is gonna die—maybe not the same way, maybe not a kid even, maybe some grandmother or the father of four. But someone else is going to die. And instead of using the first death to your advantage, it becomes just another liability."

"And Brooks says?"

Lyttle looked at Hatch. "She says Saturday morning would be best." Lyttle nodded. "And she's right. Arrest someone on Friday and it shows up in Saturday's paper, which no one ever reads because everyone's too busy Christmas shopping. She says you need to make the arrest sometime—anytime—after the deadlines for Saturday's paper, which basically means sometime early, real early Saturday morning. Then, the newspapers have all day Saturday to write some nice, long pieces recapping everything for the nice fat Sunday editions."

Hatch nodded. "Which means that everyone gets to read about it over Sunday breakfast."

"That's it." Lyttle took the cigarette from his mouth and flicked the ashes into the ashtray. "Brooks says three days is almost the perfect time. It allows enough time for public outcry, your response, and a quick, clean conclusion, demonstrating efficiency, dedication, and deliberateness."

"Nothing new in any of that." Hatch rubbed his chin.

"Right. Execution is the key. Efficiency is most important for us, she says. She says we don't want to get into something where we're pulling eight terrifying black faces in off the street hoping to get lucky. That could just as easily turn into a witch hunt, make it look as though we're panicking. Oh, yes, she also says it's best to bring in just one suspect, and make sure that he's the one. That's the efficiency part. Quick ... and sure. We have to look like we know what we're doing." Lyttle paused. "Do we?"

Hatch leaned back in his chair. He ignored the question.

Lyttle put the cigarette back in his mouth and took a short drag. He looked at Hatch, saw he was getting no response, then continued. "Then, on Sunday, the voters go to the service of their choice and pray that Rickey Jefferson's killer gets his ass hung, and just before they walk out the doors of the chapel, they thank their Lord that their city—and you, their honorable mayor—has rushed this animal to justice."

Hatch leaned back in his chair. His hands were clasped on top of his head. "Saturday morning."

"That's what she says—tomorrow."

"What about TV?"

"Screw TV. No one watches news on Saturday or Sunday. She says the Sunday paper's the best PR gimmick we got. Besides, because no one watches TV news Saturday or Sunday, the stations will make a big deal about it all over again on Monday. It's almost as if we arrest the guy Saturday *and* Monday."

Hatch nodded. He reached for the phone and dialed Frank

at home. Lyttle reached forward to hand Hatch the report from Brooks. Hatch waved it away. The phone rang six times before Frank answered it.

"Sims."

"Took you awhile."

"I was in the shower."

Hatch leaned back in his chair. "I think we need to talk."

"The Brooks report?"

"You seen it?"

"Last night. Had to squeeze it out of her, though. Tough cookie. Loyal."

"And?" Hatch jammed the phone between his ear and shoulder and fussed with his shirt collar.

"We're not wasting any time, Marty. I think we can do it. I'm meeting with Colbane in a few minutes. Keep cool. Stay calm. I'll call you after I talk with Bill. You be in?"

"Let's see. Nine-ish? Nope. I'll be meeting with the preachers."

"I'll get to you later, don't worry."

"Frank . . ." Hatch cast a quick glance back at Lyttle and lowered his voice. "I assume we're getting this thing done."

"I'd tell you to cross your fingers if I thought we needed it."

Hatch smiled. "You're a good man, Frank."

"I'll be in touch."

Hatch grinned, then looked again at Lyttle to see if he was listening. He wasn't. He was re-reading and underlining portions of Brooks's report. The intercom on the mayor's desk buzzed. It was Nancy. "The ministers are here, Mayor."

Hatch pressed the Talk button. "Show the reverends to the conference room, Nancy. Make sure they get coffee. Chet and I will give them a few minutes to cool down."

Hatch got up and walked to the mirror. He smoothed his jacket and ran a hand softly over his hair. It was grayer now than ever, but it looked good. In fact, the operation, until the recent glitch, had started to put the spring back in Hatch's step. Hope had been rekindled. And it had showed.

Lyttle stood and extinguished his cigarette. "What did Sims say?"

Hatch smiled. "He said to tell you that he wasn't dangerous." The mayor turned and headed for the door, then stopped and looked back at Lyttle. "And to make sure you tucked in your shirt, pulled up your tie, and wiped the rest of last night's dinner off your clothes."

Lyttle shook his head. Then, he did.

◇ 17 ◇

Bill Colbane was smiling and relaxed when he arrived at Frank's house. He was dressed in slacks and a sweater.

"Pretty casual today, Bill." Frank was about to head to the office. He was dressed in a dark blue suit.

Colbane grinned. "I'm taking the day off."

Frank was leading Colbane to the study and was about two steps ahead of the judge. He slowed his pace to let Colbane catch up. "A day off?"

Colbane nodded. "Haven't had one in a while. Just going to sit around the house. Nothing special."

Frank opened the study door and let Colbane enter first. He started speaking while Colbane still had his back to him. "This may not be the best time to do that, Bill." Colbane turned around. He was still smiling; Frank wasn't. "In fact, it's pretty bad timing." Frank shook his head. Colbane's smile began to fade. "You call in sick yet?"

"Yes . . . I mean, no."

"Well?"

"It has nothing to do with being sick. I just decided to take the day off."

"Can't." Frank shrugged.

"Can't?" Colbane's voice was uncharacteristically stern. "Hold on, Frank. I just told you I'm taking the day off."

Frank shook his head again. "Well, I say you're not. Not today."

Colbane gritted his teeth. He didn't say anything. He balled his fists, but kept them at his side.

"Not today, Bill. Not tomorrow. Not until I say." Frank was standing at the window now, looking outside, with his back to Colbane. It was snowing. Frank's backyard looked like a Christmas card. A blue jay lit on a tall, snow-dusted pine tree. Frank liked jays. They were tough. Ferocious fighters, and bullies. Frank looked back toward Colbane. The judge's head was bowed.

"I need the time, Frank." Colbane sat down on the couch.

Frank shook his head slowly. "We all need the time, Bill. But we can't have it right now."

"I need . . . one day." The judge's voice now was more whimper than whisper.

Frank was still looking out the window. He closed his eyes and drummed his fingers on the windowsill. Once. Twice. He turned and faced Colbane. The judge had his head in his hands. "I was up all last night."

"And?"

"I was sick."

Frank walked to the couch and put his hand on the judge's shoulder. "We all respond to pressure a little differently, Bill."

Colbane lifted his head out of his hands. "Pressure? *Pressure?*" His voice began to rise. "This isn't pressure, Frank. This is murder."

Frank moved his hand from Colbane's shoulder. "We don't—have—a day—to waste." His voice grew a bit louder with each word. *"You*—don't have—a day—to waste."

Colbane straightened and took a deep breath. "I'm not sure I can keep this up."

Frank walked to the bar and grabbed the silver carafe. He offered Colbane some coffee. The judge shook his head. Frank poured himself a cup. "Well, then what? What do you do?"

Colbane shook his head. "I don't know."

Frank took a sip of the coffee. It was too hot, and he licked the burn from his lips. "Of course you don't. There isn't anything to know." He put the cup down and walked to the couch and pulled up a chair right in front of the judge. "There is nothing else to do. We finish what we started." He lowered his voice almost to a whisper. "And if we are smart, and quick, we finish real soon."

Colbane rubbed his eyes. "This morning I was in my boy's room and I realized what . . ."

Frank knew what was coming. He also knew the soft sell wasn't working. He grabbed Colbane by the collar and pulled him forward, hard and fast. "Realized what? What you had done?" A few moments ago, Frank's voice had been soothing. Now, it was a vicious whisper. He caught himself, and began calmly spitting out the words through his teeth. "What? What your kid's going to think of you if he finds out what you've done?" He yanked at Colbane again. "We don't have time for that kind of shit, Bill. Knock off the crap. And knock it off now."

Frank stood and lifted Colbane to his feet. "Look at me, goddamnit. We're not talking about some fucking little misdemeanor here." Frank went to his desk and picked up a newspaper. "We're talking about front-page news, Bill." He tossed the paper at Colbane's feet. "Think of it. In *The New York Times*. The goddamn *New York Times*. Murder investigation implicates one of Detroit's—one of the nation's—most prominent black judges. That's reality, Bill." The way Frank said the word—"reality"—made it sound obscene.

Frank sat behind his desk. "I'll tell you something else about reality." He leaned forward. "You talked to Abe this morning—did he talk back?"

"Of cou . . ." Colbane caught himself. He knew what was coming next: Missy. Frank didn't even have to say it.

"Seems you've forgotten why you got involved in this in the first place."

Colbane didn't nod, didn't move, didn't blink. He just stood silent.

"So, Bill, I say this." Frank paused. "I say you are going to work today, and I say here's what you are going to do. Today is Friday. By noon, I'll have a list of suspects to bring in for questioning. We will have a suspect in custody sometime early tomorrow morning and we'll have him arraigned in the afternoon." Frank stopped and looked down at his desk calendar. "By that time, you'll have figured out how to get yourself scheduled for his prelim on, say, the day after Christmas."

"The twenty-sixth?—me?"

Frank smiled. "You."

"Why me?"

"Insurance, for starters, and why not?"

Colbane shook his head. "I'm not sure where I am in the rotation for preliminary exams."

Frank sighed with exasperation. "I don't give a shit where the *rotation* is."

Colbane shook his head again. "I don't know how . . ."

Frank leaned close. "You're not hearing me, Bill. I don't give a fuck how the schedule is arranged."

Colbane was beginning to plead. "I'm telling you I'm not sure I can do that—the twenty-sixth? That's too quick. They usually get at least ten days to prepare."

"You're still not listening, Bill. You're the goddamn senior judge over there. I'm not asking if you can do it. I'm telling you." Frank slammed his fist on the desk top. "I don't care if you boys spin a goddamn bottle or draw fucking straws. I'm just telling you to get the short one—understand? And on the fucking twenty-sixth."

Colbane didn't move, then began to nod, slowly.

Frank sat back in his chair. "Then"—he was calm again—"you preside over a quick and easy preliminary examination and we send this motherfucker on to trial and then"—Frank paused—"we send him away. For life."

Frank smiled. "He's dead. There isn't a jury on this planet, or a judge, Bill, going to let this asshole walk—is there?" Frank laughed. He hadn't mentioned Julius Cooper's name, but Colbane knew for certain now from Frank's cackle whom he was talking about.

Frank shrugged. "You starting to understand? You get to put this guy away. Get the ball rolling next Friday. Justice—finally. It's like, basketball. We run a play for you, set a pick for you, and you get to sink the big shot." Frank got up and walked to the couch. "And Bill"—he lowered his voice to a whisper—"it's a goddamn slam-dunk." Frank put his hand on Colbane's shoulder. "Questions?"

Colbane shook his head. "I've never done anything un-ethical in my entire career."

Frank shrugged; his voice was conversational. "You probably never killed anyone before, either."

Colbane looked up at Frank. "I didn't pull the trigger."

Frank stared him down. "Tell that to your kids—and a jury."

Frank sat on the arm of the couch. He straightened his tie, then his jacket. "I talked to Stone yesterday. He thinks he's got himself in on the prosecution team. I'd say we're in pretty good shape."

Colbane had his head in his hands again. He began nodding slowly.

"We made a little mistake, Bill. That's all. We can go on. You have to go on, or we all sink." Frank paused. "And I'm not going to let that happen. *You're* not going to let that happen."

Frank stood and went to the bar. "Need a drink?"

Colbane shook his head.

"You okay now?"

Colbane nodded.

"Good." Frank walked to the couch, took Colbane by the arm, and led him toward the study door. Marlyss was coming down the hall. Her eyes were red. She didn't look at Frank and only mumbled good morning to Colbane. The judge didn't respond. He didn't even see her. He was staring at his feet and heading for the front door. He felt an aching urge to hug Missy, hard and close, to tell her that he loved her, to see some sparkle in her eyes again.

Colbane stopped at the front door and Frank reached for the doorknob, but the judge pushed Frank's hand away and opened the door himself.

Suddenly, Bill Colbane wished he were wearing his gun.

He and Frank were finally on the same wavelength.

And Frank knew it.

◇ **18** ◇

Shooter exhaled hard, then rolled to the side of the bed, off the lithe, young woman spread-eagled beneath him. He squeezed his eyes shut and tried to catch his breath.

The woman, her black G-string yanked to one side, rolled onto her stomach. Her hair was matted and tangled, her shoulders covered with tiny beads of perspiration. "C'mon, I'm not finished, baby." Her voice was thin, whiny.

Shooter had lost interest. He stared at the ceiling and said nothing for a few seconds. He could feel her frustration, but ignored it. "Where'd you get the name?"

"Fine Thing?" She turned her head toward him and propped herself up on her elbows. "I made it up." She sounded rather proud of herself. "My real name's Dolores."

Shooter laughed. "No one's real name is Dolores, Dolores."

"Mine is." She sounded more hurt than offended.

Shooter glanced at her. "Well, Dolores, you're a helluva lot better in person." He wiped his forehead with the corner of a pillowcase. "A real fine thing. That shit on stage was terrible."

The girl paused and stared at him; now she seemed genuinely hurt. "You liked it."

"Nope."

"Gives most of the boys what they're comin' there for." She was whining again. The sound made him wince. He wanted to slap her.

He was back staring at the ceiling. "Most of the boys are fucking idiots."

"I've worked better places, you know. Classier." She was trying to talk big, but she wasn't doing very well. "This is

135

the screwiest joint I ever worked. Even the name is goofy—
Niqui's. N-I-Q-U-I-S. What kinda way is that to spell a
name?"

Shooter grunted and swung his legs out of bed and
reached for his pants on the bedpost. He began getting
dressed.

Fine Thing straightened her G-string, then sat cross-
legged on the bed. She grabbed a blanket and threw it over
her back. "How'm I gettin' home?"

Shooter didn't look up. "Cab."

She frowned. "You know, you're turnin' into quite a
chump. I shoulda known better than to leave this mornin'
with some thug who tells me to meet him outside in his car.
What? You ashamed to be seen with me?"

Shooter grinned. "I've been seen with better."

Fine Thing nodded, then began so smile. "I get it." She
began to laugh. "Okay, loverboy, I get it." She didn't.

Shooter was tying his shoes and pretended not to hear
her. It wasn't easy. His beeper went off.

Fine Thing looked puzzled. She hadn't noticed the pager.
"You sellin', too?"

Shooter shook his head and put on a serious face. "I'm a
doctor." He punched a button and read the numbers on the
screen. They weren't familiar.

"What kind?"

"Brain surgeon."

Fine Thing nodded. "Right." She looked around the
room. "Pretty simple place you got here for bein' a doc."

He nodded. "Business's been slow." He walked across the
room, picked up the phone, and dialed. Frank answered after one ring.

"Yes."

"You sitting on the phone?" There was a lot of noise in
the background. Shooter put a finger in his ear to try to hear
better. "Where the hell are you?"

"Just off the freeway at McNichols. How are we doing?"

"Just finishing my research."

"Cooper?"

"I been working on it all night."

"Don't make any mistakes."

Shooter smiled. "Not a chance this time."

Fine Thing was sitting on the edge of the bed. She'd dressed quickly and was fidgeting, getting angry. "Am I gonna get home this morning?"

Shooter took his finger out of his ear and raised it to her. He nodded.

"You there?" Frank was yelling over the street noise. He was in another impounded car and didn't have his cellular phone. He was at one of those drive-up booths in a parking lot at a McDonald's.

"Yeah."

"We have to start making some contingency plans."

Shooter smiled. "Let me guess."

Frank didn't say anything.

"Here comes . . . the judge."

Frank still didn't say anything.

"He's a chickenshit."

Frank saw a police car at a light about half a block down the street. he turned his back to the traffic. "Well?"

"Be a bit trickier." Shooter winked at Fine Thing. She was biting her fingernails. He dropped his voice. "Cost a little more."

"But?"

"No sweat. Just tell me when."

Frank watched the patrol car disappear around the corner. "We'll talk."

"Anything else?"

"Just no more mistakes. That's all. No more fuck-ups."

Shooter smiled at Fine Thing again. "Don't worry, Frank." She wasn't looking. She had a shoe off and was fiddling with a loose heel. "Don't. Worry."

Frank hung up and Shooter put down the phone. Fine Thing was glaring at him now. "Cab fare."

Shooter smiled. "My boss. I got a few more minutes."

"Big fucking deal."

"You rich enough to pass up another C note?"

"Two hundred." She sounded more like a tough business-man now than a kid.

"One fifty."

She began smiling again—and slipping off her shoes.

Shooter shook his head. "No." He wanted her to stay dressed. "We'll make this quick."

Fine Thing smiled even wider. Easy money. "Whatever you say, doc."

He smiled back and headed toward her. "Tell me about Coot's good stuff one more time."

She frowned like an exasperated kid. "Coop. *Coop.* Jeezus, man." She paused. "Main crack house on Eastlawn. Steady crib at Audubon an' Bedford."

Shooter smiled. "And I can use your name?"

"Name?" Fine Thing laughed at him. "You drive me there now, baby, and I get you in. Cash and carry. Key's right here." She tapped her purse.

Shooter smiled again. "Good stuff?"

Fine Thing nodded. "The best."

"Like you."

She smiled. "Like me, baby."

Shooter walked across the room, grabbed Fine Thing by the hips, and turned her away from him. She felt even more fragile than she looked. Her waist was so thin. He began to lift her skirt.

Fine Thing started to lean forward. "Say, doc, maybe we can make this a regular . . ." She stopped suddenly and reached back frantically for her neck, gouging herself with her nails like some mad animal. But the wire garrotte wouldn't budge. Her bloodshot eyes bulged out in horror, and her body was limp in a matter of seconds, her tongue drooping grotesquely out of the left side of her mouth. She was dead in another few.

Shooter dropped her onto the bed. "Fine mess you got yourself into . . . Fine Thing." He bent over and pulled down her skirt, then shook his head. "Shoulda stuck with Dolores."

Then he dumped her purse on the bed and rummaged quickly through the contents. He found a West Virginia driver's license—Dolores La Rose Elkins, seventeen—and a key ring. There were only two keys on the ring, and one was for luggage. He looked down again at the teenager, lying fully clothed in a still, neat heap. He shook his head again. Dolores LaRose. Seventeen. From West Virginia. Yeah, she shoulda known better.

◇ 19 ◇

Jenny Kochinski was sitting at the kitchen table, cuddled modestly in a white terrycloth bathrobe, her silver-blond hair hastily pinned back. She wasn't wearing makeup. She had the day off—the beginning of Christmas vacation. Petey had spent the night at a friend's house; he was still gone. Jenny was smiling the good-morning smile she gave her second-grade students. Her green eyes were radiant.

"I liked you a whole lot better when you were a ball-player, Stosh." She tried to keep the smile from fading. She wasn't sure if she was succeeding.

Stan was sitting sidesaddle on the bench across from his ex-wife. He was still wearing his tweed overcoat. His gloves were on the table next to his coffee. The room smelled of toast and bacon and the sweet, light fragrance of Jenny's perfume.

"Place looks the same, Jen." Stan looked around the room. "Same clock over the sink. Same hibiscus in the corner. Same old placemats with the same old ducks." He laughed and picked up the mat in front of him. "God, I hated these when you bought them. Look, these ducks still look like chickens."

Jenny took a sip of coffee. She wrinkled up her nose, then rubbed it. "You haven't been gone that long, Stan."

"Three years. Feels longer." Stan looked around. "I always liked this house. It always felt like home. Smelled like home."

Jenny put down her cup. The steam from the coffee

fogged the window next to her. "You were never really happy here."

Stan shrugged.

"The only time I ever saw you really happy was when you were pitching."

Stan waggled his finger at Jenny. "You're changing the subject."

Jenny shook her head. "You did first." She was still smiling.

Stan took a drink of his coffee and reached for the sugar. "I was a kid playing a game. What did I know?"

"You knew."

"Well, then maybe I just forgot."

Stan poured some sugar into his coffee. "Go easy on me, Jen. I just dropped by to take you up on the Clown Café."

Jenny felt a twinge of embarrassment, and looked up at him in mock seriousness. "Well, we're still available, detective, sir. Date confirmed."

"Noon?"

"Noon it is."

Jenny took another sip of her coffee. "Mary Stimic called the other night. Said she's working on the same story as you, this Jefferson thing."

Stan nodded. "We talked. She hasn't changed."

"She's a good kid."

Stan nodded politely again.

"Know what else she said? That she saw your rookie baseball card at some place . . . some exhibit—that's it, Briarwood Mall in Ann Arbor." Jenny grinned. "Thirty cents."

Stan chuckled. "Thirty cents?"

Jenny nodded. "Topps. Near mint condition—you and someone named Howie Koplitz. Fifteen cents for very good condition." She paused. "Good—three cents."

Stan looked at Jenny, and they both smiled, a bit wistfully. It should have been time to go, but he didn't want to leave yet. She didn't want him to go, either, not that she said so.

"It was good, Stan, wasn't it?"

Stan was confused. "What?"

"Baseball."

Stan forced a smile. "Yep."

Jenny forced a better smile, brighter and happier than Stan's. "How much were you making back then, in the beginning?"

"Not much. I don't even remember."

"And we were rich." Jenny took a sip of her coffee. "God, remember St. Cloud?"

Stan nodded. "Minnesota. Single A. The St. Cloud Rox—what in the hell was a Rox?"

Jenny laughed. "Better than the Aberdeen Pheasants—a little, anyway." She pointed at Stan. "Remember the lady who ran the motel—Borgland, Berland, Bergstrom, something like that—was always talking about all the lakes. The land of one hundred thousand lakes."

"I think it was ten thousand."

"Not according to her."

"The woman with the orange hair?"

"It was pink."

"Right." They laughed.

Jenny put her hand on her forehead. "Remember our room?"

"It was more like a closet."

"It was ours."

Stan nodded.

Jenny's eyes were sparkling again. "What do you remember most?"

Stan ran his hand through his hair. "The air. It was cold and crisp—too fucking cold, too goddamn crisp. My fingers would go numb when I was pitching. And the food. It was terrible." He stopped. "You?"

Jenny shrugged. "You. I remember you. God, Stan, I loved you so much."

"You loved the uniform."

Jenny laughed. "They were dingy and gray . . . and baggy."

"You loved . . ."

She stopped him. "I loved you, Stosh." Jenny crossed her chest with her arms and hugged herself. "I'd go to those games against the . . . Canaries. Wasn't there some team named the Canaries?"

Stan shrugged. "There was the Goldeyes—Winnipeg."

"Maybe. I don't remember. I'd just go to those games and watch you pitch. I never saw anyone who was so right for what he was doing." She paused. "God, the look on your face. The way you walked."

Stan looked at his watch. "It . . . wasn't real."

Jenny shook her head. "It was more real than any of this cops-and-robbers hero stuff." Her smile was fading.

Stan walked to the refrigerator and leaned against it. "I didn't decide to stop."

"Yes, you did."

"Rogine."

She shook her head. "That's an excuse."

"Maybe. Then, why?"

"Maybe you were just afraid."

"Of hitting someone else?"

"Of yourself."

Stan put his hands in his pockets. "Ever wonder . . . what happened to us?"

"Sometimes."

"No, not sometimes. Do you really wonder?"

Jenny shook her head. "No, I guess not. I'm not sure I want to know." She slid back toward the wall and pulled her feet onto the bench. "I think finding out would be too sad."

"Why?"

"Because"—she looked at Stan—"if I think about it too much, I'm sure I'll see it didn't really need to happen."

No one said anything for a few seconds. Jenny felt a chill and pulled her robe tight. "You talk like this with her?"

Stan looked away. "Sometimes."

"Do you love her?"

"I think so . . . sometimes."

"Have you told her?"

Stan shook his head.

"If you love her, talk to her. Don't be afraid of her. Don't be afraid of being happy, Stosh."

"I think . . . I'm just afraid of being wrong."

Jenny nodded. "That, too."

Stan smiled. "You got me all figured out?" Jenny

shrugged. "I come over to make a date for the Clown Café and my ex-wife reads me my tea leaves."

Jenny laughed. "I never wanted to be your wife, Stosh. I wanted to be your friend."

"I know."

"You just wouldn't let me."

"I know that, too—now."

"You shut me out, pitch."

No one spoke again for a few seconds. Then Stan walked to the table, picked up his gloves, and headed toward the hallway. He turned and looked back as he reached the front door. "The Clown Café."

Jenny had followed him. "The Clown Café."

"Eleven."

"Noon, Stosh. Noon."

Stan winked at her. "Just checkin'."

Jenny smiled back. "Petey will be excited. He misses you."

Stan opened the door, then stopped. "Thirty cents?"

"Thirty-two—with tax." Stan started to leave. "Stan?" He turned back toward her. "Even the best cops need a break sometimes."

Stan nodded. "Thanks."

Jenny smiled. "Anytime, Stosh."

Marlyss shut the door to her office, sat down behind her desk, then pulled open a drawer, took out the phone book, and searched for the page that listed area codes. She took a deep breath, then dialed long-distance directory assistance.

The phone rang twice. "What city?"

Marlyss had no idea. "I'm trying to contact a minor-league baseball team."

"Where?"

"Somewhere in Alabama."

The operator sniffed. "I need a city."

Marlyss stammered. It was that panic again. She fought it. "I don't know what city." She slowed herself. "Don't you have some sort of listing for baseball teams?"

The operator sniffed again. "I'll check." Marlyss waited

about thirty seconds. It seemed longer. "Under sports teams, we have Huntsville, Birmingham . . ." She paused.

"Is that all?"

". . . and Montgomery."

Marlyss nodded. "That's it."

"Do you want the number?"

"Yes . . . please."

Marlyss copied down the number and hung up, sat there for a few seconds, then got up and locked her door, sat back down and dialed. An older woman answered. "Montgomery Rebels Baseball Club." She had a pleasant voice.

Marlyss cleared her throat. "The owner of the team, please."

"Well, dear, there is no team yet." The woman giggled a bit, as though she were telling some secret. "But you could speak with Mr. Albert Thorsgren."

Marlyss had no idea who she wanted to talk to. "Do you know if he used to be a major-league baseball player?"

The woman giggled again. "I don't know, but wouldn't that be something if he was." She sounded pretty excited. "I'm new here. I can ask for you."

Marlyss shook her head. "No, that's all right. I think I'd like to talk to him."

"Can I say who's calling?"

"No, I mean, yes." She rubbed her forehead. "This is . . . Mrs. . . . Kochinski."

"Can you spell that?" Marlyss did. "Thank you, Mrs. Kochinski. Just a moment."

The line went quiet for a few seconds. Then a big-voiced man came on. "Thunder Thorsgren here, Jen. Long time. How's it going?"

Marlyss nodded, but she didn't answer.

"Hello? Jenny?"

Nothing.

"Jenny?"

Marlyss hung up the phone, closed her eyes, and took a deep breath. It felt good. Maybe Alabama wasn't just another mirage, after all.

◇ 20 ◇

Big Time was trying to squeeze through the doorway of his apartment with three bags of groceries. He was more upset than surprised when he saw Stan sitting on a chair in the darkened living room.

"C'mon, man, gimme a hand." Time was stuck.

Stan got up and took one of the bags. "What do we have here?"

Big Time smiled. "Staples."

Stan looked into the bag. "Corn chips. Pretzels. Cupcakes. Cookies. Donuts. Cheese doodles."

Time nodded. "Staples." He followed Stan into the kitchen and put his bags on the table.

Stan put his bag down and opened a box of pretzels. "Lock your door next time."

Time shrugged and dipped his hand into the bag. "No key."

Stan reached across the wall and flipped the light switch. "No electricity, either."

Time nodded. "Turned if off late last night. That's where I was this morning. They said it would be back on later today."

"And no girl?"

Time scratched his head. "Left sometime last night. Last time I saw her, she was nodded out on the couch. Maybe went to work." He began unpacking the bags. "She'll be back in a few days. Always is." He offered Stan a chocolate donut. Stan shook his head. Time opened a can of Hawaiian Punch and poured himself a glass. He dunked his donut in it.

Stan winced. "So, you got out last night."

145

Time nodded. "And how." He dunked his donut again. "I'm thinkin' of puttin' in for combat pay."

Stan found a chair and sat down. "Think again."

"Almost lost my ass." Big Time nodded. He finally bit into the donut. It was a mess. "Almost."

"I'm all ears."

"Sure you don't want some?"

Stan shook his head.

Time looked around the room for another chair, but didn't find one, so he sat on the corner of the table. "Well, ol' Coop ain't in the best of moods."

"Shame."

"I found him last night at a crack joint on Eastlawn, just where Fine Thing said he'd be."

"And?"

"He tried to jam his pistol through my fuckin' head."

"You're still here."

"Yeah"—Time finished one donut and reached for another—" 'cept it wasn't his pistol."

Stan shrugged.

Big Time dunked the second donut and stuffed the whole thing in his mouth. Stan closed his eyes. Time swallowed in two gulps. "This took me some time to figure out, man."

Stan shook his head. "I don't have much time."

Big Time ignored Stan. He reached for the cheese doodles. "Everyone knows Coop's fancy piece."

Stan shook his head. "Everyone, evidently, but me."

Time nodded. "That's why you're payin' me, boss." He smiled. Stan didn't. Time continued. "I seen it more than once. It's silver-plated. Ivory grips. Got carvin' all over it. Boys who know say he's always a fuckin' cowboy with that thing, waving it aroun'. It's as big a part of him as his dick—and he's never without it. Leastways, he hasn't been since sometime recently hereabouts."

Stan rubbed the back of his neck. "I hope this gets better."

Time ignored Stan again. "Never uses the damn thing. Mostly keeps it stuffed in his pants to impress some bitch. Uses it for show. He uses other pieces for his regular business. Must have a goddamn emory full a' weapons."

"Armory." Stan reached for a donut, laughing at himself for bothering to correct Time. Time offered Stan his glass of fruit punch, but Stan waved it off. "Maybe he was gettin' it polished. Maybe he pawned it. Maybe he lost it in a crap game."

Time frowned. "I'm not sure you're appreciatin' this information."

Stan nodded. "I'm not." He rubbed his eyes. "You've been watching too many cop movies."

Time shrugged. "It was just strange seein' him without it. Like seein' . . ."

"So, maybe he did the kid and dumped the gun."

Time shook his head. "You ain't been listenin'. I'm tellin' you, Cooper don't use that gun for business. Usin' that thing on some payback'd be suicide. He drills someone with it, and you motherfuckers trace it back to him in a goddamn New York minute."

Stan put his hand in his pocket and pulled out a quarter. He tossed it to Big Time; Big Time caught it.

"What's this?"

"What you've earned so far. I need more than a goddamn lost-and-found report."

"This is, man. Somethin' strange goin' on here . . . This ain't the Twilight Zone."

Time shrugged. "Is if you fuckin' live here, boss."

Stan shook his head.

Time shook his right back. "That boy is naked without that gun."

Stan put his donut on the table. He hadn't taken a bite. "That's it?"

Time shrugged again. " 'Cept for all the complainin' about this Gintry motherfucker."

"Who?" Stan was losing his patience.

"Gintry."

Stan shook his head. "Never heard of him."

"Gintry. Gintry." Stan had a confused look on his face. he was still shaking his head. Time was yelling now. "Gintry."

Stan rubbed his hand across his face. "You already said that."

"Some crazy-ass Nazi cop been bustin' heads around here after midnight. Off-duty."

Stan yelled back. He was getting angry. "Sounds like just what this goddamn neighborhood needs."

Time shrugged. "Gintry . . . it'll come to me. Just wait."

Stan checked his watch. It was 11:15. He had to meet with Frank at noon. He had to hurry. "I wish I could wait. The accommodations are great. The service is wonderful. The menu's terrific. Let me know when it comes to you."

Time nodded. Stan was halfway out the door when it did. "Mack Gintry. That's it."

Stan stopped. "Mack Gintry?" It sounded familiar. He repeated the name over and over in his head until it started to run together. "MackGintry. MacGintry. McGintry." Stan stopped. "McGinnity."

Time nodded again. "That's it. Mack Ginnity."

Stan shook his head and headed out the door. "I'll get someone from IA to talk to you."

Big Time shrugged and grabbed another donut. "Okay, boss, just tell him I don't work for nothin'." Big Time opened his fist and studied the quarter in it. "No pocket change, neither." He shook his head. "Damn."

Stan arrived at headquarters at 11:49. Dawlson was at his desk, drinking coffee and reading the *Free Press* sports section. He didn't look up. "Stosh, where you been?"

"Hell and back."

Pete laughed. "Let me guess—been doin' Time again?"

Stan nodded.

"Still as fucked up as always?"

Stan nodded. "Worse." He hung up his coat, walked to his desk, and fell into his chair.

"He's worthless."

"He's all I got." Stan rubbed his eyes. "You got anything new?"

Dawlson shook his head.

"Got that list for Frank?"

Dawlson laughed. "Stoshie, my boy, I had that done two minutes after we left his office last night."

"Who you givin' him?"

"**Whom** do you think?"

"Cooper."

Dawlson laughed again. "Not just Cooper, Stooshie—Cooper, Cooper, Cooper and Cooper."

Stan shrugged. "Good a place to start as any."

"Start and stop, Stosh. Frank wants Cooper, he gets Cooper. This one's carved in goddamn stone. We got some wino who saw him at the scene about an hour before the kid gets blown away."

"You that sure about Cooper?"

Dawlson smiled. "Why not?"

Stan shrugged. "I got a wild-ass what if."

Dawlson smiled. "Stoshie, Stoshie, Stoshie. You're an open book. You come back from talkin' to Time, who's been talkin' to his douchebag buddies about how hinky life is in the goddamn streets, and the name that is about to cross your lips belongs to"—Dawlson closed his eyes and put his hand to his forehead—"Al McGinnity, renegade cop, vigilante headbanger, off-duty scumbag—subject of the most recent IA investigation."

"So?"

"So, I can't even begin to talk about that."

"Tell me something, anything."

Dawlson scratched his head. "I'll tell you this. No cop's going to fry for this one, and McGinnity's still a cop."

"That's it?"

"No, I'll go one better." Dawlson sat up in his chair. "Why?"

"Why what?"

"Why in the hell would he take out a kid?"

Stan shrugged. "A mistake."

"You're pissin' into the wind."

"Then what about Cooper?"

"What?"

"Same question."

Dawlson's lips curved into a wide smile. "Frankly, Stoshie, when it comes to Cooper, I don't give a ratfuck why." Dawlson stood. "And that's it, pard—game, set, match . . . life at hard labor." He clapped Stan on the back.

"Excuse me, but I've got to see a man about a horse before our little rendezvous with El Franko."

Stan sighed and closed his eyes. Maybe it was better this way, simpler. The phone rang.

"Stan?"

Stan took a quick glance around the room. Pete was gone. "Hi. How are you? You at work?"

"No, I left."

"What, you out practicing a double lutz?"

"Uh-huh." She was smiling, he could hear it in her voice. "Stan?" Now it was gone.

"What's wrong? Something happen last night?"

"No. This morning."

No one spoke for a few seconds. Stan rubbed his forehead hard with his left hand. His right hand squeezed the receiver until his knuckles turned white. "Okay. Let's get together this afternoon . . . or tonight?"

Marlyss shook her head. "I don't think that's a good idea. Besides, I need a few days. I've got to think some things out. It's okay. I'll be all right."

Stan glanced at the clock. It was 11:53, seven minutes to the meeting with Frank. "Tonight. My place."

"No." She rubbed her neck. "You know it's not good like this."

Stan shook his head. "It doesn't matter."

Her voice was quiet, calm, almost reassuring. "It does . . to me." He hadn't said much and he didn't know what else to say. Marlyss was whispering now. "I've got to go. Tell Petey Happy Birthday for me." She stopped. "I love you. Stan."

Stan still had the receiver tight to his ear when Sandy Stone knocked on the squad room door and stuck his head in. "Ko-chinski, where's Dawlson?"

Stan cupped his hand over the phone. "He'll be right back."

Stone nodded. "Frank's ready."

Stan waved to Stone, waited for him to leave, then turned back to the phone. "Mar?" The only answer was the dial tone. Stan held the receiver against his cheek for a few seconds, then hung up, and got up to meet with Frank. His fists were balled tight. As he walked down the hall, he tried his best to relax them.

◇ **21** ◇

"**Y**ou two know Sandy Stone?" Frank was sitting at his desk, shuffling through a short stack of papers. He was wearing reading glasses, and he didn't look up. Stone was seated in a chair to Frank's right. He acknowledged the introduction with an almost imperceptible nod and smug smile that included a hint of disdain for the cops seating themselves in front of him. Stan and Dawlson nodded back. Stan knew almost nothing about Stone, except what he'd read in the papers—and that the other assistant prosecutors called him Gall-Stone.

Frank still had his head down. "Sandy will be working with the prosecutors on this case, so I thought it would be best to get him involved as early as possible." Stone flashed a tight smile and sat as though he were ready to take notes. Frank pushed the papers to the side and took off his glasses. He looked at Dawlson. "Got that list, Pete?" Dawlson ripped the top page off his note pad and handed it to Frank. Frank studied it and smiled. "One name. Cooper." Stone grinned a flunky's grin. Frank nodded, then winked, at Dawlson. "Any objections?"

Dawlson cleared his voice, stole a glance at Stan, and looked at Frank. "Only that we're moving awfully fast here."

Frank nodded. "No choice." He put the paper on his desk. "Stan, any problems?" Stan shook his head.

"Okay, Sandy, you're up."

Stone stood, walked to the corner of Frank's desk, and sat down. His feet dangled about four inches from the floor.

Frank sat down again and began rearranging the piles of papers on his desk. Stone looked back at him. Frank waved. "Go on. I'm listening."

Stone rubbed his nose. "We nail Cooper early Saturday morning, sometime after four A.M. That gives us plenty of time to get search warrants together and for you two"—he nodded to Stan and Pete—"to coordinate this thing with Narcotics. We'll need the narcs for the bust at Cooper's crack pad. From what I'm hearing, I expect we'll find him there."

Stone paused. Dawlson took a toothpick from the pocket of his sports coat and put it in his mouth. Frank stood and walked to the coffeemaker behind the detectives. Stan didn't notice him. He was looking at Frank's desk. Something looked different. Marlyss's picture. It was gone. Suddenly, Frank was standing right behind Stan, resting his hand on the back of Stan's chair. Stan tried, unsuccessfully, not to flinch. He wondered if Frank noticed.

Stone droned on. "Stan, you'll head up the crew at the bust. Pete, I understand Cooper's got a place on Bedford." He looked down at his notes and read off a number. "Least that's what we're hearing."

Dawlson took the toothpick out of his mouth. "From who?"

"From whom." Stone shrugged. "Doesn't matter. It's a good number."

"How do you know?"

Stone grinned again. "We know."

Frank was back at his desk, glasses on, fiddling with his papers. He smiled, but didn't look up.

Stone jumped down from the desk. "I ... we ... want you, Pete, searching Bedford the same time Stan's putting the collar on Cooper at Eastlawn." Stone walked behind Frank's desk. His posture was perfectly erect. "Any questions?"

Stan and Dawlson looked at each other. Everything seemed pretty routine. They shook their heads.

"Good. Frank?"

Frank looked at Stan. "What'd you get on the kid?"

Stan shrugged. "Not much. He wasn't into drugs—not yet, anyway—but he had a record at kid court."

Frank nodded. "A couple B & Es."

Stan shook his head. "Five."

Frank sat forward in his chair, put his elbows on the desk and his fingertips together. "Two. Five. Eleven. It doesn't make any difference. From here on out, the kid's an angel."

Stone nodded and smiled. "St. Rickeyboy Jackson."

Frank smiled. "Jefferson." His eyes were focused hard on Stan. "An urban martyr. And we're going to fry one big-time asshole for blowing him away."

Stan rubbed his forehead. "You that sure about Cooper, Frank?"

Frank's smile faded. "No. What I'm sure about is that you two are gonna find a way to hang him."

Dawlson took the toothpick out of his mouth. "We've tried before."

Frank nodded. "This time, we don't try. This time, we do."

Stone was grinning another ass-kisser smile. "Any more questions?"

Stan said, "I've been hearing McGinnity's name."

Stone's smile faded dead away. Frank shrugged. "So, what's new?"

"A dead kid."

Frank shook his head. "No way, Stan. No fucking way."

"Even if he did it?"

"Don't waste your energy."

Stan nodded. "Right."

Frank folded his hands, smiled and looked around the room. "Anything else?" No one spoke up. Stan and Pete stood to leave.

"One more thing." Frank stood, too. "Pick up your pink carnations from my secretary." Frank fingered the flower on his coat lapel. A black ribbon was attached to the stem. "You'll have a fresh one every morning. Don't be seen on the street without it."

Pete shook his head. "Who thought this one up?"

"The NAACP."

Dawlson smiled. "Try again."

"Some nice little old lady?"

"Name?"

"You know, I don't think we got it."

Dawlson shook his head. "I wouldn't think so."

Frank smiled. "We'll all meet back here at three A.M."

When they got to the hallway, Dawlson put his arm around Stan. "Just be glad we're not wearing black armbands."

Stan was having trouble pinning the flower on his lapel. He stuck himself. "Do you believe this horseshit?"

Dawlson squeezed Stan's shoulder. "It'll be over soon."

Stan finally got his carnation attached. "Where do you figure Stone got Cooper's address?"

Dawlson squinted at Frank, "Who the hell cares—if it's a good one?" Dawlson paused. "Maybe the midget is buying his shit from Coop."

Stan shook his head.

Pete stopped and grabbed Stan by the arm. "C'mon, Stoshie. Go with the flow. The kid's dead. Nothing's gonna bring him back. Maybe we can nail Cooper."

"The wrong way."

"The only way, pard."

"If we even can."

Dawlson clapped Stan hard on the back. "We can, Stoshie. We will—Frank says."

Sammy Ferguson, the day desk sergeant, called to Pete as he and Stan walked by. "P.D." Pete looked over. "You're the next guy up." Ferguson pointed to the assignment board. "Quick stop on the west side. Hooker in a dumpster. Some hophead called it in. Says the body's still warm—some parts still warmer than others, in case you're interested."

Ferguson, a dour, obesely fat man, handed Pete an Incident Report with nearly indecipherable scribbling on it.

"Roger, Fergie." Pete grabbed Stan's arm hard. "While I'm gone, you attend to our boy Stanky, here. He's having an attack of conscience, a bad one." Dawlson winked at his partner. "Get him some oxygen—fast."

There were no second thoughts in the chief's office. Frank was standing at the window behind his desk. It was warming up outside, and the snow was turning to mush. In a few hours, the city would look like itself again, sloppy and gray. Frank brushed at his hair, and looked at Stone. Sandy was watching him.

"We need to lose those kid-court files on Jefferson. They aren't available to the press, but I'm not taking any chances that some nosey, lucky reporter is going to steal any of our . . ."

Stone's smile was a mile wide.

Frank noticed. "What?"

"Done. Last night."

Frank smiled back. "Nice work."

"One question, though. Kochinski."

Frank nodded, as though his mind were suddenly elsewhere. "Don't worry."

Stone persisted. "I do. What say he finds out the kid's records got ditched?"

Frank shook his head. "He's a cop. Cops don't fuck other cops."

Stone bit his fingernail. "I don't know. Something tells me he's onto something." He dropped himself into Frank's chair and put his feet up on the desk. "You notice how he hardly looked at you this morning?"

"Yep." Frank nodded. "You see him shiver when I put my hand on his shoulder?"

Stone shook his head.

"Like he was taking a thousand volts." Frank walked across the room. "You see the look in his eyes when he saw Marlyss's picture was missing?"

"No." Stone looked confused.

Frank walked to his desk, bent forward, put his arm around Stone and his face in Sandy's. "I'm disappointed in you, son." He chuckled. "I thought you had everything on everybody." Frank eased to the side and whispered in Stone's ear. "Detective Kochinski is simply the victim of a guilty conscience, my lad." He stopped and stood tall. "He's onto something, all right—he's onto my wife."

Stone's jaw dropped. "Marlyss?"

Frank shrugged and walked back to the window, then

laughed loud and hard. "Yep. Detective Stanislaw Baseball Hero Kochinski has it bad for Mrs. Frank Sims."

Stone shook his head. "What are you going to do?"

Frank smiled. "Nothing . . . right now. I figure his unfortunate infatuation might come in handy sometime." Frank turned toward the assistant prosecutor. "What do you think, Mr. Stone?"

Frank's boy didn't answer. He didn't have to. He just grinned.

◇ 22 ◇

"**P**olice." The man flashed a badge at Marlyss. "I need to ask you a few questions, ma'am."

Marlyss had opened the door only about a foot. It was dusk, and she had a hard time making out the man's features. She was barefoot, dressed in a dark bathrobe. Her hair was half up and half down. The man was wearing a full-length coat and aviator sunglasses, his collar pulled up to his ears. Marlyss was more confused than afraid.

"I, ah . . . don't . . ."

The man interrupted. "You have, of course, the right to remain silent . . ." He paused. Marlyss looked at him, studied him carefully, warily. He tilted his head forward and peeked over the top of the glasses. Marlyss slid her hand from her forehead to her mouth, then began to smile and reached for him. He backed up and began to whisper.

"I'm parked a few blocks from here, on Lincolnshire. Meet me at the Comerica lot down Woodard in ten minutes."

Marlyss shook her head. "I can't." She whispered back, then laughed at herself. No one could hear them.

Stan put his badge away and nodded. "Can. Will."

"No."

"Twelve minutes, tops."

Stan turned on his heels and headed down the walk and back to his car. Marlyss got there fifteen minutes later. The bank's lot was empty; it was dark now. She parked and walked about one hundred feet to Stan's car, got in, and hugged him tight. "I told you I needed some time, detective." Stan put his fingers to her lips and kissed her softly on the cheek. She shivered, then relaxed in his arms. "That was insane. What if he had someone watching the house?"

"He doesn't."

"How do you know?"

"I don't." He lifted her chin and kissed her, then slid his hand inside her coat. "So, let's go—now. New York? Los Angeles? Spokane?"

"I can't. This is nuts, Stan."

"Zap, North Dakota—my last offer." He smiled; she did, too. "Okay, then. My place." She nodded.

It was a twenty-minute drive to Stan's duplex via the freeways, and at least twice that on the side streets. Stan took the longer route. It was snowing again, and there were lots of Christmas displays along the way. Drivers were taking it slow. The ride would take longer still.

Marlyss put her hand on Stan's and squeezed his fingers. "You like Christmas?"

Stan looked at her. "It's okay."

"No—I mean, really like it?"

He flipped on the windshield wipers. "Every year should have one."

Marlyss lowered her voice. "So says Detective Stanislaw McScrooge."

Stan laughed at himself.

"You buy a Christmas tree?"

"If Petey asks."

"Does he?"

Stan laughed again. "Every year."

"How big?"

He shook his head. "Small." He smiled. "Very small."

"Buy one this year?"

Stan nodded. "Maybe."

"A really, really big one?"

She sounded like a kid. He nodded again.

"Maybe I could help pick it out."

Stan was stopped at a light. God, she was beautiful when she smiled. Stan was still nodding—and still smiling. He chuckled. "Sure."

It was snowing heavily when they arrived at Stan's place. The house was chilly, and Stan dialed the thermostat to seventy-six, then went into the bedroom and grabbed two quilts. He put the blankets on the living room floor, then went to the kitchen. Marlyss was making coffee. When she heard Stan enter the room, she stopped and turned toward him. "Why me, detective?"

Stan stopped, confused. The question had come out of nowhere. A lot of them had lately.

"Why us?" she said. "You don't even know me."

Stan shrugged. "I know all I need to know."

She shook her head. "I'm not sure you do."

Her answer took him by surprise.

"When I was nine, my little brother got very sick—did I ever tell you about him?" Stan shook his head. Her voice was low. "Alex was about three then. He was my best friend." Marlyss smiled a soft, tired smile. "He was in the hospital—leukemia or something like that, I'm not sure. It was the same time my father was planning to move us across the country. The middle of winter. I'm not sure why we had to move. I was too young. Besides, it seemed like we were always moving somewhere." She was staring past Stan. "But I would go to bed at night and lie there worrying that Alex would die before we moved and that we would have to bury him there, in the frozen ground, all alone, just him—and then leave." She stopped and looked at Stan. "I'm afraid of that sort of loneliness, Stan—dead, cold, left-behind loneliness."

He didn't say anything.

"I'm not afraid of him . . . Frank, I mean." She paused. "I am—but I'm not. Do you understand?"

He shook his head.

She nodded. "You know what I'm really afraid of?"

He shook his head again.

"You." Her voice was soft. "Me. Us. I'm afraid that someday you won't want me anymore, that someday I won't want you, that someday we won't want each other." She laughed. "Isn't that crazy?"

She finished making the coffee, then took his hand and led him out of the kitchen.

The living room was dark, and warm now, almost too warm. Stan sat on the couch, Marlyss on the floor, on one of the quilts. The smell of brewing coffee was strong, but they both ignored it.

"Do you ever tell Petey bedtime stories?" she asked.

Stan shrugged. "Sometimes. I'm not a very good storyteller."

"Happy stories?"

"I'm a cop." Stan laughed quietly. "I don't know many happy stories. Not anymore, anyway." He looked at her and scratched his head. "I guess I forgot most of them."

"Tell me a story about us, Stan."

He shook his head, feeling foolish.

"Then just tell me the ending. Is it happy?"

"I don't know."

Marlyss nodded. "Yes, you do." She looked away from him. "You do."

The silence grew heavy and they didn't speak for a while. When Stan finally looked at Marlyss, she had her head down and was struggling to unbutton her blouse. Her hands were trembling. Stan leaned forward and took her fingers in his, put them to his lips, and kissed them lightly. Then he began buttoning her blouse. "Not tonight."

He brushed her head softly to his shoulder and pulled her to the couch. He was still sitting. She was on her knees on the sofa, next to him, leaning forward on him. He felt her warm breath on this neck. It came slowly, softly, in quick intervals. He ran his hand along the curve of her buttocks and up her side, then leaned back and pulled her gently on top of him. He put his hand over her eyes and softly pulled her eyelids shut, keeping his eyes open wide in the darkness. He listened to the creaky house noises, and the stillness, and felt Marlyss's warmth, and her heart beating softly against his chest, and he held her, gently, as he would hold a frightened child.

Then he did something he hadn't done since Petey was a tiny baby. He began humming. He wasn't sure what, at first, but as he hummed, "Silent Night" came out, softly, quietly, slowly. Marlyss heard none of it. She was already asleep, dreaming about the little brother she had lost. She was nine again and Alex was still three and he was alive, not cold and not lonely, and not left behind.

It was 10:30 now. Marlyss had slept for about two hours, fitfully for some stretches, in perfect calm for others. When she'd awoke, she'd nuzzled Stan's neck, kissed his cheek, then gotten up. They'd tried the coffee, but it had cooked on the burner for too long. Now they were driving in silence back to her car.

Marlyss broke the quiet. She was looking out the front window. "It wasn't always like this . . . with me and Frank, I mean." She turned to Stan.

Stan shook his head. "You don't have to explain anything to me."

"I know." She smiled softly and turned back toward the window. "But I think it's time."

She held her face in her hands for a moment, and then she began.

"We met at a football game in Miami. Browns-Dolphins, I think, I don't know. I was working at a small, seashore-type boutique in Hollywood, just getting by, that's all. Frank was a junior attorney with some mid-level Detroit law firm. I forget the name. He was in Florida with some old college friend—Bubba something." She smiled. "Honest." Then she laughed quietly. "We bumped into each other just before the second half kickoff, literally. I got drowned in Coke. Down my blouse—everywhere. Frank apologized like a bashful teenager, told me I was the most beautiful woman he'd ever seen, and asked me to meet him after the game. I did." She nodded, still smiling. "I remember waiting outside the Orange Bowl under this gorgeous pink Florida sky, all sticky with pop. My God, it was wonderful." She nodded again. "He was wonderful.

"We got married two months later—on a gray, drizzly Christmas Eve—in a plain old civil ceremony downtown— here." She squinted a bit as though she were actually seeing everything. "Frank gave me a single red rose to match the red velvet ribbon in my hair. Carried me across the threshold of our room at the Book. He held me all night. The next morning, snow was everywhere. It was like waking up inside one of those glass ornaments, the ones you shake, and it snows." She looked at Stan. "It was like a dream, Stosh. It really was."

Stan was parked now, on the side street near the Comerica lot, about one hundred yards from Marlyss's car. The ignition was off. Marlyss was staring out the front window again. Her voice dropped a bit. "Things didn't change right away, or maybe they did and I didn't see. I don't know." She bit her lip. "You hear about those things happening to other people. I guess I just wanted to be Snow White forever."

She laughed softly. "Eventually, I saw." She shook her head. "Frank's brilliance—God, he was something—began to seem more like, I don't know, conniving, and his incredible energy started to feel like some sort of mean ambition. Like he was greedy for something—or everything. He always had this strange need for organization." She smiled. "You should see his sock drawer." The smile disappeared as quickly as it had bloomed. "I thought it was some simple sort of obsession with, what?—order? But it turned vicious." She stopped and shook her head again. "It was in everything—the way he'd say things: 'No.' 'Don't.' 'Stop.' to me. To others. Not in public, never in public. But in private. Quietly, usually, but fiercely. It was in his eyes. Hard and hateful, almost—and deep. It was there, then it was gone. Like that." She shook her head. "That fast. But you never knew when. There was no reason to it.

"I remember when I finally understood what had happened. It was watching some old black-and-white horror movie at home. It was a Friday night, with Frank. And I'm watching this woman in the basement of this old castle and I suddenly realize that she was me—I was the one who had pushed open the dungeon door and stumbled upon a dark, terrible secret. I knew Frank Sims, knew *about* him—me, only me, no one else."

She stopped and shrugged. "I was terrified for a while—I couldn't go near him for days after that movie." She laughed again, softly. "It seems a little silly, now, but only because I taught myself to live with everything." She paused, and lowered her voice. "All of it." She stopped. Stan knew what she was talking about. He'd seen some of the bruises.

Marlyss shook her head. "How? I don't know. Maybe it was just some sense of refuge: Someone was finally taking care of me. Maybe it was just that I knew I had already resigned myself some way to being his wife—an object. That's all. Nothing more. A thing. A possession. An ornament. Frank would even tell me that. He'd say he made me what I was, that he'd dressed me, told me what to say and how to say it, told me who to talk to, flirt with, and who to ignore." She nodded and smiled, almost in admiration. "And he was right."

Marlyss paused again, this time for more than a moment. She shivered. Stan put his hand on her thigh. "It's getting late."

She nodded, still looking straight ahead, then continued. "I threatened to leave him once. Oh, it was far too late, but I did it. A few years ago, during his campaign for county prosecutor. I screamed at him. First time. Ever. Told him I'd had enough." She laughed at herself. "I was pretty dramatic—Grade-B stuff. Even opened the closet door and showed him my bags. Told him they were packed."

Marlyss placed her hand on Stan's and squeezed it, almost reassuredly. "Frank nodded. It seems almost funny now. It was as though he had prepared for something like that. I guess he probably had." She shrugged. "He was probably waiting. Frank always seems to be a move or two ahead of everyone else." She nodded. "He said, quite calmly, that he understood my concerns but that he really needed me right now, that, yes, of course, I was very valuable to him and that leaving would be totally unacceptable. He actually used those words—understood, valuable, concerns, and unacceptable. I wanted to laugh at them, and almost did." Marlyss stopped. Her eyes widened, then tightened up again. "Then he stopped as though some light had gone on and everything I'd said had finally sunk in. I felt this strange glimmer of hope—I did. Like some sort of prayer had been answered. He shrugged and told me not to worry, then circled behind me and put his hands on my neck. His fingers felt good. I can remember that, the feeling. They were strong—somehow, some way, sort of . . . purposeful. Then he kissed my neck and asked me not to leave, asked me to unpack. Then he left." Marlyss shook her head, almost embarrassedly. "I waited until he left the room, then just closed the closet door. I hadn't even packed my luggage, Stosh. I'd just been bluffing."

Marlyss put her hands on her shoulders and held herself tight. "The next morning, I got this huge bouquet of flowers with a note that said, 'I'm so very, very sorry.' I wasn't sure what to think. I cried a little, I guess. About fifteen minutes later, Cindy, ah, Rollins or Rawlings, I never was sure, a neighbor from down the street, rang the bell. She was hysterical. She said my dog, Marbles, this tiny, nothing little mutt I got at the pound, maybe four months earlier, was dead in the gutter near her place."

Marlyss's voice wavered a bit and grew quieter. Her eyes were watery, her arms back in her lap now, her hands folded. "About an hour later, the vet or someone from animal control called. Needed some more information, he said, then said it was the strangest hit-and-run he'd ever seen. I remember exactly what he said. He said, 'Dog's neck's broke, ma'am. But there's nothin' else.' " Marlyss's voice began to fade some more, then it grew stronger again. " 'No other trauma. Nothing. Almost like someone . . .' And that was it. He stopped. I knew what he was going to say. It was almost like someone had . . . snapped it.

"I should have left that day, right then. I know. But I was too scared, and Frank knew that." She laughed again, quietly, sadly. "Frank knows a lot of things." She paused. "Then, all of a sudden, it was too late. A week or two after he won the election, my mom called from her place near Pensacola and said a strange man—a short man in a suit— had been by her place. He was from up north, she said. She could tell. His accent. His skin was too white. He was ask-ing questions. She was scared." Marlyss nodded. "And I was trapped."

Stan was confused. His voice was low, quiet. "What? Did Frank have someone threaten her?"

Marlyss shook her head. Her voice was low, too, almost inaudible. "No . . . he didn't have to." She looked over and saw the question in Stan's face. "I can't say any more, Stan. I'm sorry."

The wind was blowing hard now, and they finally heard it. It was whistling through a half-inch crack in the rear win-dow of Stan's car. Snow swirled in little eddies up and down the street. Marlyss was staring at the floor. Her voice was flat. "He's not going to let me walk away, Stan."

The car was cold, the windows fogged. Stan started the engine and turned on the defroster. They had been parked for only a few minutes, but it had seemed like an eternity. Marlyss was staring out the window again, and she reached over, without looking, for Stan's hand. "Have you ever killed someone?"

Stan shook his head.

"Have you ever wanted to kill someone?"

He nodded. "Everyone has."

"No, really." She was looking at him now, hard. "Really. Could you *kill* someone?"

Stan turned to her. It seemed as though her eyes were pleading with him. "I don't know."

She nodded, then closed her eyes, sat there for a second, shaking slightly, then opened the door and swung her feet onto the wet pavement. She turned halfway back to Stan and shook her head. Her voice was a whisper. "I think he knows, Stan." She looked away. "I'm so sorry." She sat there for a moment, then she stood and walked slowly through the darkness and blowing snow to her car.

◇ 23 ◇

Mary Stimic slid out of bed, padded to the full-length mirror on her closet door, and stretched. She turned on her toes and studied her body. She had just turned thirty-nine; she figured she could pass for about thirty. Her breasts weren't as sassy as they used to be. Whose were? They were more low-slung now than perky, but the sag, and it was slight, made her, if anything more womanly. Her butt was still packed tight. Her thighs were a bit thicker, but her stomach was still pretty flat. She held up her hair, struck a fashion model's pose, and pouted at her reflection. Yep, except for the puffy eyes, she liked herself, all right.

She went to her dresser, tossed her hair back, ran a brush through it six times, and pinned it, then put on a robe and hurried down the hall toward the front door. She told herself to slow down, but she didn't, couldn't. She felt pretty chipper now, but much of her get-up-and-go was nervous energy. It had to be. Saturday had been a long, hectic, exhausting day. She'd gotten to bed late and fallen asleep later. She rubbed her eyes and checked the clock in the hallway. It was only 7:15. She should still be asleep. Would be, too, if Ted Enders hadn't sweet-talked her into writing the lead story for Sunday's paper. Yes, Enders had promised Mary that she wouldn't get sucked into the meat-grinder daily coverage of the Rickey Jefferson murder, but he had asked, not ordered, her to help Saturday afternoon. And the case had received lots of national attention. The murder's growing notoriety, as much as Enders's polite pleading, had seduced her.

Now, she was simply eager, as always, to judge what she had written. The words almost always seemed to read better in print than they did on the newsroom terminals—and what she had written Saturday evening in Enders's office had read pretty damn good already.

It was about fifteen degrees outside, but it felt colder than that when she opened the front door and reached onto the porch for her paper. It wasn't there. It wasn't on the steps, either. The paperboy had left it in the snow, about three steps down the walk. "Asshole kid." Mary looked up and down the street. Wayburn, a modest street mostly of duplexes on the Detroit-Grosse Pointe Park border, was quiet, almost deserted on Sunday mornings. Mary decided on a quick, barefoot dash. She gritted her teeth. A stiff gust of wind blew her robe wide open, but she ignored the flash of indecency, sprinted for the paper, grabbed it, and leaped back onto the porch and into the house.

She stood inside the door for a second, hugging herself tight, trying to stop shaking and to catch her breath. Her feet burned from the snow. She shuffled to the living room, sat on the couch, and stuffed her toes under one of the cushions, then opened her eyes wide, pulled the first section of the paper from the rest of the bundle and dropped the remainder at the foot of the coffee table.

She was still freezing—and shivering—but she smiled. Her story was stripped across the top of Page One with a huge headline: SUSPECT NABBED IN JEFFERSON KILLING. She pulled her robe tighter, propped the paper on her knees, and began reading.

An alleged drug kingpin was arrested early Saturday morning and charged in connection with the execution-style slaying last week of eleven-year-old Rickey Jefferson.

Julius Caesar Cooper, twenty-two, was arraigned on one count of first-degree murder Saturday afternoon. Bond was set at ten million dollars.

Cooper, whom police official depicted as one of the city's most vicious and elusive young outlaws, was collared at about 4:30 A.M. during a raid at the crack house on Eastlawn on Detroit's lower east side. Eight weapons, all believed to belong to Cooper, were confiscated during a simultaneous search of Cooper's residence on Bedford, near East Outer Drive. Among the arsenal: an Uzi submachine gun; a high-powered rifle with a night scope; a semiautomatic handgun; a snub-nosed .38, and a revolver police described as a .31-caliber nickel-plated six-shooter. Police said ballistics tests would be conducted on all the handguns to see if the weapons match up with slug fragments from the Jefferson shooting.

Homicide detective Stan Kochinski, who led a combined narcotics-homicide team—twenty-five officers—in the crack-house raid, said that shots were exchanged with people inside the house during the arrest, but that no one was injured.

"There was nothing really out of the ordinary," Kochinski said.

Homicide detective Pete Dawlson led a fifteen-person crew that executed the search warrant at Cooper's residence. Dawlson said that no one was home when the officers arrived and that the search was conducted without incident.

Neither officer would comment further.

Police chief Frank Sims was wearing a grim, but confident, smile following Saturday's arraignment. "I think we have a good suspect," he said before waving off reporters.

Embattled Mayor Martin Hatch was effusive in his praise of Sims and the police.

"We worked fast," Hatch said. "I said we would react quickly to this terrible, terrible tragedy and we have. I hope this sort of efficiency will help restore some of the faith our public once had in its police force."

When reminded that Cooper remained only a suspect in the case, Hatch smiled and said, "At the present time, yes." He then smiled again and said, "Just give us a few days."

The Rev. Robert Lincoln, head of the Black Pastors Alliance for Justice and one of the metropolitan area's most influential black civic leaders, was not so quick to praise the police or Hatch. But the Rev. Lincoln was much less antagonistic toward the administration than he was Friday, when he met privately with Hatch at the City-County Building, then went outside and joined a group of picketers calling for Hatch's resignation.

"Justice has yet to be served," the Rev. Lincoln said. "We are wary. But this may be a start."

A preliminary examination has been scheduled for Tuesday, December twenty-sixth, in Judge William Colbane's courtroom.

Mary stopped reading and nodded her approval. Okay, not great—but not bad, either. The story continued for thirty more paragraphs, but Mary had read enough. The copy desk had been kind—or maybe lazy. There'd been few changes—a word here or there, but nothing substantial. The piece was solid, no-nonsense journalism. The wire services would undoubtedly pick up the story and send it to papers all across the country. Mary liked the thought of that. She'd probably be able to parlay the piece into a few interviews on local radio and TV. She'd become something of a celebrity already, since being named columnist. This could only stoke her rise. She smiled, then tossed the paper to the floor. It was almost eight. She went to the kitchen, and put on some water for tea, then picked up the phone on the wall next to the refrigerator, and began dialing. The phone on the other end rang five times.

"Hello." It sounded more like a groan than a greeting.

"Kochinski? Stan?"

"Who is this?" It was a challenge, not a question.

"Mary."

"What the hell time is it?" Stan still had his head on the pillow. The phone was propped next to his ear.

"Time to get up, Chipper." Mary chuckled and reached for a tea bag above the sink.

"Jesus Christ, isn't this Sunday?"

Mary poured the hot water into her cup and inhaled the steam. "Didn't want you to miss the mass for shut-ins again."

Stan coughed. "Fuck you."

"Your grasp of the spoken word is exemplary." Mary rubbed her eyes. "Actually, I forgot to thank you yesterday for that great quote for my story." Mary lowered her voice to a growl. " 'There was nothing out of the ordinary.' "

Stan coughed again. "Next time, just make something up for me."

Mary laughed. "Maybe I will." She took a sip of her tea. "So, tell me, this thing over?"

Stan's voice was husky with sleep. "How the hell should I know?"

"Best guess."

Stan cleared his throat. It didn't do any good. "Yeah. Sure."

"You don't sound . . ." Mary mimicked Stan again by clearing her throat. ". . . sure."

"It's eight-fucking" —He opened one eye and looked at the clock on his nightstand, closed the eye, and coughed again—"seventeen on Sunday morning."

"Humor me."

"Fuck you." Matter-of-fact.

"You wish."

"Mary . . ."

"You got this guy nailed?" Her belt had come loose and she pulled her robe closed again.

"I don't know." Stan rolled onto his stomach.

"You don't?"

He propped himself up on his elbows, his eyes still closed. "What difference does it make what I know? We're going to stick it right up his ass, anyway."

Mary smiled. "On the record?"

"Fuck you again, Mary. *That's* on the record."

Mary grabbed a cookie from the cookie jar and took a bit. "Gof de gub?"

"What?"

"Sorry." She swallowed. "Got the gun?"

Stan nodded. "Sims seems to think so."

"Already?"

"If all we handed him was a straw and a spitball and told him it was Cooper's, he'd a been happy."

"You?"

"I'm just a dumb Polack, Mary. Ko-chin-ski. I keep telling you that."

Mary's eyes narrowed; she stared at the wall across from the refrigerator. "Okay, then tell me this." She paused. "Doesn't all this seem just a little bit too simple, after a kid gets its execution-style?"

Stan took a deep breath and puffed out his cheeks as he exhaled. He rolled onto his back and opened his eyes—halfway, anyway. "Who cares? Look, what are the chances we solve any hit? Even one a year? What are the chances?"

"Don't know."

"My ass you don't. They're lousy, and you know it." Stan stopped and rubbed his eyes. "Kid gets his ticket punched on a deserted street corner—bang bang. And how long we been after Cooper?"

"Long time."

"Too long, Mary. Case closed. Interview over."

Mary was wringing out her teabag. She didn't say anything.

"Besides, the kid didn't get it 'execution-style' "

"Wrong, Stosh." Stan didn't say anything. Mary smiled. "He did . . . if I wrote he did."

"A simple bullet in the brain's not enough?"

Mary shook her head. "Not always."

"You mean not for Mary Stimic."

"I mean not for the eight hundred thousand people who want grit and guts with their Sunday-morning Wheaties."

It was too early for all this jousting. Stan rolled back over onto his stomach and sunk his head deep into the pillow. "If that's it, I'll be going back to sleep."

"Okay, Stosh, okay. No more cop talk." She paused. "I talked to Jenny last night." Mary's tone of voice had changed. It got Stan's attention. He knew what was coming—some of it. "She and Petey didn't have a very nice time at the Clown Café . . . alone."

Stan had gotten tied up with the Cooper arrest reports and had forgotten about Jenny and Petey. By the time he'd remembered, it had been one o'clock. He'd called the restaurant and had the manager page Jenny, but the manager had come back on the line and said Jenny wouldn't accept the call. Stan propped himself up again.

"She wanted to know if I would be talking to you. She had two messages."

Stan nodded.

"Some guy named Thorn-something called her Friday evening from somewhere. Jenny didn't talk to him. He left a message for her—or you—on the machine. Something about returning a call of hers. She was confused."

Stan rubbed his forehead. The name didn't register immediately.

"She also said that Roger asked her to marry him." Mary paused. "She said to tell you that she was going to tell him . . . yes."

Stan knew it was coming, but still felt as though he'd been sucker-punched in the kidneys. He lost his breath, then struggled to catch it, nodding slowly, biting his lip.

Mary waited for Stan to say something, but he didn't. "I'm sorry, Chipper."

He squeezed his eyes shut tight. "No, it's okay."

"My ass."

"She'll be happy."

Mary shook her head. "She'll be taken care of, that's all." She paused "Roger will show up at the Clown Café."

Stan rubbed his head, rolled onto his back again, swung his legs off the bed and sat up. He felt dizzy. "I've got a great idea, Mary. Why don't you leave me alone for a while?"

Mary's voice grew quiet. "You okay?" She was trying to be nice.

Stan nodded. "Yeah." He cleared his throat again. "Okay." Then he hung up.

Mary finished her tea and walked back to the bedroom, unpinned her hair, took off her robe, and crawled back into bed. She shivered under the cool sheets. Her skin turned into a blanket of goose bumps and she curled into a ball. She'd told herself she wasn't going to get involved in another story like this, another dead kid, but it was happening again. Enders had known it would. It always did. She laughed. It was that damn Professor Watts.

Eugene Watts had been Mary's journalism advisor at Eastern Michigan. Professor Watts—the kids had called him "Huge Gene"—had waddled into the room the very first day of Mary's very first newswriting class, Reporting 104, and plopped his tired, two hundred sixty-five pounds down on his desk in a thick, sorry heap and said, in a loud, curmudgeonly voice, "I am about to give you the most important advice you'll ever get in this slimy, decrepit business, so listen up." He'd waited for a second until the chatter had died down, looked over the top of his reading glasses, then lowered his voice to a thick rumble. "When you're interviewing someone, anyone—and I don't care if it's the pope, Jehovah, Allah, or even Jesus himself—I want you to look him dead in the eye and then ask yourself one simple question: Why"—he broke into a wide, fake smile—"is this sonofabitch *lying* to me?" Then Huge Gene dismissed the class.

The thought made Mary smile. Always did. There were a lot of liars out there: Sims all but says it's Cooper; Cooper's going to say it wasn't him; and Stan says he doesn't give a shit. Someone, at least one of them, wasn't telling the truth. The trick was finding out whom. Mary pulled the covers tighter. It wasn't such a bad way to make a living. It was almost entertaining. She smiled and closed her eyes. She'd done good so far; she'd do even better before she was through with Rickey Jefferson. She was sure of that. Damn sure.

◇ **24** ◇

The hallways of the district courthouse were cold and gloomy on Sunday mornings, particularly on gray, winter Sunday mornings. But Bill Colbane knew what to expect.

He knew the building at all hours, seven days a week, even sometimes on holidays. He also knew what he needed. He had already read and re-read the stories in the Sunday paper about the arrest of Julius Cooper. Now, he had to get out of the house, had to go somewhere to think and be alone. He scanned the deserted corridor as he headed toward the elevators at the far end of the street-floor concourse. He wanted to make sure he was alone. Best he could tell, he was. He arrived at the elevators and pressed the orange Up button with his right hand; his left hand held the copy of the *Free Press* that he had bought at a drug store on the way downtown.

Bill Colbane looked around again. The place didn't look much like a courthouse. It was new, too new, and too cold; it looked like some sort of processing center. It didn't feel at all like the grand old post office building downtown, where the federal courts were located—where Bill Colbane's father used to work.

Sam Colbane had been a janitor at the building at the corner of Lafayette and Washington, and at least once a week when he'd been a kid, Bill Colbane would stop by after school to visit his dad. First, Sam Colbane would ask his son about his schoolwork—what he had learned, what he might expect to learn tomorrow. Then, Sam Colbane and his boy would talk about baseball, even in the dead of winter, Baseball was Sam Colbane's passion. Word was that "Broomstick" Colbane, a strong but reed-thin catcher, who would tell people that he was "quick as lightning in July," had had more than enough talent to play in the major leagues. But blacks weren't welcome in the big leagues in those days, so Sam Colbane ran trash and mopped the floors at the post office building during the day and, during spring, summer, and early fall, played in local semi-pro leagues at night. During the summer months, he coached as many amateur teams as he could handle.

Sam Colbane was a dreamer, and some days, as many as he would chance, he would usher his son into the elevator and tell him to go up to the federal courtrooms—"the empty ones, boy"—and just sit awhile. "Soak in the solemnity." But Sam Colbane was also a no-nonsense sort, and as soon as he saw one, just one attorney or judge—or, worse, a police officer or courthouse guard—cast a stern glance at the ragtag black boy hanging about the courthouse, he would wrinkle his face into a grimace and shoo his son home with a quick slap on the rear. One winter evening, after one of those afternoon sendoffs, and after dinner, Sam Colbane called his son to the basement. The elder Colbane was standing at the makeshift work bench in the far corner of the damp, dimly lit cinderblock room. He did some repair work on the side and was fiddling with the frayed cord of an electric fan that belonged to Addie Watson down the street. He asked his son what he had noticed most during his visits to the building.

Bill Colbane shrugged. He was only ten. "I don't know."

Sam Colbane didn't look up. "Think, now. Don't be afraid."

Bill rubbed his head. "This about baseball?"

Sam grabbed a roll of black tape and began bandaging the fan's cord. "Nope." He smiled, still without looking up. "You take a good cut at this one, now."

Bill nodded. He felt bad about what he was about to say, and spoke softly. "That pushin' trash and a broom all day, well, unless you an' me are talking about baseball, seems . . ." He stopped.

"Seems what?" Sam was still focused on the broken fan.

Bill swallowed hard. Sam could feel his nervousness. "Be honest now."

". . . seems like a crummy job."

Sam looked up and laughed. "That's good. That's right." He rubbed his boy's head with mock gruffness. "It's no job for a man of talent and intelligence to have." He grabbed a knife and cut the tape. "Now, what you been learning from what you seen in those courtrooms, and hallways, and such?"

Bill had no idea what his father was getting at. He shook his head.

Sam Colbane straightened up and looked down at his son. He was more than a little disappointed, but he tried not to show it. His voice was low. "Well, from now on you think about what you're seein'—and you watch those men up there. You watch them, son. You study those men. Hear?"

Bill Colbane nodded. And from then on, he did all of that. He talked less and less with his father and concentrated instead on how the lawyers and judges dressed, how they carried themselves. He listened to how they talked, and what they said to each other, and he watched them stride proudly and purposefully through the hallways and into the large courtrooms with the high ceilings and mahogany walls. And slowly, surely, he began to understand what his father wanted him to learn.

Now, more than four decades later, Bill Colbane was one of the men his father had told him to study; one of the men his father had greeted with a smile, day in and day out, while emptying their wastebaskets. Bill Colbane had worked his way into the big leagues. He was an insider. There was only one problem now: He was too far inside. And there was no easy way out. Maybe no way out at all.

The elevator stopped with a jerk at the fifth floor, and Colbane stepped out. He took a quick left, walked twenty-five feet and took another left, then went about one hundred feet further down another corridor and turned right. He was at the back door to his chambers. He unlocked the door and entered, then relocked the door from the inside. He shivered—the room was cold—he dialed the thermostat to seventy-five, made certain that the other door to his chambers, the one that opened out into the courtroom, was locked, and sat down behind his desk, leaving his coat on.

He placed the *Free Press* in front of him, opened the top drawer to his desk, grabbed a pair of scissors, picked up the paper, and began cutting out Julius Cooper's picture. He worked slowly, deliberately. When he was finished, he put the scissors back in the drawer, slid the remainder of the paper into the wastebasket next to his desk, and stuffed the clipping into his shirt pocket. Then, he reached down and unlocked his bottom desk drawer and took out his gun.

He pulled the gun out of the holster and laid it on the desk and studied it for a moment, much as he had a few days earlier, and wondered, for the first time, who'd owned the gun before he'd bought it. He wondered if someone had killed someone with it; if someone had been raped with it; if someone had defended himself or won murderous revenge with it. He took the gun in his left hand and pointed it at the underside of his chin, then pushed it up and to the left along his jaw bone until the tip of the barrel nestled snugly into the hollow behind his ear. It fit there almost perfectly. The metal felt cool against his skin. He flinched, but only a bit. He switched the gun to his right hand and held the barrel under his nose. The smell was strong, masculine—steel and gunpowder. No surprise. He held his breath and pressed the tip of the barrel against his lips, outlining the "o" with the tip of his tongue, then against his teeth. He pushed the barrel into his mouth; the metal tasted bitter. He expected that, too. He pulled the barrel out quickly, took a handkerchief from his pocket and wiped it off, then slid the revolver gently back into its holster and put it back into the desk drawer. He was breathing heavily, in big gulps. He was sweating, too. His shirt was soaked; his hands were shaking.

He sat for a moment, without moving, trying to calm himself, then began fishing in his drawer for the letter he had begun writing a few days earlier. It had slid to the back. He pulled it out, then checked his watch. It was 9:45. He'd left Molly a note saying that he would be home in time for the noon church service. He had no time to write. He would do that later. He replaced the letter and closed the bottom drawer, then reached into his top drawer for a roll of Scotch tape, got up, unlocked the door to his left, and walked into his courtroom.

Bill Colbane stood behind the bench and studied the room. It was dark. He left the lights off. He had never seen his courtroom quite like this. The place looked too small to him and too ... what? Modern? It certainly wasn't as stately as those federal courtrooms he'd visited as a young boy. He looked at the burnt orange rug, the recessed lighting, the acoustical tiles in the ceiling, and nodded. The place *was* too modern, almost like some tacky room at some chain motel, really. Or maybe that was the way it was supposed to feel—cold and impersonal, the perfect setting for doling out assembly-line justice to an endless stream of faceless criminals. Colbane sat in the darkness for a few minutes, then reached for the phone to his left and dialed. A woman answered. Her voice was gentle. Bill Colbane tried to sound as pleasant. "Mr. Samuel Colbane, please."

"Who's calling?"

"His son, Bill."

"Just a second, sir."

The woman put him on hold. Her voice was replaced by Christmas Muzak.

"Judge Colbane?" It was a different woman.

"Yes."

"This is Mrs. Sumners. How are you?" Todi Sumners was a nursing supervisor.

"Fine. Is my dad up?"

"Yes." Colbane was certain he'd met her. He tried to picture her face, but couldn't. "It's not one of Samuel's better days. He's slipping in and out a lot."

Colbane closed his eyes and nodded. "Can I speak with him?"

"Sure." She sounded very nice. "Hold on a second while we get him settled."

He could hear Mrs. Sumners speaking to his father in a loud voice. Sam Colbane had grown very hard of hearing. Bill Colbane could hear grunting and heavy breathing on the other end. "Dad?" He spoke loudly. His voice rattled around the empty courtroom. "It's me, Bill."

"Bill?"

"Yes."

"Where the hell are you? I've been waiting for you. What time'd school get out?"

Bill didn't answer.

Sam was lashed in a wheelchair; he was leaning forward against the restraints. "You finish that math project?"

His son nodded. "Yes."

"Well, what did you get?"

Bill smiled. "I got an A, Dad."

Sam nodded and sat back. "Good work. I knew it."

"How are you feeling?"

Sam rubbed his wrist. "Damn elbow is killing me."

"You fall?"

Sam scratched his head. "I wonder if ol' Satch's elbow hurt him after throwin' a stiff nine?"

Bill didn't answer.

"Couldn't hardly get the ball to second base. My first throw skipped three damn feet front of Willie's glove."

Bill sat up and leaned forward on the bench. "Molly says hi."

"Bill?"

"Yes."

Sam's voice turned to a whisper. "Smuggle me outta this place."

Bill whispered back. "I will, Dad."

"I got to play—*tomorrow.*"

"I know."

"Got to . . . you say Molly?"

"Yes."

"Missy, too?"

"Yes."

"Fine girl. Fine girl. Looks jus' like her grandma did."

"I know, Dad."

"You been studyin'?"

"All the time, Dad."

"What honors you seen on seven today, son?"

Bill rubbed his yes. "Judge Corrigan, Dad."

Sam nodded. "Fine man. Always had a kind word. Big baseball man." Silence. Then Bill heard his father grunt. Sam's voice was a low growl now. "Goddamn motherfuckers. They ever find those boys?"

Bill nodded. "That's why I called, Dad. They did—one. On Saturday."

"They gonna make 'em pay?"

"Yes."

"You sure?" Sam was yelling.

The judge nodded. "Settle down, Pop." He stopped. "I'm going to make sure."

Sam's voice trailed off to a whisper again. "You really think you can break me outta here?"

His son whispered back. "Sure. Tomorrow."

"I'll be waiting. I'm supposed to start tomorrow, bat

cleanup. Big Ben Bowman's throwin'. We're supposed to play those white boys from Toledo."

"It's okay, Dad."

"I'm counting on you."

"I know you are, Dad."

"You make 'em pay, those motherfuckers."

"I plan to, Dad."

"Missy said hi, too, huh? Damn."

Bill nodded. "I love you, Dad."

Sam looked around the room to make sure no one was looking, then lowered his voice to a whisper. "Bring my catcher's glove, son, the one with the deep pocket. Damn busybodies here stole mine. I think nursie here's using it for a pincushion."

Sam Colbane didn't say goodbye. He simply dropped the phone and called to Mrs. Sumners and told her he had to go to the bathroom. Bill Colbane listened to the chatter on the other end for a few moments, then hung up. He rubbed his eyes again, then looked at his watch. It was almost 10:30. He didn't have much time. He reached into his back pocket, took out his wallet, reached into the fold and retrieved the newspaper photo of Rickey Jefferson and a picture of Missy. He took the picture of Julius Cooper out of his shirt pocket and knelt behind the bench, lifted the corner of the carpet and pushed it back, then placed the three pictures—Missy, then Rickey Jefferson, then Julius Cooper—in a row and taped them down. He studied them for a moment, then replaced the carpet, and stood and looked once more across the empty room. He was shaking again as he picked up the phone.

"Molly?"

"Get all caught up?" Her voice sounded good.

He steadied his voice. "Yes. I'll be home soon."

"Good."

"I love you, Molly."

She was in a hurry, he could tell. "And I love you, too, Bill. Now, get a move on."

Bill Colbane nodded and hung up the phone. He took one more good look around the empty courtroom, then walked slowly through his chambers to the hallway and took the stairs to the street floor. He needed the exercise. The sky was a deep blue, and the sun was bright when he stepped outside. It felt warm. Colbane liked feeling the sun on his face on brittle winter mornings. He wondered if Julius Cooper liked that feeling, too, or if he even noticed. Bill Colbane would miss the sun; he would miss it a lot. He would miss his father, too. He wondered if Julius Cooper would miss his father. He wondered if Julius Cooper had a father. He wondered if he had a daughter.

◇ **25** ◇

Stan was sitting in the corner of one of those too-cute, fern/sports/yuppie shopping-mall restaurant-bars, reading the *Detroit News* and eating a bowl of gumbo, the only thing he could bring himself to order on a menu that listed things like "seafood salad croissant" and "fried mozzarella cheese." Marlyss knew he'd be here. It was their meeting place: every Sunday noon, Ruby Tuesday's, at Briarwood in Ann Arbor, in the booth right under the poster of Barbara Hershey in *Boxcar Bertha*.

Marlyss hadn't talked to Stan since Friday night, when she'd told him about her and Frank. A day and a half seemed like two weeks. She'd missed him terribly, especially when she'd thought about having to end everything, sometime, somewhere. Especially since she'd admitted to herself, finally, that it could come to that—goodbye.

She was late, but she stopped near the bar and watched him for a few seconds. He looked tired, older than his years. His hair was thinning on top and graying on the sides. His clothes didn't fit very well. Not bad, but not so great, either. Early on, she would wonder just what was so special about him, and she'd finally come to a simple conclusion: Stan was solid. That was it. Not solid normal or solid average or solid reliable and dependable. No single dictionary definition fit. Stan's solid was all those, but different, too: better—warmer, somehow. Good, solid Stan Kochinski. Marlyss couldn't help but smile. She knew at that moment that there could be no sad goodbyes today. She walked to the booth, sat down, and snuggled against him.

"So, how's Dick Tracy on this snowy Christmas Eve?" Marlyss was wearing gray, stone-washed jeans and a black sweater. She kissed Stan on the cheek and rested her hand lightly on the inside of his thigh.

Stan had been waiting for an hour, hoping that she would show up. He'd missed her, too, a lot. He smiled, then shrugged. "Haven't got to the comics yet."

Marlyss took the front page from him. "Paper says you got your man." Stan didn't say anything. She looked at him. "What? Too excited to talk?"

He pushed the rest of the paper across the table, then smiled. "Yep."

"Are not." Marlyss wrinkled up her nose and walked her fingers slowly up his thigh.

"Okay, not yet. But I'm getting there."

They both laughed, she heartier than he, then stopped and looked at each other as if they were alone in some movie. And they were alone, just about. Ruby's was empty except for a busboy setting tables across the room. Stan wanted to kiss Marlyss full on the lips, to pull her to him, to hold her and not let go. It was the skating-rink feeling all over again. He stared deep into her eyes, then reached up and pushed the bangs off her forehead. That was it. "It's nice to see you."

She nodded. "Me, too." She shrugged, then smiled a little nervously. "He's busy all day with Hatch." Stan kissed her forehead. She wrinkled up her nose again and rearranged her bangs, then grabbed Stan's hand and squeezed it. "Let's go shopping."

"Not hungry?"

Marlyss began to slide out of the booth. "Nope. Let's shop."

Stan stopped her. "Frank had it right, you know—you're the most beautiful woman I've ever seen."

It was the first time he'd said anything like that to her, and she blushed. Her voice soft and low, she shook her head. "It's not me, Stosh, it's you. You make me feel beautiful." Marlyss put an arm around Stan's neck and hugged him tight.

He closed his eyes for a moment, then opened them wide. "What for?"

"Shop?"

"Yep."

"For me." She smiled like a teenage flirt. "You bought me a Christmas present yet?"

"Nope."

"Good, I'm not sure I trust your taste."

Stan grinned. "You don't know my taste."

Marlyss laughed. "Oh, yes I do, detective—if it fits, you wear it. Let's go."

They left Ruby's and window-shopped until they turned the corner into the main mall. The sports-card display Jenny had mentioned was still there, in the middle of the aisle. Stan tugged on Marlyss's arm. "Let's stop here a second. I want to check something out." He walked up to the center table; Marlyss followed.

As far as Stan could tell, the exhibit was manned by a single salesman. His nametag said Wooly. Wooly was wearing Coke-bottle glasses, a faded Michigan State sweatshirt that was a size too small, and a Santa Claus hat that looked about two sizes too big. He was bent across a counter, shuffling through a stack of football cards, trying to help another customer. Stan cleared his throat. Wooly didn't look up. Stan looked back at Marlyss and shrugged, then turned back toward Wooly. "Excuse me." No answer. "I'm looking for a rookie baseball card of a guy named Kochinski, used to pitch for . . ."

Wooly still didn't look up. "Twins. Guy was a Roman candle—bright flame, then the fizzle—big time. Got one down there on the end." He pointed right. "The '66 case, Topps—thirty cents. He's some local DJ in Flint now, or somethin'." Marlyss giggled and poked Stan in the back.

Stan turned and headed down the aisle. "Thanks."

"Get it while it's real hot, pal." Wooly was still fussing with the football cards. "I got two other calls this week. Musta been the guy's old lady."

Stan and Marlyss walked to the last case. It took them only a minute to find the card. Marlyss spotted it first. It was laying between a $14.50 Roger Maris card and a $115 Willie Mays. Most of the cards were in protective plastic sleeves; Stan's wasn't. Marlyss studied the picture. "You look like a kid, Stosh."

"I was." He touched the glass with his finger, then smiled, a little wistfully, but only a little. Marlyss was watching him. She noticed.

"Buy it."

Stan shook his head. "Not on your life. I don't know this guy."

"Come on."

"Nope. I just wanted to see if it was here—it is."

"How good were you?"

"He wasn't bad." Stan had moved on. He was looking at cards in the case marked "1967."

Marlyss was still watching him. "How good could *he* have been?"

Stan smiled. "The best. At least that's what Laddy always said." He laughed, softly, self-consciously.

"What happened?"

Stan looked at Marlyss. "No guts." She caught the embarrassment in his eyes before he shrugged and looked away. "The story of my life."

Marlyss put her hands on Stan's neck and pulled his cheek to her lips. She kissed him softly, then put her lips to his ear. "The real thing is worth more than thirty measly cents."

Stan smiled. Her breath tickled. Her perfume was terrific, too. He nodded. "Four bits, easy."

"And you do too have guts." She jabbed him in the soft part of his stomach. He laughed.

They left the display and window-shopped some more, mostly in silence, for another half hour or so, until Marlyss found an empty bench in the central concourse, across from the "Briarwood at the North Pole" exhibit. She sat down. The line to visit Santa snaked past them through the mall. Stan was still standing. He watched the families in line. Most of the parents looked perturbed; the kids looked antsy, or scared. Stan got that homesick feeling in the pit of his stomach. He wished for a second that he were there, in line, waiting with the others, with Jenny and Petey.

Marlyss was watching him again. "What's on your mind, detective?"

Stan didn't answer right away. "Christmas." He paused. "Nothing." He shook his head slightly.

Marlyss watched him watching the families. "Petey?" Stan didn't answer. "Ever think of having more kids?" Still nothing. A few more seconds passed. "Jenny?" Stan still didn't respond. Marlyss nodded. "It's okay." She took his hand in hers. She was a little jealous, but she tried not to let on. "Can't ignore it."

"I know." He took a deep breath. "I know."

She rubbed her hand across his knuckles. "You ever wonder about me, Stan?"

He looked down at her. "All the time."

"Like this?" She looked around the mall. "In the middle of everything?"

"Yep."

"Do you ever wonder where I came from, what I've done besides marry Frank Sims?"

"Sometimes." He wasn't looking at her. "I figure you'll tell me all that when you're ready, just like you told me the other night."

Marlyss nodded, bit down on her lower lip, and patted the spot on the bench next to her. "Sit down." Stan looked at her, then did. "You know what I wonder sometimes about you?" Stan shook his head. "I wonder what you're afraid of. Anything?"

Stan smiled, sort of. "I told you back there." He nodded toward the sports-card display. "Everything."

She laughed softly and shook her head. "I doubt that."

A teenage boy dressed like a Santa's helper walked up to Stan and Marlyss and handed them candy canes and wished them a Merry Christmas. The kid had trouble keeping his eyes off Marlyss. He almost tripped over his elf shoes walking away.

"Are you afraid of me?" Marlyss stared at Stan. He felt her gaze.

"Sometimes."

"Why?"

"Because of who you are and who I am."

"That frightens you?"

"Scares the shit out of me." The mall was buzzing with noise, but Stan heard none of it. He grabbed his sweater and tugged on it. "Look at me. I'm nothing special—a forty-two regular, a dime a dozen. You should have figured that out by now."

"That's all that frightens you?" Marlyss scrunched her face into a question mark. "Me waking up and realizing you're not, who?—Prince Charming? Warren Beatty?"

"No."

"What, then?"

"I'm afraid of you because my life isn't mine anymore."

"That's my fault?"

"Yes, it is."

Marlyss shook her head. She was confused, and a little hurt. "I don't understand."

"You've stolen my life."

"You mean your heart. That's what I'm supposed to do." She didn't want to sound defensive. She was just trying to explain herself.

"No, I meant my life." Stan rubbed his eyes, then turned and looked at her. "Jenny stole my heart once. Petey did too. What you've done"—he shook his head, ever so slightly—"is nothing like that at all."

"Is that good or bad?"

Stan shrugged. "I don't know. It's never happened to me before."

She nodded to herself. "What *do* you know, Stan?"

"That I think about you more than I should. That I want you more than I should. That weird, strange things happen in life and I think this is one of them."

"Is all that so bad?"

"No. It's just . . . dangerous."

"Frank?"

Stan shook his head. "No, not Frank, Marlyss . . . us."

She knew that. Of course, she did. She nodded, got up, stood in front of the bench for a few seconds looking across the mall, then turned back to Stan. Her eyes were shiny. She forced them to smile, held out her hands and pulled him up. "Let's walk some more, Stosh."

They did, slowly, in silence again, for another half hour, with Christmas carols playing in the background, until Marlyss stopped in front of the Lord & Taylor department store. She put on a nice let's-be-friends smile and tugged playfully at Stan's arm. "Let's buy me a Christmas present."

Stan checked out the mannequins in the window; they were dressed in elegant, formal evening gowns. He followed Marlyss inside and took a quick look at a few price tags, then pulled Marlyss close. "Now, this . . . is really scary." They both laughed.

"Guts check time, Kochinski." Her eyes were sparkling again. She nuzzled Stan's cheek and spoke in a breathless whisper. "We're here"—she tickled him in the ribs—"to have fun."

Stan nodded. "Fun."

"That's right. Stick with me, Kochinski."

Marlyss took Stan's hand and led him to the escalator. They rode to the second floor and Marlyss pulled Stan right, toward the lingerie department. It was empty, except for a saleswoman who was almost as tall as Stan and about his age and looked like she'd just stepped out of *Vogue*. She smiled a tight, formal smile at Marlyss, and raised an eyebrow at Stan.

"Can I, um, help you?"

Marlyss smiled politely at the woman and pulled Stan close. She put on a pout and turned on a thin Southern accent. "Mah daddy wants to buy me somethin' special." Marlyss looked at Stan and tugged on his arm.

Stan nodded.

"Well, what'll it be, babe?" Marlyss giggled. "Some lacy black panties or that see-through bra you been fussin' about?" Stan tried hard not to look embarrassed. Marlyss smiled at the woman and spoke in a stage whisper. "His eyes say it'll be the bra." She giggled again.

The woman looked as if she wanted to throw up. She raised her hand and pointed toward the back of the department, by the wall. Marlyss nodded. "Thank you."

Stan stood off to the side, trying his best to disappear, while Marlyss sifted through the bras. She caught Stan's eye, held up a bra in front of her, and winked. The garment, what there was of it, was made out of a diaphanous black material, trimmed in lace. Marlyss raised her hand to her cheek and motioned to Stan with her finger, smiling. When he got close, her eyes suddenly blazed with mischief. "Let's go . . . try it on."

She led him to a fitting area with four small stalls inside one large room. Stan waited against the outside wall while Marlyss went in. She came out a few seconds later and grabbed his arm. "Come in with me. There's no one in the other rooms." Stan looked around nervously. Marlyss didn't. "It's okay." She kissed him on the cheek. "Don't worry."

Stan took another quick look around, then followed Marlyss into the tiny stall and sat on a bench along the back wall. Marlyss locked the door, then stood in front of him, facing a mirror on the wall to the right. She unbuttoned her sweater. She wasn't wearing anything underneath, and her breasts swayed a bit as she took off the sweater and slipped on the bra. "It feels nice." She ran her hand over the material, and caught Stan's eye in the mirror. "What do you think?" She smiled softly. "I'll only wear it for you."

She turned to him—he was looking at her now—and motioned to him again with her finger. Stan shook his head, but she held out her hand and left it there until he took it. She pulled him to her, then spun slowly, tightly, into him, her back to his chest, facing the mirror. She smiled, and spoke in a whisper. "Come on, Stosh, tell me if you like me in it." She took his hands and placed them under her breasts, then put her hands on his and pulled his hands up slowly, running them gently over the thin, silky material until he took over the caress, fondling and squeezing her softly, until her nipples hardened. She leaned back, with her head on his shoulder. Her whisper grew quieter still. "That's nice, Stan."

She watched him in the mirror. Her eyes were half-closed; her lips curled into a satisfied grin. She let out a tiny gasp. "God, I love the way you touch me."

She began to move slowly against him, then stopped and turned to him. Her chest was already flush with excitement. She put her arms around his neck and pressed herself into him, her dark eyes on fire. "How's this for dangerous?"

Stan didn't make a move. He smiled—nervously. "Great, I can see it now: 'Homicide dick caught playing dress-up with chief's wife in changing room.' "

Marlyss giggled nervously, too, then shook her head. "We ain't done nothin' yet, lieutenant." She glanced around the cubicle. There was a four-inch space between the bottom of the door and the floor. She pulled off Stan's coat and grabbed her blouse and jeans and purse and blocked it off.

Stan watched her. "You've done this before?"

Marlyss put her finger to her lips and shook her head, then put her arms around Stan's neck and kissed him hard. "Now, Stan . . . right here. Hurry." She took his hands and placed them on her thighs, then pulled them up to her stomach. Stan broke away from her kiss and looked over her shoulder and watched their reflection in the mirror.

"Here?"

Her eyes glistened with urgency. "Yes. Here." She took his hands again and put them on her waist. Both their hands were shaking. He undid the button at her waist, unzipped her jeans and began pulling them down, then dropped to his knees and pulled off her shoes and jeans and panties, and spun her around. She placed her hands on the mirror and leaned forward. The reflection of her taut, tensed body was breathtaking. Stan stood, then watched the intense look on her face, eyes closed, teeth gritted tight, as he quickly entered her. She squeezed her eyes shut even tighter, and bit down on her bottom lip to keep from crying out, then placed her cheek against the cool glass and pushed back hard against him, forcing him deep—deeper, it seemed, than he'd ever been in any woman. Their movements were furtive and silent and breathless and, finally, as feverish as they could be in public.

When they were through, Marlyss turned and wrapped

her arms around Stan's neck. Her back was dotted with perspiration. His shirt was damp. She was still trembling and
struggling to catch her breath, but she kissed him hard
again, anyway, and hugged him the same way. She put her
lips against his ear. "Don't be afraid of me, Stan." She
paused, still gasping. Her voice was a whisper. "Please. I'm
ready to leave with you. Anywhere." She kissed his neck
once, twice, three times. "Let's just go."

Stan nodded. He held her tight and looked over her shoulder, into the mirror again, into his own eyes, then back into
hers. "We will. After the Cooper trial."

She kissed his neck. "Promise?"

Stan placed his hand on the small of her back and moved
it slowly up to her shoulder, then to her neck. He pulled her
head gently to his chest. "Yes."

They held each other for a few seconds, then Marlyss
pulled away. Stan stood behind her and watched her take off
the bra and put on her sweater and jeans. She smiled at him
in the mirror, her eyes gleaming. He had that urge again, the
skating-rink one, the one in the deli, to take her and hug her
hard, to grab hold of her spirit, her spunk, her happiness.
This time, he could. And this time he did.

Then he went to the door, retrieved his coat, and stepped
aside. Marlyss left, but he remained for a moment, looking
once more into the mirror. He was tempted to wipe
Marlyss's smudges and fingerprints from the glass. Why he
left them, he wasn't quite sure. But he did. It seemed like
the right thing to do.

◇ **26** ◇

Julius Cooper was waiting in an eight-by-eight interview
room on the fifth floor of the Wayne County jail. The lime-

green cinderblock room smelled like stale cigar smoke; it was empty except for a table and three chairs. Cooper was sitting in the chair farthest from the door. He was chewing on a toothpick.

"Goddamn thing makes me look like the fuckin' Great Pumpkin." He was dressed in a faded orange jumpsuit about four sizes too big, with "CITY JAIL" stenciled on the back in the dark blue. He looked at his feet. He had been issued shower thongs about two sizes too big. "An' look at this shit."

Randall Smithson looked up from the papers he was reading. Smithson was the best defense attorney in town, and did a lot of work for Dickie Broedinger and his boys. He glanced at Cooper's feet, then returned to his reading.

Cooper picked at the bandage with his left eye. The stitches were beginning to itch. Cooper's cheek had been opened to the bone during his arrest. "We gonna find out who did this?"

Smithson didn't waste his time on bullshit. He didn't look up, either. He laughed. "Nope."

"I was on my stomach when I got hit, man."

"We've got more important things to worry about."

"Motherfucker did me with . . ."

Smithson continued shaking his head.

"Fuck you, then."

Smithson smiled. "Okay. Fuck me, then."

Cooper took the toothpick out of his mouth. "Yea, you and Broedinger." His voice was rising. He put the toothpick back between his teeth. "Where the hell's he been, anyway?"

Smithson shrugged. He kept on reading.

"I been in here since Saturday mornin', and here it is Sunday night, Christmas goddamn Eve, and I ain't seen his faggot ass yet."

Smithson shrugged again. "He'll be in here."

"When?" Cooper stood and walked toward the attorney. "Goddamnit, when?"

"He said seven." Smithson still hadn't looked at Cooper.

"Fuck what he said."

Cooper was standing in front of Smithson now. He was

reaching down to grab the papers out of the lawyer's hand when Broedinger walked in. Dickie Broedinger was dressed completely in black—black slacks, black shirt, and black sports jacket—which made his pale complexion seem even paler. He smiled and spoke in a delicate voice. "You know Julius, they can hear you out there." He sat at the table. "And they're laughing."

Cooper sat down across from his boss. "I don't give a damn what they hear an' what they're doing." He sat forward in his chair and stared hard at Broedinger. "Where the hell you been?"

Broedinger reached into his pocket, pulled out a pack of cigarettes, and placed it on the table.

"No smokin' in here, man." Cooper reached for the pack.

Broedinger grabbed it first, took out a cigarette, and lit a match. "Let's remember who's in charge here, Julius."

Cooper grabbed the match and extinguished it between his thumb and middle finger, then he snatched the cigarette out of Broedinger's mouth, crushed it in his fist, and threw the shreds to the floor. His face screamed at Broedinger, but his voice was almost a whisper. "I said, where the hell you been?"

Broedinger looked at Smithson. Smithson shrugged. "I had a lot of things to do."

Cooper wrinkled his face into a grimace. "Man, I ain't talkin' about errands. I'm talking' about me being here in this goddamn stinkhole."

"I had to talk with Randall, here. I had to get someone to replace you. I . . ."

Cooper looked at Smithson, then turned back to Broedinger. "Replace me? What the fuck are you talking about? I been here before, and I been out fast. This shoulda been a one-night stand."

Broedinger looked down at the table. He took out another cigarette and tamped it on the face of his watch. Cooper didn't try to stop him this time. "It's not the same this time, Julius." Broedinger looked at Smithson. "Figure this place is clean?"

Smithson nodded. "I checked it out before you came. I think we're all right."

Cooper sat back in his chair. The look on Broedinger's face scared him. He forced a laugh. "What's all this stupid shit?"

Broedinger rubbed his nose, lit his cigarette, then took a long drag. "No shit here, Julius. This isn't going to be easy."

Cooper put his head back and looked up at the ceiling. It was spider-webbed with cracks and the paint was peeling. He didn't notice. "Don't be fuckin' with me, Dickie."

Broedinger shook his head. "You talk to him, Randall."

Smithson stood and walked to the far corner of the room. He leaned against the wall and folded his arms across his chest. "I've been talking to some of my friends in the prosecutor's office, Julius, and they say the cops got you dead, pardon the expression."

Cooper sniffed. "Says?"

"Don't worry who says, Julius. The word is they're just waiting on the ballistics test to write you a life sentence."

Cooper laughed nervously. "My ass." He spit his toothpick onto the floor and took another from his breast pocket and began chewing on it.

"They say they have the murder weapon."

Cooper laughed again. He fingered the empty earring holes in his left earlobe. The guards had confiscated his jewelry when he was booked.

"They say that fancy six-shooter of yours is gonna match the slug fragments found at the scene . . ."

"My six-shooter." It was a statement, not a question. Cooper stared at Smithson for about three seconds, then broke into a huge grin. Then he started laughing, loud and hard. There was no gallows echo to his guffaw. Broedinger and Smithson looked at each other.

"It seems, Randall, like you said something funny." Broedinger was beginning to smile, too.

Cooper slapped the table. "That gun—my ass." Broedinger was smiling hard now. Even Smithson was beginning to grin.

Cooper stood and lowered his voice to a whisper. "Man, I lost that piece weeks ago—*weeks.*"

Broedinger began to nod. He was still smiling. "Says who?"

Cooper began moving around the room. "Says me, man."

Broedinger kept nodding, but his smile was fading. He looked at Smithson. "Says him." Smithson shrugged.

Cooper caught their glance. "Listen to me, goddamnit." He clenched his fists. "I was parked on the street this night and some big motherfucker sneaks up on me, pulls his piece, and cops ol' Betsy. Guy was dressed like some damn night stalker or somethin'. I ain't had the pistol ever since." Cooper stopped in the corner across from Smithson, turned toward the table, and leaned against the wall. He was breathing hard.

Smithson put his hand to his lips, then pointed to Cooper. "Who?"

"Who what?"

Cooper was still being too loud. Smithson put his finger to his lips again. "Who's going to corroborate your story?"

"Ain't no story."

Smithson nodded. "It doesn't matter whether it's a story or the truth."

Cooper gritted his teeth. "It's ... the ... truth."

Smithson shook his head. "Not good enough, Julius."

"Fuck you. Get me someone else, Dickie."

Smithson waved for Cooper to be quiet. He was completely unperturbed. "When the tests come back matching the slug pieces from the kid's head to your gun—and you better figure they're going to—you're going to what? Waltz up the judge and jury and tell them you couldn't have killed Rickey Jefferson because you lost your gun?"

"Not lost. It was stolen." Cooper sneered at Smithson. "And I ain't gonna say a goddamn thing. You are—or ..."

Smithson looked at Broedinger. "We need more, Richard."

Broedinger nodded. He began to say something, then stopped. No one spoke for thirty seconds.

Cooper broke the silence. "There is more." His voice was low, cold, a bit nervous.

"Like?" Broedinger looked up.

"Like there was a witness."

"To what?"

"The robbery." Cooper nodded. "I was with ... some-one."

Broedinger smiled. He took a deep drag on his cigarette, exhaled, then waved the smoke away. "Who?"

Cooper stared at Broedinger. Five seconds passed, then ten, then twenty.

"Who, Julius? Come on."

"Wendy."

"Who?"

"Your wife."

Broedinger shook his head and laughed. "Not a bad concept, but it'll never work, Julius."

Cooper flew out of the corner like he was shot from a catapult. "It's no fucking concept, Dickie."

Smithson walked to the table, "Easy, Julius."

"Fuck him."

"Let's hear it."

Cooper sat down and stared at Broedinger. Broedinger puffed on his cigarette and looked right through Julius. "Mrs. B's been chasin' my ass for years. So this one night last summer she calls me, like she does all the time, and tells me to meet her. I usually just say no, because I don't need no forty-year-old play. But she says Mr. B is out of town and she needs some stuff for her girls at the joint, and we meet and before I know it, she's on me. A few minutes later, this asshole pulls open the door, says a few motherfucks for show, takes my piece, and says, 'Don't fuck with the Shooter.' Somethin' like that, somethin' about Shooter. Then I get the hell outta there."

"Wendy." Smithson's voice was low.

Cooper's wasn't. "She's still alive, ain't she?"

Smithson nodded. "This gives us a chance, Richard."

Cooper nodded, too. "Told you."

Broedinger didn't move, didn't say anything. He sat staring at the tabletop for a few seconds, then dropped his cigarette to the floor, crushed it, gathered his cigarettes and matches, stood, put on his coat, and started for the door.

Cooper grabbed him by the arm. "Man, it wasn't me. It was her."

Broedinger stopped and flung Cooper's hand away with his right hand, then straightened his coat, and with a quick, powerful move, slapped Cooper hard with his left. Then he composed himself, looked down at Cooper, smiled, and shook his head. Then he walked out.

◇ **27** ◇

Niqui's All-Star Revue—Girls! Girls! Girls!—was shoehorned between a waterbed warehouse and an auto-parts store on Eight Mile, just east of the state fairgrounds. Before Dickie and Wendy Broedinger had taken over Niqui's, it was called Silk 'n Satin, and before that, Ginny's Girls, and before that, back in the '50s, simply, The Roxy. Back then, The Roxy was a three-and-a-half-star night club. Today, Niqui's was simply a thin cut above the other sordid stops on the fading skin-show circuit—"a cut above" meaning that Wendy Broedinger had a strict hiring policy: "No C-scars, stretch marks, or tattoos." Niqui's did an okay business. It gave Wendy Broedinger something to do.

The place had a decent-sized main room, with a runway that bisected the bar, and four tiny rooms in back where girls performed behind Plexiglas windows for private audiences. Wendy's "little ladies," as she called them, were paid about four hundred dollars a week, in cash or drugs. Most took half and half. Some of the best performances came from amateurs working off their dope debts to Broedinger. Wendy Broedinger called the amateur shows Girl-Next-Door Nights. Tonight was one of those nights. The parking lot was packed when Dickie Broedinger arrived.

Dickie Broedinger was an extremely cautious driver. It usually took him about twenty minutes to get to Niqui's from downtown; tonight, despite the slippery, slushy streets, he made the trip in twelve. He pulled his navy Mercedes to the back door of the club, got out, handed his keys to the security guard, and hustled in. The back hallway, where the private rooms were located, was dark. It smelled of cheap perfume and sweat and strong, musky, female odor. Two women were huddled in the shadows in a corner near the door, waiting to go on stage. The brunette looked stoned. The blonde looked pretty spacey, too. Broedinger squinted through the darkness at the women. He grabbed the blonde.

"Where's Wendy?" He had to shout over the rockabilly music rolling in from the main room.

The woman stared at him, then shrugged. "Who knows?" Broedinger eased closer. The woman was harsh-looking, but reasonably attractive. Good body. Older. Maybe thirty. She apparently had no idea who he was. She pulled her arm away. "Try her office."

Wendy Broedinger's office was the third of five rooms along the outside wall—two rooms for private shows, Wendy's office, then two more private rooms. The door to Wendy's office was closed. Broedinger turned the knob slowly and eased the door open. Wendy was sitting behind her desk, dressed in tight jeans and a white, deep-cut blouse. A redhead, who couldn't have been more than nineteen or twenty, was stripping in front of her. The girl was taking off her bra when Broedinger closed the door behind him. "Audition's over, honey." The girl looked at Broedinger and covered her chest, then looked at Wendy. Her face turned scarlet.

Wendy looked at her husband, nodded, and made a note on the scratch pad in front of her. "It's all right." The girl grabbed her clothes and ran out of the room.

Wendy sat forward on her chair, still looking at her notes. "I hope you didn't spook her." She tried to sound stern.

Dickie Broedinger shook his head. Stern hadn't worked. It couldn't hide the tiny, nervous flutter in Wendy's voice. He knew right then that his wife knew why he was there—and that Cooper had been telling the truth. He nodded toward the door. "She did look a little concerned."

Wendy Broedinger kept up the small talk. "She owes us three grand, Richard. With that body, she can make up more than that." She continued to scribble on the pad. "She's even willing to do a little work on the side."

Dickie Broedinger put his hat and coat on a chair. "Ah, yes, the moonlighting part." He ran his hand through his thinning, crewcut hair and reached into his shirt pocket for his cigarettes. Wendy was straightening her desk. He walked across the room and flicked the switch on a small control panel built into the west wall. Four black-and-white TVs flashed on. The screens, fed by wall-mounted cameras, monitored the four private rooms, mainly for the safety of the girls. There was action in one of the rooms; the other three were empty.

Broedinger pointed to the picture from Room One. "I met blondie in the hallway."

Wendy looked up at the screen, then back down at her desk, avoiding her husband's eyes. "She puts in an honest day's work."

Dickie Broedinger watched her dance. "Seems to enjoy it."

"I don't know about that." Wendy Broedinger looked at the screen again. "Believe it or not, she works at a day-care center. She just got divorced. Needs the extra money—real bad."

Dickie Broedinger nodded, walked over to a deep red plastic couch, and sat down. The room was dusty and smelled like cedar air freshener. The floor, covered by a dingy Oriental rug, vibrated to the pulsating bass of the music in the main room. Broedinger lit a cigarette, then leaned forward with his elbows on his thighs. "Speaking of moonlighting"—his voice was politely conversational—"tell me about the night our friend lost his gun."

Wendy didn't look up. She continued writing. "Who?"

"Julius."

Wendy stopped, but just for the briefest of moments. She still didn't look up. "I don't know what you're talking about, Richard."

Dickie Broedinger laughed. He was looking at the TV across the room, but not watching it. "Yes, you do."

Wendy Broedinger said nothing.

"Did you fuck him?" Dickie Broedinger's voice was still controlled, even. He still hadn't looked at his wife.

Nothing.

He stood, walked across the room and sat on the corner of her desk, and leaned toward her. "Maybe it was difficult for you to hear me from way over there." His voice was ice cold now.

Still nothing.

He took a deep drag on his cigarette, flicked the ashes on the floor, then rested his arm on his knee. The red-hot tip of the cigarette was about a half-inch from Wendy's neck. She could feel the heat. "Now, let's start over again. That night"—she still had the pen in her hand, but she wasn't writing. She was staring at the blotter on her desk— "Did you fuck him?"

Her eyes were lit with fear. She looked up and stared into his, but she still said nothing, even when she felt the tip of the cigarette sear her skin. She pulled back, whimpered, and gritted her teeth in pain.

Dickie Broedinger pulled the cigarette back, took a deep drag on it, then aimed it at her neck again. "Was it the first time?"

Nothing. She was breathing harder. He nodded. This time he grabbed her hair, then pushed the cigarette in hard and held it there longer. The first burn was already beginning to blister. She could smell the burned flesh from the second. She stuffed her hand into her mouth and bit down hard, stifling a scream.

"That night—he said you called him."

Nothing still. He moved the cigarette close a third time. She closed her eyes tight. Dickie Broedinger pulled the cigarette back, let her go, then stood and walked to the corner of the room. "He said"—he stood for a second alongside the bookcase, then reached out, picked up a brass candlestick, looked at it, then threw it at the Room One monitor—"you goddamn called *him*." The blonde disappeared in a shower of glass. He was breathing hard now, and shouting. "I don't need this—Cooper and you, this Shooter shit—heard of him?—whoever in the hell he is." Broedinger took the cigarette out of his mouth and threw it on the floor. "You know what's going to happen, don't you?"

Wendy Broedinger had her head down, her eyes closed, and her hand across her neck.

He walked to his wife, grabbed her by the hair again, and lifted her head. He put his face into hers, his breath stinking of cigarette smoke. His voice was terrifyingly calm now. "They're going to call you to the witness stand and have you testify that you were screwing Cooper when his gun was stolen." He shook his head, then hers. "And you know what?" He tugged harder on her hair. "No one's going to listen to your story and figure Cooper's innocent. No, his ass is long gone, no matter what. What everyone's going to hear is that this street-fuck nigger was servicing my wife. In my car. Behind my back." He paused. "Now, that's bad enough." He paused. "You know what's worse?"

She didn't move. Couldn't.

"Everyone's going to be laughing at me." He shook his head again. He put his mouth next to her ear and lowered his voice to a whisper. "That's not too good for this kind of business, is it?" He shook his wife's head again. "Now, what do you suggest?"

Her body was trembling. She was crying. She cleared her throat and caught her breath, her voice raspy. "That I . . . lie."

"Good." Dickie Broedinger released her hair. "Very good. You will lie. Perfect."

The office door suddenly swung open. It was the blonde from Room One. Dickie Broedinger looked at her and waved her away. "Not now."

"This'll only take . . ."

He walked over to her, a thick smile on his face. "Excuse me, but are you hard of hearing?"

The blonde was dressed only in a G-string. She put her hands on her hips and twisted her face into a sarcastic grin. "No."

Dickie Broedinger put his face very close to hers. She was still sweating. He could feel her heat. "Then please listen up, because I don't have time to repeat this." His smile widened. "If you don't leave right now, I'm going to push your face through the fucking wall." The smile disappeared. "Understand?"

She removed her hands from her hips, turned, and left the room.

Dickie Broedinger turned back to his wife, went to the desk again and sat down, wiped the sweat from his forehead, and pulled a notebook out of his pocket. He fumbled through the pages, then picked up the phone and began dialing. "You'll lie." He chuckled, grabbed his pack of du Mauriers, then pulled a cigarette out with his lips. "Brilliant idea, my dear." He ran his fingers under her chin, then squeezed it hard. "Too bad you weren't smart enough to have someone else scratch your itch." A woman answered his call. Broedinger let go of Wendy's chin, sucked hard on his cigarette, then realized it wasn't lit. "Frank Sims, please." He threw the cigarette on the desk.

A few seconds later, a voice came on the phone. "Sims."

Dickie Broedinger snuck a deep breath, trying to rinse the hint of panic from his voice, then slapped another smile across his face. "We've never met face-to-face, Chief Sims, but I think I might have some important information for you on this Rickey Jefferson case."

Frank didn't even ask who he was talking to. "I doubt it."

Broedinger's conversational tone didn't change. "I don't." He smiled at Wendy. "I've got someone right here with me who will testify that some clown who calls himself the Shooter, or something like that, stole Julius Cooper's gun off him long before the kid was killed."

"So?"

Broedinger paused. "I'm talking about that Fancy Dan six-shooter you're going to use to put Julius Cooper away. Cooper didn't have it the night the boy was murdered. He hasn't had it for at least three months. If that gun killed the boy, Cooper didn't."

Frank didn't reply for a few seconds. "I don't know what gun you're talking about."

"Right." Broedinger nodded.

"Who is this?"

That was it, there it was. Dickie Broedinger was waiting for the tiniest crack in Frank's calm. He began to smile. He was close. "I think the introductions can wait until we meet."

"That may be awhile."

Broedinger shook his head. "I doubt that very much."

Frank paused.

Broedinger held his breath.

"Look, I'm willing to talk to anyone who has information on the Jefferson shooting . . ."

Broedinger nodded. His smile widened. He had won. "Fine. Two hours."

". . . in my office—tomorrow."

Broedinger laughed, loud. "Nope."

Frank paused. He waited for Broedinger to break the silence. He needed time—seconds, minutes—to think. Broedinger didn't bite. Frank shook his head. "I can't get anywhere in two hours, not on Christmas Eve."

"Suit yourself."

Frank rubbed his forehead again. "Where?"

"There's an old moving company on Lakeview, just off Jefferson. Three-story brick building. KEEP OUT sign on the door. The light will be on in . . ."

Frank shook his head. The area was too chancy, too dark, and too close. "No way." He thought for a second. "Okay—the truck stop on 280, just across the Ohio line—Stony Ridge."

Broedinger looked at his watch. "That's some drive." Frank said nothing. Broedinger was still looking at his watch. "All right. Ten-fifteen. Don't keep me waiting, Frank." He paused. "And come alone."

Broedinger hung up, then hopped down from the desk. He walked to the chair and grabbed his coat and hat, then studied the three operating TVs. All three rooms were empty. He flicked off the monitors. "Let's go, Wendy, my dear. We have an appointment to keep."

Wendy locked her desk, then walked to the closet and got her coat. Dickie Broedinger came over and helped her put it on. "Was he any good?"

She was staring at the floor. She shook her head.

"Shame." He shook his, too. "A real shame." He slid his arms around her waist and squeezed her. "At the very least, it should have been good." Dickie Broedinger kissed his wife softly on the cheek. "No, it should have been better." He chuckled. "For what it's going to cost you, it should have been the experience of a lifetime." He ran his hand gently through her hair. "Do you know what I mean, my dear?"

She did.

The only sounds in Frank's car were breathing and the steady squeak of the windshield wipers. The quiet was almost eerie, not that Frank noticed. He was too busy trying to stay on the snow-covered highway. He had run into a major squall about fifteen miles up the road and now the lane markings were obliterated and the gusty wind was jabbing hard at his car, making it feel as though he were driving on skates. It was dark as pitch, and everything in his headlights' beam was white. He was going only about twenty. At least he wasn't far from the truck stop. The sign a few minutes ago said two miles. He wiped the sweat from his forehead and told himself to stay calm. He took a deep breath and glanced down at the steering wheel. His knuckles were white. He relaxed his grip and flexed his fingers. They were stiff. No accidents tonight. Couldn't afford any. Not out here. Everything had to be slow, steady, sure, even though he was already fifteen minutes late.

He looked out the right side of the windshield. The lights from the truck stop suddenly bloomed out of the darkness. He must have missed a sign; he almost missed the turnoff. He swore, then held his breath as he eased onto the exit ramp. The car swerved to the right, then came back. He was okay.

The road curved to the right, alongside a corn field, then took a sharp right turn into the truck stop. Frank pulled to the side of the lot and killed his lights. He was behind the restaurant. He held his breath and looked around. The place was busy, too busy for this kind of meeting. He shook his head. Must be the holiday travelers—and the weather. All the gas pumps and diesel stations were being used. He pulled ahead at a crawl, past rows and rows of idling semis, around the front of the restaurant. The parking lot there was filled with cars. People were rushing to and from the building. Those heading toward their vehicles were leaning into the wind. Those heading out of them were being pushed ahead. The snow was still coming down wet and thick.

Frank wasn't sure what he was looking for, but he figured he'd recognize it when he saw it. He'd completed one circuit around the plaza when he noticed a woman walking a small dog in the field to his left. No, it was a man. Wasn't it? He stopped the car. He was at the outskirts of the complex now. He looked to his right—cars and trucks, the restaurant, and service station. He looked to the left—the field. He gazed straight ahead—nothing—then turned to his right again. A dark luxury sedan was pulled alongside the grass near the back border of the lot, about one hundred feet away. No lights, but maybe a stead ribbon of exhaust. Frank couldn't tell for sure. In daylight or better weather he would have spotted the car much sooner. It might even have been there the first go-round. The figure with the dog was about twenty-five feet in front of Frank's car now and appeared to look at him, before heading toward the other car.

Frank was wearing jeans, a sweatshirt, sneakers, a handgun in a shoulder harness under his winter overcoat, a seven-shot Derringer up his sleeve, a bullet-proof vest, and a tight, tired, sullen look. He felt for both his weapons, then yanked up the collar on his overcoat. He pulled ahead, slowly, until he was about ten yards behind the car. Then he stopped—and waited. The man with the dog walked past the car and toward the restaurant. As soon as the man neared the building, the driver's door on the car ahead opened and someone got out. It was hard to tell much about the figure in the darkness, and Frank didn't spend much time trying. He got out, too. The men got within five feet of each other, then stopped. Frank couldn't see the man's face. It was too dark. All he could see was a cigarette. The wind whipped between them. It was still nastier than hell out.

"I figured you're armed, Chief Sims." It was the voice from the phone. "I also figure you've thought about what you're going to do here and that you came to the correct conclusion—that there's no need for anything rash." The man tugged his coat tighter. "I suppose you could kill me and this witness of mine, but I think that whole thing would eventually get rather messy." The man eased closer to Frank and took a long drag on his cigarette. Frank finally caught a glimpse of his face in the reddish glow. Now he knew. He hadn't recognized Broedinger's voice, but he knew his face. "And I think you're a lot like me, Frank—neatness counts."

Frank looked around. The man with the dog was gone. Frank saw nothing that looked too suspicious, though it would have been easy for Broedinger to stash a few men somewhere here. Frank wondered for a second about the man with the dog. He had no idea where he was.

Broedinger motioned to his car. "Shall we go inside?"

Frank shook his head. "This is just fine."

Broedinger shrugged and stuffed a hand deep into his overcoat pocket. "Have it your way." He tossed his cigarette to the ground, then pulled out a pack, got another cigarette and struggled to light it. It took about four clicks of his lighter before he finally got it smoldering. He took a deep drag, then coughed.

Frank took another look around, then glared at Broedinger. "I don't have all night."

Broedinger grinned, cockily, nodded, laughed, then rubbed his hands together. He wasn't wearing gloves. The cigarette dangled from his lips. He turned and headed toward his car and motioned for Frank to follow. He did, slowly. Broedinger spun around and began walking backward. "You know this Shooter person?"

Frank didn't answer."

"That a no?"

Still nothing.

Broedinger shrugged. "If it is, I think you're probably lying." He was at the passenger door. "But no matter—not yet, anyway." Broedinger yanked open the door. Wendy was sitting in the passenger seat, staring straight ahead. Broedinger reached in, grabbed her chin roughly and twisted her face toward Frank. Her eyes were swollen, her hair was a mess of yellow, and her right cheek was streaked red. She had a pair of dark spots—moles, Frank thought, maybe beauty marks—on the left side of her neck. Broedinger smiled. "This is my wife, Wendy. She was with

Julius Cooper when this Shooter character stole the, um, murder weapon." He shook his head. "Wendy, here, is not feeling too well tonight. She's a little upset. Just before we came, she had a little accident." Broedinger twisted her head even further to the right. Frank recognized the marks now; they weren't cosmetic. Broedinger let her go and shut the door.

"What's the point?"

Broedinger shook his head and frowned at Frank as though he were a father disciplining an impudent child. "Don't play dumb, here, Frank. It's too fucking cold." He smiled. "Cooper didn't use that gun on the kid. You know that, Cooper knows that, I know that, and *she* can testify to it. And I think that possibility might put a crimp in your plans to frame my boy."

Frank studied Broedinger's face. He saw no sign of worry or fear—or bluff. Broedinger knew what Frank was looking for. He clapped him on the shoulder as though he appreciated the effort. "Don't worry, Frank. I'm here to bury Julius Caesar Cooper, not save him." He laughed.

Frank didn't; he backed away.

"He's yours." Broedinger smiled and opened his arms wide. "Yours—all yours. You're the hero. You get to solve the Jefferson case and get Public Enemy Number One off the street. Two for one. Quite the deal." Broedinger paused. "This is possible." He raised his eyebrows and nodded.

Frank didn't answer.

Broedinger's grin suddenly faded. "Cooper was my best man. The best field man in the city, maybe the Midwest. I'm losing thousands of dollars a day with him gone, and I'm going to continue to take big losses until I find someone to take his place." He scratched his forehead. "I can make most of my losses up in due time." He paused, and took a drag on his cigarette. It had gone out. He flipped the butt to the ground, reached inside his coat for his pack, and lit another one. "And I will, quite quickly. Especially if I move my operation."

Broedinger was studying Frank's face now. He was the one looking for a reaction. There was none. "I've been wanting to move to the west side for a while. The east side is losing its appeal. I have a nice network set up, but there's too many splinter groups now. It gets tiring. Beside, my best sunburn customers get spooked driving down those deserted streets. What I need is . . ."

Frank shook his head.

Broedinger looked at him. "You're pretty quick on the trigger for a man who could lose really big, Frank." Broedinger stopped and tried to temper his impatience. He was aware of the next edge to his voice, and he didn't want to get into a pissing contest. "Anyway, I don't need protection, exactly." He smiled. "Was that the word you were afraid of?" He chuckled. "I'm sorry. No, what I need is . . . a honeymoon period."

Frank shifted his feet.

"You call off the boys in the designated area on the west side—say, a four-block area for starters—and keep me informed when you've got to do something for show." He nodded. "See, I'm willing to make a few sacrifices. I want this to work for everybody. I might even surrender a few kids now and then to make you look good." He motioned behind him with his head. "Anyway, we reach some sort of agreement, Frank, and lovely Wendy here doesn't sing the wrong, sad song when she's called to testify." He lowered his voice to a whisper. "She might even disappear."

"*If* she's called to testify."

Broedinger recognized the look in Frank's eye. He shook his head. "Like I said before, Frank, don't fuck with me and don't play me for the fool. She'll be called to testify."

Frank shrugged. "Who's going to believe her?"

Broedinger smiled. "That's your gamble, Frank, not mine." He took a drag on his cigarette.

"This isn't good publicity for you."

"I know." Broedinger nodded. "It'll hurt me in the short run, but certainly not as much as it's going to hurt you if you can't pull off this once-in-a-lifetime double-play."

Frank nodded. "That it?"

Broedinger nodded back. "Almost."

"What's left?"

"You answer."

Frank shook his head. "Tomorrow."

Broedinger laughed and shook his right back. "No, no, no." He paused. "Now, Frank." His smile faded. "Now."

Frank looked over Broedinger's shoulder. The moon was out now and the snow had tapered off to a soft flurry. The wind had died down, too. The truck stop had begun to empty out.

Broedinger smiled. "Cooper's not going to walk, Frank, not if we play square with each other. You know that."

Frank stared at Broedinger. Then he nodded. Broedinger smiled and held out his hand. Frank ignored it and turned toward his car.

"Mr. Shooter?"

Frank heard the question but didn't stop.

"Maybe we can talk about him at some later date?" Broedinger began retreating toward his car, then stopped. "Frank?" He smiled. "Merry Christmas."

The meeting had lasted only about seven minutes. Frank shivered as he sat in his car. He turned the heater on high, rubbed his eyes, then looked at Shooter. Frank exhaled long and low. "We're still okay."

"So?"

"Cooper's squeeze, the night you copped the gun, was Dickie Broedinger's old lady."

"No shit—the painted-up blonde?" Shooter rubbed his head.

"Yep."

"I come up?"

"A couple times."

"Not so bad."

Frank nodded. "It could have been worse."

"So, do we add Broedinger to the list?"

Frank nodded again. "At the top."

"When?"

"We'll find the right time."

"Now?" Shooter nodded toward Broedinger's car. It was still sitting there.

Frank shook his head. Broedinger was right—too messy. "I wish."

"What about Mrs. B?"

Frank started his car. He shook his head. "I got the distinct impression she was already spoken for."

Frank put the car in drive and headed for the highway. "Colbane and Broedinger—our list is growing."

Frank nodded. "We can handle it." But for the first time in days, he wasn't feeling so confident. "We have to."

◇ **28** ◇

Stan shivered, rolled to the edge of the bed, and reached to the floor for the covers he'd thrown off during the night. He wrapped himself in a wool blanket, put his head under his pillow, and peeked at the clock radio on the nightstand. It was 5:10. There was no reason to get up at 5:10—or 6:10, 7:10, 8:10, or even 9:10, for that matter. He had no one to see, no place to go. Marlyss was spending the day entertaining with Frank, and Jenny and Petey—Stan still hadn't talked to Jenny since standing her up at the Clown Café.

Stan closed his eyes, then opened them again. It was 5:11. He tried once more. They wouldn't stay closed—5:12. He rubbed his neck, and reached for the radio and switched it on. The dial was set to WNUZ, an all-news talk station. But even Double-u-News, as it called itself, was playing Christmas carols this morning. Stan switched off "O Holy Night" in mid-chorus and rolled out of bed, walked to the window and peeked through the blinds. Everything glistened, even in the early-morning darkness. Four inches of powdery snow had fallen during the night. Christmas morning looked wispy and wintry, just like it was supposed to look. The scene made Stan want to smile, but it was too much of an effort.

He left the window, shuffled into the bathroom, and stared sleepily into the mirror. He saw the same thing that he had seen yesterday and the day before and the day before that—his father. He'd been prepared for the inevitability. He just hadn't thought it would happen so soon. He wondered for a moment if Laddy had ever stood before a mirror studying his own reflection, and he wondered who Laddy'd seen.

He dressed slowly, and, after eating a bowl of cereal and a piece of stale coffeecake, and washing both down with a glass of luke-warm pineapple juice, decided to drive to headquarters and do some paperwork. At least he would have some company there. It was 6:34.

The street outside Stan's place was deserted. Smoke rose straight into the dark blue sky from just about every chimney on the block. Most families were still sleeping. As Stan drove slowly down the street, he saw Santa Claus step out of a station wagon and hurry into a neighbor's home. Stan remembered the time he'd played Santa for the police union's Christmas bash. Jenny had been Mrs. Claus. They'd made a great pair, at least that night. The union had asked them to do it again the next year, but by the time Christmas had rolled around, he and Jenny were separated, so Stan had gone alone. He wasn't as jolly then, and everyone knew why. Stan reached for the radio, then stopped. He would drive downtown in silence. He didn't want to hear Christmas music right now.

The homicide offices were quiet. If New Year's Eve was a cop's nightmare, with people getting drunk, arguing, and shooting each other, Christmas Eve wasn't far behind. Any December twenty-fourth could turn police headquarters, homicide especially, upside down and inside out. Every December, the *Free Press* and *News* ran stories about holiday violence on frustration and holiday tensions. Stan figured all the bloodshed had more to do with booze. By this time of the morning, though, everyone who'd had a few too many was either sleeping off a drunk or had already been shot. The pace had slowed. Pisarcawitcz had his feet on his desk and was reading a book.

"*Connie Does It All,* Stoshie." The desk sergeant looked up and laughed. "Real literature."

Stan nodded and looked around for the donuts. There weren't any.

"Sorry, Stosh some idiot threw up on 'em." Pisarcawitcz went back to his book. "A real fuckin' nut case. Shot his wife in the head 'cause she spent all his money on some shit for the kids, who weren't even his—or so he said. We booked him on murder ... and destroying police property." Pisarcawitcz chuckled, then pulled his feet off the desk and paged quickly through his book. "Here, read this. This is unbelievable. You being an ex-jock would appreciate this more than the normal dick-face." A wide smile lit up his stubble-dotted jaw. "I didn't think a broad could do this with ..."

Pisarcawitcz held out the book, but Stan waved it away. "I just went to confession last night."

The desk sergeant laughed. "You're a fuckin' wimp."

Stan smiled, nodded, shrugged, and headed out of the office and toward his squad room.

Pisarcawitcz went back to his reading. "An' don't wake Dawlson."

Stan didn't. Pete was already awake when he got to the room. He was sitting at his desk making notes on a yellow legal pad. His clothes were rumpled again, and his hair was poking out every which way, but his eyes were clear. He seemed startled by Stan's arrival, but the surprise quickly faded. "This is not place to be on a bright Christmas a.m., Stanley."

Stan nodded. "Okay, so what are you doing here?"

Dawlson shrugged. "Homework. Couldn't sleep. Just getting a head start on Tuesday's hearing."

Stan took off his coat and tossed it onto the couch. "New stuff?" He went to the coffeemaker and finished off the pot—half a cup. The coffee was lukewarm, and strong, bitter. Stan drained his cup in two gulps, then shook his head.

"Ballistics, Stoshie. Got the report a few minutes ago. Boys been working overtime. I was going to wait until eight to call you." Dawlson looked at his watch. "Seven? What the hell are you doing up this early?"

"Santa woke me trying to get up the chimney."

"You give his fat ass a kick for me?"

Stan chuckled. "What'd the report say?"

"It said Cooper's a goner. Perfect match, Stosheroo." Dawlson smiled. "Merry fucking Christmas, Julius Caesar Cooper."

Stan walked to Dawlson's desk. Peter handed him the report. It was a single page.

"Game, set, match, Stosh. We better start planning the victory party."

Stan shrugged. "Ballistics usually aren't enough to convict."

Dawlson went back to his writing. He didn't look up. "Bah, humbug, to you, too, Mr. Scrooge. Thirty-one is a pretty odd caliber, Stosho. And this is a high-profile case."

Stan nodded. "And the defendant is Cooper."

"And . . . bingo." Dawlson tapped his pencil on the desk. Stan nodded. "Boys up here are going to love this."

Dawlson nodded, too. "I do think it's party time, Stosh."

Stan put the report on Dawlson's desk and looked over his partner's shoulder. Pete had a thick file open before him. "What's that?"

Dawlson sat back and ran a hand through his hair. "Everything we got on Coop's boss, Dickie Broedinger. For the post-mortem. I figure we might be able to get Cooper to sing a little Christmas carol—and maybe, maybe, even nail Broedinger." Dawlson shrugged. "Actually, it's the boss's idea. Frank suggested it when I called with the ballistics report."

"Wishful thinking."

"The only kind in this business, Stosh."

Stan rubbed his eyes. "I'm running low."

Dawlson still hadn't looked up. "It'll come back."

Stan went to his desk and sat down. "So, what's the plan?"

Dawlson was back to work. "No plan, yet. I'm just making a list—and checking it twice—of Broedinger's addresses, known hangouts, joints, residences. Simple shit."

Stan got up and walked to the coffee maker. "More coffee?"

Dawlson shook his head. "I'm gone in a few minutes. Got to go home, maybe catch a little shuteye and clean up."

"Big Christmas doings?"

Dawlson looked up and smiled. "Mary Stimic invited me over for dinner."

Stan smiled back. He was surprised—then again, he wasn't. Mary knew how to work a story, even on Christmas Day. "You got some sort of trade agreement with her?"

Dawlson shook his head and smiled. "Not me, Stosh."

Stan nodded. "Right." He winked at Pete. "What? You got a thing for her?"

Pete laughed. "She's a looker, Stan, but she's not my type." He looked back down at his paperwork. "Believe it or not, Stoshie, we're going to church. The cathedral service."

Stan laughed. "You?"

Dawlson feigned a hurt look. "My father was a preacher."

Stan stopped grinning. "You kidding?"

Dawlson laughed. "Yep. How about you?"

Stan shook his head. "Nothin' doin'. Christmas Day'll be like any other."

Peter looked up again. "Come over to Mary's."

"Naw. That's okay. I got stuff to do here and at home."

Dawlson nodded. "Right, sure. Come on."

"Nope, three's a crowd."

Dawlson began cleaning up the papers on his desk. "I'm tellin' you Stosh-man, this is gonna be Beaver Cleaver meets Shirley Temple." He checked his watch, hurried for his coat, picked up his papers and headed for the door. "There's plenty of room for Dennis the Menace."

Stan shook his head. "You taking the file on Broedinger?"

Dawlson nodded. "I need some good reading for the can."

Stan gave his partner a semistern look. About a month ago, Stan had been named records liaison officer, which was a sentence, not an honor. It meant that he was the fall guy for the Records Department when one of the detectives screwed up and misplaced a homicide folder. The records officer always caught a lot of crap. "You sign it out?"

Dawlson stopped, and glanced at his watch again. "You're takin' this job too seriously, Stosh. I was records officer here for three years and no one ever knew." He winked at Stan. "I'll get it tomorrow, mom. You just quit worryin' about cop stuff, now, and go find yourself some holiday cheer." He held out his hand. "Merry Christmas, pal."

Stan smiled and shook Pete's hand. His partner had a good solid grip. He nodded to his friend, then sat at his desk. The room was too quiet and too empty now. Stan pulled out his file on the Jefferson shooting and reviewed his notes. Dawlson was right. With the ballistics report, Cooper's conviction was a grand slam, and a rather spectacular one. Stan closed the file and stared at the wall. Church. He chuckled at the thought. But it really wasn't such a bad idea. He hadn't been inside a church since he'd split with Jenny. He had nothing else to do.

He got his coat and was headed out the door when the phone rang on Dawlson's desk. Stan answered it. Wrong number. A woman was trying to reach the pharmacist at some place called Banger's Drugs. She sounded embarrassed when Stan told her that she had reached the Detroit homicide department, but she was polite. She wished Stan a Merry Christmas before she hung up. It made him smile.

Stan put down the phone and turned to leave when he noticed that the top drawer of Pete's desk was open a couple of inches. He saw what looked like a manila envelope with the bold, black letters IA stamped on it. Stan slid open the drawer. The I and A were only part of the envelope's inscription. The entire marking read: CONFIDENTIAL: IA ONLY. A name, Alfred Tony McGinnity, was written in a thick, felt-tipped pen in the upper left-hand corner. Stan looked at the file, then at his watch. If he hurried, he could make the 8:15 mass at St. Kate's. A little snooping through McGinnity's file could wait a few hours. Stan closed the drawer. He felt a little better now. Mass, then McGinnity. Perhaps Christmas Day wouldn't be a total waste.

◇ 29 ◇

St. Kate's was a tiny, threadbare parish on the far east side that drew churchgoers from the entire metro area to its single simple Sunday service. The worshippers were rich and poor, white, black, brown, red, and yellow. Some, more than a few, were non-Catholic. It was a people's parish. A priest presided over the Mass, which was celebrated on a schoolhouse lunch table and held on a worn, creaky wooden basketball floor in a dingy gym. But more often than not, members of the lay community gave the sermons, which really weren't sermons at all. Three Sundays earlier, a young nun had told about her experiences as a nurse at an AIDS hospice. A few Sundays before that, the principal of a lower east side elementary school had talked about her students, most of whom lived in poor, drug-infested neighborhoods. The previous summer, a police officer who had shot and killed a teenage robbery suspect had spoken about violence and being a cop and trying to deal with the death of a kid he had killed. Some of the speakers were invited; some requested the opportunity. There were no guidelines. In fact, Father Bernard Cook, St. Kate's crusty six-foot-five, stoop-shouldered pastor, had only two simple, but absolute, rules:

One: Keep whatever you have to say to twenty minutes. And two: "Tell the goddamn truth."

Today's speaker was Bill Colbane. Colbane wasn't Catholic, but he had been a friend of Cook's since their grade-school days in the Parkside projects out near City Airport, back when Cookie, lanky and loud, had been the only white kid on the block, and Willie C. had been the runt among the blacks. Colbane had been outside, replacing burned-out

Christmas lights, a few days earlier when his friend had phoned to recruit him. Molly had called her husband in.

"Willie?" The priest was the only person who called him Willie. "Cook here."

Colbane couldn't help but grin when he heard his friend's voice. "Father Bernard, it's so nice to hear from you, sir." He brushed the snow off his jacket onto the floor, then caught Molly's disapproving look from the living room. He grabbed a paper towel, bent down, and wiped up the mess.

"Knock off the crap, Willie." The priest's fake growl turned into a gruff, but sincere, chuckle. Bill Colbane laughed, too. "I know it's late, but I need a warm body to deliver the Christmas homily."

Colbane laughed back. "Well, if it's warmth you're seeking, Brother Cook, I nominate you."

"Go to hell."

"You know I'll see you there."

The men chuckled together. Sharp, often brittle needling always preceded any serious conversation. It was part of their gritty past. It was like a strong handshake, a warm hello.

"Anyway, Willie, I choose not to accept his year." Cook cleared his throat. "People are tired of hearing me prattle on."

"Ah, but my wonderful monsignor, you slight so terribly your captivating eloquence."

"Fuck you, again."

"There it is right now. So succinct, so concise, so well put."

The men laughed once more. Cook paused and turned serious. "I've just been thinking that with this Jefferson thing being such a big deal . . ."

Colbane interrupted his friend. "I've got the Cooper prelim on the twenty-sixth, Bernie. I couldn't talk about it."

"I understand. I don't want you to mention the shooting. I just want you to talk about . . . hope."

The word hit Bill Colbane in the gut. "Hope?"

"Sure—how we can't afford to give up and give in. The long, hard road. Good, tough, grab-'em-by-the-throat stuff. I know you, Willie, you understand all that, you believe that, you *live* that." The priest stopped and waited for Colbane to answer. He didn't. "I think you'd give the folks a Christmas to remember."

Colbane exhaled slowly. He still had the paper towel in his hand. He rubbed his forehead with it. The towel was damp and cool. It felt good. He turned toward the living room. Molly was watching him. She was setting up the Nativity scene on the fireplace mantel. She smiled at him, and he at her. "I don't know, Bernie."

"You owe me one."

"For what?"

"For being your goddamn friend all these years." Goddamn came out as two words, both heavily accented.

"Hell, that hasn't been hard."

"Says you."

Colbane chuckled and shook his head. He thought for a long second, then buckled. "Okay. For you, Brother Cook, only for you. How long?"

"You know the rules."

"Twenty minutes, no bullshit."

"One thing. Don't go soft on me now."

The judge nodded. "No pap."

"Just the straight shit."

Colbane smiled. "I'll see you in a few days."

"Thanks, Bill."

"You're welcome, Cookie." Colbane paused. "You have been a good friend, you know."

The priest nodded. "That's what I'm talking about, Willie. Give 'em hell, not hokum."

Colbane smiled again and nodded. "Right."

And so, on Christmas morning, Bill Colbane, impeccably dressed in a black, pinstriped suit, a blindingly white shirt and cranberry red tie, walked briskly from his seat of honor in the first row of folding chairs, aligned neatly with the out-of-bounds stripe, climbed the single step to the lunch-table altar, strode to where his friend had stood only moments before, and turned and faced the churchgoers. Stan hadn't figured on the parking mess outside the church and had arrived about ten minutes late. But he was there in time, though barely, standing in the aisle in the jam-packed room with the other late arrivers, to watch Colbane take the three-by-five note cards from his right hand and stuff them into his suit pocket, then smile at Molly, Missy, and Samuel, and wink at Abe, and begin what many churchgoers would indeed tell family and friends later that afternoon was the most powerful Christmas Day homily they could remember, or even imagine.

Bill Colbane, trim, erect, and distinguished, started slowly, noting the simple despairs of everyday life that gnaw at happiness and moral resolve. But as his sermon drew on, as he began talking about being brave in the face of adversity, of the need for an unshakable, intractable belief in what is right, of always doing what is right—unexceptional concepts, really—he also began speaking more quickly, with more energy, more verve, more feeling, as if he were somehow divinely inspired, or even possessed. It was that combination, the style perhaps much more than the substance of his simple words, that held the congregation spellbound.

As he neared the end of the homily, Molly Colbane found herself thinking that her husband was standing taller and more self-assured, and sounding more confident and committed, then ever before.

"Christmas"—Bill Colbane paused; he looked down at the altar for a split second, then back at the congregation—"is not just about the birth of the Son of God." He paused again. "It is about the rebirth of hope. About renewed stamina. Renewed strength. Renewed courage and a renewed commitment toward a better, more just and more peaceful life." He gazed across the room. He could feel everyone hanging on his every word. He had never felt such pure, perfect power. He raised his arms, with fists clenched. "It is about being able"—his voice crescendoed in pitch and volume—"to continue on." His voice got even stronger. "It is about continuing"—then, he lowered his voice to a strong, burly, throaty whisper loud enough for all to hear—"on."

The church was eerily silent when Bill Colbane bit off that final tiny word. There was no rustling, no bustling now. Even the babies, screeching, whining, and babbling throughout the church just second before, were quiet. But the silence lasted only for a long moment. Then, the worshipers began applauding and, row by row, standing, and cheering, until everyone was up and clapping, hard, feverishly, almost in cadence. When he returned to the pew, to the continuing ovation. Molly gave her husband a quick hug and kissed him softly on the cheek. She was crying.

And for a moment, for a fleeting second, and for the first time in days, Bill Colbane had second thoughts about what he had chosen to do. No, what he must do. Then he remembered his friend's words—hell, not hokum—and realized that nothing had changed at all. Nothing could. He smiled at Molly, and kissed the tears from her eyes, then reached for Missy and hugged her and his heart stopped for a moment. He thought that maybe he had seen tears in her eyes, too. But he was too afraid to look, so he didn't. He simply buried his face in her hair and held her tight.

◊ 30 ◊

Stan zipped his pants, walked to the sink, and washed his hands. The men's head in the Copper's Kettle was empty—no surprise on Christmas Day, but it felt strange nonetheless. Stan couldn't remember ever being in there alone. The place was usually elbow to elbow with cops. He punched the hand dryer. Nothing. The towel dispenser was out, too. He shook his hands dry. No big deal. He was just glad the tavern was open. It gave him someplace to go besides the office.

Stan was one of three customers in the place. The other two—Charlie Stout and Vickie Morrison—were necking in a booth in a back corner. Stout and Morrison were married, but not to each other. Morrison was a sexy, hard-bitten undercover vice cop who liked to fool around. Stout, another undercover cop, was supposed to be posing as Morrison's boyfriend pimp. He was doing a bang-up job on the boyfriend part this morning. Stan knew them both pretty well, but didn't stop to say hello. They were too busy with each other. He headed straight to the bar and sat down. Within minutes, Danny Donati, the bartender, had placed a cheeseburger and fries in front of Stan—the Bunco Burger Combo.

"Merry Christmas, junior." Donati winked at Stan. The food was on the house. The burly, balding Donati was a retired homicide dick and part owner of the bar. The tattoo on his feet forearm read: "Semper Fidelis, Gloria." An ex-Marine, too. He'd done some serious cop time with Laddy Kochinski. "Want a side dish of cranberry sauce?"

Stan shook his head.

"Lemme know if you change your mind, kid. We got a can open." He shrugged. "Leftover from Thanksgiving, but it's still good. Stuff's shot full of preservatives."

Stan smiled and nodded, then turned toward the TV set above the bar a few stools down. Donati had a football game on. It was a replay from the night before on one of those all-sports cable stations. He pointed to the screen. Minnesota was playing Mississippi State in some bowl game somewhere down south. It was raining like mad. Both teams were wet and muddy. Fourth quarter. They looked bored. Donati pointed to the screen. "How'd ya like to be floppin' around in that crap, Laddy?"

Stan smiled at Donati's slip. He watched absentmindedly for about twenty minutes, until one of the announcers said something that caught his ear. Donati was gone, so Stan leaned forward on his stool and reached across the bar for the remote control. He punched up the volume.

" . . . right, Ernie. Here it is again on reply. Stoneman sidesteps the Gophers' pulling guard—whoosh—number sixty-five there, cuts neatly to the inside—there, there—and brings down Otis Kelly—wham. Nice play."

"You bet, Tony. And for anyone counting, that tackle by Stoneman was his fourteenth, breaking the single-game Bulldog record for solo tackles held since 1967 by P. J. Dawlson."

"I remember Dawlson, Tone. He was a hitter."

"You got that right, Ern."

Stan jumped off the stool and headed quickly to the back of the bar. The pay phone was on the wall next to Stout and Morrison's booth. The couple stopped groping each other and looked at Stan. Morrison had both hands under the table. Stout didn't. Stan picked up the phone and dialed Mary's number. She answered after one ring.

"Merry Christmas, Mary. Pete there?"

"Sure . . . Stan?"

"Yeah, hurry up."

"Stan?" It was Dawlson. "What's up?"

"You watching that game on SportsNet?"

"Nope." Pete laughed. "We're making a Christmas pie— Bakers Square was closed."

Stan laughed back. "Great. Listen, some kid Mississippi State linebacker named Stoneman just broke some record held by P. J. Dawlson—that you?"

"Yeah. Heard about it late last night." He laughed. "Maybe that's why I couldn't sleep. I kept seeing all the tackles I missed in that game. Shoulda had twenty-five. God, we clobbered Georgia Tech by twenty-two."

Stan chuckled. "I didn't know you were such a big man on campus."

"My last record."

"You had others?" Morrison and Stout were ignoring Stan now.

"Two more—interceptions and blocked punts."

"No shit. You never told me."

"You never asked."

Stan shook his head and smiled.

Dawlson covered the phone for a second. Stan could hear Mary's voice in the background. Pete came back on. "You coming over?"

Stan shook his head. "Naw, I got some stuff to do."

"Suit yourself." Dawlson paused again. "Sure?"

"See you tomorrow." Stan hung up and headed back to the bar. He sat down for a second, got a dollar's worth of quarters from Donati, grabbed the cheeseburger and went outside. He walked to the phone booth in the back corner of the parking lot, put the sandwich on the ledge inside the booth, dropped a quarter in the slot, and dialed. A man answered. It was Roger, Jenny's fiancé. Stan didn't answer his hello. He hung up, took a deep breath, then took another quarter out of his pocket and dialed again.

Another male voice. This time Stan answered. "Chief? Stan Kochinski here." Stan paused. Frank was talking to someone. Stan waited for him to finish.

"What's up?"

"Sorry to bother you, but that ballistics report is in. You seen it?"

"Yep." Frank was interrupted again. The voice in the background sounded like Marlyss's. Stan strained to hear if it was her. He felt a little like a school kid, and a little like Morrison and Stout. Both feelings made him uneasy. Frank was back on the phone in a few seconds. "The report. Right. I got it a few hours ago."

"Just wanted to make sure."

"That's okay."

"Merry Christmas."

"Same to you, detective."

Frank hung up. Stan did, too, then picked up the cheeseburger and left the booth, then stopped. He looked at the sandwich and tossed it into a nearby dumpster, turned and walked back to the phone.

This time Marlyss answered. "Hello."

"It's me."

"I'm sorry, ma'am, but you must have the wrong number." Marlyss's voice was loud. She paused, then giggled, then lowered her voice to a whisper. "I knew it was you before. I love you, Stanley. I love you for calling back."

Stan gripped the receiver tight. He rubbed his forehead. "I just called before to say . . . Merry Christmas."

"Merry Christmas, Stan." Suddenly, Marlyss sounded as lonely as Stan felt. "Why aren't you here with me?" She also sounded a bit tipsy.

Stan shrugged. There was no answer to the question. "I'll talk to you later."

"Tomorrow?"

"Okay."

"I do love you, Stosh."

Stan nodded, "I know."

Marlyss hung up; Stan didn't, not right away. He stood there, in the booth, in the corner of the parking lot, dwarfed by an old, sagging, brick apartment building that was half gone to demolition, and spoke, to no one but himself, in an almost inaudible whisper. "I love you, too, Marlyss Sims."

Then he hung up, checked his watch, and looked to the sky. It was after three now, and it had turned cloudy, and the holiday melancholy that had, indeed, lost out for hours to Bill Colbane's inspirational homily was returning. Stan shivered. He got in his car and drove home.

It was only four when he got back to his place, but it was already beginning to get dark. He tossed his coat on the couch and plugged in the small Christmas tree that Marlyss had bought and decorated as a surprise one afternoon while he was at work.

He sat on the couch, staring at the tree and began thinking about Christmases past.

He remembered the Christmas when he was nine, when his mother gave him his first baseball glove. He remembered taking the glove to bed with him that night, putting it next to his pillow, right next to his nose, and falling asleep to the sweet smell of the new leather. He remembered the Christmas three years later, the first one after his mother, Maggie Kochinski, had died quickly and unexpectedly of cancer, and how he'd slept with his glove that night, too, and how it smelled different and how he'd cried for the old smell, and for his mother. He remembered his last Christmas with Laddy and his first Christmas with Jenny, and their first with Petey. Then he figured he was remembering too much, and he stopped.

He got up, went to the kitchen, and began rummaging through a stack of Christmas cards. He found the one he'd gotten from Thunder Thorsgren two weeks earlier. On the front was a caricature of a war-toughened Confederate soldier carrying a bat over his left shoulder and wearing a Christmas wreath around his neck. Stan opened the card and re-read the message; "Still looking for some help reviving this team. Pay ain't great, but the backbreaking work makes up for it. (Little joke) Love, Thunder." Stan nodded to himself. Maybe it was worth a call. Tomorrow, after the hearing. Stan nodded again. He felt much better. He would do it. He would.

It was about six now. Stan popped open a beer, went back to the living room, and lay down on the couch. He had completely forgotten about the McGinnity file in Dawlson's unlocked desk drawer. He did wonder, for a moment, why Bill Colbane had flinched when Stan had stopped in the church parking lot to congratulate him on his sermon. Maybe Colbane had just been surprised to see one of Sam's old ballplayers. Stan had played for Sam Colbane one summer and he and Bill Colbane's father had become good friends. Maybe that was it. The judge hadn't said anything, but that must have been it.

Then, as the lights on the Christmas tree in front of him twinkled, some blinking on and off, Stan quit thinking about Bill Colbane and his dad and closed his eyes and just tried to picture Alabama. He could be free. They could be free. Maybe just one phone call. A few days. It could be all over.

Outside, in the crisp, windswept, Christmas night, a group of carolers paused outside Stan's house and sang a loud, lively rendition of "God Rest Ye, Merry Gentlemen." Stan didn't hear them. His eyes were already closed. He was already feeling a subtle, welcome sense of peace. He thought he was finally there.

◇ **31** ◇

Bill Colbane rapped his gavel once, then again, then paused and waited for the murmuring in the packed courtroom to settle to a low buzz, and finally to respectful silence. It always did. Colbane had a good hand with the gavel. Some judges tip-tapped politely. Others used the mallet without rhythm or purpose, as though they were shooing flies. Not Bill Colbane. He let all assembled know who was boss in his courtroom. His raps rang out sharp and powerful, with dignity and cadence.

Colbane put down the gavel and took a good long look at the scene before him. To his right sat Julius Cooper and his attorney, Randall Smithson. Cooper was dressed to kill in a deep, dark-purple pinstriped business suit, a white shirt, and a color-splashed tie, with a blood-red hankie in the breast pocket of his jacket. His long, Jheri-curled hair had been cut short. He was clean-shaven, rid of his moustache and goatee. He wasn't wearing any gold, not even his Rolex. He looked rakishly handsome and perfectly harmless. He could have passed for a *GQ* model or a Wall Street broker. He sat forward in his chair staring at his hands, which were neatly manicured and folded on the table in front of him. He seemed relaxed. He was predictably impassive.

Smithson sat to Cooper's right. He was digging through his briefcase for some papers. He was not a big man, and he looked a bit like an egghead in his horn-rimmed glasses. He was anything but. He was about as street-smart as they came. Colbane liked him. All of the judges did. Smithson knew his stuff. No bullshit. No theatrics. He truly was the best defense lawyer in town.

To Colbane's left sat Ned Moster, the husky, florid-faced county prosecutor. Moster and Colbane went back more than twenty-five years. Both had started out in the public defender's office doing nickel-and-dime cases for two-bit hookers, street bums, and penny-ante con men. Their oldest children were about the same age. Penny, Moster's oldest child, was a freshman at the University of Michigan. Though his manner was less formal, more conversational, Moster was every bit Smithson's match in the courtroom. Colbane chuckled to himself. It would have been one helluva trial, he thought.

Sandy Stone sat on Moster's right. He was busy separating documents and meticulously placing them in specific spots on the defense table. Colbane was careful not to make eye contact with him. A pair of armed officers stood guard at the courtroom door. The guards were not regular courthouse officers but members of the police SWAT unit. They were dressed in navy blue jumpsuits and black bulletproof vests. Because there was no need for a jury at a preliminary examination—the hearing would merely determine if, indeed, there was enough evidence to try Cooper on the first-degree murder charge—reporters and a trio of artists doing sketches for local TV stations were permitted to sit in the jury box to Colbane's right.

Sims and Hatch and their aides were seated directly behind Moster and Stone. Stan and Pete were behind them. Although she had been invited to sit with Hatch and Sims, Myrtle Jefferson chose to sit with relatives. Jefferson, wearing a faded, flowered spring dress, a red winter coat, and a pink carnation with a black ribbon, sat with two sisters and a brother. Theirs were the only black faces on the left side of the room. They sat in the last row of the gallery.

Mary Stimic, who arrived too late to claim a seat in the jury box, was one of the only white faces seated behind Cooper. The crowd behind the defendant was dominated by Cooper's friends and relatives. Everyone except Colbane, the defense team, Sims, Hatch, and the police guards had been herded through a metal detector and frisked before entering the courtroom.

Colbane glanced at the clock on the wall to his right. It was 9:10. He was surprised that he felt so fresh. He hadn't expected to. He'd slept very little Christmas night. He'd had his in-laws over for dinner and had stayed up late after they'd left and helped Molly do the dishes. They'd finished about one. Molly had headed off the bed, but the judge had gone into the family room at the rear of the house and sat in his favorite chair until he was sure his wife was asleep. Then he'd got down on his knees in front of the large cabinet against the back wall and pulled out the family picture albums, the early ones, and paged through them until he found the photo he was looking for. It took a while; he hadn't been through the albums in years. He was searching for a photo of Missy—one taken when she was about seven.

He found it sandwiched between a snapshot of Spider, the family's first dog, and little Samuel sitting at the piano, pretending to be Stevie Wonder, glasses and all. The photo of Missy made Bill Colbane smile. Missy had just climbed out of the neighborhood swimming pool on a chilly early-summer morning and was standing pigeon-toed and dripping wet, with her arms across her chest, staring directly into the camera. She had a wide, innocent, happy grin on her face. Her eyes sparkled with life. It was the image of his daughter that Bill Colbane wanted to carry with him. He removed the photo, put the albums away, sat back in his chair, and studied every little detail of the snapshot, trying to feel, not just remember, the moment he snapped the picture. He wasn't sure how long he sat there. It didn't matter, anyway.

It was about 4 A.M. when Bill Colbane finally climbed into bed. He couldn't sleep. He didn't really want to. He snuggled close to Molly, fitting his body gently into the curve of hers as she slept with her back to him. He listened to the soft purr of her breathing while waiting for the dawn. But he couldn't outlast the darkness. He arose at 5:10, showered and shaved and dressed quickly, then began making the rounds through his kids' bedrooms, whispering quiet goodbyes as he watched them sleep. Before he left Missy's room, he put his hand gently on the top of her breast. The throb of her heart was faint but steady. He removed his hand and threw a soft kiss to his daughter, then went back to the master bedroom to say goodbye to Molly. She was still asleep. Bill Colbane placed his hand gently on her cheek, then bent down and kissed her tenderly on the forehead. He watched her toss for a moment, then turn over and go back to sleep, and he wished that they had made love one more time. Then, he walked downstairs and out of the house.

He was the first person to arrive at his chambers. His clerk, his court reporter, the guards, and all the others would begin arriving at eight. He had almost a full hour of quiet. He unlocked his bottom drawer, removed a thin stack of papers, wrote for a few minutes, signed the last page, neatly placed the five pages in an envelope, sealed the envelope, and placed it in the middle of his desk. Then he removed his revolver, took it out of the holster, made certain it was loaded, placed it back in the holster, and strapped the holster to his leg. The leather felt cool and a bit prickly against his skin. Foreign. It usually did when he first put it on. An hour later, he didn't feel it anymore.

Colbane was staring now at Cooper, who was whispering into Smithson's ear. He wondered if Cooper had experienced that same sensation with his weapons. Did they become so familiar to him that they became an extension of his body? Colbane wanted to call a short recess and take Cooper into his chambers—just Cooper, no one else—and ask him that very question. And while he was at it, he would ask Cooper how it felt to kill a human being, to squeeze the trigger, to watch life explode out of someone's head. But he couldn't. Of course he couldn't. He laughed at himself, to himself. Silly, foolish even to think it.

"Judge, I think we're ready." Francie White, Colbane's clerk, looked up from her desk. Her raspy voice jolted him back to reality. It sounded like thunder. In fact, she was speaking in a low whisper. Colbane nodded to White and took another quick glance around the room. The court reporter was in place. The guards had closed the doors. It was 9:17. Colbane rapped twice with his gavel, then nodded to Ned Moster. Colbane had met with Moster and Smithson late Sunday. He listened politely to their gripes about having such little time to prepare for the exam, then instructed them to be succinct. "This isn't the trial, gentlemen. This is a preliminary hearing. Let's save the passion and whatever theatrics you care to muster for the jury. I've known both of you a long time. No need to impress me. Make it plain. Keep it simple."

Moster did. He nodded to Colbane, then Smithson, then circled in front of the prosecution's table and walked to the podium in the middle of the aisle. "Your Honor, the state is here to show that Rickey Jefferson was shot and killed on or about December twenty-first, and that the defendant, Julius Caesar Cooper, is guilty of murder in the first degree. We have a witness who will place the defendant in the vicinity of Drexel and Kercheval at the time of the shooting. We will also introduce into evidence the murder weapon, which, we will show, belongs to the defendant and was found during a search of his residence." Moster returned to his table and sat down.

Smithson didn't leave Cooper's side. He stood, put one hand in his pants pocket and used the other to grab a pencil, which he used, lead end out, as a pointer. "We will argue, Your Honor, that the defendant was nowhere near the scene of the crime at the time of the shooting and show that the gun allegedly used to shoot the deceased did at one time belong to my client, but had been taken from him weeks earlier during a robbery. We will argue further that the gun was planted in the defendant's residence by police or some agent of the police in order to frame him."

Smithson's allegation of the police conspiracy drew little reaction from the crowd. For a week now, stories in the newspaper and on TV and radio had outlined prosecution and defense strategy. Smithson was not revealing any secrets. He took his hand out of his pocket and sat down. Cooper turned back to the gallery to his right and caught Frank Sims's eye. Cooper smiled. Frank didn't.

The hearing unfolded quickly. Moster introduced a witness who said he had seen someone who looked like Cooper near the scene of the shooting about ten minutes before Rickey Jefferson was killed. The DA then called the coroner, Dr. Klaus Kernstetter, who testified that Rickey Jefferson was, in fact, deceased, and that a bullet did rip through his skull, entering at a point an inch down and to the right of his left ear, and exiting in the general area of his right temple.

Kernstetter sat at attention on the witness stand. His speech was slightly broken. His manner was stiff, his voice cold. "Death was almost assuredly instantaneous."

Moster then called a police ballistics expert to testify that markings from bullet fragments retrieved at the scene and found imbedded in Rickey Jefferson's skull matched perfectly those found on .31 caliber slugs fired from the six-shooter confiscated during the search of Cooper's apartment.

Sergeant Leonard "Bulls-eye" Rottinger had testified at hundreds of hearings and trials. He said he had never been more certain of a match. "No doubt." The hint of a sneer that wrinkled his mouth as he looked at Cooper made it quite plain that, in a different setting, he would have interjected "fucking" between the "no" and the "doubt" and made one word out of it.

Smithson maintained an inquisitive, entertained look throughout the testimony. Cooper simply looked bored. When it came Smithson's turn, he didn't waste time calling witnesses. There was no need. Colbane was going to order a trial. Any judge would. Colbane had asked him to keep things simple, and he was going to comply. There was no reason to piss him off, nothing to be gained by it. Smithson did some perfunctory cross-examining, but that was all.

Bill Colbane was unaware that the attorneys were following his pre-hearing admonishment so wonderfully. He was listening to little of what was being said. He spent most of the time keeping one eye on Cooper, and wondering about him—where he came from, why he ended up the way he did, what his parents thought of all this. He wondered if they knew what their son had become. Then he wondered if Julius Caesar Cooper really was evil. He even found himself wondering if Julius Cooper believed in God.

Then, as Smithson plodded toward the conclusion of his cross-examinations, Myrtle Jefferson put a handkerchief to her face. The sudden movement, the white material against her dark brown face, caught Colbane's eye. Rickey Jefferson's mother looked exhausted, smaller, older, more scared, and more alone than anyone else in the courtroom. As he watched her daub at her eyes, Bill Colbane remembered what she had said in one of the newspaper stories: "I have nothing left." The statement was terrifying in its simplicity. It was not original, however. Bill Colbane had heard it, or strikingly similar sentiments, dozens of times before, from widows, from widowers, from parents of other murder victims. But it sounded different, hearing it from her. It echoed more, reverberated in his mind as he replayed the four words in his head in Myrtle Jefferson's thin, tired voice. "I have nothing left." Suddenly, Bill Colbane felt himself sweating profusely. He began wondering anew. He didn't have to do this, did he? Wasn't there some other way left to him? He wanted to stop and wave some sort of magic wand, cast a spell, and put everything into a state of suspended animation. He wanted time now to rethink what he had planned to do, to rethink whether he had to do it. Then he remembered the pictures. He had taped them to the floor for just this reason, in case he began to waver, to lose his courage. He slid his chair back two inches or so and lifted the edge of the rubber mat with the tip of his shoe. He stole a quick glance to the floor. Missy was still there, and Rickey Jefferson, and Julius Cooper. They all stared at him. Bill Colbane's mind raced. He wondered if anyone was reading his thoughts, if anyone knew what he was going to do, what he had to do, if anyone would try to stop him—if anyone could.

"Judge?" It was Francie White again. She was staring at Bill Colbane with a confused, concerned look. The judge looked at her, blinked twice, then gazed out into the courtroom. Moster and Stone were staring at him, too. So was Smithson. They also had puzzled looks on their faces. The only one who didn't was Cooper. He was smiling. It was a street-wise, fuck-you smile.

"Judge? Judge?" The clerk was talking in a stage whisper now. "Mr. Smithson said he was finished." Colbane looked back at her. He nodded. He looked down one more time at the pictures—Missy, Rickey, and Cooper.

Colbane nodded to himself, then looked to both attorneys. "Gentlemen and Mr. Cooper, please approach the bench." Moster and Smithson looked at each other. Now, they were totally confused. There was no need for this sort of bench caucus, not during a preliminary hearing. There had been no arguments, no major objections, no controversy. Everything was cut and dried, plain and simple. The men obeyed, walking forward slowly. The lined up in front of the bench, Moster to Colbane's left, then Smithson, then Cooper. Sandy Stone followed. He stood behind the defendant.

"Gentle . . ." Bill Colbane's forehead was covered with beads of sweat. He was oblivious to them. He wiped his arm across the top of the bench, knocking his pen to the floor. "Please, ah . . . excuse me for a second."

It was getting comical. Stone thought Colbane had

cracked. He turned slightly and stole a glance at Frank. Frank was getting edgy, but he tried not to show it. He shrugged. But Francie White had a look of panic on her face, and Moster was worried about his old friend. He thought that Colbane might be having a heart attack. Julius Cooper was having a hard time keeping himself from laughing out loud.

Colbane stole a quick breath and reached for the gun. He grabbed it, and felt a surge of energy, authority. No, not authority. It was arrogance, a rush of blind, vicious arrogance. So, this was what it really felt like. This was what made punks like Julius Cooper feel so goddamn tough, so omnipotent. And that was it—omnipotence. There was only one thing in the universe that could give animals like Cooper such absolute control, and now Bill Colbane held it comfortably, coolly, in his right hand. He smiled. He felt himself stop sweating—as though a faucet had been turned off. He sat up in his chair with his right arm in his lap. He had ducked under the bench a frightened man and had emerged courageous. He wanted to laugh at the bewildered faces in front of him. Fools, all of them. They had no idea. No one had any idea—except, perhaps, Julius Cooper. He took one more glance at the pictures. Missy. Rickey. Cooper. Then he began.

"Julius Caesar Cooper." His voice was even, but low. He studied Cooper, looking for some fear, some apprehension, a twitch, anything. He saw nothing. "A little over twelve months ago, you orchestrated and participated in the abduction, rape, and sodomy of one Melissa Stewart Colbane."

Smithson shook his head. Moster scratched his. There had been rumors about what had happened to Missy. Some were close to correct. But there had been no reports, no investigations, certainly no names. Never. Frank had kept his word about keeping everything quiet.

The reporters in the gallery were leaning forward now, straining to hear. They began whispering feverishly to each other. A few began scribbling. Cooper began laughing. "What the fuck is this?"

Colbane remained calm. He nodded. "And today, I pronounce you . . ."

"Bill!" It was Moster his voice was sharp. Colbane ignored him.

". . . guilty . . ."

Cooper laughed even harder. "Fuck you, old man. You're fuckin' crazy."

". . . and sentence you . . ."

"Bill, c'mon Bill." Moster again. His voice was lower. He had moved closer to the bench. He was pleading now.

"Fuck you, you idiot nigger." Cooper spit the words at Colbane.

Moster was reaching for Colbane now. The judge waved at him. "Back off, Ned." He stared Julius Cooper dead in the eyes. ". . . to death."

Francie White screamed, and in one fluid motion, the Honorable William Baxter Colbane stood, pointed his right arm, the long arm of justice and truth and the law, at Julius Cooper, smiled, said something under his breath that one TV newswoman would later report as "Judgment Day, Julius," and fired. The revolver was hidden inside the draped sleeve of Colbane's robe, but Cooper knew what was coming. He only got out. "What the . . ." before the apocalyptic red flash exploded from Colbane's sleeve. The bullet that followed beat the "fuck" out of Cooper's mouth and wiped the sneer from his lips. It blasted a neat gap a half-inch above his right cheekbone, leaving a dark red hole where his eye had been. The second bullet, fired as Cooper reeled backward, glanced off the side of Cooper's skull and struck Sandy Stone dead in the heart. Colbane didn't even seem to notice.

Then, as panic-filled screams, sobs, and what-the-fucks ricocheted through the cramped courtroom, as almost everyone dived to the floor, and as the two SWAT officers lay motionless, stunned, their weapons trained on the robed warrior behind the bench, Bill Colbane dropped his arm to his side and turned toward Myrtle Jefferson. She was still there, still small, still alone, hankie in hand, the only person in the courtroom not cowering for cover, for she really had nothing left to lose.

Colbane's voice was low, rushed. He began to sob. "I'm so sorry, Mrs. Jefferson. We didn't mean to . . ." And as Bill

Colbane jerked his arm quickly toward his pursed lips in what was going to be his final act, the absolution following his obscure confession, two shots rang out. One hit him in the forehead, killing him instantly. The other bisected his neck, puncturing the jugular, releasing a splash of red, and sending his lifeless body clattering down the steps behind the bench. As William Baxter Colbane's body came to a halt, a strange stillness washed over the courtroom. It was a sickening, horrifying stillness that you could smell and feel and hear. It was a stillness that one *Free Press* columnist would later call "the true sound of violence." It lasted only a split second.

As the renewed screaming and sobbing pierced the deathly quiet, Frank Sims scrambled to his feet to see who had fired the shots that had brought the short-lived calm. Only one gun was smoking—and it was in the steady hand of police officer Al McGinnity.

$$\diamond \ \textbf{32} \ \diamond$$

It didn't take long, even in the chaotic wake of the deaths of Colbane, Cooper, and Stone, for Frank Sims to make one thing perfectly clear: "The Rickey Jefferson murder case is now closed."

Less than two hours after the bloody courtroom scene, Frank Sims was presiding over a hastily called press conference in a makeshift briefing room at police headquarters. His hair was perfectly matted with sweat; his shirt was nicely stained with it. A butterfly bandage near his right temple, a tastefully understated red badge of courage, held shut a two-inch-long gash he'd suffered when he dived to the floor after Bill Colbane's first shot. The shoulder holster he never wore during TV interviews hung loose beneath his left arm. He looked the part of the humble, victorious lawman—and he knew it.

He was sitting at the end of a long table. Three TV cameras were trained on him. The local stations were going live with the press conference. The chairs around the table were filled by reporters; the walls were lined with them.

"I can answer questions for a few minutes." Frank glanced around the room. The glare from the TV floodlights made it nearly impossible to identify the reporters, but he could feel their anticipation.

The first question came from Frank's left in a high-pitched male voice. "Why did Judge Colbane apologize to Myrtle Jefferson?"

Frank shrugged. His demeanor was calm, solemn, sorrowful. "I wish I knew."

The second question came from the back. "What about McGinnity?"

Frank nodded. "Al McGinnity was part of a five-officer plainclothes force assigned to surveil the crowd."

Another different voice, this one female. "Meaning what, sir?"

"Meaning that we were concerned about Cooper's associates."

"Why didn't any of the other officers shoot?"

"We will interview all who were present while we try to determine whether Office McGinnity acted in haste."

"Did he?"

"No comment."

"Did Cooper rape Judge Colbane's daughter?"

Frank shook his head slowly, but surely. "We've run a quick check, and we have no report on that."

"Well, what about Judge Colbane's . . ." The voice came from the far end of the room.

Frank held up his hand, looked down at the table, then back up into the lights. "Bill Colbane was a good friend. I'm sorry for what happened today. I feel even more sorry for his family."

The reporter interrupted right back. "So if Judge Colbane was . . ."

Frank interrupted the reporter again. "I'm sorry, but I have no idea what he was saying or . . ."

"What about this Shooter person who supposedly stole Cooper's gun?" Randall Smithson had just completed a similar interview at the courthouse. Smithson had stood slumped against a wall, his suit jacket covered with Cooper's blood. The attorney had caught his client when he was blown backward. Smithson was still shaking a bit, but he spoke quietly and with remarkable calm. He'd told reporters that the Jefferson murder weapon had been stolen by a street thug who called himself "the Shooter" and that he'd heard there was an eyewitness to the theft.

Frank turned toward the sound of the voice. He tried to stare through the glare, then stopped. It was no use. It would only make his face look tense and pinched on television. "I never heard of someone called Shooter, or *The* Shooter." Frank could hear notepad pages being turned.

"What about this eyewitness?"

"Same." Frank paused. "Look, I respect Mr. Smithson's reputation and his admirable loyalty to his client's . . . good name. But I think we all know that the alibi was rather preposterous. Next question."

A different voice. "So there's nothing to this police frame-up theory?"

Frank shook his head. "I think I just answered that question."

Another voice piped up. This one was closer. "Back to the stolen gun . . ."

"We have no proof that a gun was stolen—period." There was a lot of snap to Frank's voice now. Too much. He noticed it and cautioned himself about it.

Different voice. "What's McGinnity's status?"

"Officer McGinnity is being reassigned to desk duty until we complete an investigation of the shooting. Standard procedure. Most of you are aware of how that goes."

"We hear there was a note."

Frank nodded. "It's been turned over to the family."

"What did it say?"

"You'll have to ask them." Frank put his palms on the table and began to rise.

"One more question, Chief." It came from the back of the room. Frank relaxed into his chair. "Can you sum up what all this says about ..."

Frank recognized the type of question. He couldn't see the questioner, but he knew instantly and for certain that it came from a TV reporter and that if his answer was good, it would be used throughout the evening's prime-time programming as a teaser for the late news. He was being tossed a home-run pitch—and he was ready to take the big swing. He paused, trying to appear thoughtful, then shook his head and stared hard—it was time—into the lights, trying to focus on the questioner. "Say?" He paused again. "Two good men are dead today, and for that I have no answer. One vicious young gangster is gone, too." Another pause. "And to that, I can say nothing other than ... good riddance." Frank stopped. He half expected the room to ripple with applause. It didn't, though quite a few of the reporters were nodding. "We did our job. We brought Cooper to trial. We had our man. I'm not sorry for that."

Frank stood and half-felt his way along the aisle and toward the door. The reporters moved quickly out of his way as he left the room. He heard the floodlights click off as he walked through the doorway, and he took a deep breath as he entered his office. He exhaled hard, closed and locked his door, buzzed his secretary and told her to hold his calls, then picked up the red phone, the special hotline to Hatch's office.

"Hatch here." The mayor sounded as though he was battling his nerves.

"You alone?"

"No."

"Get alone."

The mayor was back on the line in less than a minute. He didn't say anything. Frank could hear him breathing.

"How're you doing?"

Hatch nodded. "I don't know."

Wrong answer. Frank was afraid of that. It was the first time he and Hatch had spoken since lying nose to nose on the courtroom floor. Hatch had kept repeating "Oh, my God," until it came out sounding like one word. He'd looked as though he were going to cry. Frank had said nothing then. No time. He realized now that he should have called Hatch sooner. Frank gritted his teeth. He hoped he hadn't made a serious mistake. "It went great with the press."

Hatch nodded again. "I watched." His voice sounded weak, shallow. He rubbed his forehead. "This Shooter talk worries me."

Frank sat down and leaned back in his chair. "We're okay, Marty." His voice was soft, calm, reassuring.

"Sure?"

"Yep." Frank nodded. "I'm sure."

"What about McGinnity?"

Frank rubbed his eyes. "What about him?"

Hatch paused, as though he were afraid to ask the obvious question. He was, but he did anyway. "Is it him?"

Frank shook his head and laughed quietly. "You know the rules, Marty."

Hatch laughed back, but it was a jittery, nervous laugh. "You sure we're okay?"

Frank nodded into the phone. "Sure as I can be."

"Well, what about this eyewitness?"

Frank shook his head. "She doesn't exist."

Hatch didn't catch Frank's slip. "Gone?"

Frank nodded. "Good as."

"It's not us—is it?" Hatch sounded really panicky, now. "No more, Frank."

Frank exhaled long and low. This was bad, doing this over the phone. Hatch needed to hear this stuff face to face. But he had no choice. "No, not us."

Hatch paused. "What about the suicide note?"

"It was a soppy mess. Same shit as in the courtroom. A lot of I'm sorry this and I'm sorry that, forgive me, Missy, this, forgive me, Molly, that."

"Us?"

"Not a word." Frank's voice was still even, solid. "Ol' Bill, bless his heart, was faithful to the end. In fact, he was our goddamn savior."

"Did Cooper really rape Missy?"

"No comment, Marty."

"If he did, and I'm just saying if"—Hatch sounded as though he were afraid of Frank—"how's Molly Colbane going to react when she hears you said the rape never occurred?"

Frank felt his anger rising. He wasn't supposed to have to explain all of this to Hatch. It was like he was dealing with some scared little kid. "Frankly, Marty, I don't give a damn."

"Makes Colbane look like a liar."

Frank stood and arched his back. It was sore, stiff. Must have strained it when he hit the floor in the courtroom. "On top of being a murderer and a goddamn fruitcake." Frank paused. "Relax, Marty. She's got her hands full."

Hatch nodded. He felt a little better, a little. Frank sounded confident. But Frank always sounded like he was in control. "What about the press?"

"What about 'em?"

"What do you think they'll write?"

Frank smiled. "At this point, Marty, you shouldn't give a shit."

"Meaning?"

"You just do what we planned. We move on the east side hard now, while you milk the hell out of Cooper's arrest and the end of this Jefferson crap."

"And?"

"And?" Frank paused. God, he wanted to grab Hatch and shake some sense into him. "And? C'mon, Marty. You got your city back. You got your future back."

"I wasn't thinking."

"Well, start." Frank was getting perturbed. He was ready to yell at Hatch. He caught himself. His voice was stern, not angry. "Start thinking about cleaning this goddamn place up and getting the fuck out."

"Out?"

"Governor, congressman, senator—out." Frank took a deep breath and shook his head. "What does Lyttle say?"

"Same. We do some fix-up, and we maybe get the backing to move on."

"When did he say that?"

Hatch shrugged. "Saturday, Sunday."

"Call him back—now. Tell him to make some calls, get a real feel for how things are right now. Tell him to get his fat ass to work."

"Right." Hatch nodded. He took a deep breath. He looked out his window at the teeming downtown scene below. His city, again. "What about Stone?"

"Casualty of war." Frank sniffed. "We'll send flowers."

Hatch nodded. He still sounded shaky. "We'll send pink carnations."

Frank closed his eyes and nodded, too. "Of course, Marty. Pink carnations."

Mary Stimic was at a desk deep in a corner of the *Free Press* city room. She was twirling a pencil between the fingers of her left hand. In her right, she had a telephone receiver. She was holding it a full six inches from her ear.

"Goddamnit, Mary, I don't have time to talk now." Stan was overwhelmed. He sounded frustrated and angry—and loud. "This place is a fucking zoo. I got paperwork and reports out the ass, and Pete's been in the can for half an hour."

Mary counted slowly to ten. She kept her voice calm, but didn't back off. "We're off the record, Stan." She waited for an answer. She got none. "There's something real wrong here."

Stan rubbed his cheek, then his eyes. "No time."

Mary nodded. She whispered hard into the phone. "Listen to me, goddamnit."

"No time." Stan's voice got louder.

So did Mary's. "Make. Fucking. Time."

Now Stan was the one counting to ten.

Mary tried to calm herself. "C'mon, Stosh, there are too many holes here—the stolen gun . . ."

Stan shook his head. "Alleged stolen gun."

". . . eyewitness . . ."

He shook his head again. "Alleged eyewitness."

". . . this Shooter . . ."

He put his hand over his eyes. "This isn't a goddamn TV movie, Mary."

". . . Colbane drilling Cooper, then apologizing, for God's sake, to Myrtle Jefferson . . ."

Stan nodded. "He just blew a rod. Lots of us idiot gladiators end up swallowing our guns."

". . . the rape that isn't on the books."

He was shaking his head again. "No rape, Mary.

"Have you ever looked at that kid, Stan? She's a frickin' zombie." Stan took a deep breath. "Then there's the kicker: McGinnity."

He laughed. It was an exasperated, please-leave-me-alone laugh. "So what? He's a trigger-happy cowboy."

"That all?"

Stan bit his bottom lip. He didn't answer the question. He didn't know how to. "So what's it all add up to, Ms. Marple?"

"That this case isn't even close to being closed."

Stan shook his head. "That's not what Frank said."

Mary slammed the pencil down on her desk. She lowered her voice to a street-tough whisper. "Fuck Frank, Stosh. What do you think?"

Stan leaned back in his chair. "I'm tired of thinking, Mary."

"Listen, if you know what I know about McGinnity—and I bet you do—I figure you've had a few thoughts about him."

"No comment."

"Chickenshit."

"Sticks and stones, Stimic."

"Motherfucking chickenshit."

"Go to hell."

Mary paused. She had to slow down and think. She was getting nowhere. Stan sounded pissed, but he hadn't hung up. "Okay, truce." She waited. Nothing. She half-pleaded. "C'mon, Stosh, what's your gut say?"

He rubbed his stomach. "That I got gas."

Mary laughed. Maybe she had been pressing a little too hard. But Stan had to have some of the same doubts about the whole thing—had to. Maybe. "Okay, I'm sorry."

"Are not."

"Okay—not." Mary smiled. "But give me two minutes tonight."

"You'll want two hours."

"Look, just come over to my place. We'll make it . . . I don't know . . . a real-life game of Clue—Mary in the ballroom with the rope."

Stan laughed, sort of. "That's what I'm afraid of."

"Okay. Low key. I promise."

"Call Dawlson."

"Uh-huh. He told me to go to hell. He thinks I'm all wet." Mary paused. "You, on the other hand, don't."

Stan ran his hand over his head, then rubbed the back of his neck. "Wrong."

"Am not."

Stan shook his head, then nodded. "It'll have to be late—real late."

Mary nodded back. "I'll pour a couple pots of coffee into my veins." She'd won Round One. A tight, tired smile wrinkled her face. "Just be there, Chipper. Just be there."

Marlyss was in the middle of an aerobics class at the club when she heard about the shootings. Terry Miller, the fitness director, pulled Marlyss out of the class to tell her what she had heard on the radio—that three people were dead in a courtroom shootout downtown during the Cooper hearing. Miller had been on the phone in her office when the bulletin came over the radio. She thought maybe one of the names she'd heard was Frank's. She wasn't sure.

Marlyss ran to the locker room and struggled to get out of her clammy leotard and tights. Miller had followed, protectively, and offered to help. On any other day, Marlyss might have been uncomfortable undressing in front of the redhead. Though she didn't advertise it, Miller, stylish and in her forties, was a rather free spirit and enjoyed flirting with Marlyss. But Miller didn't look the least bit the seductress now. She was chalky pale. Her assistance was perfectly clinical. Marlyss didn't shower. She was undressed and dressed again in about five minutes. Miller gave her a gentle hug as she left.

"Frank's okay, Mar, I can feel it."

Marlyss nodded. She ran outside. It was bitterly cold; the wind was blowing hard. By the time she got to the car, her damp bangs were brittle with ice. She started the car, put the heater controls on high, and turned on the radio.

". . . switch you live now to, um, Joanie Arnex just outside Courtroom 5039. Joanie, you there now?"

"Thanks, Stew. I'm here outside the courtroom, and just to recap: There was a shootout in Judge William Colbane's courtroom about half an hour ago. Three men are dead. They are: Judge William Colbane; murder one defendant and reputed drug gangster Julius Caesar Cooper; and . . ." Marlyss held her breath. Arnex stopped. "Excuse me for just a moment." The sound of rustling papers came over the speaker like a burst of static.

"Come on." Marlyss's teeth were ground tight. "Come. On."

"Excuse me there, Stew. I was beginning to mention police officer Al McGinnity, who shot and killed Judge Colbane." Marlyss shook her head. "I'll get to that in a moment." Arnex paused again. She was a rookie reporter; she sounded a bit flustered. "The third victim . . . here it is . . . was assistant prosecutor Sandy Stone." Marlyss closed her eyes, then leaned forward and put her forehead on the steering wheel. Stan was okay—but so was Frank. She turned off the radio. She didn't need to hear any more. Tears welled up in her eyes. She sat back, took a deep breath, put the car in reverse, backed up, and started pulling out of the parking lot. She stopped when she got to the driveway, and looked in the rear-view mirror. Terry Miller was still standing watch at the door. Marlyss waved, then took her foot off the brake, then stopped again—it hit her, all at once. It was over. If Cooper was dead, wouldn't Frank close the Jefferson case? And if he did, if it was over, Stan would take her away. He'd said that. He'd promised. He had. He would know what to do, how to handle everything. Marlyss began to smile, then laugh, then cry, all at once. It would be finished—finally. She began to sob and shake. She rested her head on the steering wheel again for a few seconds, then wiped the tears from her cheeks with her jacket sleeve. She took a deep breath and another look in the rear-view mirror.

Miller was gone. Terry would have expected Marlyss to turn right, to head downtown to make sure Frank was okay. Frank would have expected the same. He would have wanted her to provide photo and film opportunities for the media—the concerned wife rushing to her gallant husband's side, film at eleven. Marlyss checked once more in the mirror. Still no Miller. She pulled out of the driveway and turned left—toward Stan's place.

The duplex was dark when she arrived. Marlyss took off her coat and opened the blinds in the rear of the kitchen and, for the first time in the dozens of times she had been in the house, stopped and studied the view. The backyard adjacent to Stan's was littered with snow-covered junk: an old, discarded stove with its oven door open; a pile of tires; a mangled push lawn mower with only one wheel; a rusting, rotting car with no doors at all. Stan would shrug, sometimes a bit embarrassedly, and call it "urban landscaping." Late one night, over a final cup of coffee, he'd told her about his crazy dream he'd had once, how he'd visited the Grand Canyon and found it filled to the rim with discarded Frigidaires. She'd laughed; he had, too. Sort of.

She looked at one of the kitchen chairs. She had sat in the same chair many times before, but now she noticed that the edge of the seat cushion was ripped and that a large piece of black electrician's tape covered the tear. She ran a fingertip along the fissure. It felt rough, uneven. She brushed her hair back with her hand and looked around the tiny room. A broom stood in a corner, next to a messy pile of old newspapers. Dirty dishes were piled in the sink. The refrigerator door was covered with fingerprints. Stan had tossed empty beer and pop cans into a grocery bag next to the wastebasket—his one concession to recycling. He'd missed twice. She remembered rebounding some of those misses once and telling him he needed a woman's touch around the house. He'd said, "I was thinking more along the lines of . . . Earl the Pearl Monroe's." Then he'd laughed; she had, too. Sort of.

She went into the living room and opened the drapes there also, and sunlight streamed into the room. The gray couch, where she and Stan sometimes made love in the flickering light of the TV, and sometimes just plain fucked in the pitch black, was terribly worn. He'd gotten it at a police auction. The end table nearby was nicked and scratched—garage sale, down the street. She laughed softly. Stan was proud of them. Thirteen bucks for the sofa; ninety-five cents for the table. She remembered the first time she'd sat there, in the darkness, and how Stan had slipped his arm around her like some kid on a first day and held her gently and how nice his voice sounded when he said her name and how special, how perfect, everything felt.

She walked down the hall toward Stan's bedroom. She stood in the doorway and gazed across the room. It certainly was more cramped than cozy. She walked to the dresser and picked up the photo of Stan and Petey that was stuck in the mirror. She had held and studied the picture several times before. It was a wonderful photo. Stan and Petey were sitting underneath a tree on a picnic bench in a park, with the fall colors at their crispest. Father and son were smiling grandly. Stan had asked Marlyss once if she wanted to keep the picture. She'd giggled and teased him then. "And what would I do with it, my dear, Stanislaw? Put it on my dresser? Frank would love that." Stan had felt foolish, embarrassed; Marlyss had felt bad she'd made him feel that way. She'd kissed him lightly on the cheek and said she would love to have the picture, but that she would leave it right there, on his dresser, for safekeeping, for now. It was still there, waiting for her.

She walked across the room and sat on Stan's bed. It was unmade. The blankets and sheets were twisted into a ball near the foot of the bed. The pillows were on the floor. A shirt, a recent birthday gift from Jenny, hung from one of the bedposts. Marlyss gently lifted the shirt off, held it to her face, and inhaled. It smelled like Stan. It was Stan—plaid flannel. Jenny knew him, too. Marlyss felt a twinge of jealousy, but only a twinge, then smiled, hugged the shirt to her, lay back on the bed, and closed her eyes. She wanted Stan there right now. She thought of calling him, but didn't. There was no need.

She wasn't sure how long she stayed there, on the bed. Maybe she'd even fallen asleep. She couldn't remember.

What she would remember, later, was that it was almost dark outside when she got up and went to the kitchen to get her coat, and that she saw Stan's reminder to himself to call Alabama. And she would remember taking the note and stuffing it into her coat pocket. He wouldn't need it; she would do the reminding. She wanted to be there when he called.

She took another look around the house now, as she put on her coat. It wasn't like her and Frank's place. Theirs was custom tailored. This was more like your basic . . . forty-two regular. She smiled. And messy. But it was solid. She looked at her watch. What was she—hours, a day, two, from being free, from being rescued? Yes, soon. Stan would take care of her. Solid Stan Kochinski. The Jefferson case was closed. She'd even heard Frank say that on the radio. Yes. Yes. Yes. She'd survived.

Then, Marlyss smiled again, and her smile turned into one of those wide, sparkling hug-me smiles, but no one was there to finish it off. She thought for a moment about just waiting there for Stan. He would take her in his arms. But things were probably a mess at headquarters and he might be really late, and, besides, maybe it was time to go home and finally pack those bags. Maybe even load up the car. Maybe it was time. Maybe.

◇ **33** ◇

Mary Stimic was boiling. "The stinking politics of this mess is what gives it away."

Stan rubbed his eyes. He'd started to have doubts a few minutes earlier, but he was certain now that he shouldn't have come to Mary's apartment. He shook his head. "Are— stinking politics *are* what gives it away."

Mary glared at him. "Go to hell."

Stan shrugged. "Won't stand up in court, anyway. Conjecture. Bullshit. Wishful thinking."

Mary would have thrown something at him if she'd had something to throw, anything. All she had in front of her on the table was an antique teacup. She had to tell herself not to pick it up. "I didn't say it would, goddamnit . . ."

Stan rolled his eyes. "I heard it in your voice."

She got up from the table. "You're not just an asshole, Kochinski, you're a complete fucking asshole."

Stan tried smiling. "C'mon, Mary." He was patronizing her and she could tell.

"Fuck you, Stan. Fuck you to hell."

He shook his head. "Here we go again."

As usual, it hadn't taken long for their discussion to degenerate into confrontation. Mary had been dressed in a white blouse unbuttoned over a loose-fitting black tank top and a pair of jeans when she'd answered the door a half hour earlier. When she'd turned and moved away from the door, her breasts had swayed a little, naturally. Barefoot, and with her hair pinned back—well, she hadn't looked like such a pain in the ass then. Plus, she had one helluva smile. She'd whispered, as she invited him in. "Don't worry, Stosh, my parents aren't home."

Stan had laughed and apologized for being late, even though he had dragged his feet in getting there.

From there, they'd moved to the dining room. They'd been civil, even friendly, to each other for a good twenty minutes. Mary had made herself a cup of tea and poured Stan a beer. He'd actually been enjoying her company. Then, gradually, she'd gotten all wound up, and her pulpit fervor was being fueled by Stan's stubbornness.

The white blouse was long gone now, Mary's hair had fallen sternly to her shoulders, and the friendly teasing was a memory. Stan was ready to plead with her to ease up.

"Why can't you just let this be?"

Mary gritted her teeth and nodded. "Because, Stan, unlike you and your shit-for-brains colleagues, I like to get things done right—not just done." She landed hard on the last word. "I *need* to get things right. It's in here." Mary pointed to her chest. "And here." She jerked her thumb toward her stomach.

Stan rubbed his eyes again.

"C'mon, Stan, I had you going on the phone this afternoon." There was no letup in the tone of her voice or its volume. She was still challenging him.

"That was this afternoon."

She put her hands on her hips. "What happened?"

"Nothing." He shook his head. "I'm just tired of all this, Mary. Can't I be? Just goddamn tired?" He stood, but he wasn't going anywhere. He struggled to keep his voice conversational. "So what if Cooper didn't pop the kid? Who cares? He was a motherfucker. Capital M. Capital F. And now he's a dead motherfucker." Stan walked from the table to the refrigerator and got himself another beer. "And so what if the cops—if *we*—are framing Cooper? He's an animal. Big. Fucking. Deal."

Stan looked at Mary. He could see veins popping out in her neck and shoulders. She sneered at him. "Gutless."

He popped open the beer. "Go to hell, Mary."

"Gutless again."

Stan was losing his cool. He wanted to slug her. He would have if she weren't a woman. And right about now, he was pretty close to wondering why in the hell that made any difference. He didn't say or do anything.

"Motherfucking gutless."

Silence.

"What do you know about guts?" Stan's voice was low. So was Mary's. "I know about yours."

"I doubt it."

"I'm Jenny's best friend . . . remember?"

Stan took a deep breath.

"Which means that I know, Stosh."

Stan nodded. He pursed his lips, then bit down on the bottom one. He shrugged. "I'm just through with being a cop, Mary. Period. You ever get tired of being a reporter?"

Mary shook her head. She wasn't going to get sucked into that. "Well, you can rest later, for the rest of your life, lieutenant, for all I goddamn care."

Stan nodded again. No one spoke for minutes. Mary's

face was red, her bangs damp with sweat. She went to the kitchen and boiled more water for tea. Stan watched her, but she didn't seem to notice.

The tea kettle whistled. The cooling-off period was over. "Care to start fresh?" Mary's voice was relaxed now. She was pouring the steaming water over her tea bag, and she took a deep breath. She was trying to smile. The effort was admirable, but hardly effective.

Stan caught himself staring at her body, and looked away. "One more time—that's it."

"The politics?"

Stan had his head down. He nodded slowly. "Go ahead."

Mary returned to the dining room and sat down across from him again. Her voice was calm now, but her eyes still blazed. "It's just all too simple. Kid gets shot, a city gets the hots to find the killer, and the cops arrest the meanest, nastiest, vilest asshole in the history of the state. The asshole gets blown away by a respected judge, who then gets blown away by a maverick cop. Meanwhile, who the fuck is this Shooter character?" Stan took a slug of his beer. Mary tapped her temple with her finger. "Nothing happens like this, Stosh."

Stan took another swallow of beer. "Okay, tell me how it happens, detective."

She ignored his sarcasm. "Borderline kid gets drilled." She shrugged. "Stumblebum cops find no one." Shrugged again. "Idiot mayor goes down the tubes. End of kid. End of administration." Mary held her hands out, palms up. "Life trudges on—and who punched Rickey Jefferson's ticket becomes another of its many unsolved but solvable mysteries."

Stan smiled. "No one buys the book."

Mary smiled back. "No one should buy this story."

Stan nodded.

Mary watched him carefully. Something was coming.

He rubbed his cheek. "Okay." He stopped. "Three days."

There it was. Mary knew immediately what Stan meant. Three days would be enough, for starters, at least. Once Stan was hooked, she'd have him. She tried hard to sound disappointed. "That's all?" She pretty much succeeded.

"We don't show something more than all this cop-novel crap in seventy-two hours, I'm off it . . ."

Mary stared hard at Stan. She nodded back. There was another period of silence. This one was far shorter.

Stan drummed the table with his fingers. ". . . because you still haven't convinced me."

Mary knew better. Or at least thought she did. She smiled.

Stan looked away. "First things first: Alfred Tony McGinnity. Let's have it."

Mary nodded. "How much?"

"Everything."

It took her about twenty minutes to go over her notes on the cop who'd shot Bill Colbane. Stan knew some of it, the basic stuff. McGinnity was thirty-five and black, had been a cop for twelve years, and had worked in the Fifth Precinct, then narcotics, sex crimes, homicide, and back to the Fifth. He had a reputation as a mean son of a bitch who'd grown up on the lower east side and, according to street talk, had some self-imposed soldier-of-fortune mandate to liberate the east side from the drug gangs. Stan also knew— hell, who didn't?—that McGinnity had been under investigation by Internal Affairs for some off-duty nutcracking, some vigilante stuff. He didn't know to what extent. But Mary had it all. And it wasn't the isolated, penny-ante stuff Stan expected.

According to Mary, IA was investigating eight cases of alleged assault—late-night shakedowns—by McGinnity. The victims, mostly drug-gang scum, were told to get the hell out of town, then pistol-whipped or shot in the hand, foot, elbow, or kneecap, then threatened with worse if they went to the cops. All IA had so far were statements from dirtballs.

She smiled smugly. "And listen to this: At least three victims say they knew McGinnity's little brother and that little Billy McGinnity was shot and killed by . . ."

Stan nodded and interrupted. "The late Julius Caesar Cooper."

Mary nodded.

"Too good, Mary." Stan nodded. "But interesting, and

somewhat worthwhile." Stan went to the refrigerator for another beer. "But if this McGinnity is this Shooter—if, and I'm guessing that's your next profound leap—why does he drill Colbane?"

Mary shook her head. "Meaning?"

"Meaning if he's some secret, midnight superhero, why draw all that attention to himself? He could've let someone else pop Colbane, or let Colbane do it to himself, which he apparently was planning to do."

Mary didn't have an answer.

"And why do we even assume Cooper is telling the truth? Maybe he was just taking advantage of someone's— McGinnity's?—reputation."

Mary was listening hard.

"And why is it that this Shooter's name hasn't cropped up before?"

"Maybe it did."

Stan shook his head. "We would have heard. That kind of shit gets around."

Mary nodded.

"And why would McGinnity shoot Rickey Jefferson?"

Mary shrugged.

Stan took a gulp of his beer. "By the way, where'd you get all this?"

Mary shook her head. "Nope."

"I gotta know."

Mary shook her head again. "No way."

"Dawlson?"

"Forget it, Stosh."

Stan smiled. It was okay—for now. He rubbed his forehead. "Okay, here's the deal." Mary leaned across the table. Stan could smell her perfume. It was slightly sweet, slightly tart. She was sexier than hell, and she knew it. "You go to work on Colbane."

"Why?"

"Because I said so."

"What do we need?"

Stan smiled. "We?" He chuckled. "Anything."

Mary was still confused. "Be more specific."

Stan nodded. "Okay—get everything you can."

Mary looked down at the table. She was making a note. "Give me a hint."

Stan smiled. She wanted to play cop, he wasn't going to coddle her. "I just did."

Mary looked up and smiled. This was going to be all right.

Stan took another slug of his beer. "I'll make some calls, and I'll get together with Al McGinnity."

Mary nodded. "Is that smart?"

Stan shrugged. "Who knows? I keep telling you, Mary, I'm no Rhodes scholar."

"Than what?"

Stan stood. "Three days."

"Three days, what?"

"Don't play stupid, Mary." Stan smiled. "It's unbecoming." He grabbed his coat. "We don't come up with something in three days, I'm through."

Mary figured it was a good time to lobby for more time. "It's ..."

Stan saw it coming. He didn't even look at her. "Three days."

She backed off quickly and held out her hand. "Deal."

Stan shook his head. "I don't make deals, Mary."

Mary nodded, and smiled, almost apologetically. "I'd do all this myself if I could."

"You could."

"Naw." She shook her head. "Plus, I don't think it'd be as much fun."

Stan nodded. "We'll see how much fun it is three days from now." He took his beer can to the sink. "Am I excused?"

Mary nodded. "Unless you want to stay for the social hour."

Stan smiled. "You'd eat me alive, Stimic."

"I doubt it, Chipper." Mary shook her head. "I think you're probably tougher than you let on."

Stan buttoned his coat. "We'll meet again tomorrow night. Eight. My place. Bring a shitload of evidence." He opened the door. "I'd get started if I were you."

* * *

It was after two when Frank pulled into his garage. He had just gotten off the phone again with Hatch. Marty still sounded jittery, and a little drunk. Frank was worried about him. He worried about Hatch's drinking. He had to get him through the next few days. That was all. Hold his hand for a few days until everything settled back to normal. He laughed—normal? Soon. Very soon. He felt it coming. He stared out the windshield, or tried to. He could hardly see anything. The glass was covered with salt from the highway; he'd run out of washer fluid on the freeway. He was surprised he hadn't gotten killed on the way home. He could see the headlines: POLICE CHIEF SURVIVES COURTROOM SHOOT-OUT, DIES IN CRASH CAUSED BY DIRTY WINDOWS.

He got out of his car and looked around the garage for some washer fluid. He had a jug of the stuff somewhere, but he couldn't find it. Marlyss's car—she would have some, in the trunk. She dumped everything in there; it was overflowing with junk. It used to be a joke between them: Something was lost, anything, they'd look in her trunk. Frank opened it. Nothing. No washer fluid—nothing. It was empty, cleaned out. Frank shook his head. He knew right away, and she was disappointing him. He'd thought she was a little smarter than this. Maybe she wasn't. He'd have to have a talk with her, but not yet. For now, he just slammed the trunk closed as hard as he could. He wanted her to hear it all the way in their bedroom.

And she did.

◇ **34** ◇

Stan took a big gulp of coffee. It was cold and he grimaced. He checked the clock—6:22. He looked at the thick stack of paperwork in front of him from the Cooper case and grimaced again. At this rate, he'd be at his desk all night. He got up to stretch, and yawned. He hadn't slept well last night. He felt like an inmate planning an escape. The time was getting closer and he worried that maybe he was just running away—that's all, just running away. Every now and then he felt his nerves rattle, could almost hear them. He had been anxious about things before, but it was never like this. That scared him, a lot.

"Pete?"

"Yep." Dawlson didn't look any fresher than Stan. He was slouched forward, over his desk, writing. He had bags under his eyes. He didn't look up.

"Mary says you laughed her off on this Shooter thing."

"Yep."

"You sure?"

Dawlson continued to write. "Yep."

"Sure, sure?"

"You want it straight?"

Stan nodded. "Okay."

Dawlson put down his pencil and turned toward Stan. He put his hands to his face and rubbed his eyes, then his forehead, then his cheeks. He opened one eye, then the other. "I know women like Mary, Stosh. She's drop-dead gorgeous, and she's got this intensity, this energy, somethin' special inside, that can burn you up if you get caught up in it. Hey, I been around her. I can feel it." He shrugged. "But she's no cop." He tilted his head and raised an eyebrow. "Good newspaperman, maybe, I guess. But no cop—period, end of answer."

Stan shrugged. "She makes a few good points."

Dawlson shook his head. "But cops feel things in here, Stosh, you know that." Dawlson put his hand on his stomach. "And what do you feel?"

"Not much."

"Bingo." Dawlson turned back to his desk. "So, what did you tell her?"

Stan felt foolish. "I gave her three days to show me something."

"Think she will?" Pete was writing again.

Stan shook his head. "No." He wasn't sure he was telling the truth.

"Just take it eas . . ."

"What?"

"Goddamn motherfucker. Look at this shit." Dawlson had reached across his desk and knocked his cup of coffee into his lap. The dark brown liquid was splattered all over his khaki trousers. "Goddamn." Dawlson got up and threw down his pencil. He headed for the bathroom. "I'll be back in a few minutes."

He wasn't gone more than fifteen seconds when Pisarcawitcz stormed into the room. He was pulling double duty again, he was out of breath, and he looked pissed. Pisarcawitcz was carrying another one of his fuck novels, and he started waving it around.

"You motherfucking idiots, you goddamn shitheads, you gotta learn to put the phone back on the goddamn receiver. Jesus and Mary. You think you were one or two goddamn years old. How'n the hell am I going to transfer calls in here when the cocksucking phone's off the motherfucking hook?" Pisarcawitcz went to Dawlson's desk, picked up the receiver, and slammed it hard into the cradle.

Stan didn't say anything.

The desk sergeant's face was red. He was breathing hard. "Where's Dawlson?" And he was still yelling.

Stan shrugged. He was struggling to keep from laughing. "The can."

Pisarcawitcz sniffed. "Figures. Down there playing with his dick. Goddamn."

Stan nodded sympathetically. "What's up?"

Pisarcawitcz looked around the room as if he expected to find Dawlson hiding under a desk somewhere. "Some broad on the phone wants to talk to him about Cooper's dead ass."

"I'll take it."

"She said she wants Mr. Playingwithhisdick."

Stan nodded. He finally smiled. "I got it, Johnny."

Pisarcawitcz took one more look around the room, nodded, then checked to see that the receiver he had slammed into place was, in fact, resting properly. It was. He gritted his teeth, hissed, then turned and headed for the door. "Give me a few goddamn minutes to get back to the desk." The phone rang within thirty seconds.

"Lieutenant Dawlson?" Since the shootout, Stan and Pete had been receiving calls on the hour, every hour, about Cooper and the whole frame-up conspiracy thing. Most callers had been loud and vulgar—Cooper's friends, Stan had guessed. But this call was apparently going to be different. The woman's voice was soft, low, even.

"No, this is Lieutenant Kochinski. I worked the case with Pete." He paused. "Can I help you?" There was no reply. He waited a few seconds longer. "Hello?"

"Julius Cooper didn't shoot the boy."

Stan paused again. For some reason, probably the caller's manner, he wanted to make sure he was polite. "We've heard that before, ma'am."

"Not this way."

Stan remained silent. He was nodding politely . . . and waiting for more.

"I was with Julius when the gun was stolen." Stan and Pete had heard that before, too. But this time was different. The woman's voice was still soft, still low, still even, but there was an eerie purpose to it now.

"I'm not going to talk about it over the phone."

"Where, then?" Stan couldn't believe he had said that. The woman could be anybody, any fucking idiot. Jeezus, was Mary doing this to him?

"Meet me in twenty minutes at Belle Isle." Belle Isle was a city park plopped in the middle of the Detroit River. "Park in the aquarium lot. I'll be along the curb behind the giant slide."

Stan nodded and took a deep breath. He reached under his right arm to make sure his .38 was there. The move was instinctive. The gun was in place.

"You're not alone and I'm gone." The woman paused, her voice still controlled, almost monotone. "You're late and we all lose." She waited for a moment, then hung up.

Stan waited for the dial tone to kick in, then hung up, too. He rubbed his eyes with his open palms, then headed toward the door. He almost bowled over Dawlson as he turned and hustled down the hall.

Pete was still wiping at his pants. He had a ball of soggy, brown paper towels in his hand. "Hot date, Stosh?"

"Later." Stan hurried toward the stairs. "I'll tell you about it later."

Dawlson went into the squad room, then came rushing out. "Stan. Your coat." He shook his head; he was too late. "It's snowing out there, man."

Pisarcawitcz heard the clamor and stuck his head into the hallway. "Musta been some hot call."

Dawlson shrugged. "Who?"

"Sweet-voiced dame called for you. Said she had big-time shit on the Cooper thing."

"Me?"

Pisarcawitcz nodded. "That'll teach you to be in the shitter during workin' hours chokin' the chicken." The desk sergeant wasn't angry any longer. He leered at Dawlson, laughed, then half-jogged down the hallway toward Pete and pulled his book from his back pocket. "But while we're on the subject, read this, right here." Pisarcawitcz fished for a dog-eared page and handed the book to Dawlson. "Here. Page one-twelve. It's unbelievable, Pete. Unfuckingbelievable."

Dawlson took the book and scanned the page, but only pretended to read it. "Sure is, Pisser. It sure is."

Stan was sitting in his car, waiting, when the dark, late-model Mercedes pulled up to the curb across the street. The car was moving slowly, feeling its way, with its lights off in the pitch dark. It stopped right where it was supposed to stop. Stan reached behind his head and flicked a switch on the dome light. He didn't want the bulb flashing on when he opened his door. He took a quick look around, pulled the .38 out of his holster, then got out and began walking slowly toward the car. It was parked about twenty-five yards away. Stan shivered. The wind was blowing hard. The big, wet, heavy snowflakes were coming at him sideways. By the time he got to the car, the left side of his gray-tweed sports jacket was white.

Stan had tried to sneak up on the woman, but the passenger door clicked open as soon as he approached the car. He opened the door and looked in. A bleached blonde sat behind the wheel. The woman took a good look at Stan, and he at her. Then Stan reached around and unlocked the back door and opened it. The backseat was empty. He closed the door, put the .38 in his holster, and climbed in the passenger's side.

It was dark, but Stan figured the woman looked about forty-five. She was almost attractive in a rough, hard way. Her makeup was thick. Her straight hair was pulled back severely. She was wearing an expensive fur jacket and held an unlit cigarette in her left hand. Her right hand was on the steering wheel. The hand trembled. Stan started to speak, but the woman shook her head and removed her hand from the steering wheel and motioned for him to be quiet. Her fingernails were painted a deep red, but they looked black in the darkness. Later, he would remember them, especially. Black fingernails, like those you would imagine on a witch.

"I'm going to keep this short and simple." The woman's tone of voice was no different from the phone. Her hand shook, but her voice didn't. She sounded as though she was in control. Stan continued to stare at her face, trying to place her. She pulled a fancy gold lighter out of her coat pocket and lit the cigarette. Her face was illuminated now, but Stan still didn't recognize her, and she could tell. "And I'm not going to repeat myself."

She took a drag and blew the smoke out the left side of her mouth, steaming the driver's window. "My name is Wendy Broedinger. I'm Dickie Broedinger's wife." She turned back to Stan. "I'm sure you've heard of him."

Stan nodded. He continued to study the woman. Her neck was either wrapped in a white scarf or loosely bandaged. He couldn't tell which for sure.

"I was with Julius Cooper the night his gun was stolen." She took another drag, and this time exhaled while she talked. "It happened just the way you probably heard by now—this Shooter character and all." She took another drag on the cigarette. This one was deep, and hard. "He took Julius's gun, chased him off, then left with it."

"What did this . . ."

She shook her head. "No questions—not yet."

Wendy Broedinger reached forward and pulled open the ashtray. She crushed out her cigarette. "A few days ago, right before the hearing, Dickie met with your boss ..."

"Frank Sims?" Stan could hear the surprise in his own voice.

So did she. She sniffed and smirked. "Yep." She looked out her window. "They cut a deal. Sims got Cooper, and Dickie got a brand new start on the west side."

"West side?" Stan acted incredulous, but it made sense. Parts of the east side were becoming almost too deserted, even for the drug gangs.

Wendy Broedinger nodded. She reached for the ignition. "That's it."

Stan reached over and put his hand gently on hers. "This Shooter ..." There was a twinge of pleading in his voice.

She pulled her hand back, then shook her head and shrugged. "Nothing more to tell. Big, but not too big. It was dark." Wendy Broedinger was staring out the windshield now. "Like tonight."

Stan waited. He was holding his breath. He didn't want to interrupt, and he didn't want her to stop. He remembered what Dawlson had reminded him of about cops and gut reactions. He could feel this one: If she stopped now, she was gone.

"There was something a little strange about him." She looked at Stan and nodded. "Something out of place—the way he walked—carried himself, maybe even talked." She reached into her coat pocket and pulled out a silver cigarette case. "Julius noticed it, too. It was different."

Stan looked puzzled.

"The way he talked, especially. There wasn't a lot of street to it. Not enough jive. Not enough"—she tamped her cigarette on the steering wheel—"nigger."

"Was he black?"

She shook her head. "I don't know."

Wendy Broedinger paused again. The moon had broken through the clouds and cast a bright strip of light on the snow outside. Stan could see her better now. She looked tired, and scared.

"Why?"

"Why what?" She lit her cigarette.

"Why this?"

Wendy Broedinger took a short pull on her cigarette and smiled a small, sad smile. "I looked in the mirror tonight, just before I decided to call, and finally figured out why Dickie hadn't fucked me up real bad. I had been waiting, you know." She glanced into the rear-view mirror and gently touched her neck. "He's going to make it look like suicide." She laughed coldly. "I should have known. No one's going to be able to tell."

She reached for the ignition again, and this time started the car. "I just figured if I'm going to hell—and I am, lieutenant, very soon—some of them are coming with me."

Wendy Broedinger's voice hadn't changed, but her eyes were watery now. She touched a switch on the panel to her left and Stan's door popped open. She shifted the car into drive. "Get out."

The meeting had lasted no longer than five minutes. Stan returned to his car and sat in the dark, thinking. In all the years past, through all the hinky, stinking cases he had investigated, a stark testimony like the one he just heard from Wendy Broedinger would have been enough to convince him that something was pretty screwed up. That, coupled with everything else, would have been more than enough. But this wasn't then. This was now, and Stan didn't want to follow leads. He didn't want to go from A to B to C, connecting the dots. He didn't want to play G-man anymore. He was too close to cutting loose, to being free. He just wanted to be finished, through, done. He was a pilot flying his last wartime mission before being shipped back to the States—and he wanted a milk run into the sunset.

So, Stan told himself he needed more than a preponderance of evidence. He told himself he wanted something beyond a reasonable cop's doubt. He didn't want more—he *needed* it. He slammed his hands against the steering wheel, then gripped it tight. He wished now he hadn't been so polite to Dickie Broedinger's wife. He wished he had slapped the cigarette out of her hand and screamed at her that he needed something even more fucking dramatic than some bizarre confession in some dark, smoke-filled car. He wished he had taken her hard by the goddamn fur jacket, shook her and told her that he wanted something motherfucking absolute; something more than he said, she said; something more than Shooter this and Shooter that; something for sure, something final.

And he had no idea what.

But Wendy Broedinger, bless her black little heart, did.

◇ **35** ◇

Stan was on the phone with Big Time when Mary knocked.

"Hold on a second, pal."

"My time's your money, boss."

Stan shook his head. "I doubt it." He put down the receiver and opened the door. Mary was waiting patiently. She was dressed in a black overcoat, an oversized gray sweatshirt, neon-purple tennis shoes, and black jeans. She looked a lot more relaxed tonight, but it was still early. She smiled. Stan nodded. "Come in. I'm on the phone." He headed back to the couch. "There's a frozen pizza in the oven." He pointed toward the kitchen. "It should be done in about three minutes."

Mary put down the stack of papers she carried under one arm, took off her coat, and headed toward the kitchen. Stan picked up the phone again. "You were saying."

"I was sayin' that I think I'm gonna be needin' a bonus." Stan could hear the grin in Big Time's voice, but he was in no mood for bullshit. He was on edge. He had left Wendy Broedinger only forty-five minutes earlier, and on the way home had decided that three days was stringing out this Shooter thing way too long. He would decide tonight either to hit it hard or forget it. Either Mary had something, or she didn't. He hoped she had gotten stuck with another assignment today. He hoped she hadn't come up with anything. Stan didn't figure Time had, but his cop's conscience told him he was worth a listen.

"Go to hell."

"Whoa, boss. What lunk sum was it we agreed upon?"

Stan ground his teeth. "A *lunk* sum of one hundred—now, knock off the horsecrap."

"I'm gonna be needin' three bills."

"My ass."

"Goodbye."

Stan took a deep breath. He was trying to keep his voice low. He didn't want Mary to hear anything. "Better be good."

"May I commence?" Stan didn't answer. Time didn't care. "It seems that in the course of this 'vestiga ..."

Stan leaned forward toward the coffee table and picked up a pencil and squeezed it until his knuckles turned white. "Cut the crap, BT." He spit out the words between clenched teeth.

"A cop."

Stan winced and bit his bottom lip until it hurt. "You lost your goddamn hear ..."

"I ain't lost nothin'. I'm tellin' you, man—a goddamn cop."

Stan pressed his thumb against the pencil point. "What the fuck does that mean?" The pencil point broke off.

"It means everyone I talked to, all my 'sociates, anyone who would know or hear a peep about this Shooter character—and the pickin's were mighty slim, boss—said there was somethin' strange about him. Somethin' that wasn't quite right." Time stopped and took a breath. "Big guy. Tough. Tough talkin'. Scary mean. That's what everyone remembered."

Stan snapped the pencil in half. "Well, stop the fucking presses." His voice was too sharp, too loud. He was sure Mary could hear.

"I will. I will." Time took a deep breath. "Listen to me, brother." Stan winced. He hated it when Time called him brother. "No one could put a finger on what was so weird. Then someone did." Big Time paused.

"Who?"

"Prince William."

"Who the fuck is that?" Stan's face was wound into a tight grimace. He almost began to laugh. He rubbed his forehead. This was getting stupid.

"Wino hangs out at some party store 'round Mack and Rohns. Or Mack and Bewick, at the Greater True Vine Temple, somethin' like that."

Stan couldn't help but laugh. "Prince William?"

"Right. Well, the Prince, she's . . ."

"She?"

"Yeah, well, he thinks he's a she. We give him benefit of the doubt." Stan shook his head. Time continued. "Anyway, the Prince is sort of a street busybody, sees a lot of shit other folks miss. She . . ."

"He." Stan laughed.

". . . right—confides in me this little tidbit and I retrace with all the rest of the people I intervened . . ."

"Interviewed."

". . . right—and it's like this bulb goes on in their eyes—snap, crackle, flash."

"And?"

"The Prince says this Shooter guy—what info she's heard, now—acted a little too much like a cop, talked a little too much like a cop, walked a little . . ."

Stan nodded. "Thanks. I get the idea."

"Even smelled like a cop. He weren't no street nigger, that's for sure. He was a little too smooth, but not street smooth—honky-like, middle-class, light-beer smooth. Get me?" Time paused. "Us niggers can see that shit comin' a mile away."

This wasn't irritating anymore. It wasn't fun, either. Big Time's description of Shooter was beginning to sound a lot like Wendy Broedinger's, and they both sounded a lot like someone like Al McGinnity. Stan shook his head. "A cop." It was a statement.

"That's what I been tellin' you, boss. My humble opinion

is that ya'll got some crazyass headknocker out there calls himself Shooter—and he's carryin' a badge, just like you."

It wasn't what Stan needed to hear. What he'd wanted to hear was that Time had found nothing. Zip. Zero. Then, he stopped and thought for a second. He considered the source. Prince William? He laughed. "A cop."

"Three bills." Stan didn't answer. "After all, boss, wasn't I the first one told you that Cooper was missin' his favorite piece? Remember?"

He had. Stan nodded. "A cop." He laughed again.

"Thas right—a cop."

"By the way, did you or the Princess happen to get this cop's badge number?"

Time sighed exasperatedly. "Don't be fuckin' with me, boss."

Stan nodded. "Check's in the mail, pal."

"C'mon, man . . ."

Stan hung up. Mary heard Stan put the phone down, waited a few seconds, then returned to the living room. She was carrying two plates of pizza. Stan took one and thanked her. "Let's get to it."

Mary nodded. "Right." She sat on the far end of the couch.

"How'd it go?" Stan was hoping for the worst.

"Not bad. A good start."

"Let's hear it."

Mary took a bite of pizza, then put it down and wiped her mouth. "For starters, I'd say Missy Colbane was raped."

"Says?"

"I found a guy at St. John Hospital says he remembers seeing someone who looked like Colbane coming in there late one night about a year ago. Showed him a picture of the judge. The one we ran yesterday. He said that was the guy. Man saw something and went to pieces, he said. Staggered like he was drunk. Kept mumbling something like 'Sissy, Chrissie.' " Mary shrugged. "Missy?" Stan didn't say anything. "Then, I got a cousin of a cousin who's a secretary for a rape crisis center in Southfield said there was some talk early this year about some bigshot's kid getting ripped up pretty bad. She wouldn't give me a name. I asked her if it was Melissa Colbane. She wouldn't answer. And . . ."

"A cousin of a cousin and, what . . . an emergency room intern?"

Mary shook her head. "Security guard . . ."

Stan laughed. "Great."

". . . and my guy in Sex Crimes." Mary watched Stan's smug smile disappear.

"Who?"

Mary shook her head. "Not on your life, Stosh. This guy thinks Sims is a scumbag of the first order, but he kept the thing quiet when Frank told him to, because of the girl. I had to promise him I wouldn't use the information."

Stan shook his head. "Then what good is it?"

Mary looked him dead in the eye. "Might get you off your dead ass."

"Not yet." Stan shook his head again; he didn't like all the thoughts welling up inside it. He was done, damnit, done. He had promised . . .

"As for Cooper?" Mary shrugged again. "Nothing for sure."

Stan nodded. "So, Colbane just flipped, taking out all his pent-up rage in some dramatic, theatrical execution. Case, Ms. Stimic, still closed."

Mary continued. "You already know, I'm sure, that Colbane killed Cooper and Stone with a Saturday-night special."

Stan nodded. He'd known that before Cooper's body was cold. All this no news was still good news.

"Right." Mary nodded, too. "Then, just for the hell of it, I got a pal over at the courthouse to pull a printout of Colbane's docket for the last nine months."

Mary paused. Stan didn't say anything this time. "Well, I run through the list and I start recognizing some of the names—Timothy 'Capone' Stallings, Sammy Malzone, 'Flatface' Wilston, Randy 'Dr. Funk' Borden, Markie . . ."

"Not exactly your litany of the saints."

"Nope."

"All members of the Knights."

"Former members." Mary handed Stan a list of those

names and two others. "They're all dead." Stan studied the list. "All hit, less than a week after walking out of the courthouse."

"How do you know?"

"I took a flier and ran their names through the *Free Press* computer. Our cop reporter keeps a disk with all the homicide victims. Gets the info from your police records."

"So, they're dead." Stan took a bite of his pizza. It was cold. It tasted like cardboard. "Big deal."

"So, I call Homicide." Mary stood. "You recognize some of these stiffs, right?" Stan nodded. "No big-timers, right?"

"Punks."

"But recognizable names."

"To us and the narcs, maybe."

"Would you remember if their cases were open or closed?"

"These guys? Maybe. Probably." Stan sat back against the couch. "In fact, I'd be willing to guess, especially with the way this line of questioning is headed, that all the cases are open."

"Why?"

"We're talking about itty-bitty wise-ass motherfuckers here. Low-level idiots. They get knocked, who cares? One more shithead down. We wave at cases like these and file 'em away. They wanna kill each other off, great."

Mary nodded.

"I'm guessing that doesn't surprise you one helluva lot." Stan was acting smug again. "In fact, I can tell you for sure that at least three of those cases are wide open."

"How?"

"They were mine—Stallings, Wilston, and this other jerkoff, number six—and I didn't give a shit."

Mary shook her head. "All closed, Stosh."

"What?"

"Solved, apparently."

Stan shook his head. "My ass."

"Okay." Mary stood and shrugged. Now, she was smiling—smugly.

Stan was on his feet now, too. "Says who?"

"Our files . . ."

Stan smiled, but it was an effort. "Great. Your files." He walked up to Mary and poked her in the chest. He was careful to avoid her breasts. He hit her breastbone. "Well, *your* files are wrong, flat-ass wrong."

She poked him back, same place. ". . . and *your* files, Chipper." Stan was stunned. Mary nodded. "No shit." She was in Stan's face now. She held up a photocopy of one file—Sammy Malzone's. It was stamped closed. "Signed off by Chief Scumbag."

Stan felt like a boxer on the ropes. He tried to bounce back. He even surprised himself by trying to defend Frank Sims. "He signs off on all the closed cases."

Mary countered flawlessly. "Even when they're not closed?"

Stan didn't say anything for a moment. "Okay." He threw up his hands. "An accounting mistake."

Mary shook her head. "An accounting mistake is when you add two and two and get a tax writeoff and the IRS finds out. These are stiffs, dead people, shitheads that no one cares about. Why lie?"

Stan shook his head. "It's explainable."

Mary sniffed. "You gotta be kidding."

"We're in the nineteenth century up there, Mary. None of this crap is even on a computer. We're still doing everything by hand."

Mary's eyes weren't flickering any more; they were on fire. She was angry. "There's something here, Stosh. You know it, and I know it." Stan didn't say anything. Mary poked him again. Hard. "Is it you?" Stan looked at her like she was crazy. "Are you Frank Sims's inside guy?"

Stan shook his head and laughed. "Go to hell."

"He needs someone."

"Not tonight, Mary."

"Then when, Stosh?" She threw her hands up. "Maybe you worked for Colbane."

"Colbane?"

"Sure. Maybe he was the Shooter."

"Bill Colbane?"

"Sure, he goes out on these guerrilla missions looking to take out all the Knights he can find because one of them

raped his daughter and he shoots the poor sucker kid by
mistake, then apologizes to the kid's mother and tries to
blow his own brains out."

"That's some flying leap." Stan looked at Mary as though
she had said the sky was falling.

She didn't care. "You got a better theory?"

Stan was sitting again. He didn't answer. He felt as
though he were on a runaway train, reeling back and forth,
from one side of the track to the other, and he wanted to get
off. He quickly started to review everything. Mary was convincing enough. Not about Colbane. That was pretty far-
fetched. Stan figured he had just shorted out. But everything
else? Especially Sims. Signing off on the cases? Why? A
mistake? Maybe. Maybe. Wendy—the deal with Broedinger.
That was the key. That was it. But how did he know for
sure if *she* was telling the truth? How could he know for
sure? Stan put his head in his hands. Something was still
missing. He could feel it. And it felt both bad and good.

"Well?" It was Mary. She was going for the kill.

Stan nodded. He was ready to speak when the phone
rang. It was Pisarcawitcz.

"Eff-wise-eyes, Stosheroo. Just callin' to keep all you big
homeboys up to speed."

Stan didn't have time for his happy horseshit. "Speak En-
glish, Pisser."

"Fuck you, Stosh." Pisarcawitcz's voice turned into a
whine. "What? I interrupt something?"

"I'm not in the mood, pal."

"Well, fuck me all to hell, then." His voice was still sing-
songy. Pisarcawitcz paused. "Excuse me."

Stan sighed. "Let's just have it."

Pisarcawitcz grunted. "You know this Dickie Broedinger
asshole?" All of a sudden, Stan knew what was coming.
It was coming. He didn't say anything. "You there,
dickhead?"

Stan nodded.

"Little wifey gassed herself in the car tonight. Happened
just a few minutes ago. Early call is suicide, clean and simple. Over and out."

Stan didn't say anything.

"You there, shithead?"

Nothing.

"Answer, for chrissakes."

Stan nodded. "Right." He paused and took a deep breath. "Thanks."

Stan put down the phone, slowly, gently. Nothing was missing anymore. He couldn't explain away Wendy Broedinger. It was all there now, all stacked up, too many questions, all the convincing he needed. He could feel Mary's stare, that's all. Everything else was numb. He went into the kitchen and stood at the counter. He looked down—for the note he'd written to himself a few nights ago, on Christmas, the reminder to call Alabama. It wasn't there.

Mary had followed him into the kitchen. "What're you looking for?"

Stan stopped, when to the refrigerator, and got himself a beer. "Nothing." He popped open the can and took a long, cold gulp, then headed back into the living room. He sat back down on the couch. "Looks like we got more work to do."

Mary nodded. "So, you're in?"

Stan didn't say anything. He just looked at her. He wasn't going anywhere, not now, anyway. He was still a cop to-night, and there was no escaping that. He shrugged, then looked away.

Mary smiled. "You were born to be a cop, Chipper."

It was the high, hard one. Stan flinched. Maybe Mary was right. Maybe she was goddamn right.

$$\Diamond \ 36 \ \Diamond$$

Frank studied Marty Hatch's eyes. He didn't like what he was seeing. Hatch's eyes didn't just flicker with terror, they smoldered with it. The mayor was sitting in a chair in Frank's study with his elbows on his thighs, his chin in his hands, and his face to the floor. He was on his fourth double Scotch, and he looked it. His tie was down. His hair was mussed. The left side of his pink carnation was crushed. Frank watched him carefully. He said nothing.

"This . . ." Hatch stopped, shook his head and looked up, at the trim, prim Christmas tree in the corner. The tiny red lights flickered like hundreds of miniature flames. His voice was low. "Jesus Christ, Frank, what have we done?" The mayor's hands were shaking. "Bill Colbane, for chrissakes. Stone."

Frank nodded. "No more, Marty."

Hatch shook his head. He laughed, softly, to himself. "Right. But no guarantees, huh? Isn't that what you said, here, a year ago? No guarantees."

Frank shrugged. He really didn't remember. He had said a lot of things, here, that night, a year ago. He had said everything he had to say.

Hatch stood. His eyes were wet again. His hands were still trembling. He walked to the bar and struggled to put his glass down. He did, then waited until it clattered to a stop. "And someone's going to find out, Frank—then what?"

Frank shook his head. He'd brought Hatch to the house to try to calm him. He thought it would be different with Hatch than with Colbane, but he was beginning to realize he was wrong. Marty Hatch was panicking—big time. The courtroom scene had really spooked him. Worse, he was drinking too much, way too much. Frank had watched and listened to Hatch's edges unravel stitch by stitch the last thirty-six hours. He'd told Hatch to stay cool, what, at least fifty times, counting the twenty-five minutes they'd been locked in Frank's study? But Hatch wasn't listening to anyone but himself. Marty Hatch was a great frontrunner. Campaign bosses loved him when he was ahead. He listened when he had a lead, went for the jugular, put his opponents away. But when he got behind, big, tough Martin Hatch III got scared. He stopped paying attention and began flailing away. And he was reverting to form now. Frank kept trying to get through. He had no choice.

"No one will find out, Marty." Frank's voice had started out friendly and comforting when they'd entered the study. Now, it was stern, and businesslike. Frank was working hard to keep it from becoming impatient and angry.

Hatch shook his head. "I believed you before, Frank, when you talked to Bill, told him things would be all right, okay, over and over again. You call this okay? Look at us."

Frank stood and walked to the bar. "No, Marty, not us— you." Hatch looked Frank in the eye. Frank stood tall and straightened the mayor's lapels. He primped up his carnation, brushed his hair back with his hand, and took a cocktail napkin and wiped the sweat from the mayor's forehead. "You." He was whispering now. "It's you. Not me. I still believe." Frank nodded. "We're still the only ones who know. Just us, now, me and you. It's even safer this way." Hatch shook his head. Frank didn't. "Us two." The mayor reached for the bottle of Scotch. Frank got to it first, grabbed it politely, and placed it back on the shelf. "Us. Two."

Hatch turned away and walked to the Christmas tree. He stood there, still shaking his head. Frank followed him. "Look at where we are, Marty." Frank's voice was low. "Eleven days ago we were in this same room—and we were dead. All of us." Frank nodded. "A stupid mistake, and we turned it around. Sure, you believed me then, that we were okay. But I didn't know, not for sure. But I had to convince you and Stone—and Colbane." He backed toward the bar. "And I did. And I was right. And here I am again. And now I am sure, again. We—are—okay."

It was the same sort of speech Frank had given Colbane in private. Hatch was staring at the floor. Frank was sitting on the couch now. "Marty." Hatch was listening to his own little voice again, Frank could tell. "Marty! Colbane killed Cooper, we didn't! We didn't do anything. Anyone starts snooping around with some sort of wild conspiracy theory and we lay it right at Bill's feet." Frank shrugged. "Right there. He was the Lone Ranger, a bug-eyed parent avenging his daughter's rape."

Hatch looked at Frank. Frank nodded. "Someone tries to

tie us to the courtroom, I just leak that police report on Missy Colbane's rape."

Hatch looked surprised. "You said . . . I thought it never got into the system."

Frank shook his head. "It didn't. It never got into the system." Frank paused. "But don't underestimate me, Marty. Don't ever do that." Frank stopped again, got up and went to the fireplace and grabbed the poker. He turned back to Hatch. "We're reborn, Marty. You and me—us. We can go forward from here. We were wallowing in shit before, but not anymore."

Hatch was sitting down. Frank had gotten his attention. "The Shooter?"

Frank shrugged and poked at the logs. "What about him?"

"What if he decides to blackmail us? Then what?"

Frank shook his head. "He won't."

"How do you know?"

Frank shrugged. "Because I know."

Hatch began smiling. It was an odd, almost crazed smile. "Is it you?" He pointed his finger at Frank. "If it is, then it would really be just the two of us." Frank was losing him again. "I knew it. I knew it. You—the Shooter. I knew it. Perfect, Frank. God, I knew it." Hatch began laughing, crazily, almost hysterically.

Frank dropped the poker, walked to Hatch's chair, and stood before him. Frank's face was cold and blank, but only for a moment. He yanked Hatch to his feet with his left hand and slapped him hard and quick with his right. "Knock off the crap, Marty. Now." But Hatch couldn't stop laughing—or crying. Frank shook him. "Now listen." He shook him again. "You hear me?" Hatch was trying. He nodded. He was breathing in gasps and staring at Frank. "Number one, no one knows—no one." Frank's teeth were clenched. The words came out in vicious hisses. "Two, Cooper is gone and we're goddamn heroes. Hell, even the preachers have disappeared like fucking cockroaches back into their crummy, hellhole storefront churches. Three, Falwell from PR called me today and said Myrtle Jefferson has agreed to do some PSAs for us—support your local cops, that kind of crap." He threw Hatch back into the chair. "Believe that?" Frank wiped his forehead with the back of his hand. He was sweating now, and smiling, almost wickedly. "That's where we stand, Marty." Frank's eyes were blazing. "Clean. Clear. Ready to move ahead. Understand?" Hatch didn't move. His chin was on his chest. Frank reached down and grabbed the mayor by the jowls. He twisted Hatch's face toward his. "Understand?"

Hatch nodded, slowly, avoiding Frank's gaze.

Frank let him go. "We stop looking back, right here and right now. You will stop looking back." He went to the bar and poured himself another drink. "No more whining about what happened in that fucking courtroom. No more whimpering about poor old Bill. He was an imbecile. An idiot. Weak. Gutless. Jesus, Marty, didn't you see that?" Frank slapped the top of the bar. "Can't you?" He took a hard gulp from his glass. "We aren't. Us, Marty. We survived. We made it."

Frank stopped and walked to the sofa. He was out of breath, and sat down. For the first time in the forty minutes they had been sequestered in the room, Frank heard the soft Christmas hymns playing in the background. It had been there all along—"Angels We Have Heard on High," "Away In a Manger," "O Come, All Ye Faithful." Now, it took all the edge off the terrible silence. Frank took a deep breath. His neck ached. He rubbed it, then took another slug of his drink. Hatch was staring straight ahead, into the fireplace. "I . . . talked to Chet today." The mayor's voice was soft, almost monotone. He was afraid to look at Frank. He was weeping again. "He says we aren't reborn at all, Frank. He says we aren't heroes."

Frank looked at the mayor, shook his head, and squinted across the room at Hatch. "What the fuck's that mean?"

Hatch's voice was still low. "It means my political future is here, Frank, and nowhere else." The mayor looked at Frank, then away. "Lyttle was on the phone all day and says I can probably salvage another term here—maybe. But that's about it. He says, he put it, I'm tainted—damaged goods. That's what the party says now, that I fought the good fight, made a helluva comeback, but it took too long, all these years." Hatch was staring at his shoes. "They got some guy in Grand Rapids and another in Kalamazoo. I didn't even recognize the names." He stopped. He was sobbing. "I'm done, Frank." He wiped his eyes. "I'm sorry."

Frank nodded. He didn't have anything to say. Didn't know what to say. He hadn't planned for this. He'd been too busy with everything else. Nothing was geared toward this. Everything was set for saving themselves, then moving up and out—moving Hatch up and out. He wanted to talk to Lyttle himself. Maybe Hatch was just panicking again. Maybe he'd gotten it all screwed up. But what if he was right? Frank was in line behind the mayor, and for how long? This was wrong, all wrong. Frank couldn't leapfrog over Hatch. Not now. It was too soon.

Frank felt his chest tighten. He was struggling to breathe. He fought himself for control. Hatch was watching him. He had to get out for a second. He loses it bad here, and Hatch blows for sure. Frank walked to the door, opened it, entered the hallway, and closed the door behind him. He leaned against the wall, his chest heaving, calmed himself, then slammed his fist against the wall. He gritted his teeth and began thinking.

Hatch was going down and the yellow sonofabitch was taking Frank with him . . . or was he? Oh, Christ, he was a fool. Frank Sims was a fool. He had been wasting his time in the study trying to talk some sense into Marty Hatch, when he'd known all along that Hatch wouldn't get it, couldn't get it. None of this was about saving Marty Hatch, anyway, ultimately. Frank shook his head. He'd been making things too complicated. Way too complicated. He locked the study from the outside, then hustled down the hallway to the phone. He picked up the receiver and dialed quickly. A voice answered. Frank didn't waste time saying hello. "It's Sims. The mayor needs a ride home. Now."

Then he hung up.

◊ 37 ◊

"**H**ow long you been here?" Stan leaned up on one elbow in bed and looked across the room. Marlyss was sitting with her legs tucked under her in the chair near the window. She was wearing only the flannel shirt that had been hanging on the bedpost.

"I don't know. Not long, I guess."

He squinted at the clock on the nightstand—1:08—and tried to blink away some of the sleep. It wasn't easy, and it wasn't working.

"Where've you been? Work?"

"No—out. Driving. Then I came here. I needed some time to think."

"Done?" Stan smiled, tiredly.

Marlyss brushed her hair back. It was a nervous habit that Stan recognized. "No, not yet."

He could tell she wanted to talk. "What've you been thinking about?"

"Lots of things—crazy things. Mostly us." She smiled bashfully, as though she were embarrassed. "Except, right before you woke up, I was thinking about the second grade, and St. Cecilia's."

Stan rubbed his eyes, then got up. "St. Cecilia's, huh?"

"Sister Cosette picked me to crown Mary during the May ceremonies. I'm not sure why. I never thought she liked me much. Maybe she felt sorry for me. Suzanne George was her favorite." Marlyss paused and nodded. "Her mother— George the Gorge—baked cookies for the sisters. I think Suzy ended up being a nun." Marlyss laughed, softly. "I wore my mother's old Communion dress. It was brittle and prickly around the collar, and had two huge yellow spots on

274

the skirt. And it was so hot that day, about ninety, at least. But I felt so . . . pure . . . or something. The way only a young girl can feel. Sometimes." Stan was in front of her now; she looked up at him. "I'll never forget feeling that way, Stosh." She smiled and shrugged. The flannel shirt fell open. "Silly stuff, I told you."

Stan smiled back. "I was an altar boy."

Marlyss laughed again. "Of course you were, Stanislaw."

Stan knelt before her. She looked so tiny tonight. He leaned forward, carefully, resting his arms on her, and tried to gaze into her eyes. It was too dark. He looked down, instead, and touched her stomach, then lightly traced the dark, thin line of down that began just below her navel and ended in perfect lushness in her lap. Marlyss put her hands on his head and caressed him, pulling him to her. Neither of them moved for seconds, a minute, two.

"Stan?" He pulled back and looked up at her. He still couldn't see her face very well in the darkness. It sounded like she was smiling; she wasn't. "Tell me that we can leave tonight, Stan, right now."

"And where would we go?"

"Anywhere." She wasn't looking at him anymore. She was shaking her head and staring across the room. "Not tomorrow. Not the next day. Not next week." She was nodding now, mostly to herself. "Now, Stan." She paused to take a deep breath, then looked down again, this time deep into his eyes. "I'm ready. Tonight. Anywhere."

"You packed?"

She shook her head. "I'm serious, Stan. Dead serious."

Stan stood, slowly, then turned and stole another glance at the clock—1:33. He rubbed his eyes, then turned to the window, walked to it, and looked out the frosted glass, trying to buy time, trying to think. A car was heading down the service drive to the freeway, its headlights bouncing into the darkness as it cut across the icy ruts in the road. The vehicle stopped when the driver saw the WRONG WAY sign.

Stan watched the car back up and was suddenly, horribly awash with the sickening sensation he'd had the split second before that pitch crushed Billy Rogine's face so many years ago, when he'd screamed for time to stop in some sort of freeze-frame so he could pull Rogine out of the picture; when he'd wished so hard for the inevitable somehow to be avoided—and it couldn't be. Something, he knew, was going to happen and he wasn't going to be able to stop it.

Leave tonight? Not with what he knew about Jefferson and Cooper and Wendy Broedinger. That was one road he had to follow to the end. And now with what he knew about Frank Sims, he understood, as surely as he was standing there, that he could not go anywhere with Frank Sims's wife now, maybe not ever. And, even worse, he could not tell her why. He saw Marlyss's reflection in the window. She was standing behind him.

"Not out there, Stan. I'm in here."

He spoke to her reflection. "I can't."

She took him by the arms and turned him around. He could see her dark eyes clearly now, flickering with hope and fear. "You said after the Cooper investigation—you said that was it."

"I know."

"Well, it's *over*, Stan." She was whispering, but her voice was strong. She let go of him, but he could still feel the burn where her fingers had held him. "It's over. Cooper is *dead*. What's left?"

"I'm not finished."

"I don't understand." She attempted to camouflage the anger that was creeping into her words, but her voice was low and steely. "What is this, some kind of cop talk?"

He shook his head. "No. I can't explain now, Marlyss. There's just . . . more work to be done. It's bad timing."

"Bad timing." She nodded. "Bad timing." She walked to the bed and sat down. "Will it ever be over, Stosh?"

"Yes. Soon."

"Soon? Then what, Stan?"

"Then we talk and—"

"Talk? *Talk?*" She grimaced, then sprang from the bed. "We've already talked, Stan. What are we going to talk about? This isn't a vacation." Her eyes were lit again. Her voice was still low, but the tone was growing sharper. She grabbed his arms. "We're talking about us. Not a vacation in the mountains, or some luxury cruise, or some sweaty weekend fuck in Alabama!" She paused. She hadn't wanted to mention Alabama, but it was out there now. "What was Alabama, Stosh, some funny, little joke? After all this time, I thought you'd understand. I can't just leave him. I need someone to take me *away*. Don't you know that? Haven't you been listening to what I've been saying—to what I *haven't* been saying?" She faced him, balled her fists, and shook them at him. "I can't—just—leave him."

Stan shook his head. "Why not?"

"You don't know me, Stosh." Marlyss's shoulders sagged. Her voice was suddenly soft. "From second grade to Marlyss Sims . . . there's a lot in between."

"Then tell me."

She began to say something, but then the phone rang, ripping through the room like thunder. Stan answered it, reflexively, and wished he hadn't. It was Mary. He took a deep breath, his voice almost inaudible. "Not now, Mary."

She paid no attention. She didn't care. "I've got something very . . ."

"Not now."

"But, listen . . ."

He finally had to yell. "Not. Now." He lowered his voice. "Tomorrow."

He hung up the phone, sweating now, and looked at Marlyss. "What, Marlyss? What is it?"

She shook her head. "Stan, I—"

The phone rang again. This time Stan let it ring, but the answering machine kicked in.

"Kochinski. This is Sims. It's an emergency. Hatch has had some sort of accident. Meet Dawlson at the curve on Rochester near Coach Lamp in Oakland Township as soon as possible. I need . . ."

Stan took a deep breath and picked up the phone. He talked to Frank for a few seconds, then hung up and looked at Marlyss. She was sitting in the chair again, just as she was when he'd woken, legs under her, staring across the room at him. "I've got to go now. The mayor . . ."

She nodded. "I know." she smiled a thin, almost invisible smile, just like the ones Jenny'd used to smile. "You always have to go, Stosh."

* * *

Marlyss sat, unmoving, in the dark, for a few minutes after Stan had left, waiting for the phone call she knew was coming. It arrived less than five minutes later. She walked to the table, tugged the flannel shirt tight, and picked up the receiver.

The voice on the line was hard and low. "It's time to come home, dear." The announcement was followed by a sharp laugh. "You know why."

Marlyss nodded.

Frank was right.

She did.

◇ **38** ◇

"**O**nce more on a few things here, Frank, just to make sure I've got it all straight."

Frank was on the phone in his office. The voice on the other end belonged to Wally Charles, a crusty police reporter with the *News*. Frank checked his watch. It was 7:54. He'd been fielding calls and answering questions on Hatch's fatal accident for almost two hours, and he probably would be at it for at least another hour. Frank switched Charles to the speaker phone, put down the receiver, and stood to stretch his legs. He ran a hand through his hair, then held out both hands in front of him. They were steady. He nodded to himself, then looked down at his phone. Three of the four remaining lines were blinking. Only the yellow light—the last one on the right, the private line—was out. He put both hands on his desk, leaned forward, then buzzed his receptionist, Debra Crowell.

"Yes, sir?" Crowell's voice still trembled a bit. The secretary, a stiff woman in her early fifties, had worked in

Hatch's office for five years. Before that, she had worked on his campaigns. She had transferred to Frank's office only at Hatch's urging. She was a Hatch loyalist, and the morning was taking its toll. Frank didn't much care for her. He thought she was stupid.

He rubbed his eyes. "Take the names and numbers of the rest, will you? Keep them in order. I'm taking a break after this call."

"What?" It was Charles.

"Not you, Wally. Hold on." Frank put Charles on hold and pressed the intercom button again for Crowell. "And more coffee, Debra. Lots—strong and hot."

Frank took Charles off hold. "Okay. Let's finish up." Frank sat down and put his feet on his desk. He had decided not to hold a news conference until later in the afternoon, when the autopsy results would be official. This one-on-one stuff was tiring. Every reporter asked the same questions. But this was a new beginning, and Frank, speaking in a low, solemn, businesslike voice, was trying to be as patient and polite and straightforward and accommodating as possible.

"Hatch's car was found on its hood at the bottom of that thirty-foot ravine at . . ." Frank knew Walters well. He was in his late fifties, would've been perfect for one of those old movies about newspapers. He spoke in a monotone that made him sound almost bored.

"Right. On the way to that cottage of his, or summer home, getaway, whatever it was, out by the lake." Frank paused. "You going out there?" Frank's eyes burned. He squeezed them tight, then opened them again. It didn't help. The sting didn't go away.

"Someone else already did. Some mess. He went through the windshield?"

"He was thrown from the car." Frank patted his forehead. The gash near his temple had needed five stitches, and the sutures were itching. He played with the bandage.

"Medical—let's see, you said . . ."

Frank switched off the speaker and picked up the phone. "Make sure you double-check all this with the morgue. This is all preliminary."

". . . right—a fractured skull, a broken leg, and two punctured lungs and . . . a broken neck."

"Two legs, one lung. They found him at the base of a tree." Frank saw his door begin to open and quickly swung his feet off the desk. Crowell was coming in with the coffee. Her face was more tightly pinched than usual. She poured Frank a cup, and he took a sip. "You going to print all that?"

"Dunno. The car was discovered by a motorist who noticed tire tracks leaving the road?"

"Correct."

"Time?"

"About 1:15."

"Time of accident?"

Frank shrugged. "Not sure."

"Death?"

Crowell was slow leaving. Frank cupped his hand over the phone. "Thanks, Debra."

"Huh?" Charles again.

"Coroner says instantaneous."

"Skid marks?"

"The road was snow-covered, Wally. It's pretty dark out there. Looks like he just overdrove his headlights."

"Right. Who you got on it?"

"Dawlson and Kochinski. But Traffic'll take it soon as we finish the preliminary report." Frank pulled open a side drawer and propped up his feet. "Another hour."

"Contributing causes—besides the weather?"

"Later, Wally."

"When?"

"This afternoon. We'll get everyone together. You'll be contacted."

"One more thing. Off the record. The mayor's job— you?"

Frank paused. Charles was a lightweight among the local media and Frank didn't owe him an answer. Still, Frank wanted to sound perfect, if for no other reason than to practice. The answer had to be right. Frank could seem neither too interested in the possibility nor too offended by the question. Sincere. Honest. Humble. A bit emotional. Tired, but not exhausted. Matter-of-fact, but conversational. Obtuse. Smooth, but not slick. All that. "Come on, Wally, Marty hasn't been dead—what?—six hours." Simple, but nice. Especially the tone, and the way his voice faded at the end. He would remember that. Nice touch.

"Right. Had to ask."

Frank had been perfectly disarming. "I know." Just a twinge of disgust.

He put down the phone and took a deep breath, chugged the rest of his coffee, and buzzed Crowell. "Break time. Hold my calls."

"Yes, sir.

Frank took a deep breath. He still felt calm, relaxed, but his palms were clammy. The flashes of anxiety and paranoia would fade with time. You had to stave off the panic early, stay away from tiny mistakes, misstatements. Frank nodded. He would be okay. After all, there was no Colbane, no Stone, no Hatch. Just him. He would rise or fall on his own now. He smiled. He couldn't have planned everything like this if he'd tried. Except for a few nasty speed bumps along the way—Colbane, Hatch—it really had been easy. And he owed it all to Rickey Jefferson, some nowhere, nobody, nothing kid, who'd stopped a bullet meant for someone else. He laughed out loud. He couldn't stop.

He walked to the closet, looked in the mirror, straightened his tie, and smiled at himself. Only one thing could make everything even better. Frank checked his watch—it was eight. Any time, now. He went back to his desk, sat down, put his fingertips together, and stared at the phone. Nothing. Nothing. Nothing. Nothing. Then, almost as though he had willed it, the yellow light at the end of the string lit up. Frank picked up the receiver.

"Sims."

"Chet Lyttle, Frank."

Perfect. The dominoes just kept right on falling—his way. Frank smiled, but disguised it in his voice. "Yes, Chet."

"Sorry."

"Me, too."

"Listen, two things." Frank could hear the mayor's press secretary take a hard drag on a cigarette. "I hear Marty was at your house last night and that preliminary tests show alcohol in his system."

"Where are you getting your information?"

"I have my sources." Lyttle coughed.

Frank nodded. "He left about midnight. He had a few drinks."

"Then what?"

"You're asking the wrong guy, Chet. Marty and I were close, but I wasn't his brother and certainly not his keeper."

"You know he went through a tough alcohol rehab four years ago?"

Frank tried to gauge Lyttle's tone. He couldn't tell for certain if it was informational or accusatory. Frank played it straight. He had to. "I'd heard bits and pieces." Frank lied. Sandy Stone's file on Hatch had had every detail of the supposed fishing vacation Hatch had taken to Minnesota almost five years ago, down to the wallpaper pattern in the mayor's bathroom at the Hazelden rehab center.

Lyttle sucked hard again on the cigarette. "Not many knew." Informational, Frank was certain from Lyttle's tone. He relaxed again. Lyttle exhaled loudly. "He had a tough battle with the bottle. Almost killed him. Word was he was staying pretty sober." Lyttle paused and waited for Frank to say something. Frank was silent. Lyttle hesitated some more, then finally continued. "Listen, I've already been on the phone with the state party chairman." He took another drag. "The old news is that they had no intention of running Marty for governor next fall. Too much baggage."

Frank nodded. "I'd heard something like that. Nothing official. It didn't surprise me."

"It would have been a big gamble, even with the Jefferson turn-around—even though everyone got a hard-on a mile long when you took Cooper down."

Frank nodded again.

Lyttle paused. "You like politics, Frank?"

Frank fought off another smile. "I like challenges."

Lyttle coughed again, hard this time. "Well, the party's got a lot of money, and they got these two decent guys outstate. But I gave them your name a few minutes ago. They think you're worth, as they put it, *cultivating.*"

Frank cleared his throat. "This is all moving pretty fast, Chet."

Lyttle grunted. "No speed limit in this game, Frank. But lots of shadows. We get around pretty good."

Frank stood and walked to the window and looked out. The streets were slush-covered, the sky was gray. The forecast was dreary—snow mixed with rain. Frank took a deep breath.

"First thing we need to do is get you into the mayor's mansion. You interested?"

"Between you and me?"

Lyttle sniffed. "Frank, don't ever talk to me like I'm some snot-nosed idiot reporter."

Frank nodded. He had to be more careful. "Maybe." That was too careful.

"Don't play around, either, goddamnit. I know you. And to tell you the truth, I'm not sure I like you." Frank went back to his desk and sat down. "Someone could probably even convince me over a few beers that you went out there last night and pushed Marty's car off the road."

Frank said nothing. He wondered if the silence sounded incriminating.

"No, I don't like you very much at all, Frank Sims." Lyttle took another drag on his cigarette. "But, then again, I don't have to."

Frank didn't know what to say. He guessed. "What do I do?"

Lyttle extinguished his cigarette, fished around his desk for another pack, found only a half-smoked butt, and lit it. "Sit tight. The city charter says the council president takes over until the next election or until the council sets up a special election."

"June Foster's the president."

"Right." The speed of Frank's reply wasn't lost on Lyttle. "She can be, let's say, convinced to hold a special election—pronto. And there's really no one else, Frank, not in the wake of the Cooper thing."

Frank said nothing.

"So, just be patient. Lie low. You meeting with the press today?"

"Later, four, five, somewhere around there."

"Make it 5:15. Make it a TV press conference." Another drag, another cough. "In fact, let me arrange it, discreetly, of course. I'll work through Debra."

"Okay."

"You thought about what you're going to say?"

"Mainly answer questions."

"Okay, but let's make a big deal out of the cause of the accident."

"Meaning?"

"The alcohol."

"Marty was a good friend, Chet."

Lyttle sniffed. Frank couldn't tell if it was disbelief or a small hint of disdain for the late mayor. "Don't bullshit me, Frank." It was a little of both.

"Okay." Frank nodded. "Why?"

"Because you're clean. You don't drink and drive." Lyttle chuckled, this time in amusement. "You are clean, aren't you?"

Frank tried to make a joke. "Last time I looked."

"Well, you're the upstanding candidate now, Police Chief Frank Sims. You nailed Cooper. You take over for a man with well-known, documented weaknesses for women and alcohol." It sounded to Frank as though Lyttle was making notes as he talked. "You're a tough lawman and you're married. You have a stylish, classy wife. The party, quite frankly, was getting tired of Hatch's catting around. They'll love you—and Marlyss, especially. And the idiot public is tired of addicts and drunks. Especially addicts and drunks in public office. They'll eat this up."

Frank didn't answer.

"Be smart. You're sorry Marty did this to himself. He was battling the disease. One day at a time—all that stupid shit. Just make sure it's at the very top of the contributing causes."

"That it?"

"Yep. This is the big time, Frank. I'll take care of you— the party will take care of you—until you're not worth taking care of."

"Okay."

Lyttle took another deep drag. "One more thing, Frank." He paused. "Make sure you're wearing a pink carnation for the news conference."

"For the last time."

Lyttle grunted again. "You don't like looking like a fucking Shriner every day?"

"From now on, it'll be a white rose."

Lyttle nodded. "Not bad, Frank. Innocence. Nice touch." He laughed softly, knowingly. "I think maybe you can play this game, Frank."

Frank laughed, too. *Play?* Lyttle was as big a fool as the rest of them.

$$\diamond \ 39 \ \diamond$$

Al McGinnity took a slug of beer, swallowed it, then turned away and spat. He hit the floor, not the trash drum, but it didn't make any difference here. "You're a motherfucking idiot."

Stan had finished his half of the paperwork on Hatch and split to take a run at finding McGinnity—and he'd gotten lucky on his first guess. He was sitting next to the stocky, light-skinned black cop at a greasy table in a dank, shitkicker pool hall—Margo's—downriver in Ecorse. Stan and McGinnity were alone, except for the bartender across the room. McGinnity was wearing cowboy boots, faded jeans, a dark brown turtleneck, a black leather jacket, and a three-day-old beard. Stan was sure McGinnity was carrying a gun, but he couldn't figure out where. No bulges. Stan certainly didn't ask where it was, and McGinnity hadn't pulled it out—yet.

It was only 2 P.M., but McGinnity already had four empties lined up in front of him. He was about to make it five, then stopped. "My old man was Irish, Kochinski, and the Micks had a saying for assholes like you. Let me see if I can remember it." McGinnity paused. "Sure, of course, it went something like this: Go fuck yourself." McGinnity half-sneered and half-laughed. Stan just nodded.

McGinnity had been suspended with pay while the police review board investigated the Colbane shooting. The investigation was standard procedure. Cutting an officer loose wasn't. Usually, the officer would be assigned some boring, harmless desk job while the board completed its probe—exactly what Frank had told reporters immediately after the shooting. But Al McGinnity wasn't the usual case. None of the police commanders wanted him, not even behind the desk. He was spring-loaded, a troublemaker. Frank had just sent him home.

McGinnity turned and spat again, this time across Stan's chest, hitting the trash can on the other side of the table. "You're a fucking idiot, Kochinski. You and all the rest of the sorry jerkoffs like you. Fucking TV cops." He sniffed. "Assholes. Cooper's nigger ass is dead, a score of his pals are out there dicking their eighty-year-old grandmothers and hooking kiddies on crack, and where in the goddamn hell are you?" McGinnity was in Stan's face. His breath was hot and smelled of beer and cheap cigars. His eyes were dark and hard, borderline vicious. He didn't blink. "You're here, fucking here, asking me if I'm this Shooter motherfucker, who, by the way, probably don't even exist." McGinnity finished the bottle and slammed it down hard on the table. "What'd you expect me to say—*yes?*"

Stan shrugged. "Maybe."

The answer made McGinnity sputter with laughter, then roar. McGinnity put his arm around Stan and put his mouth to Stan's ear. McGinnity's lips were warm and wet. "Why don't you just get the fuck out of here before I kick your sorry cracker ass all the way back downtown?"

Stan nodded. "Right." He grabbed a handful of peanuts from the dish on the table and shoved them in his mouth, then he stood. "Right." He turned to leave, then swung back slowly, as though he had one more thing to say, and slid one foot behind the leg of McGinnity's chair and, in one lightning-quick motion, grabbed the back of the chair with his left hand, yanked it back hard, reached behind his back with his right, and pulled his gun out of the waistband of his pants.

Suddenly, Al McGinnity was on his broad back staring up the barrel of Stan's blue-steel .38. He was a bit stunned, but unfazed. "Boy Scout move, Kochinski."

Stan nodded and slowly swung the barrel of the revolver south, until it was trained on McGinnity's crotch. His voice was low. "Maybe." Stan was stone-faced. "But I bet I get a merit badge for blowing your dick off."

McGinnity didn't move.

Stan nodded again. "Get up, nice and slow. And don't tempt me, asshole."

Stan kept the gun on McGinnity while he rose; he frisked him when he was on his feet. He found McGinnity's police revolver in his hip pocket and removed it just as the bartender arrived. McGinnity had his hands up, palms in, at about chest level. He nodded to the barkeep. "It's okay, Chico."

Chico didn't get it. "I'm calling the cops, Al."

Stan was holding McGinnity by the shoulder of his jacket. He still had his gun aimed at McGinnity's zipper. Stan nodded to Chico. "I am the cops, dickhead." Chico looked at McGinnity. McGinnity nodded, too. Stan watched them. "You got a backroom here?"

The bartender said nothing.

"A fucking backroom, asshole—you got one?" Stan was screaming now. McGinnity shrugged, and Chico nodded, nervously. He led the way to a small, cramped room at the end of a short corridor, where the restrooms were located. The place reeked of piss and whiskey. Stan took a quick peek in. It was a storeroom with cases of liquor stacked against all four walls. The hardwood floor was filthy, and the desk near the far corner was dust-covered and piled high with papers, cans, bottles, and other trash. Stan nodded. "Okay. Now disappear, Chico." The bartender hesitated. "Now!" He did. Stan kicked the door shut, then shoved McGinnity toward a stack of liquor cartons. McGinnity stumbled against them, caught his balance, then turned and plopped down rather cockily on one. Stan backed up to the desk, swiped the mess from one corner onto the floor, and sat down. "Now, we're going to talk."

McGinnity was chewing on a toothpick, his arms folded across his chest. "Blow me."

Stan shook his head. "Not smart."

McGinnity smiled. He wasn't convinced. "Maybe I need a lawyer."

Stan had the .38 pointed at the floor; he raised it a few inches and fired. The bullet tore into the box at McGinnity's feet, sending a river of yellow fluid onto the floor. The box said it was bourbon. Stan shook his head and waved his gun. "Mr. Prosecutor, here, says no."

Chico stuck his head in the door. Stan saw him, but didn't look over. Instead, he swiveled his arm toward the door and fired. The bullet hit the top molding on the doorway and sent a shower of splinters into the air. Chico disappeared again.

Stan retrained the gun on McGinnity. "You might need a lawyer, Al. But not now. Now, you just need to be a little more co-operative."

"Fuck you, Kochinski."

Stan aimed about a foot below McGinnity's crotch, at the *J* in J&B.

McGinnity shook his head, slowly. "I don't know nothin' about this Shooter shit."

"Nothing?"

"Nope."

"Keep talking."

McGinnity nodded again. "I roughed up a few guys."

"But . . ."

"But I never took nobody out."

"No one?"

"Not the Jefferson kid."

"Prove it."

McGinnity wound his face into a tight, painful grimace. "You gotta be shittin' me."

Stan fired again. The bullet went right between McGinnity's shins and into the bottom of the *J* on the carton. More liquid—but this time no Chico.

"Hey, you fucking crazy?" McGinnity was getting nervous.

"Left nut next, pal."

McGinnity nodded, his teeth clenched. He wasn't so sure anymore that Stan was all talk. "I.A. got all that shit."

"What shit?"

"Everything."

"What the fuck is everything?"

"My whereabouts. When the kid was shot."

"Where were you?"

McGinnity shrugged. "Sleepin' one off in a holding tank about ten miles south of here."

"They got that?"

"Fuck you. Haven't you seen the files?"

Stan didn't answer.

"You ain't workin' for I.A.?" McGinnity was confused. "What the fuck then?"

Stan nodded. "Just keep talking."

McGinnity shook his head, laughing to himself. "They got the records."

"Who?"

"I.A."

"Tell me about Cooper's gun."

McGinnity laughed out loud, hard.

"Share the joke, Al."

"You think if I find Cooper with his pants down, that I'm gonna waste my time stealing some fuckin' gun?"

Stan said nothing.

"I find Cooper with his dick in the breeze, and he loses it. Fuck the gun."

Stan lowered the .38 a few inches, then brought it back up. "What about Colbane?"

"What about him?"

"Why'd you shoot?"

"I wasn't interested in waiting around to see if he wanted to do someone else."

"No one else fired."

"No one else?" McGinnity roared and shook his head. "Everyone else was scared shitless. Not me."

"You got copies of the I.A. file?"

"Fuck you."

Stan nodded. He should have expected as much. "We're going to call."

"Who?"

"The desk where you spent the night."

"Go to hell."

"Where?" Stan's voice was stern and strong. McGinnity didn't answer. *"Where?"* Stan's voice was louder.

McGinnity ground his fist into his palm, but he nodded. "Flat Rock."

Stan reached for the phone across the desk, called information, and got the number for the Flat Rock police, then dialed it. A dispatcher answered.

"Police and fire."

"Duty officer, please."

"Hold on." The phone went dead; then another voice answered. "Thomas, here."

Stan lowered his voice. "This is Captain Hallson, Detroit I.A."

"Yes, sir."

"Just double-checking this McGinnity thing."

Thomas whistled. He sounded young. "Man, what'd that guy do now?"

Stan was staring at McGinnity. "Nothing. I just need the booking sheet from the twentieth."

Thomas sounded confused. "I sent a copy about a week ago, captain."

"Right."

"The first time you called."

Stan said nothing.

"Hold on, let me check my files." The officer was gone for maybe thirty seconds. "No, I faxed that way back on the twenty-second. Late. Ten P.M., to a P. Dawlson."

Dawlson? Now Stan was confused. "Well, we must have misplaced it, then. Refresh my memory, will you?"

"Yes, sir." Thomas cleared his throat. He was trying to sound extremely official. "I was there."

"Where?"

"On the run. We're pretty small out here, sir."

Stan was keeping a good eye on McGinnity. "Okay."

"Took three guys to handcuff that guy. Drunk as hell, a real sonofabitch. Blew lunch all over my partner. We found out he was a cop, and we called your headquarters. Didn't charge him. Just let him sleep it off."

"How long did he stay?"

"It should all be in that report, sir."

"Right. But how long?"

"We rolled him in at about nine P.M. and had him here till about one the next afternoon."

Rickey Jefferson was shot about midnight. Stan nodded. "Thanks."

"No problem, sir."

Stan put down the phone and rested his .38 on his thigh. McGinnity was staring at him. "Satisfied, motherfucker?"

Stan said nothing. He was more confused than ever. McGinnity with an alibi? Amazing, but possible. But that wasn't what bothered him so much. Dawlson? Had Pete known about McGinnity all along? Maybe that was why he'd laughed off the McGinnity-Shooter theory. But if he'd known about McGinnity getting locked up, why hadn't he shared the information? Why not pass it on? I.A. security? Maybe. But he could have told Stan. They were partners. They trusted each other. He could have let him know straight up that Mary had him off on a big-time wild-goose chase. Stan shook his head. And why was Pete still working McGinnity almost two days after Frank had pulled him off the case? Stan was trying hard to think. He'd lost his focus on McGinnity, and almost didn't see him come flying across the room.

Almost. Stan reacted quickly, with one well-placed shot. The loud blast from the .38 was followed by a sharp, sickening crack. By the sound of it, Stan figured McGinnity's left kneecap was shattered, if not simply blown off.

He didn't hang around to find out. On his way out, he sent Chico back with a Band-Aid.

◇ 40 ◇

"**Y**o, Stoosh-face." It was Pisarcawitcz. Stan was in no mood for the desk sergeant's act. The thirty-five-minute trip downtown had taken hours. First, he'd gotten sideswiped on the entrance ramp to the freeway and ended up in a ditch. Then, it had taken the tow truck forty-five minutes to get to him. Then, the tow truck's winch hadn't worked. Then, after a second truck had pulled him free, he'd found himself smack dab in the middle of rush-hour traffic—and a sleet storm. All that—and Dawlson, too. The mess had given him too much time to think. His mind was still reeling. Was Pete somehow covering for Sims? But *why?* There were simply too many questions—and no answers, none. Stan was running on adrenaline and nervous energy when he arrived downtown. He had begun to sweat, heavily, as soon as he entered headquarters.

"Not now, Pisser."

Pisarcawitcz bowed and stepped nimbly out of Stan's way. "Suit yourself, babe."

Stan blew past Pisarcawitcz and blasted into the squad room. It was dark, and he flicked on the lights. No one. He spun around and headed back down the hall. Pisarcawitcz was still standing there with a stupid grin on his face. Stan was out of breath. "Seen Dawlson?"

The desk sergeant pulled his arm out from behind his back and held out the envelope. Stan reached for it, but Pisarcawitcz pulled it back. "No, no, Stoshie, boy. Say, 'May I have the envelope, Mr. Pisarcawitcz—please.' "

Stan grabbed Pisarcawitcz by the collar and snatched the envelope, then pushed the desk sergeant against the wall. He ripped open the envelope. Inside were a ticket and a note:

"Too much work makes us dull boys. You owe me one, Stosh. Scared up two beauties for tonight's game. Meet me there. Just like old times. Pete."

Pisarcawitcz's grin was gone. He was holding his neck. "I'm going to sue your goddamn Polack ass, Kochinski." Stan ignored him and checked his watch. It was 6:05. The game started at 7:30. The Palace, the arena where the Detroit Pistons played, was in Auburn Hills, a good half-hour drive in decent weather. Stan ran back to his car.

The teams were in their final pregame shoot-arounds when he arrived. The player introductions wouldn't begin for another fifteen minutes or so. The Palace was about half full. Stan checked his ticket and found his seat. It was in the third row, just about midcourt. Great seats. A buxom cocktail waitress with a flirtatious grin asked him if he wanted a drink. Stan shook his head. He was busy looking for Dawlson. He sat down and took a deep breath. Maybe he was too wound up about all this. Maybe everything was just a coincidence. Maybe, but he doubted it. Something really was out of whack. He took another deep breath. It didn't make him feel any better. The seats to either side of him were empty, but he felt claustrophobic, as though he were suffocating. He reached up to loosen his collar. It was already loose. He stood and continued to scan the crowd. He didn't notice the short, fat, grandfatherly man staring at him from the press table to his left.

"Say, aren't you Stan Kochinski?"

Stan looked at the man and tried to act polite. He nodded. "I remember you."

Stan smiled. "Thanks." He didn't need this now.

"No, really, I remember." The man walked up to Stan and held out his hand. "Roy Lockner. I'm with the enemy." He smiled and nodded toward the basketball floor. "Sort of, anyway. I cover the team for the *Constitution*. In Atlanta."

Stan had never been to Atlanta and never heard of the paper. "Right." He shook the reporter's hand. "Nice to meet you."

Lockner shook his head. "Oh, no, no, no. We've met before."

Stan tried to look embarrassed, but he didn't do very

well. "I'm sorry, I don't remember." He was staring over Lockner's shoulder now.

"Oh, you wouldn't. Probably, anyway. It was back in the rookie leagues. Maybe down south." Lockner nodded. "Or up in the Northern League—the Goldeyes? Long time ago. You were something."

"Thanks." Stan wanted to make Lockner disappear.

"Listen, you look sort of preoccupied, but you could do me a big favor if you'd give me just a few minutes. This really is my lucky day. I've been doing a piece on this guy Pete Dawlson, and somebody told me you were in Detroit and were actually his partner, and I figured, great, I'd give you a call tomorrow, but, hell, here you are now."

"Pete?"

Lockner watched Stan's eyes light up, and followed up quickly. "Yeah, used to play monsterback at Mississippi State. Had all these defensive records. Last one was broken a few days ago." Lockner pointed at Stan. "He is your partner, right?"

"Right." The arena was filling up. The piped-in rock music was blaring. Stan took another look around. No Pete. Maybe Mary had talked to him. Mary—he should call Mary. A man and two small boys brushed Stan on the way to their seats, pushing him into Lockner. Stan glanced toward the press table. There was plenty of room down there. He looked back to Lockner. "Can I use your phone?"

Lockner smiled as another fan squeezed past. "You give me a few minutes, and the dime's on me."

Stan nodded and followed Lockner to the press table. Lockner rifled through a ratty briefcase for a notebook; Stan picked up the phone and dialed Mary.

"Mary? Stan."

As usual, Stan was about to regret the call. "Where the fuck've you been, Chipper?"

Stan sat down at the press table and rubbed his face. "C'mon, not now, Mary."

"Go to hell, Stosh."

Lockner looked down and winked. He could hear a female voice. He figured Stan was having girl problems.

"I've been trying to call you all day."

"Well, here I am."

"Where?"

Stan shook his head. "Just talk—and make it fast."

Mary was still heated up. "You first. Tell me about McGinnity."

Stan shook his head. "Forget him."

"Why?"

"Just forget him, that's all—it's a dead end."

"No—why?"

"Goddamnit, Mary." Stan was trying to keep his voice down. He wasn't doing very well. Lockner looked somewhat amused. He still hadn't found the notebook.

"Okay, okay. Later?"

Stan nodded. "Sure."

Mary was standing at her desk in the rear of the *Free Press* newsroom. She sat down. "I finally got that cretin Stevens to let me look through the homicide records." Carl Stevens was a sixty-two-year-old homicide dick put out to pasture in the records department, which meant he sat in his office eight hours a day and watched TV and read dog-eared girlie magazines.

Lockner was standing at the ready now, with notebook and pen. Stan held up his finger. Lockner nodded patiently. Mary continued. "Well, Stevens remembers most of these files, but for a different reason."

"Go on."

"Someone checked most of those out, but never signed for 'em."

"He know who?"

"Yep. And the reason he remembers who, is because he always was arguing—good-ol'-boy stuff, the way he tells it—with this guy about signing them out. The guy would say, 'I'll get it later,' 'Tomorrow,' that sort of thing. Once he caught him trying to sneak a couple back in."

"Who?"

Lockner tapped Stan on the shoulder. "We only got a few minutes before tip-off, Stan."

Stan nodded. "Right."

"What?" It was Mary.

"I got two things going on here, Mary." Stan winced. "Hold on." He turned toward the sportswriter.

Lockner nodded. "What's he like now?"

Stan scratched his forehead with the receiver. "Low key, laid back, quiet, really pretty unexcitable."

"Stan?" Mary again.

Stan put the phone back by his ear. "In a minute, Mary."

Lockner shook his head. "People change, I guess."

Stan nodded. "I guess."

"Stan?"

"Hold on, Mary."

"Never gets excited, though, huh?" Lockner looked surprised.

Stan shook his head.

"Stan?" Mary was almost screaming now.

"One guy played with him in college said . . . wait, let me find it."

Stan nodded politely to Lockner, then pulled the phone tight against his lips. The teams were heading to their benches for the pregame ceremonies, and the crowd's enthusiasm was growing. Stan tried to whisper over the noise. "Just a second or two, Mary."

"No, Stan, listen now."

Stan nodded. "Okay."

"What?" Lockner looked up from his notes.

"Nothing."

"Stan, you there?" Mary again.

"Yep." He stuck a finger in his ear trying to block out the noise.

"It was Pete, Stan."

"What?" Stan would have bet on Sims. "Pete?" Stan was yelling now over the jeers and boos for the visiting team.

"Pete." Mary nodded. "Pete, Stan. Pete was the one who wouldn't sign out the files. Pete. Why?"

Stan took a deep breath. "Mary, that information you got on McGinnity—anything about an arrest late on the night of the twentieth?"

"The twentieth?" Mary shook her head. "The night the Jefferson kid was killed? No, of course not. I wouldn't have suggested we chase after—"

Stan cut her off. "But you probably didn't have the complete file."

She nodded. "Yes, I did."

"Everything?" Stan was still yelling. Lockner didn't seem to notice, or at least wasn't bothered. He was still flipping through his notebook.

"Stan, I had the fucking original file—the I.A. original."

Stan was stunned. No one got ahold of I.A. files. He remembered the file and Dawlson's open desk drawer. Had Pete wanted him to see it, too? But why?

Lockner tapped Stan on the shoulder. He was laughing, but Stan couldn't hear him. The lights were dimmed and the home team was being announced now. The crowd was going nuts. Everything was too loud. "Guy here—listen to this . . ."

Stan wanted to push him away. He couldn't.

"Stan?"

"Hold on, Mary."

"I can't hear you." Stan was shouting at Lockner. Lockner shouted back.

"Guy who played with him—Monty Malone, something or other, Mahoney—said Dawlson would get so fired up after a great tackle that he'd run up to the guy who made the play . . . let's see here . . . oh, yeah, then cock his finger like a gun and stick it right in the guy's chest or between his eyes . . ."

Stan closed his eyes and nodded.

"Stan?"

"Yeah, Mary."

". . . and he'd say the same thing every time." Lockner was yelling so loud over the din that his face was turning red.

Stan nodded again. He was getting pissed.

"He'd say, 'Way to go, big shooter'—or something like that—always shooter something."

Stan lost his breath. He felt his jaw drop. "What?" It came out like a gasp. He stood and grabbed Lockner by the shirt and pulled him closer.

Lockner looked scared, his eyes wide as saucers, his face two inches from Stan's. He looked down at his notebook and began stammering. "Something like . . . um, way to go, big shooter." He looked like he was going to cry. "Something like that, Mr. Kochinski."

"Stan? Stan?" Mary was screaming again.

Stan still had a tight grip on Lockner and the phone jammed between his ear and shoulder. "Mary?" His voice was loud, but calm, even.

"What?"

"Who gave you that file?"

"Nope."

"Who?"

Mary didn't say anything.

"Who, goddamnit, who?" Stan was red-faced and screaming at Mary and jerking hard on poor, pudgy, frightened Roy Lockner.

Stan was about to yell even louder, when the arena lights went on and a calm, even voice came out of nowhere, softly filling his right ear.

"It was me, Stan. But you have that figured out now, don't you?"

Pete reached around and unclasped Stan's hand from Lockner's shirt and took the phone from Stan's other hand and gently hung it up. He nodded to the three security guards, who'd been summoned by the other sports writers. "It's okay, fellows, I'll take care of my friend."

Then Stan felt a stern poke in his back. Pete was still speaking in a soothing, conversational voice as the crowd stood for the National Anthem. "Be smart now, pard. Be polite. Be cool. And let's take a little walk."

They did. By the time the crowd was finished singing, Stan and Pete were in the parking lot. And by the time Pistons forward Spider Salley brought the capacity crowd to its feet with a thunderous, alley-oop slam-dunk for the first points of the game, Stan and Pete were speeding back toward town, with Stan behind the wheel of Pete's car, and Pete riding shotgun—armed with Stan's .38.

◇ **41** ◇

"**I** could have explained most of this, Stosh." Pete shook his head. "And we wouldn't have needed this." He waggled Stan's .38 in the air, then retrained it on his partner. "Those case files?" He shrugged. "Hey, I was just on the same thing you were—Frank Sims and open investigations that ended up closed." He stopped. "I didn't sign for those files because I didn't want Frank to know what I was up to."

Stan said nothing.

"The I.A. file in my desk? Hallson let me keep it because he'd told me I'd be back on the case as soon as the Jefferson thing blew over." He nodded. "The missing arrest report on McGinnity?" He scratched his forehead with the barrel of the revolver and raised his eyebrows in mock surprise. "Oops, must have slipped out. Sorry. It's there, in my desk."

Silence.

"And me giving Mary the file? She asked for it, Stosh. Begged for it. How'd I know she thought McGinnity was the Shooter. I thought she was cooking up some big story on asshole cops." Pete paused and smiled. "How'm I doing?"

Still nothing.

"And then, when the McGinnity lead falls through, you just finally say the hell with it all." Dawlson nodded. "You were this close, already, pard." He held his thumb and forefinger about an eighth of an inch apart. "Cooper was dead and gone. The case was closed. Who cared? One tired, goody-two-shoes cop and a reporter? That's all. Pretty soon, all that's left snooping around is Stimic." Pete paused. "And she may be good, Stosh, but she's not *that* good."

Pete poked Stan with the .38. "Neither are you. No one

is good enough to get this whole thing straight. We made a tiny mistake—otherwise, it's the perfect game." Pete stopped and chuckled at using the baseball analogy on Stan. "Plus, you got lucky." He paused and waved the gun at Stan, then shrugged. "Or unlucky."

Stan didn't look at Pete, but Pete was right—on all counts, especially one: Stan was that close—probably closer—to getting the hell out of here. Now look where he was—driving through a sleet storm on the way to where? Frank's place? That was a good guess, with his partner holding a .38 in his right ear. Stan flipped the wipers on high. He thought briefly about making some sort of move— what? Swiping at the gun? But Pete had his own .22 stuffed into the waistband of his pants. Opening the car door and jumping out? He could probably slow the car enough to survive the dive. But if Frank was the brains here, and he was, wasn't he? Then what about Marlyss? Was she safe? Jesus, did she know? Stan could feel himself sweating. He guessed she didn't. He hoped not. His fingers wound tighter around the steering wheel. No, she would've told him. He relaxed, but only a bit.

He was angry at himself. He should have listened more to Mary, been more careful. He'd gotten himself into this. He'd been too helter-skelter, like some fucking pinball. He was all over the place on this thing. He stopped. No, he was wrong—he shouldn't have listened to Mary at all. He should have just left, gone with Marlyss. He should have rescued her, taken her away like she wanted. He did love her. He wished he had told her, just once. That's all she'd wanted—just to know it, just to hear it.

Pete jabbed him again with the gun. "Next one." Stan checked the exit sign. If they were headed for Frank's place, they only had another few minutes.

Pete was still watching Stan closely. Stan could feel his gaze. Dawlson was a tough, hard-nosed cop and smart. He didn't miss much. It always amazed Stan how Pete knew exactly how—and what—the scumbags were thinking. Stan remembered thinking once that Dawlson, dressed in those commando-black outfits, would have made a terrific assassin. One step ahead. Always, one step ahead. Like your shadow with the sun at your back. And cool.

"How much I tell you about the tunnels in 'Nam, Stosh? At Cu Chi."

Stan knew Pete had been to 'Nam—they'd talked about it a bit—but he still didn't answer.

Dawlson smiled. "I'm disappointed in you, Stanislaw. You were always such a good conversationalist." He shrugged. "The tunnels." He laughed. "Spiders big as fucking saucers, Stosh. Bats that'd squeeze right down your pants. Once, I saw a guy take a .45 and try to blow one off his balls." Pete shook his head. "That's what this is all about, Stan—don't you see?"

Stan was staring out the windshield. He was seeing a lot, but not that.

Pete slid closer. He lowered his voice to a whisper. "Ever been on your belly face to face with a rat, Stosh?" Pete placed the tip of the revolver softly against Stan's cheek, then slid it into the curve of his nose. "So close you could feel the putrid little motherfucker's wet, sloppy kisser?"

Pete pulled the gun back. "One time I heard something different—wasn't a gook or a rat or bat or the hornets or snakes they'd drop down there for laughs. It was something else, moved strange, and it was coming closer." He paused. "I held my breath, Stosh. I held it so hard and so long that I could hear myself sweat. I could feel the blood pumping like a hammer through my dick, for chrissakes. I waited and waited and waited until the son of a bitch got so close, until I thought my brain was going to explode." Pete was staring hard at Stan, his eyes open, scary wide, and his forehead dotted with sweat, but with a calm, cool, crazy smile on his face. "Then I fired—once, twice, three times. Seemed like six times, maybe eight, ten, like a goddamn machine gun. But it was three. Always three—only three." He stopped again, then laughed, softly. "I swear I come up with the asshole's snot and spit all over my face. Some nights I can still hear the scream. Some nights I can even hear the poor sucker's teeth shatter." Pete shrugged, still smiling, sort of. "One of ours, Stosh. Vietnamese kid. Wasn't supposed to be down there, stupid motherfucker. A casualty of war . . . just like Rickey Jefferson."

Pete stopped, then laughed again. "Everybody wonders about those years I was gone. I didn't run off with any broad, didn't go off to take care of mama. I was undercover, Stosh. Deep. Drug ring, from here to Southeast Asia. Then, I wake up one day stinking like stale sex in this flophouse in Thailand with this six-bit hooker and finally realized where I was." Pete's smile, what was left of it, faded even more. His voice grew angry. "I was back in the fucking tunnels, on my belly with creeps and scum, squeezing through the fucking holes, ending up face to face with stinking rats . . . again." His voice dropped, but his teeth were clenched and he was breathing through them. He looked at Stan as though Stan had no goddamn chance in hell of understanding what he was saying and why was he saying it.

"Then I come back, here, to the department, and you know what I see—again?" Pete stared hard at Stan. "C'mon, Stosh, you know what I saw—*c'mon.*" His voice was hard, rising, impatient, agitated. He stabbed at Stan with the gun.

"I saw that the fucking tunnels were everywhere now"— Pete's voice was suddenly a whisper—"that we were all on our bellies, all the fucking time, Stan—you, too—crawling in some sleazy fucker's piss, coming nose to nose with jive-ass shithead rats with stinking fucking breath, fighting for inches, not yards." He sniffed and laughed. "Not fighting for neighborhoods or cities, but fucking inches. Quarter-inches. Like fucking 'Nam. Just like motherfucking 'Nam." Pete was out of breath. "It's all a joke, Stosh, what we do—a dirty, shitty joke." Silence again.

Pete leaned back against the door. "That why, Stan. I knew you were thinking it—why." He paused. He was still out of breath. Stan had never seen him this way. He looked as though he'd gone mad.

Pete nodded, inhaled deeply, then chuckled. "Bet you didn't know Frank was a tunnel rat, too?" He nodded again. "He was the junior officer in my platoon, Stosh. Crazy son of a bitch. No fear, none. Especially not in the tunnels. We called him the Prince of Fucking Darkness. Not just the Prince of Darkness—the Prince of *Fucking* Darkness." Pete paused. "He's the Devil, Stosh. I know that." He shrugged. "But you make strange friends in hellholes, and when I come back to the department and the first thing I realize is that I'm back in the darkness, sucking in shit again, but this time with an empty gun ..." He shook his head and the gun, always keeping his eyes on Stan. "Frank knew. He *knew*—and he loaded it for me." Pete nodded. "What he was paying didn't mean shit. Someone down there, down *here,* needed a fucking loaded gun. He made it all right again."

Pete bit his lip and poked at Stan again with the .38. He laughed, then took a deep breath. "You got it all figured out yet, Stoshie? One, two, three, four ... then, bingo-bango—Cooper. We were taking 'em out, pard. Boom, boom, boom. Just like we did at Cu Chi. In the darkness—*their* darkness. One at a fucking time." Pete's eyes were lit up.

Stan shook his head. He took a deep breath. Some of it was starting to fit together, at least a little: the dead punks; the Cooper frame-up; vigilante justice; some sort of conspiracy. And Rickey Jefferson ends up dead. It all seemed possible—and insane. The police chief? A top homicide detective? Who would believe any of it?

Stan finally spoke up. "How many?"

Pete laughed and shook his head. "I didn't count."

"The Jefferson kid was in fifth grade."

Pete's smile turned into a sneer. "A mistake, Stosh, like the girl in the tunnel—she was eight."

They were off the freeway now, on Seven Mile, nearing Frank's place. Pete had been quiet for a minute, maybe two.

"Cu Chi, Stosh, twenty-five miles northeast of Saigon. You go down and you don't come up the same. The darkness changes you. You want to blow the fucking things up and be done with 'em. And you do that, and they just dig more and it doesn't end, Stosh. But you, cops like you, just don't want to get that." The anger had returned to Pete's voice. "You been a cop for, what, twenty years?—and you don't want to understand that. You want to go on playing this idiot kid's game of justice for all." Pete shook his head. "Problem is, justice for all includes assholes like Cooper."

They were in Frank's drive. The sleet had turned to rain

and it was coming down hard, in wind-blown sheets. Pete was calm now, just like that. He got out of the car, went to Stan's side and pulled him out, then stuffed the hand with Stan's .38 into the pocket of his topcoat, pushed the barrel hard into Stan's back, and put his lips to Stan's ear. "It didn't have to be like this, Stoshie. Maybe if you hadn't been off playing ball. Maybe if you'd been in the tunnels with me and Frank—the three of us."

They walked to the door. Pete rang and Marlyss answered. She was wearing black satin lounging pajamas—she and Frank were apparently staying in. Pete smiled. "Season's greetings, Mrs. Sims. Frank home?"

Marlyss looked at Stan, then Pete. She was shocked, all right—Stan saw the confusion in her eyes—but she returned the smile, correctly, politely. "Sure. Come in. I'll get him."

Marlyss was back with Frank in a matter of seconds. He was wearing jeans and a sweater and his eyes flickered with surprise, too. He nodded to Pete, looked hard at Stan, then turned to Marlyss. "Why don't you head to the study, dear, and make some drinks for these two detectives who have been hard at work on Marty's accident?" Marlyss nodded, smiled again, this time nervously, and left, without looking at Stan.

When he heard Marlyss enter the study, Frank reached inside Stan's coat for his gun. Pete started to say something and pulled Stan's .38 from his coat pocket, but Frank waved him off and grabbed the .22 from Pete's waistband. He was staring at Stan.

Pete shrugged. "I had no choice, Frank."

Frank nodded. "You did ... but this is okay, too. It'll work out. What's he know?"

"Not everything, but too much."

"Okay. Frisk him."

"I did."

Frank lowered his voice to a tough whisper. "Again."

Pete did. "Wait in the car. We won't be long."

Frank watched Pete leave, then broke into another smile. This time, it was a big, wide, fuck-you smile, the kind Frank had smiled when he'd helped Marty Hatch into his car one night earlier; the kind he'd smiled in the blackness, years ago, just before the Prince of Fucking Darkness blasted another shadow to hell in the pitch-dark tunnels of Cu Chi. "How cozy. You and me—and Mar." He shook his head. "Not quite New Year's Eve yet, but still—auld lang syne." He chuckled. "This is just too good an opportunity to pass up."

Then Frank stuffed the .22 into the back of his pants and pushed Stan toward the study. "One stupid move, lover boy, and she's dead."

◇ 42 ◇

Marlyss was behind the bar when Stan walked into the study with Frank. She caught her breath when she saw Frank close the study door—no Pete. Frank was watching her closely. He smiled. "Now, now, dear, let's get a grip on ourselves. You're giving yourself away." He laughed. "I thought you'd be a little better at this."

Stan looked at Marlyss and shook his head, only slightly. He said nothing. He had to be careful. Whatever she didn't know about Frank and Pete and Cooper and Rickey Jefferson, and whatever else there was, couldn't hurt her.

Frank led Stan to the couch. "Sit." Stan didn't, right away. Frank glanced at Marlyss again. She was fussing with some glasses at the bar. Frank shrugged, went to the bar and grabbed one of the drinks Marlyss had fixed. He took a sip and looked down at his hand. It was steady. He smiled, nodded, and looked up and around. It was an odd scene: Marlyss, in her expensive new outfit; him, relaxed and preppy; and Kochinski, dressed for a wake—his. Frank loved it. He smiled. First Hatch, now this. The finish line kept moving on him, but there couldn't be too many hurdles left. He reached behind himself and brushed his hand across the butt of the .22. He let his mind wander, just a bit. Pete would hide Kochinski's body so that no one would stumble on it for a few days at least, maybe a week. Then, some stooped-over addict would find Kochinski sprawled in the basement of some rotting, abandoned house on the lower east side. Frank would call a press conference and tell the public that Detective Stanislaw Cyrus Kochinski, one of his top investigators, had been on a perilous undercover assignment when he'd met his terrible fate. He would shake his head to the TV cameras and say he was sure Kochinski'd been brave to the end. Maybe he'd even give the eulogy at the funeral. Frank laughed—and Marlyss, poor, pretty, grieving Marlyss wouldn't—couldn't—question any of it.

Frank looked at Stan and wrinkled his face into a concerned frown. "Pete give you the lecture on Cu Chi?" Stan didn't move. He was still looking at Marlyss, trying to see something—what? Frank glanced at Marlyss, then back at Stan. "I certainly hope you got the abridged version." He took another sip of his drink. "Well, I'm not going to waste your time on that, or other . . . related matters." Frank smiled. "No, I want to hear about us. The three of us. Maybe we should trade stories?"

Marlyss was staring at the floor. She shook her head. "Don't, Frank."

Frank was keeping his eyes on Stan. "Shut up, Marlyss." The words were sharp and mean. Frank looked into Stan's eyes and saw a flicker of anger; his smile widened again.

He walked to the bar, put his drink down, and wrapped his arm around his wife. "See, I know just about everything there is to know about the two of you. Where. When. How many times. The good stuff. No pictures—though I could've had some." He patted her cheek. "In fact, detective, I know a lot you don't even know about dear, sweet Marlyss here."

Marlyss was still staring at the floor. She was clearly terrified. "It's over, Frank. I'm sorry it ever happened. Please stop."

"Sorry?" Frank grabbed Marlyss by the neck. *"Sorry?"* He pulled the .22 out. Her eyes flew open wide when she saw the gun.

Frank turned toward Stan. "Let me tell you something about Marlyss here. Did you know, for instance, that her name isn't Marlyss at all? Did she tell you that? No, I bet she didn't." Frank shook his head. "Her name's really Nancy . . . Nancy Koenig." Frank saw the surprise in Stan's eyes. He liked that. "Did she tell you she's from Florida?" Frank smiled. "South Dakota. Millstone, South Dakota. Middle America. Salt of the earth. A dried-up, sucked-out little two-horse prairie town, waiting for a strong wind to blow it off the fucking map."

Frank ran his hand along Marlyss's cheek, then kissed her neck. She was staring at the floor. "It's quite a story. Sad, actually. Nancy's daddy—Frederik—was an evil man, though you wouldn't know it from outward appearances. In fact, most of the townsfolk thought he was an upstanding heartland sort. Went to church, worked hard. Weeded his garden. But Mar, here, knew better. So did Marou, Freddy's poor wife." Frank frowned. "Seems ol' Fred liked the bottle and was loosing all his demons on Marou. Beat her up, a lot. Then he began going after young, pretty Nancy, here." Frank stopped, released Marlyss, and took a drink. He put the glass down and stuffed the gun into the front of his pants so that both hands were free.

He was gesturing like an actor now, but staying close to Marlyss, just in case Stan got any ideas. "Marou didn't like that one bit. But it wasn't until Daddy . . ."

Marlyss shook her head, her voice low. "Please don't, Frank."

Frank laughed. "Please don't?" He shook his head, pulled the gun out again, and grabbed Marlyss by the hair. "But this is your life, Mar. Your suitors need to know this sort of background information."

He looked at Stan again. "As I was saying—it wasn't until the wonderful, upstanding Frederik Koenig tried to fuck his beautiful twelve-year-old daughter, that mama really did anything. Actually, it was the, what, third or fourth time, Mar, that he tried to have little Nancy that mama did anything? Then, God bless her soul, she did it right." Frank circled around Marlyss, smiled, put his arm around her, and trailed the barrel of the .22 up Marlyss's stomach, resting it under her left breast. "Four shots, Detective Kochinski. Bang. Bang. Bang. Bang. While the likkered-up slob was asleep. Coroner's report said Freddy was dead after two."

Frank reached out with his free hand and grabbed his drink. "That was bad enough. But then it got even more complicated. It seems that Marou's standing in the community was rather iffy. Seems she was having an affair during all of this—and not her first one—not that anyone could blame her, of course." He shrugged. "But it sure didn't look good. So she shot hubby and took little Nancy and split. She was scared stiff. Wouldn't you be? Still is, too. Afraid someone'll rat on her and some backwater South Dakota prosecutor and his righteous jury with nothing else to do will send her off to the slammer . . . for a long, long, *long* time."

Frank nodded. "Make a good TV movie, no? For some cold, wet Wednesday night." He laughed. "You really have to pardon my laugh, Kochinski, but I find all of this pretty entertaining—especially the thought that Nancy, here, would run away while mama's still holed up in some rickety shack in the Florida panhandle."

Marlyss had moved away from Frank and was backed into a corner now, like a scared child. Frank stopped, stuffed the gun back into his pants, and walked toward her. "Anyway, that's not Nancy's style. She's more a follower, the kind of woman that looks good on the end of your arm." He slipped her arm through his. "Don't you think? Though I suppose it would have been sort of amusing to see how long she could have lasted in hot, sweaty Alabama. Where?—in some trailer park? How long do you think the fair Lady Marlyss would last there? How long did you figure she'd be happy swatting away mosquitoes in the sweltering heat with all those stinking rednecks when she starts thinking about how she could be sitting pretty in the mayor's mansion?" Frank's voice rose. "A year? Six months? Six weeks? Six fucking *days?*"

He stopped and smiled at her. "No, she's not going anywhere. She's what I need—especially now—and she knows that. She knows the rules. They're simple, though not altogether painless. Sort of like what mama went through, I

guess, except the bruises I give usually don't show." Frank
pulled Marlyss tight again and kissed her shoulder—then
nipped it. She closed her eyes and flinched. "Funny, how
that stuff runs in cycles, isn't it? Mommy—her daughter."
He reached around her and straightened Marlyss's top. "See,
Mar, here, doesn't like uncertainty. She needs to know the
score all the time. Bing. Bang. What's up, what's down."
Frank wiped mockingly at his eyes and imitated her voice.
"Are we leaving, Stanley, or aren't we?"

He smiled. "But I like that, too, that she knows what's
expected of her."

Frank studied them both. Marlyss was still looking at the
floor. Stan was watching her. She looked at Stan, then away
again. Frank nodded, then chuckled. "What was it Pete told
you, Kochinski—the tunnels? That this is all about rats in
the darkness?" Frank laughed. "Poor Pete." He shook his
head. "It's about control, Kochinski. That's all. No meta-
phors, no symbolism, no analogies, no stupid fucking fa-
bles. It's control. Period." He grabbed Marlyss's hand and
pulled her out into the middle of the room. "You find someone's weakness, and you use it. Sometimes, if you're good
at it, they don't even know what's happening. Hell, Ol'
Marty Hatch never did get it." He laughed. "It took Mar,
here, years to figure everything out." He nodded. "She's got
it down now but can't do anything about it. She's afraid of
something happening to mama. Or ending up"—Frank
pulled out the .22 again and waved it at his wife—"like her
old man." He shrugged. "Makes sense, doesn't it?"

Frank positioned Marlyss in front of him. "Watch."
Marlyss's chest was heaving. Her lipstick was smeared. Her
eyes red. Frank fussed with her hair a bit, fixing it, then offered her the gun with his right hand. "Take it." She didn't.
"Take it." Frank's voice was rising. He looked away, at
Stan, for the briefest of moments, then slapped Marlyss hard
with his left hand. Stan stiffened up. He wanted to make a
move, but he couldn't. Not yet.

"Take it." Frank grabbed Marlyss's hand and pushed the
gun into her palm, then took the barrel and pulled the .22 to
his chest. He smiled, still holding the barrel, staring at
Marlyss. Her head was down. A thin trickle of blood was

oozing from the corner of her mouth. Her hand was shaking. Frank looked at Stan and laughed. "See, Kochinski—control."

Frank looked back at Marlyss. His smile turned into a sneer. He helped her rotate the gun toward the floor. Then, he was grinning at Stan, again. "No guts, Kochinski. No fucking . . ."

No matter how hard he tried later, Stan wouldn't be able to recall if Frank's next word was obscured by his screams or by the first blast, the one that blew a hole in Frank's left thigh and threw him to his knees. All he would remember, and so vividly, was the incredible look of surprise in Frank's eyes when the .22 fired. That, and that by the third shot, the one that actually killed Police Chief Frank Sims, Marlyss's hand seemed rock steady, her eyes focused tight, her aim perfect.

Stan was fighting for breath now, for his own control. Everything was spinning. He grabbed the gun from Marlyss's hand and sprinted out of the study, to the front door. Pete was still sitting in the idling car. He saw Stan and reached for the car door. Then he saw the gun—and pulled out of the drive—fast.

When Stan returned to the study, Marlyss was sitting on the couch, staring straight ahead. The place still stunk of gunsmoke. She wasn't crying. She was just sitting calmly, biting her lower lip. "I'm okay now. It's over, Stan."

Stan knelt next to Frank and felt for a pulse. There was none. He turned to Marlyss.

She shook her head, her voice even. "It's all right, it really is. You were right, Stan—it was me, I had to do it. Me, not anyone else. Not you." She nodded. "Everything is over, finally. You can go. I'll be alright."

Stan shook his head. "You don't understand . . ."

She nodded. "I do. I'm through running away, Stan. I don't need that anymore." She almost smiled. "I'm not afraid anymore."

"Jesus and Mary, Marlyss." Stan dropped to his knees. "*Listen* to me."

She shook her head and looked deep into his eyes. "No, you listen to me, Stosh: *It's over.*" Now she did smile, softly. "You do what you have to do—but do it for yourself this time, not for me."

Stan nodded. She was right. He backed off and looked at Frank again, then at the .22 he was holding. His mind was racing again. He grabbed a towel from the bar and wiped the gun clean, then stuffed it deep into his pocket. He looked at Marlyss. "Don't move. Don't do anything. Don't touch anything."

Then he left, took Marlyss's car and drove to a pay phone near a Burger King on Seven Mile. He dialed Mary at the paper. He'd forgotten that she'd been cut off when Pete marched him out of the basketball game; she hadn't. "Go fuck yourself, Chipper. I'm busy."

Stan gritted his teeth. "No crap now, Mary. Meet me at your place. Two hours."

He didn't wait for an answer. He hung up and headed back to Marlyss. It was almost time for her to call the cops.

◇ **43** ◇

Mary Stimic's inaugural column in the *Free Press* ran three days early, on December 29. Assistant managing editor Ted Enders edited the piece on deadline and ran it down the left-hand side of Page 1A. He called it a "killer debut." Mary's column:

The killing takes no holiday in this city that has all too often earned the appalling distinction of being not only the Murder Capital of this country but probably of the civilized world.

This time, the victim was the man whose job it was to try to somehow stem the tide of brutal, senseless violence.

Police Chief Frank Sims, the heir apparent, many had predicted, to Marty Hatch's once-powerful political machine, met his Creator last night the same way all too many people do in this vicious, unforgiving town. Sims was fatally shot in what was described by a homicide investigator as a holiday get-together that turned into an argument that turned violent, then— again, as so many here do—deadly.

Marlyss Sims, expecting a quiet evening at home at the Sims's Palmer Woods estate, enjoyed anything but that. The chief's attractive wife is known to close friends as a loving partner and a meek, mild woman. A homicide investigator said Mrs. Sims was upstairs at the time of the shooting. She would not comment to reporters.

She didn't have to. A neighbor standing in the cold rain outside the Sims home late last night said it all. Monica Collins, watching as dozens of police combed the house and yard, wiped her eyes with a balled-up tissue and said, quite simply, "Marlyss ... deserved better."

With heartfelt condolences to Mrs. Sims—and my deepest apologies: Yes, don't we all.

Homicide Lieutenant Stan Kochinski, one of the senior investigating officers on the scene, said that Chief Sims was apparently visited by an old friend early yesterday evening and that an altercation ensued and that the gunshots—three or more—apparently came without much warning. He said that shortly after the last shot was fired, the front door of the home slammed shut and a car was heard screeching out of the driveway. A neighbor returning home from the grocery store reportedly identified the getaway vehicle.

Kochinski said that although police had not located the murder weapon, the tags on the car and a preliminary examination of slug fragments found at the scene were enough for the police to issue an APB.

Police officials said they would not release the

name of the suspect until a warrant is issued. The warrant is expected sometime today.

But officers were clearly numbed by what had happened and the prospects of what now must follow—a manhunt to find Frank Sims's killer.

Police hunting . . . a policeman.

"We don't expect this suspect to turn himself in," Kochinski said.

Hardly. Not here. No, not here, where things never come easy, and where tragedy comes flying at us so fast that we can only duck out of its way and hope to keep moving on, because something else, something often even more ghastly, is usually hard on its heels.

Mayor Hatch's tragic death was one thing—a horrible accident.

But Chief Sims?

New Year's is but two days away. The question is, can we hope for anything better in this city, for this city, in the coming months?

Christmastime is a season of hope—and I wish I could say yes.

I can't.

I'm sorry.

$\Diamond$ **44** $\Diamond$

Stan rubbed his eyes. He was sitting at Mary's dining room table and squinting at the screen on her portable computer terminal. Mary was sitting across from him, watching.

He finished, then nodded. "Nice column. Tough stuff."

Mary nodded back. "They wanted a columnist—they got one." She leaned back in her chair and stretched. "Think they'll find him?"

Stan shrugged. "I don't know. Pete's pretty smart." He stood and picked up his coat, then his coffee cup. "Resourceful. Was one of those tunnel rats in 'Nam. Strange characters, I guess. Maybe he snapped or something." Stan finished the coffee. It was cold. "I have a feeling we've seen the last of him—alive."

Mary kept her eyes on Stan. It was after two and she was still hard at work. "But say they do—what do they need?"

Stan put on his coat. "They find Pete's gun, and he's a goner."

"Will they?"

Stan shook his head. "Like I said—he's smart. He probably wiped the gun clean and ditched it."

"Then what—if they find it?"

"The usual—ballistics tests. He was there, no doubt. The neighbor across the street—Potter, I think, or Porter—saw Pete's car blow out of the drive. And Pete carries a .22. Not many of us do." Stan stopped. "Plus, Pete and Frank were old buddies—Vietnam."

Mary stared at Stan. "I didn't know that, either."

Stan shrugged. "Me neither, till recently. Maybe ol' Pete had some bad memories—post trauma." He winked at Mary. "Maybe there's a motive there."

Mary wasn't buying that. "This have anything to do with records or this Shooter thing?"

Stan shrugged and headed for the door. "Who knows? I doubt it. Beside, I'm tired, Mary. Find Pete, then we'll talk."

"Any clues?" Mary was stalling now, he could tell. Stan shook his head and she smiled. "All right, all right. I'll stop for now. Care to stay for breakfast?"

Stan grinned and shook his head. "Maybe some other time."

"What now?"

He put on his gloves. "Home."

"Not going to work this one?"

Stan shook his head. "No. Too close to it."

"What, then?"

"Sleep. A phone call or two."

"Must be important."

Stan nodded. "Maybe. An old friend named Thunder."

Mary smiled. "Sounds like a movie."

Stan smiled back. "I'll tell him you said that. He'll like that." He held out his hand.

Mary took it and shook it. "Nice working with you, Chipper."

Stan nodded, smiled again, then left. The hard rain had turned to a thick, soaking drizzle. He closed the door and headed for his car, stopped, took a deep breath and shook his head, then nodded. He had to keep thinking clearly. His car was still at the Palace, at the basketball game. He was still driving Marlyss's car. He would get his own tomorrow.

He pulled up his collar and started to walk the two blocks to where he was parked. He passed Mary's Toyota on the way and noticed that the driver's door was unlocked. He felt for Pete's gun in his jacket pocket. It was still there. He was half-tempted to leave it on Mary's front seat as a little present, but it was too soon, way too soon. Maybe later—if he had to.

It was almost three when Stan got to his place. The drizzle had stopped halfway home, then turned to a downpour again. Stan was shivering a bit, chilled from the walk to the car. He was tired of being cold and wet. He sat in the darkness, waiting, Marlyss's car running, the heater on high. He reached up to rub his head and brushed a handful of papers stuck in the sun visor. The pack fell to the floor and Stan picked it up. One envelope stood out—standard, legal-sized, and stamped and addressed to Det. Stan Kochinski. The handwriting was smeared, but was clearly Marlyss's. She hadn't mailed it yet—or maybe she'd just decided not to. He opened the envelope. Inside was his rookie baseball card and a note, written at the bottom of a receipt for thirty-two cents:

You've given me back my dignity, Stosh. I could never repay you for that—but I tried anyway. I love you, Mar.

Stan re-read the note, then smiled, gently slid the piece of paper and the card back into the envelope, and stuffed the envelope into his coat pocket. He looked outside. It was still black as hell, but the rain had eased up just a bit. He turned off the ignition and took a deep breath.

Maybe it was finally time to make a run for it.